The Last Original Ranger of New York

A Novel

Bryan Reilly

This book is a work of fiction. Any references to historical events, real people, or real places and used fictitiously. Other names, characters, places, and events are products of this author's imagination, and any resemblance to actual events or places or persons, living or dead, is entirely coincidental.

 For information write Reilly Publishing LLC, 80 Columbia Ave, Hartsdale, NY 10530. Bryanreilly65@gmail.com

First Edition November 2023

Cover design by Romain Bonnet
Photo of author by Tia Tiedt

ISBN 979-8-218-31906-9

For Quinn

Based on true events…

The Original Roster

Clarence "Taffy" Abel #4 – Defenseman

Frank "Raffles" Boucher #7 – Center

Billy Boyd #8 - Center

Lorne Chabot #1 - Goalie

Bill Cook #5 – Right Winger

Fred "Bunny" Cook #6 – Left Winger

Ivan "Ching" Johnson #3 - Defenseman

Reg Mackey #2 - Defenseman

Murray Murdoch #9 – Left Winger

Ollie Reinikka #11 - Center

Paul Thompson #10 – Right Winger

Hal Winkler #1 - Goalie

Lester Patrick – Head Coach

Harry Westerby – Trainer, Traveling Secretary

Sam Crawford – Water boy

Chapter One
February 1994

The snow crunches beneath my boots.

I can see the frozen lake through the trees as I carefully make my way along the path. I use my stick like a hiking pole.

I am too old to risk slipping and breaking a hip on this trail. Soon, I'll be safe on the ice.

Their skates glide along the surface, and I can hear every turn and stop the children make. The sound of pucks slapping against stick blades as another kid yells for a pass. These are sounds I've been around my whole life. I stop and just listen for a moment. By sound alone I suspect none of them has the gift.

But I hear their laughter before I see their smiles. I know they are having fun as I reach the edge of the ice.

That's all that matters.

The trees are leafless, and the sky is bright and clear. The wintry air reminds me of home. Clean and crisp in the lungs as I breathe deeply.

I suddenly crave a cigarette.

Ahead is the small shack. An older man, yet certainly twenty-five or more years my junior collects five dollars from every skater through a window. I marvel that people now pay to skate on a frozen pond. But this is not Lucknow or Edgerton.

This is Westchester County, some twenty miles north of Manhattan and behind a women's college. Here the local fire department checks to ensure the ice is safe. A green flag by the road and people can skate. Red and they drive on. The shack sells hot chocolate, coffee, and snacks but they've long since stopped selling cigarettes.

There are wooden benches for the parents who don't venture out onto the ice. I can't hear what they're discussing but it seems vitally important, something about annuities and stock options I imagine.

Not all the parents are on the sidelines. Several mothers and fathers are skating with their children. I didn't know that experience as a child. Mom did not like the feel of skates on her feet. Dad was just too tired. He would often come home too exhausted to even talk.

"Those are antiques" the man in the shack comments with a chuckle at the skates hung over my shoulder and the wooden 'Northland' stick in my hand. My skates and stick are older than the man in the booth.

I notice the rectangular bulge beneath his sweater. I put down a ten-dollar bill.

"That's for two skaters and I wonder if I can bum a smoke?" I ask.

He reaches under his sweater and pulls out a pack of the quintessential American brand. He shakes it just so and extends his hand. From the hole in the foil, I pull out a stick.

I hesitate before putting it to my lips. It's been some years since I quit. I'm about to break many promises to my Marie and Joan, but whatever guilt I harbor vanishes as he strikes a match.

I am ninety, and I do not have many, if any, winters left. I inhale and immediately cough. He's chuckling. I smile and reply, "It's been a while." and I take another drag.

"Canadian Aye? My name's Nick, nice to meet you. Here with one of your great grandchildren aye?"

I have less patience for people these days, and mimicking a Canadian accent has me wrapping this conversation up quickly.

"Thanks, my friend will be joining me shortly." I offer, "He's a tall guy in his early thirties, will look like an athlete." waving the cigarette I turn and head over to the edge of the lake.

The snow-covered ground is a good six inches above the ice level. Judging from all the boots lying around, skaters still use this spot to lace up and launch themselves onto the ice. As they have for decades.

I decide it's a nice place to enjoy my smoke as I wait. I sit on an empty bench, far from anyone, and watch as a young girl celebrates after scoring a goal. She's dashing around with both her arms raised and smiling. I immediately recognize who's pose she's emulating, and I chuckle at the irony. She's even wearing his number 11 jersey. My smile grows, delighted the hockey gods still have a sense of humor.

I scan the ice and take in the other activity. A group of kids are racing each other. A teenage boy skates to join the pickup game at the far end. A young father supports his child's weight by lifting the kid's hands. The child's blades are barely touching the ice. I admire the father's intent, but the child isn't going to learn and the father's only going to mess up his back.

A hawk glides over the trees. The sky is such a bright blue.

Joan is insisting I move to South Carolina and live with her family on Pawleys Island.

I know this will be the last visit I make here. I've come every few years and ponder what might have happened. To remember and honor. I can't help but wonder what might have been.

Ching, Sam, and I skated together on this very spot. Lester asked for volunteers during our Christmas dinner to visit a local orphanage. Sam put the whole excursion together. The building that once housed the orphanage is now part of the women's college behind me.

After all these years I still remember their laughter. It was a beautiful and snowy day. The smile on those kids faces. And the boy who clung to Ching! Ching was as tough as any man I've ever met, but that moment stayed with us both. We never learned if that young child could skate. But Ching knew the kid wasn't clinging to his hand for balance. The kid craved contact. And that January afternoon Ching was happy to oblige. I miss Ching. He was a good man.

The darkness comes over me like a wave. He was a good man. I miss him. I miss them all. They are all gone.

My hand, it shakes as I take a drag from my cigarette.

I am the last.

It was sixty-eight years ago that we last saw Sam. I've asked myself many times, how could someone I'd known for such a brief time, just a few months really, have such an impact? Although he was only 15, seven years my junior at the time he was so…gifted.

He had more potential than any player we had ever seen. We were in awe. We were certain, even those of us who were afraid and jealous of his gift, that he was destined for greatness.

This large frozen lake is now part of a series of interconnected reservoirs that are a vast system that feeds water to the city.

But back then, with Sam, Ching, and the kids, this was just a large frozen body of water to play on.

The sound of another kid celebrating a goal brings my attention back to the ice but only for a moment. Here in this peaceful serenity, I close my eyes and absorb the sounds around me; the joyful yelling of childhood, a youngster crying after falling, laughter and cajoling from others. Pucks against stick blades. Skates against the ice.

Sound travels across the frozen body and in the distance, I hear a train whistle. I am not far from the river and it's the same track we traveled together. Many of our trips to Canada during those years, before the planes, were traveled up and down the Hudson. I look at the cigarette in my hand and take a last drag. Our first trip together was on that very track. When we were a new team in ‘26.

Chapter Two
November 15, 1926

The sun had been up a couple hours and we had already eaten a simple breakfast of scrambled eggs, toast, marmalade and washed it all down with black coffee.

A lot of coffee.

We remained in the Pullman food car, commandeered two tables, and played cards to pass the time.

The coffee kept flowing as fast as the porter could refill his silver pot. The rollicking cabin was thick with smoke, and no one thought to crack open a window.

Streaming past on our left were forests, farms, and small villages. The right side was dominated by the wide Hudson and mountains further in the distance.

Bunny looked up just in time to catch sight of a fire damaged medieval-looking castle standing just off the shore on a small island. He whistled.

"Thought those were all in Europe" he said to our table as Frankie showed his flush and pulled the coins toward him.

We were quickly learning that Frankie's Irish blood made him luckiest with the cards.

The young porter, explained as he refilled our cups that the castle had been an artillery depot that exploded just a few years before. "It's Bannerman Island and residents clear on the other side of the river felt the explosion."

Frankie shuffled the cards and dealt to the six of us crammed around our table. All of us dressed in our wool suits in various shades of gray and brown. More than any of us, Frankie looked most like a banker or businessman. He had that professional air about him.

He first dealt cards to Bunny Cook, whose real name was Fred. Had Bunny gone to university he would have been a frat boy.

Then next to Taffy Abel, whose real name was Clarence and the only American on the team. I had never met a man more uncomfortable in a suit. Taffy always looked rumpled, and he frequently fidgeted with his collar. He's shoulders were too large, and the seam down the back of his jacket was in constant fear of splitting open. Yet, when not on the ice, he was in a perpetual happy-go-lucky mode and seemed oblivious to his appearance.

Sitting next to him was his defensive partner, Ching Johnson. I didn't know Ching's real first name yet, but I knew he wasn't remotely Asian, so there had to be a story. Ching and I got off to a hard start but have since found our stride.

The nearly bald Ching was someone you needed to be careful around. As big as Taffy but harder and meaner looking. Both looked like steelworkers. One wrong comment might get a person in more trouble than they could handle. Ching was devastating to the body on the ice and fearless in a scuffle, as I learned all too well, but he could flash a warm smile and light up any room. His tailor seemed to have no trouble fitting him.

I sat between Ching and to my left was Bunny's older brother Bill. The Cook brothers originated from a small town deep in Ontario. At the age of thirty, Bill was the oldest player on our team and our undisputed Captain. He was quiet but he set the rules and a high bar. He had served in the War, although never spoke of it. No one voted him captain. It just happened naturally, and no one would ever dispute or question it. He had a quality about him that instantly invoked respect and command. If he wasn't born with this presence, he learned it on the bloody, gas-filled battlefields of Europe.

Bill and Ching were the only two that had served in the horrible war and seen action. Their respect for one another was not in dispute. Yet they rarely spoke to each other about any topic outside of hockey strategy. They were like two big dogs who respected each other's space. While Ching led the defensive squad, Bill led the whole team.

Winning yet another hand with three queens and two eights was the increasingly wealthy Frankie Boucher. Nicknamed Raffles for the famed fictional gentleman thief, our centerman sat, as always between our two starting wingers Bill and Bunny. The three of them comprised our forward line of skaters the press already dubbed the "A Line" for the subway that run beneath our new arena.

Bill encouraged the first line to stay in formation as often as possible. Frankie was always physically between them. Bunny to his left, Bill on his right. It didn't matter if we were eating, in the locker room, at a boxing match or playing cards. Bill wanted Frankie to see Bunny on one side and himself on the other. Bill wanted them to learn and anticipate each other's every move and decision.

The only time they were not together was at night as each had a different bunk mate at a hotel or here in the Pullman sleeping cabins.

Taffy, Ching, Bunny, Frankie, and Bill were clearly going to be our starting five skaters.

My role was made clear once the roster was settled and I made the team. That was an uncertain fate throughout training camp. I was to be the second line left wing to give Bunny a breather whenever needed.

Which wouldn't be often. The starters would play most of the game.

At the table next to us, the other backups passed the time just as we were; cards, coffee, smokes, and talking about dames and the game.

Paul Thompson and Oliver Reinikka were my likely line-mates. Ollie, the Cook brothers and Frankie were the only guys with any professional experience. Frankie was the only player on the team with actual playoff experience. Although Taffy had the distinction of winning a silver medal in the 1924 Olympics for the US squad in France. He only mentioned this achievement once before realizing Bill and Ching had been in western Europe for other reasons.

The rest played in the semi-pro leagues. I was the only person who also played for a university. Expectations around New York couldn't be high.

I was a little concerned about my line mate Paul. At twenty he was a smooth and confident player, but perhaps a little too cocky with his dark curly hair and handsome good looks. He was already at odds with our coach over playing time. He had a face that looked like it'd never been punched.

Reg Mackey was our backup defensemen and the quietest guy on the team. He was friendly enough, just very private. Happy to play cards and eat with us. But always in the background.

Also sitting at the table were our two goalies Hal Winkler and Lorne Chabot. It was assumed we would only carry one goalie during the season but we broke camp without having decided. Both were spartan, stoic men. Lorne was the larger of the two and I always preferred a big man between the pipes. He had comically large dark eyebrows and a dower expression even when happy and laughing. Lorne and Hal got along well and often kept to themselves. Goalies are a separate breed.

Hal rarely removed his cappy, even on the ice. Although a very handsome and chiseled bloke, he was balding at an early age. He was often lost in a book, content in some far-off adventure. Both men were professional and with no sense of rivalry towards the other. Good men, both. I didn't envy the inevitable choice our coach would have to make.

Our train had come to a brief stop in a village named Garrison and we all stepped outside to stretch our legs. We lit fresh smokes and admired the view.

Across the river was the imposing United States military academy at West Point. It was built into the side of an impressive and domineering mountain range well above the water.

Our train was only temporarily delayed, and the conductor informed us we would still arrive at Grand Central Station before noon. The idea that we Canadians would be living in Manhattan was surreal. Taffy was American, but only because he was born on the U.S. side of Sault Ste. Marie in Michigan. Sault Ste, Marie is two cities by the same name that literally straddle a river separating both countries. So, we figured he's Canadian in all but currency.

We all made this journey without our wives or gals. Marie would love this scene and be completely comfortable joining us for a smoke. I struggle to comprehend how we've all found ourselves moving to Manhattan to play professional hockey. But for myself, it started with a simple letter.

Chapter Three
Summer 1926

"Murray, who's Connie?" Marie asked with a playful hint of jealously through the screen door. "You have a letter in today's post from a Connie Smythe."

I struggled to push the heavy reel mower over uneven ground, half buried rocks, and patches of dirt that kicked up a choking cloud. All to cut weeds and brush that were quickly encroaching around our tiny house. It was a losing battle. A scythe might be more effective. Or better yet, a controlled burn.

I paused to wipe the sweat and dirt from my forehead and smiled. Marie puts on a show of dramatically sauntering down the porch steps in her floral sundress. She had the suspicious letter in one hand, and a refreshing glass of homemade lemonade in the other.

"So? Who's this Connie?" She offered me the letter with an outstretched hand. She kept the glass of sweetened water beyond my reach.

"I don't know a Connie my love. Why don't you read it to me while I enjoy that glass of sunshine in your other hand?"

"The envelop says she's from New York. Are you hiding a floozy from me in far off Manhattan Mr. Murdoch?"

"I will happily answer that question Mrs. Murdoch, after I've sipped from that glass you're keeping away from me. While I'm quenching my thirst, you're welcome to unseal the incriminating document and reveal its immoral and sinful contents yourself."

"Deal". She swapped hands.

As quickly as I drank from the glass, she ripped opened the envelop and unfolded a typed letter.

I teased "Oh, a romantic letter on typed letterhead! How excitingly blasphemous this portends. My oh my, this lemonade is wickedly delicious, thank you."

She read the letter silently. Her eyes flicked across the page. Her expression, stone-faced. She read it twice and dropped her hand to her side. She stared off into the distance to some far-off place.

"What does it say?" I asked, troubled by her reaction.

"We have to discuss this." She handed me the letter before turning and going back to the house.

My first semi-pro hockey season with the local Winnipeg Maroons had finished two months earlier and I was selling insurance and beating back the brush around our house for the summer. I was only two years out of the University of Manitoba, where in '23 we won the Memorial Cup. That was something of a big deal around these parts.

Marie and I were married two days after Christmas in '25, and happily settled. Marie's father died when she was only three and her mother was rarely in good health these days. We wanted very much to give her mom and my parents their first grandchild. Marie helps her sister run a restaurant that often caters to weddings and funerals.

Two decades earlier, that same restaurant was used after her father's funeral. There was little doubt, it would soon be used for her mother.

My parents supported my hockey as a hobby. But they always stressed an education so I could escape the farm. I knew Dad didn't want that life for me. He loved farming but the droughts were getting worse and the margins narrower. The business was all but impossible, even for a man with a will made of iron. He would never quit, but he didn't want me to begin that journey. I sell insurance and will soon be an accountant. I will keep mowing the weeds, the closest to farming he wants me, and Marie and I will raise a family here.

I don't know how this Connie Smythe, now presumably a male, discovered me. But his letter invited me to meet him in Duluth, Minnesota, all expenses paid if I wanted to play professional hockey in New York City. He said he would have a contract ready for me to sign.

We were dumbfounded.

Playing in New York, as preposterous as that sounded, utterly terrified, and undeniably intrigued us both. This was not anything we had ever contemplated. The offer came literally out of the blue from another country.

We knew there was only one thing to do when faced with such an unexpected quandary.

Go fishing.

We both dropped lines in the water as we sat in our Wasatch canoe at the confluence of the Red and Assiniboine Rivers. We sat in silence with our backs pressed against each other. I designed and cut the mid-bench to accommodate us both. It was our way of making fishing together more romantic.

Marie and I never tired of being in physical contact. In public we would often hold hands. Our feet would find each other under the dinner table. If not cuddling or spooning while sleeping, one of us would inevitably drape an arm over the other. It wasn't unusual to be awakened by Marie's sleeping hand across on my face.

I lite a cigarette and passed it behind me to share with her. Smoking among young women was frowned upon in these parts. My Marie was a rebellious flapper.

We took in the beauty of this favorite spot. It was peaceful with low green brush gently swaying in the breeze along the shorelines. Isolated, yet near the center of the city. The tributary had a strong current under a placid surface. Depending on the season it was gifted with a seemingly endless supply of northern pike, smallmouth bass, bullheads, walleye, carp, and sturgeon. In the winter months we would drill holes and ice fish for free dinners. An ideal spot for contemplating family decisions.

"We should just ignore the letter. Playing semi-pro puts a few extra bank notes in our pocket while I cut my teeth selling insurance." I argued. "I play locally during the week. Even the further away weekend games don't uproot our lives. In another year or two I'll land a better job. We already have a home, and our families are here. Marie, why would we consider this ludicrous letter? Our lives are good. If I even make the team, which is a silly long shot, how long could I possibly play? One season? Two if I'm lucky and don't get hurt? I could be traded at any time, and I would have no control over where I'm sent."

"That's all a real possibility Murray." She reassuringly agreed. "I can't argue with any of that logic."

"So why are we even discussing this?" I tried to ask calmly, but I know it came out snappish.

Marie, hearing this anxiety in my voice sat silently for a bit before finding her words.

"Murray, it's not every day that a letter arrives inviting you to work in Hollywood as an actor, or to run for a government position in Ottawa. You've been invited to play professional hockey, a game you love, in the biggest, most exciting city in the world. I know you're a hell of a hockey player and apparently someone else suspects it too. I think we should at least hear what this Connie Smythe has to offer. We can't make a good decision without knowing all the facts. Murray, I've barely been out Manitoba. I've followed you to some small cities in Saskatchewan and Ontario. The thought of our living in New York for a while is terrifying and yet…" She paused for just a few seconds before continuing.

"…I know you." She continued. "You'll never forgive yourself if you don't explore this. A year from now, you'll be sitting on our porch, drink in one hand, cigarette in the other, rocking back and forth. The wondering what might have been will eat you up. I don't want you to have that regret. I don't want you to get hurt either, but you're already playing and that could happen right here. By the way, I can't see your pole behind me, but I know you've had a fish on the end of your line for the last minute. Don't you want to reel it in and see what you've caught?"

I telegraphed Smythe explaining I would not be traveling to Minnesota, but he was welcome to take the train to Winnipeg if he wanted to meet. He responded almost immediately and called my bluff. He agreed to come to us.

Marie and I waited in the high-vaulted lobby of the Fort Garry Hotel at the appointed hour. It was mid-afternoon and there were only a handful of hotel guests reading papers and drinking coffees in high-backed leather chairs. We had no expectation that he would be on time. Trains were often delayed, and it was already twenty minutes past the agreed hour.

We kept an eye on the main entrance and a dainty but sharply dressed businessman impatiently strode into the room. He wore a thin pencil mustache. I stood and asked, "Mr. Smythe?"

He approached us as if uncomfortably hurried and annoyed.

"Mr. Murdoch?"

"Yes, welcome to Winnipeg; this is my wife, Marie." We both greeted him with warm, friendly smiles and outstretched hands.

"Mr. Murdoch, I wasn't expecting your wife to join our business meeting." I shake his hand, but I am unimpressed.

First impressions matter. I hold his gaze and smile. He's a cocky windbag with cold arrogant eyes. I instantly regretted this meeting and wanted to leave.

Marie kept her hand out. After a brief awkward pause, he shook it begrudgingly and as quickly as possible.

We sat down at a small round table, and he presented his proposition by sliding a contract onto the table. He placed a pen on it for effect.

He offered little new in the way of information. A new professional hockey team was forming in New York and would start practice this October in Toronto. If I made the team, there would be forty-four regular season games. We would be playing our home games at a year-old arena in the Broadway district of Manhattan.

I shared my misgivings.

"I'm sorry Mr. Smythe, but I'm not sold on this. I don't know if you can put together a competitive team or not. I don't want to live in New York for six months and lose game after game."

This meeting was proving harder than he anticipated. Not hiding his annoyance, he went on at length to brag about his credentials and how this team would have star players. Big names that would sell tickets and win game.

His promises didn't work on us.

He must have realized we were completely unimpressed, so he offered me $2,500 for one year if I made the team.

Marie spoke. "I'm sorry you came all this way Mr. Smythe, thank you for the offer but that's not sufficient for us to uproot our lives here."

Smythe barely concealed his contempt at Marie's involvement in the discussion. "$2,500 is a lot of money for Winnipeg Mrs. Murdoch. Surely you know this is nothing to sneeze at. You can buy a lot of pantyhose with this dough."

"Sir," she paused and smiled. I knew enough to sit back and enjoy the show.

"It's a very nice salary for Winnipeg, but my husband and I would be living in Manhattan. It's my understanding that pantyhose cost considerably more 'dough' there."

He sat back and begrudgingly offered $3000 with a sneer.

Marie immediately leaned forward and countered with $7000 and a smile.

"Mr. Murdoch, your wife must be joking."

"No, she's not Mr. Smythe. We're happy and our prospects are good here. Frankly, I'm not at all confident we're going to like living in New York City. $7,000 seems reasonable considering this line of work and that you need to fill out a roster."

Marie and I sat stone faced. The truth was, $3000 was a lot of money for us to leave on the table. More than that, accounting was hardly exciting, and I love playing. The semi-pro league was fine. But to play at the highest professional level suddenly starting to feel like a dream come true. A dream I never really allowed myself to embrace before that letter arrived.

"I cannot authorize a penny above $5000 for one year Mr. Murdoch. Do you accept my offer; conditional on your making the team of course."

I tried not to swallow. Marie was as cool as a cucumber. Neither of us had ever been out of Canada but I was intimidated about New York. I hesitated just a moment and, in that ever so brief span of time, Smythe blinked. He pulled out a roll of new one-hundred-dollar bills.

I could only think "who carries cash like that?"

"Of course, I understand you will need some cash advance." He explained.

He started counting out fifteen $100 U.S. dollar bills right in front of us. It was more money than we had ever seen at one time.

Marie didn't hesitate.

"No, it's not an advance Mr. Smythe, it's a signing bonus regardless of his making the team or not. That's in addition to the $5000 for the season. Agreed?"

Marie reached out her hand to shake on the deal.

The contract I signed stipulated that in September I was to travel to New York for a press event to introduce the team. Smythe explained this would coincide with a major boxing match involving Jack Dempsey and all the local reporters would be in one place.

In October, I was expected to report to our first training camp in Toronto.

Chapter Four
October 1926

I walked into the Ravina Gardens locker room and the unmistakable smell of stale sweat convinced me I was in the right place.

The small room was overcrowded, and the benches were already full of guys getting changed, smoking, and drinking from glass bottles of Coca-Cola. I placed my stick with all the others lined against the wall and a short snub-nosed fella came over.

"I'm Harry Westerby, the team's trainer and equipment manager. Forward, defense or goalie?"

"Forward" I replied.

He handed me a white sweater. On the front was a cartoon cowboy atop a rearing horse. The cowboy was waving a hockey stick over his head. It was an ugly sweater.

"Are we called the cowboys?" I asked. Harry shrugged his shoulders.

"The press is trying out names, last week I heard 'Tex's Ranchers' and then 'Tex's Broncos'." He turned away to hand out another sweater.

I grabbed a wooden chair from the hallway and took the lone vacant spot in the center of the room near the unlit wood stove. A black pipe rose to the ceiling and then vented out a side wall.

I neatly hung my suit jacket on the back of my chair while looking around the noisy room for anyone I knew.

I caught Taffy's attention and then Bunny shouted, "Hey Murdoch, over here". Both those guys I had meet last month at the bout under the most chaotic of circumstances. I was relieved to see some familiar faces.

Weeks before, on September 23rd I arrived in New York's Pennsylvania Station alone to utter confusion. I never imagined in my wildest dreams a more magnificent or complex structure. Curved steel girders held countless glass windows overhead, allowing the platform to be bathed in light. It was morning and all of humanity was hustling and jockeying past me. It was the embodiment of all I feared this metropolis would be. I hadn't even left the station platform and I felt swallowed up. It seemed I was the only person who didn't know where to go. Crushing anxiety was building rapidly. I immediately wanted to get back on the train and return home when I spotted a handwritten placard being held up by a man above the crowd at the end of our platform.

"Murdoch" was below the names Abel and Cook. I approached just as three other strangers did the same. I surmised that the four of us must have just arrived on the same train.

The man with the placard put it down and said "oh good, you're all here. That was easy."

He didn't bother to introduce himself but instead reached into his breast pocket and pulled out four envelops and handed one to each of us.

"Sorry, but there's been a change in plans. The tonight's fight is moved to Philadelphia, so all the press are there now. Your train leaves in forty-five minutes on track 37. I wrote down the name of the hotel where you'll be staying. In the envelop is both your train ticket to Philly, a ticket for the fight and a train ticket for you to return home tomorrow. The fight is outside and unfortunately, they expect heavy rain. Hope you all have a change of clothes because you're going to get wet. I'll wire the Colonel and let him know the four of you will be arriving. He'll probably met you at the station. If not, head to the hotel and wait for him there. The

Colonel and Mr. Rickard send their regards and welcome you to New York. Sorry your stay wasn't longer."

The man wished us well, pointed in the general direction of track 37 and rushed off, disappearing into the mass of people.

As we made our way to the new train, introductions revealed "Cook" on the placard was for brothers, Bill and Bunny. The other fella, Taffy Abel and I did our best to keep up. The Cook brothers seemed to know their way around this station. As we walked briskly, through the strong currents of train passengers, Bunny explained over his shoulder. "My brother Bill and I have been here before. Our sisters live in Brooklyn."

The Cooks didn't seem the least put out by this unexpected change in plans, so I just went along pretending I wasn't nearly as overwhelmed as I felt.

On the ride to Philadelphia, we compared notes. I had the least information to share. The Cooks knew our new boss was named Tex Rickard. Among other business ventures he was a highly successful boxing promoter, and this Jack Dempsey verses Gene Tunney fight was his production. Rickard originally expected the fight to be held at Yankee Stadium. But there was some issue with the New York State Boxing Commission giving Dempsey a license. Instead, Rickard hastily moved the fight to Philadelphia. But in all the bustle and jockeying, no one remembered we were coming to New York until we were already on our way. Hence, we were now shuffled down to Philadelphia. I guess it made sense that with all of New York's sports writers there for the "Fight of the Century" that would be where he'd want us.

We briefly met Mr. Rickard at the press luncheon after we arrived. Bow-tied, square jawed, and cigar in hand, Mr. Rickard might have been raised in Texas, but he certainly fit my imagination of a New York magnet.

Ironically, I learned a lot more from the sports writers than they got from me.

Mr. Rickard built and opened Madison Square Garden only the year before in 1925 to showcase his bouts, the circus, bike races and hockey.

The National Hockey League granted the first team to New York under the ownership of Big Bill Dwyer. Dwyer is reputed to be a bootlegger and local gangster and he signed a lease with Rickard to rent ice and play at the Garden during the 1925-26 season and beyond.

New York's first professional hockey team, the Americans, thus came into existence last year.

But Rickard still had open dates on the calendar and wanted them filled. He saw that the Amerks, as they were nicknamed by the press, were selling seats. He began wondering why he didn't just own his own team, in addition to renting the ice to the Americans. New York and the Garden were big enough to support two teams.

When he heard the new National Hockey League wanted to continue expanding, he sent his friend and business partner Colonel John Hammond to investigate.

Hammond, a West Point Graduate, traveled to Montreal on behalf of Rickard and discovered two things before the Garden was even built.

The movie houses closed on days when important hockey games were being played; and the Mount Royal rink was so crowded he could barely move between periods.

All this coincided with the folding of the Western Hockey League and there were suddenly many players available.

Detroit, Chicago and a second New York City franchise, this time owned by Mr. Rickard, were awarded for the 1926 season.

Rickard already had a rink for his new team. He figured all he needed were the players, staff, and a name for the team. He and Hammond hired a young up-and-coming character in Connie Smythe to be the team's Manager. It was Smythe's job to worry about all the details.

Hammond told Smythe to hire big name players to fill the seats every night. Smythe must have had another agenda because he hired the lot of us instead.

None of us were a marquee draw or could sell tickets on our name. New York already had Babe Ruth, Lou Gehrig, Jack Dempsey, and Red Grange playing for the newly formed Yankees football team, so Hammond made it clear to Smythe that big names were expected.

Instead, I was one of the first Smythe signed. I'm confident no one in New York had ever heard of Murray Murdoch.

The forecast was correct. We arrived in Philadelphia during torrential conditions and after the press luncheon and checking into our hotel, we made our way to Sesquicentennial Stadium. For ten rounds, along with 120,000 others, we watched Tunney beat Dempsey in the pouring rain.

It was a whirlwind experience, so crowded, so hurried, so wet. We did have a change of clothes, but none of us thought to bring another pair of shoes. Once in our train berth the next day, we rode back to Canada in our bare feet. Our shoes and socks laid out to dry.

After a quick handshake and backslap with Bun and Taffy in the crowded locker-room, I unstrapped my leather equipment bag and like all players I first pulled up my jock. My one-piece knee and shin pads were made of thin strips of cane held together with leather and padded with felt. I pulled up my knit stockings and I noticed everyone was wearing the colors of whatever team they previously played with. Mine were well-worn off-white with maroon stripes from my team back in Winnipeg. After one full season they were torn in spots although Marie kept them stitched together. I pulled up my padded tan pants and got the suspenders over my shoulders.

A guy across from me made a joke about my skates. Like the rest of my gear, nothing was replaced often, and I knew my skates were old. They were a gift from my parent when I started university. They had very little money, so they purchased an already outdated model. The skates were beyond their means, mom had to pull several more hours to pay for them.

This guy thought it was funny that my blades were curved equally in the front and back. I knew it was a style that had gone out of fashion some time ago, but they carried me just fine. I made note of his face and wondered if we'd be doing some checking today.

Smythe walked into the room dressed just as I had last seen him back at the Fort Garry Hotel. Dapper and polished. He stood waiting until we quieted down, but the guys weren't even aware he had entered and kept right on talking. I sensed Smythe was expecting obediencc merely by walking into the room. He was getting agitated like water reaching the boiling point in a tea pot.

From behind me came a firm "settle down and listen up." The stern voice was not loud, yet everyone in the room immediately quieted down.

We collectively turned our heads toward the source in the back corner.

I immediately recognized Bun's brother, Bill. He was a handsome veteran player, with dark slicked back hair with a strong widow's peak. Although it was morning and he was clean cut, I wasn't altogether sure he wouldn't need another shave by dinner. He was fully dressed and ready to hit the ice. We gave each other a knowing nod.

Smythe slammed his clipboard against the doorframe, loud enough to get everyone's attention directed his way. "There are twenty-two men in this room. I am taking eleven skaters and a goalie with me to New York. The rest of you are going back home to your pathetic farms and small towns. Where's Murdock?"

I stood up.

Smythe glared at me with contempt. "Where's your wife Murdock? Don't bother unpacking your suitcase. You're on the wrong NHL list."

He turned and walked out of the room.

I was utterly confused, and I felt my tempter rising fast. The wrong National Hockey League? What did he even mean?

The same jerk who laughed at my skates chuckled loudly, sensing my embarrassment at being called out in front of everyone. "He means Not Here Long. Hope you bought a round trip ticket home."

Chapter Five
October 1926

Our first practice, or as Smythe made clear our first "tryout", followed a format familiar to all of us. We warmed up with a few laps around the rink and then Smythe put us through a series of speed and agility drills. We were driven hard to gauge our endurance. After we worked up a good sweat our stick handling skills were tested. Several standouts emerged early on. It was clear who were the professionals and who were the amateurs hoping for a spot.

Bill Cook was the best player on the ice, performing each task with an intensity and drive many of the others lacked. While Smythe stood in the visitor's bench area along with his pocket watch, clipboard and barking instructions, Bill quietly lead by example on the ice.

Bill skated up to me while I was waiting to take my turn on one of the early drills. "You look good Murray, I'm sorry we didn't get to talk in the locker room earlier. And it's unfortunate Smythe called you out like that. Let's find a drink later, ok?"

I was looking forward to several of the guys searching out a hidden speakeasy and enjoying a "pop" together. It being illegal to serve alcohol in the states and parts of Canada, I found it hard to imagine how the two countries were functioning at all.

From the barefooted train ride, I learned the two brothers were originally from Kingston and later Brantford. Bill was seven years older and when he returned from the First World War the two brothers moved west to farm and play for the Saskatoon Sheiks in the Western Canada Hockey League. They were stars out west, but the league ran out of money just as Connie showed up with an offer to play in New York.

Now that we were all seeing each other skate for the first time I immediately understood how Fred Cook got his nickname, Bunny. He had a unique skating style whereby he would often appear to hop between strides. While unorthodox it also allowed for a powerful jump start and his speed was undeniable. For a big man he was quick.

After a noon break, where we each had to provide our own food; I had cold chicken legs left over from the previous night's dinner, we broke up into groups.

Defenders in blue, forwards in white and goalies in red.

From the very first drill Bunny Cook, Frank Boucher and Bill Cook grouped together as our leading attackers. The three of them would bring the puck into the offensive zone against two defensemen and a goalie. Often, they would find the back of the net. All the other forward players were interchangeable, but Cook, Boucher, and Cook were set in stone right at that first session.

Smythe would yell and find something to criticize on almost every play. I could often see guys out of position or misreading a play. But even when it seemed we were doing everything correctly he would find something to roar about. He liked to yell.

His whistle would stop plays in mid-action and he'd make us start over again. Some of his comments were fair but others left us more confused.

Bill would occasionally skate near the flummoxed player and try to explain what he thought Smythe wanted. But in truth, he wasn't always sure either.

Smythe noticed these interactions and inexplicably resented Cook's efforts to help. Although it wasn't Bill Cook's intention, Smythe overreacted as if his authority was being threatened right from the start. His response was to assert it even more forcefully and now he started berating the first line. Bill noticed the bulging veins in Smythe's neck and tempered back. But during these early hours, Smythe's insecurity was barefaced. He lost our confidence before he ever had a chance to build it.

As the day was growing late, things were not going well. Smythe's surly attitude was part of the problem. Except for the first line, the guys just weren't making plays or coming together. The two guys I was paired up with, named Mickey and Bud, were particularly weak in my estimation. Yet they both had an attitude that two roster spots were already theirs. I got the sense some of these guys came to camp assuming they had made the team. Suddenly there were twenty-two players in camp fighting for eleven spots. After a few hours it was clear five of those eleven roster spots would include the names of Bill and Bunny Cook, Frank Boucher, Taffy, and another intimidating defenseman people were calling Ching.

Everyone's mood was growing increasingly foul. As the drills wore on, we were getting more physical. Smythe had me convinced this would be my only practice. He was riding me hard and finding something wrong with my every move or decision. I knew I was a darn good hockey player but within hours he had torn away at my confidence.

It was our turn again. Smythe blew his whistle for us to go.

I skated up the left side and my center attempted to send the puck my way as he came under pressure. The pass was several feet behind me, so I let it bounce off the boards as I made a tight loop. I picked up the ricochet right onto my stick at full stride. The other defenseman squared off and tried to tangle me up. But I took the puck wide outside and was able to get around him. He knew he was beat and that I had a clear path to the net. I heard him curse at me. I felt his stick catch around my ankle. He yanked unnecessarily hard. It was more than a tripping. It felt like he was trying to ripe my skate right off my foot.

Falling, I instinctively backhanded the puck across the ice some ten feet in front of the net. It was a perfect centering pass but neither of my line-mates were in position to take advantage. The puck bounced harmlessly off the far boards, and I found myself lying flat on my stomach sliding on the ice.

An unexpected pain suddenly took my breath away. The wooden blade of the defender's stick violently stabbed me just under my ribcage as he skated by.

"What the…?" I gasped as I made eye contact with the goalie. He was only a few feet away and I could see his concern beneath bushy eyebrows. I must have looked like a fish on a frozen pond gasping to breath.

"Jeez, are you ok?" He asked but before I could answer he yelled at the defenseman "That was bush league!"

I quickly glanced back to see the defenseman skating away with a smirk. It was the same fool who had laughed at my skates back in the locker room while I was getting dressed. I picked up that his name was Sparky Vail. I smiled through the pain.

I heard Smythe screaming "Get your lazy ass up Murdoch. You're slowing us down. Go home to your wife so she can kiss your boo-boo."

My blood was boiling now. I skated back to the group of forwards near center ice. My supposed linemates, Mickey and Bud were snickering.

I was having none of this.

Smythe blew the whistle for the next line to go.

Waiting their turn next in line, Bill, Bunny, and Frank gave me a sympathetic look. They knew that neither of my line-mates were up to par. I skated up to my center and winger and asked softly but seriously, "One of you needed to be crashing the net there, you know that right?"

They looked confused and amused by my question. I looked from one to the other and said in a quiet voice, "you guys need to find another winger".

Smythe's whistle blew as the play underway petered out.

I turned and saw that the first line was now getting into position to attack. They were facing off against the defenseman called Ching…and Sparky.

I skated over to Bill Cook as he was taking position on the right side against Vail.

"Hey, mind if I take this shift Bill?"

Amused, Bill came out of his ready position and retreated to lean along the boards and watch.

"You sure you're ready, you look to still be in some pain?" he asked.

"I'm good to go, thanks." I replied.

Grinning, Frankie gave me a nod and exploded forward just as Smyth blew his whistle to start the play.

He made a quick fake to me and passed the puck sharply to Bunny on his left. Bunny took the pass and came to a hard stop, ice sprayed from his skates. The defenseman Ching, caught off guard by the quick unexpected stop, recovered to re-engage Bunny. But Bunny was too fast. He saw me coming down the right side and shot the puck clear across the ice and put it right on my blade without my having to adjust speed.

Sparky was flatfooted for just a moment, unsure whether to engage me or start backing up. I showed no such hesitation. My quick wrist shot sent the puck just past his right ear in the general direction of the net. My intent was not to hit him with it, but to distract him for one heartbeat. Sure enough, he flinched away from the puck.

I lowered my shoulder and made no effort to slow down my momentum. I threw myself into his chest. The explosive force of the open-ice check sent him flying. He landed with a hard thud.

I could hear Smythe angrily screaming in the distance while Bill, Bunny, Frankie, and a few of the other guys laughed hysterically to whoops and hollers. I imagined the rest, including Mickey and Bud, had their jaws hanging open in shock.

I skated past Sparky and warned him, "These old skates. Sometimes I can't stop quickly."

I was suddenly hit by a freight train and sent flying. I slid hard into the boards and looked up at the imposing man-monster.

"I can't let you get away with a hit like that on one of my defensemen." Ching calmly explained.

It probably should have ended right there. I knew he was right, and he didn't seem to be looking for a fight.

But I was. As I got to my feet, I dropped my gloves and sprung. The first punch caught Ching wearing an expression of surprise that I would hit back.

I landed a solid blow right on his chin and it felt as though my fist exploded against a brick wall. His face only barely moved.

I immediately knew I was in trouble as he dropped his gloves. My only chance was speed, and I threw another blow. His expression changed from surprise to a maniacal smile.

He grabbed my sweater and pummeled my face with multiple punches. I couldn't count how many, they landed with such fury. He let go of my sweater, and I dropped right down, landing square and hard on my coccyx bone. A sharp pain shot right up my spine, and for a moment, I wondered if I'd ever walk again.

The familiar iron taste of blood filled my mouth. My vision was filled with stars. I could here a few guys laughing.

A heartbeat passed and I was filled with fear.

My vision was blurry, but I could make out Ching reaching down to pick up his gloves.

To my complete surprise, my legs still worked. Although wobbly, I got back on my feet.

Ching looked at me, "it's over now, let it go Murdoch."

I raised my fists.

No one was laughing now.

A look of resignation washed across his face.

I moved in closer.

"Get your hands a little higher." Ching advised as he threw another punch that I barely deflected.

I returned fire with a left-handed upper cut that found its target. I followed with another right to his chin. It had no more effect than the first blow I threw. We grabbed each other's sweaters and kept throwing fists. Ching had me. I couldn't match his power on my best day. My arms were suddenly so heavy. He was practically holding me up now and the blows stopped.

Simultaneously other players separated us. I was too exhausted to offer much resistance. Bill Cook was pushing me away, "stand down kid, it's over."

Over Bill's shoulder, I suddenly saw Sparky Vail attacking me.

Before he could land a punch, Ching grabbed him around the

waist, picked him up and flipped him backwards like some wrestling move. Vail landed hard on the ice for the second time in minutes. Now Ching raised his voice, “Enough! We’re done.”

Sitting on my stool, I pondered my first and I assumed my last day of camp. I lit a cigarette and took a long, deep drag. The blood on the end of my cigarette looked like one of Marie’s when she wears red lipstick. My face and hands were throbbing. My ass bruised in ways I didn’t want to know about. The room was crowded like before but much quieter. Ching strode over to me, still in his skates.

“Here, these will help.”

He handed me an ice pack and one of two open colas.

We clicked our bottle together and we both chuckled.

“You did good Murdoch.”

“Thanks Ching. I wish we had more time together.”

Chapter Six
October 1926

I could hear Smythe throwing yet another tantrum. I didn't bother to turn around and give him an audience. The sound of our spare sticks, which had been neatly lined against the bench, crashed to the floor. This was Smythe's melodramatic way of adding an exclamation point to his tirade.

"None of you bums know how to skate! Play the damn body, not the puck! Watch the back door damn it, that guy is wide open! Hit that damn guy, hit him! Hit him!"

Smythe was screaming at our defensive squad at this moment but that could change on the very next drill. His fury was fickle. It was the start of our second week, and while I was still his favorite target, he hadn't sent me home yet.

Smythe hadn't sent anyone home yet. We still weren't playing full ice scrimmages, even though we had enough players and goalies. He simply had us running the same drills over and over. It was so monotonous I wondered if Smythe was simply trying to get players to quit out of boredom.

"Hey, watch that stick!" Taffy yelled as one of the forwards clipped the goalie Lorne Chabot in the shoulder, dangerously near his unprotected neck and face. It's a defenseman's job to protect his goalie, but he shouldn't have to do so during practice from his own mates.

Smythe remained silent as the forward yapped back at Taffy. Not a wise move in my estimation. The leaders on the team were left to police the riffraff. I knew things would escalate, just as they had done daily.

Sure enough, the next time that player skated into the zone, Ching and Taffy both rode him right into the boards with enough force to knock over a bull. The forward crumpled to the ice with the wind knocked out of him. Message sent.

Even though many of us were staying at the King Edward hotel we mostly split up after practice into small groups or went our separate ways.

As if our mood wasn't sour enough many of us were missing our gals something awful. A handful of the guys lived in Toronto, so they didn't stay with us at the hotel. They went home to their wives and girlfriends.

Marie and I wrote each other daily. She was a prolific writer with a perfect beautiful script. She was staying with her sister's family, and she took pleasure in describing her days back in Winnipeg. Her letters were a welcome light in the gloom.

I struggled to keep my letters to her from being painfully repetitive and dull. I took to sharing all I could about my potential colorful teammates.

I was rooming with Frank Boucher and there was no doubt he loved his wife Ag every bit as much as I did Marie. Ag and Frank were married two years and I had never witnessed a man more outwardly in love except in the Hollywood movies. Their first child was just a few months old, and I knew being parted was hard on Frank.

They also exchanged daily letters since we arrived and Frank could often be found reading and re-reading them, even sitting on his stool prior to practice. At night I would frequently wake up to see him hunched over the desk writing her by candlelight.

Frank was as much a gentleman as he was a skilled, intelligent, and hardnosed professional hockey player. I bet he could compete with the starting center on most clubs. He specialized in poke-checking the puck away from opposing players, hence his nickname Raffles for the fictional gentleman thief. Two of his brothers were also expected to be playing in the NHL this season.

Perhaps it was because he had a large Irish family, but Frank was a lover of telling stories, and he could spin tails without end.

If he wasn't writing Ag, he was telling us stories and I did my best to share them with Marie.

My dearest Marie,

I skated strong today, but the camp is still a disaster. I doubt this is going to improve. The problem is our friend Connie. Our instincts about him when we first met in Winnipeg were right. Too much time is wasted. He's unable to control the day and resorts to yelling and screaming at everyone, including the best players on the ice who are performing well. Marie, some of these guys are really good. The Cook brothers and Frankie are an outstanding line and I'm learning a lot from them. We have a defensive pairing in Ching and Taffy that no one gets through. Two of our goaltenders are especially tough. In my opinion there are about eight players that should have been cut last week. I fall somewhere between these two groups. I'd say that Connie Smythe has it out for me, but he seems to have it out for everyone.

We heard a rumor the Toronto St. Pats offered us a great player in the famous Babe Dye, but Smythe squashed the deal. I have no idea why. Toronto wasted no time and instead sold him to the new team in Chicago. We are still a team without a well-known player and I'm thinking Rickard and Hammond can't be happy. Babe Dye is a player who puts paying spectators in their seats. He scored 38 goals two seasons ago. Dye is exactly the kind of player Hammond hired Smythe to find. I think our starters are competitive, but none has a recognizable name outside of western Canada.

My roommate Frank has been in form with his stories. Here are his latest.

Like many of us, he was on the ice as a wee lad in a pair of hand-me-down skates. In his case, they were probably hand-me-downs from one of his many older brothers.

When he was six, growing up in Ottawa, he prayed that Santa Claus would bring him his own new skates and a stick. We probably all wished the same at that age. Christmas morning, he races downstairs before anyone else and sure enough, Santa delivered. Under the tree were double-runner skates with leather straps, a stick, a roll of tape, and even a puck. Eureka.

Marie, I hope you can picture Frank. Even though he's the spitting image of a banker he speaks with such enthusiasm he could captivate a bar full of patrons and bring the tavern to tears of laughter. He's Irish through and through.

Anyway, he taped up his new stick and bolted for the ice rink his older brothers had built in the back yard. But as soon as his skates hit the ice, they went flying uncontrollably out from under him. They weren't sharpened you see. All he remembers is seeing his feet above him and wondering why they were in the sky and not on the ice.

Apparently, he woke a day later with his family gathered around and a lump the size of a goose-egg on his noggin. When he was telling me this tale, he was slapping his knee with one hand while feeling the back of his head for a remnant all these years later.

With Frank, one story leads right into another.

He claims his grades were good enough in eighth grade that he was allowed to quit school. You see it was during the war and he got a job with the Imperial Ministry of Munitions as an office boy at $40 dollars a month. He was there four years during the War and when he turned seventeen a buddy talked him into joining the Mounties. His application was rejected. He was not yet eighteen and he was under the minimum height requirement of 5 foot 8.

That didn't stop Frankie. The Royal Canadian Mounted Police needed a parent's consent if under twenty-one. His mom said no, and his dad was traveling for work. He forged his father's signature and wrote a letter to the commissioner of the Mounties about his size. He argued that since his dad was a hell of a big man that he'd undoubtedly grow. Frank became a constable in the Mounted police even though he'd never been on a horse in his life.

By nineteen he was a detective in Banff. But for some moonshine stills, opium dens and peeping toms, there's not much crime during the winter months, so he kept skating.

Guess he decided he wanted to be a hockey player more than a detective. His hometown of Ottawa offered him a chance to play professionally, and he jumped at it. He moved into one of the only two houses on Crichton Street behind a Chinese laundry with some other players. They called it Shanghai Alley."

As fate would have it, Ag lived in the other house on the street. In 1924, she turned seventeen and they were married before they moved back west to Vancouver so he could play two seasons with the Maroons. Ag & Frank like to tell people they meet in Shanghai.

I know your day was much better than mine and I can't wait to read about it. Your letters are a ray of light.

Love,

Murray

On Saturday, Bill Cook arranged for us to watch a local football match together. While everyone was invited, several guys didn't show. It was a beautiful day in sharp contrast to how we all spent the last two weeks inside the gloomy Ravina Gardens. We arrived back at the King Edwards to find our trainer Harry Westerby waiting for us.

"Boys we're changing hotels tomorrow."

"What's going on Harry?" Frank asked.

"Colonel Hammond is on the train here. He's wired Smythe to meet him at the Union Depot tomorrow. I'm sorry fellas but I don't know what hotel they're moving us to."

We were all left to wonder what this meant.

Several of us returned to the lobby of the King Edwards after dinner. We moved some of the leather high-back chairs closer to the fireplace to talk and tell stories before heading to bed early on a Saturday night. Everyone in the room was feeling some level of anxiety. The positive feeling of the Saturday afternoon football game was fading fast.

I wondered if Colonel Hammond was arriving tomorrow to shut the whole venture down. I suspected a few of the guys might be thinking the same. Two weeks of practice were largely wasted. While we had a solid starting five, I failed to see how we were going to sell tickets without an established big-name star or two. No one on the team had confidence in our manager. Heck, the team didn't even have a name yet.

But we wouldn't be changing hotels if Hammond was shutting us down, I reminded myself. I found some hope in the thought.

Frank, sensing our tension shared with us the time his jaw was clocked so hard in a game that he bit through his tongue. It had to be stitched back together and he walked around with his tongue hanging out so we could see his surprisingly mangled tongue. It was in deep stark contrast to his otherwise business-like appearance.

The gross humor helped to lighten the mood.

Bill leaned over and whispered something into Ching's ear. Ching immediately excused himself and said he would be back shortly. He nodded to Taffy and the two of them vanished together.

Bill started talking about the players he knew from the old Western League.

"Amby Moran and Herb Gardiner went to the Canadiens," he commented.

"I heard Dick Irvin and Puss Traub were picked up by Chicago," Bun offered.

"Is it true Chicago also got Babe Dye?" I asked.

"I haven't seen it announced in the papers yet, but that's my understanding." Bill offered.

"What's their team's name?" Ollie asked as he placed another log on the fire.

"The Black Hawks," Bill, Bunny and Frank replied simultaneously.

Bunny chimed in with, "Clem Laughlin's with the new Detroit Cougars I heard."

"I heard the same." said Frank.

We found ourselves debating rule changes. The league rules were getting modified nearly every season and the commissioner was trying to find the right balance of scoring vs. defensive play. Forward passing isn't allowed in the offensive zone but there has been a push to open up that part of the game. Players can pass forward while getting out of our defensive zone and while in the neutral zone. But once in the offensive zone, passes can only be lateral, behind or defections. Forward passing would certainly make the game more exciting.

Ching and Taffy returned. Each comically trying to hide something under their jackets, which only made them appear more suspicious to the hotel staff and guests. They looked like mobsters concealing tommy guns, but they pulled out two brown medicine bottles and announced, "this is extremely fine 'cough syrup' headed to the States."

Bill stood up and took one of the bottles. He pulled off the cork, took a smell and then a sip. "Fine 'cough syrup' indeed fellas. Good work. Let's find something to pour these into."

"There are coffee cups over here," Bunny rushed to a sideboard. The clerk at the front desk looked at him questionably.

Bunny merely smiled back and faked a cough into his hand. "The whole team is sick, we need medicine."

Facing an uncertain future and being a Saturday night in Toronto, we quickly polished off the two bottles of bootleg booze and ventured out to find a local speakeasy.

It was the first sign of our bonding as a team.

Chapter Seven

October 27, 1926

Nursing our collective hangovers, we checked into the Peacock Hotel, which turned out to be in West Toronto and a lot closer to our practice rink. Even the guys who lived in Toronto were ordered to check in. Apparently, someone wanted the whole squad staying together. But that wasn't the biggest change.

Our equipment manager Harry was quickly becoming our inside man and reported a bomb shell. Hammond stepped off the train with hockey legend Lester Patrick in tow.

Harry said Smythe's jaw hit the platform as he muttered, "well, that's that".

We stood dumbfounded. We must have appeared mighty confused because Harry raised his voice and announced, "Smythe's been fired! Lester Patrick's now in charge!"

Several guys openly cheered. While I wasn't sorry to see Smythe tossed out in the least, it was shocking for any team to lose the head coach after only two weeks. But Bill Cook gave me a reassuring smile. He wasn't gloating in Smythe's dismissal, but he clearly approved. I wondered if Bill was at all involved in his dismissal. After practicing this past Friday, I had the misfortune of encountering Smythe on my way out of the building.

"You're still here Murdoch? I'm amazed you haven't run back to your wife yet. I thought for sure you'd be the first to quit this outfit. You're not making this team so you're just wasting your time."

After two weeks I'd grown immune to his antagonism. Or so I thought.

"No, I'm still here Sir." I replied politely. "I'm not a quitter. My daddy taught me that."

As soon as the words came out of my mouth, I knew I'd made a mistake. Just keep walking away I told myself.

"Your 'daddy'? Let me guess. A factory worker? Farmer? Miner? What unskilled labor does your 'daddy' do?"

I should have just kept walking but again, I stopped and turned. "My father is a proud farmer and he sent me to university. He's got more honor than you'll ever have, sir."

We locked eyes and he stepped right up close. Our faces only inches apart. What the hell is happening here I wondered. Why is this man looking for a fight? If I throw a punch I'm certainly done and yet my fists were clenched.

"Smythe!" Bill Cook yelled with a command that froze us both.

"Keep walking Murray. I'll see you back at the hotel later. Mr. Smythe and I need to have an overdue conversation." Bill gave me his reassuring nod. That was the last I saw of Smythe before hearing this news that he'd been fired.

Unlike Smythe, every one of us knew plenty about the highly respected Patrick Family. He and his family not only started and ran the Pacific Coast Hockey League but literally wrote most of hockey's rulebook. The league always struggled financially, even though one of their teams were perpetually represented in the Stanley Cup, the most prestigious trophy in the sport. Until just recently Lester Patrick was the head coach of the Victoria Cougars. The Cougars are now in Detroit, but they were in the championships these past two seasons and won the Cup last year.

Like so many of the small regional leagues with sparse populations, they just couldn't get a financial foothold. Players opted for the better paying and fast expanding National Hockey League with ten teams now. The Ottawa Senators, Toronto St. Pats, Chicago Black Hawks, Pittsburgh Pirates, Detroit Cougars, and Boston Bruins. Montreal had both the Canadians and the Maroons. New York had the Americans and now us.

Anxiously gathered and enjoying our cigarettes in the lobby of the Peacock it wasn't long before Hammond and the man that would change my life walked through the doors.

Lester Patrick clapped his hands together and let loose an excited laugh that filled the lobby. He looked around the room and immediately started shaking hands with each of us. Perhaps the sun was simply peeking through the clouds, but the room suddenly seemed brighter.

Lester Patrick was already familiar with Bill, Bunny, Frank, and Ollie Reinikka, the four guys in the room who played professional.

Patrick was tall, over six feet, with a thick head of wavy silver hair like Brillo wire. He looked to be in his early forties, but perhaps younger by the way he moved gracefully. A former athlete to be sure. He dressed sharply in a working man's suit and his shoes were well worn.

Making his way around the room he walked right up to me with his infectious smile and grabbed my hand firmly. His hands were deceptively powerful with long lean fingers. That his family descended from Irish blood was unmistakable.

"Lester Patrick," he said to me square in the eyes.

Still holding hands "Murray Murdoch" I replied.

"Manitoba, two years ago, the Memorial Cup. I remember seeing you play."

"That's right Sir. Thank you, Sir." I was flabbergasted that he would even remember me.

"I heard you went toe to toe with Mr. Johnson on the first day. That says something right there. My gosh that says something. He's the toughest, most intimidating player in the whole league."

"Umm, Sir. That's not exactly how it happened. Ching put me on my butt hard the first time and the only reason I didn't go down twice was because he held me up." I replied with a chuckle.

"But you got back up and went a second time. Excellent to have you on the team Mr. Murdoch."

Hammond stood beaming in the back of the room enjoying his cigar as Patrick finished his personal introductions and then gathered us around him in a tight circle. Lester's presence filled the room with an air of excitement and respect.

When he spoke, I took in his every word as if in a hypnotized trance.

"You may have heard that I am taking over the team. This is true." He continued.

"And tomorrow morning we are going to work together on building a championship hockey club."

As he spoke, he took turns very naturally connecting with each of us.

"I am not interested in managing a good hockey team. I will be managing a great hockey team and we will be competing for Lord Stanley's Trophy. In short order we will be holding it! Those fortunate to make this team will find your names engraved on that cup. They will be there forever. Believe nothing less."

Lester put his arms around Bill Cook and Ching. "And more than that, we will be a team. We will be bothers. We will win together. We will lose some games together, but we will do so as ONE team. Gentlemen, our new team will set a high standard for others to follow. A tradition of excellence starts right now."

He paused for a moment and gathered himself. Several of us now had our arms wrapped around each other's shoulders as Lester lowered his voice. We huddled in tighter still.

"Now gentlemen, I introduced myself to far more than eleven of you. We all know there will be necessary cuts to get the roster down to that number. I will not drag this process out. You will know where you stand soon. I will thank those of you who do not make the team. Those that do, you will know your role and what I will expect from you. Our first game is on November 16th at Madison Square Garden in Manhattan, New York."

"We have much work to do before we play our first game against the Montreal Maroons. They are the reigning champions. That's a title I intend to take from them. Now let us sit down and enjoy a good supper together. Mr. Hammond has graciously reserved a very long table for us just down the block. After, we will retire to our rooms, and I will write to my wife of having met each of you. Come to the rink prepared gentlemen because I am going to find your limits. I am going to push you harder than you have ever been pushed. I am going to demand much. And I am going to do it quickly. We are going to build a championship team."

My oh my, I was in awe.

The next morning, we crammed into our locker room to find Lester Patrick already laced up in skates and full gear. He would be taking the ice with us.

Harry came in holding a heavy stack of new sweaters and stood next to Mr. Patrick.

"Gentlemen, none of us cared much for that first design. Mr. Rickard personally approved of this new sweater and the name."

Lester took one off the top of the pile and held it up showing us the back of the sweater. It was royal blue, with a red strip between two white strips around both the elbows and waist. There was a large white 5 on the back. I immediately thought it was classy and timeless. He tossed it to Bill Cook. Bill stood up and pulled it over his head and down his torso. Stitched in bold white felt letters diagonally down the front was our name – RANGERS.

Chapter Eight
February 1994

"Hello Uncle Murray, you picked a beautiful spot."

Right on time. Early in fact. His strong voice was as instantly recognizable as is his commanding, lean, athletic frame. The very embodiment of a leader.

I am reminded how today's players are built differently than in my day. He respectfully calls me "uncle", but he is descended through Marie's family. We are not related by direct blood but family, however distant, nonetheless.

And we are surely the only two people at this frozen pond whose names are both engraved on Lord Stanley's Cup, let alone more than once. Mark is a five-time champion.

He puts his stick and duffle bag down and sits on the wooden bench beside me. Removing his leather glove, we shake hands. His left hand rubs my shoulder. Although his touch is intentionally gentle both hands feel like they are chiseled from marble. He is nearly twice my size as I seem to be shrinking with the years. We haven't seen each other since he was introduced to the Garden as the Ranger's newest Captain in October of '91. He arrived with the highest of expectations and the pressure has only mounted.

"Mark, I am so grateful."

"Of course, but I can't believe you drove here by yourself from New Haven. This really is a lovely spot."

The two of us sit quietly for a moment and watch the skaters.

"How are you feeling these days?" He asks.

I smile and tilt my head to look in his concerned eyes.

"I pee in short streams, and more frequently than I would prefer. All things considered, not bad for ninety". I rub his knee as we laugh together.

"And Joan? How is she?" Mark asks.

"Nagging me to move down to Pawleys Island. Eventually I'll have to. I know. But I'm not ready to leave Connecticut. I still have ties at Yale, and I enjoy watching the local kids play." Unintentionally, I pause. I try to recover quickly and spit it out, like ripping a band-aid off a wound that has not yet healed.

"I can't leave Marie, you understand."

Mark nods. "I understand."

That is all he says, and it's everything.

When Mark speaks, he means it. I can hear the sincere empathy in his voice. When he's in your presence you know he's fully engaged. He's a remarkable leader of men.

"I know how busy you are Mark. The demands on your time. I want you to know just how much I appreciate you meeting me here and giving me an afternoon."

"It's ok, we had a morning skate in Rye and I'm free for the rest of the day. I'm curious why you wanted to meet here though. I could've driven up I-95 to your house in New Haven."

He cuts right to it. I look at him and smile. Another band aid but this wound hasn't healed enough either, even after all these decades.

"I just wanted to bring you here Mark. It's a special place. I've come to realize I need to share some things with you. How it all started and a little more. You need to know our history and I'm the only person alive who can tell the tale.

Chapter Nine
November 12, 1926

As the conductor promised, our Pullman arrived in Grand Central Station shortly before noon.

We were in excellent spirits as we stepped off the train and gathered our trunks, equipment bags, and sticks. A group of teenage boys, from every corner of the earth rushed to meet us as we exited the train to help carry our gear. There was one kid directing them and he reassured us he was sent from the Garden to collect us.

We strode up the crowded ramp and into the main concourse.

We froze. Our eyes turned upward.

We marveled at the high domed green ceiling. Although I had briefly been in New York just a few weeks prior for the fight that got moved to Philadelphia, I had arrived through Pennsylvania Station. I didn't have a moment to admire that station's full size and architecture, nor did I step outside the building. Grand Central Station was just as hectic, but we weren't as hurried. I felt none of the anxiety as I did the first time. I wasn't alone this time.

That any city could have two such beautiful and majestic stations was hard to comprehend. The constellations were above us.

"Taffy, what are you doing? These kids will help." Bunny offered.

I turned around. Taffy was several yards behind us dragging his truck, carrying his hockey duffle and sticks.

"No, I'll do it." Taffy responded.

Ching grabbed the other handle on the chest and together they managed fine.

We exited the building and again, our heads collectively looked upwards. There was nothing to compare with the heights of these buildings anywhere in Canada. Perhaps nowhere in the world.

Our gear was loaded onto a waiting horse-drawn carriage. Here, Taffy allowed his belongings to be loaded.

The kid informed us, "they will take everything to the Garden. It's not a long walk and I thought you'd enjoy the stroll. There are plenty of taxis if anyone would prefer to drive though."

We all agreed to walk, and the kid sent the wagon ahead while he guided us.

We walked west on 42nd street, passed a massive library on our left, and reaching Broadway minutes later. We turned right and made our way north.

Times Square was instantly recognized. A bustle of action, smoke, smells, and noises. The streets were crowded with dozens of automobiles, trolleys, and horse-drawn carriages. All fighting and jockeying for position and progress.

Many of the countless buildings had their name chiseled proudly on their façade. The theaters had large marques announcing their production.

Oh, Kay! by the Gershwin's was playing at the Imperial Theatre on 45th street. Next door was Helen Hayes in *What Every Woman Knows.* A sign for *Pygmalion*, opening one night before us on the 15th, caught my attention. There seemed to be dozens of theatres within sight.

In addition to the marquees were even more posters and signs for every product imaginable. Enormous metal scaffolding sat atop each building with billboards for Canadian Club, Camel Cigarettes, and various types of soups, pastes, and oils.

The Paramount Building, with its clock tower, rose 33-stories above Broadway. Men, many of whom were dressed for success in their wool suits, brimmed hats and overcoats walked briskly and with purpose. Women, rarely alone, walked with parasols in the latest fashions.

There were working class folk and a surprising number of young boys running about, a few of whom were industriously selling papers for two cents or cigarettes for five. Shoeshine boys offered a polish for ten cents.

We arrived wearing our tweed caps and blended in with taxi drivers and newsboys selling the papers and cigarettes. We joked amongst ourselves we were going shopping for fedoras after we settled in.

Unrelated to our attire, people were noticing us. Evidently, even in Manhattan the sight of eleven athletic men gets a reaction. Men were nodding as we passed. I found myself blushing as women changed their course to walk by us and gain our notice.

Our large group turned at 49th street and walked one block west. There in front of us was our new home.

It was a four-story building with large glass windows dominating the top three floors of the façade. Shops lined both sides of the main entrance on 8th Avenue.

Adams Hats and a drug store were just to the left and a Nedick's soda shop and corner diner to the right.

The marquee itself arched and draped down off the second floor with MADISON SQ. GARDEN outlined in big round light bulbs. On either side of the marquee were large billboards announcing the evening's event and coming attractions. Tonight, there was a bout between two boxers I did not recognize. Below was an announcement for the Rangers debut verses the Montreal Maroons in four days' time.

The kid leading our pack knew right where to go, and we followed him through the narrow employee entrance on 49th. We made our way down the dark and damp labyrinth corridors until we found our locker room. It was little more than a cubby hole. Exposed steam pipes ran across the ceiling and down one wall. While not a large room it was big enough for those of us fortunate enough to have been chosen by Lester Patrick. There was a small office for the coach and another equipment room and an area to get patched up.

Just two days ago we learned that Lester had signed a twenty-eight-year-old amateur named Billy Boyd. None of us knew him but Lester had our complete faith, and we trusted his decision. Lester had turned our training camp around immediately. Several players were cut after the first day and he kept other's so we could have full ice scrimmages. There were no more shenanigans or fisticuffs once Lester replaced Smythe. Boyd was expected to arrive tomorrow.

All the kids from the train station burst into the room with our duffle bags and sticks. They placed them neatly against one wall.

"We dropped your chests off at the hotel." One boy explained.

We tipped the kids for their help.

But we were anxious to see the ice rink itself. We hurried like young children down another long dark corridor with light at the end, brighter with each step. We emerged and stepped into the bowl-shaped arena.

"My oh my" I uttered.

The floor was already set up for the evening's boxing match. The ice was covered over with planking and the side boards were removed to allow for folding chairs to be placed around the ring.

Still, we all stood together and took in the Garden's three tiers of olive-gray seating. Although the building was empty, a thick lingering blue smoker's haze filled the air. It was by far, larger than any arena any of us had ever dreamed of playing in.

A large speaker system and lights were suspended from the high flat ceiling while a scoreboard and multiple clocks hung from the overhanging mezzanine. The smallest of the clocks told the time. The largest measured our twenty-minute periods, and another was designed to tick off the seconds on a penalty.

They were all situated between two signs advertising Gem Blades with the tag line "Cost less per shave."

The façade of the upper deck advertised a list of "coming attractions" that included our game, a few bouts and our rival American's first home game of the season on the 18th, also against the Montreal Maroons.

The moment was not lost on us.

Bill and Bun Cook, Frankie Boucher, Ching Johnson, Taffy Abel, Paul Thompson, Reg Mackey, Ollie Reinikka, Hal Winkler, Lorne Chabot and I, the original Rangers all stood together in Madison Square Garden for the first time.

"Gentlemen! Up here" came Lester's unmistakable booming voice from the seats above us. We turned around and found him holding conference with Colonel Hammond and another man I didn't recognize. The three were sitting in a vast section of otherwise empty seats. "Welcome!" he yelled as we ascended the stairs.

Lester had left Toronto the day before us to get affairs here in order while we packed up our gear.

"How was the train?" asked Hammond as we gathered around.

"First class Colonel, thank you." Bill offered for the group.

"Allow me to introduce Mr. Dwyer" he continued. "Mr. Dwyer is the owner of your rivals, the New York Americans who also play here at the Garden.

I had heard much about 'Big Bill' Dwyer, the reputed bootlegging kingpin. He appeared much like the New York gangster I had imagined but surprisingly his smile and handshake seemed genuine, sincere, and perhaps most importantly, non-threatening.

There seemed to be no tension between Lester, Hammond, and Dwyer. Our coming along only a year after the Americans and sharing the same ice which, Dwyer had to pay to use, must have infuriated him. Yet he was congenial and polite as he spoke to us with a deep voice.

"Welcome to Broadway men. What the Colonel failed to mention was that he was also my team President until Tex decided to start his own club and stole him from me. Nevertheless, being the bigger man, you'll all be staying at my hotel just across the street for as long as each of you need to settle in and find your own places. You'll be getting a good deal on the rate, but you'll find cheaper arrangements for sure after you've learned your way around. You need anything, anything at all you just tell the front desk at my hotel. I've left tickets for the lot of you at Yankee Stadium for tomorrow's big football game."

We all must have had a confused look on our faces.

"Army vs Knute Rockne's Notre Dame?" He asked. "It's a big college game and tickets are hard to come by. Now I won't lie to you. I purchased these tickets for my boys, but the hockey Gods decided that the Amerks would be opening the season on the road. I won't have them go to waste, so you fellas go and enjoy. I imagine none of you has been to Yankee Stadium before?"

We all shook our heads and said no. Big Bill Dwyer smiled and said "well, it's a cathedral. Or it will be when it's finished being built."

"Don't worry about finding your way" Colonel Hammond said. "Sam here has volunteered to escort you up to the Bronx tomorrow".

He indicated behind us.

The teenager who led the other kids at Grand Central Station bound up the stairs towards us. He had big eyes, an infectious smile, and an intelligent face. His clothes were not new, and I noticed that he had the faint smell of a farmer as he got close.

"Hello, I'm Sam Crawford. It's really an honor to meet you fellas."

"Sam's our water boy and will be helping Harry Westerby with your equipment, keeping your skates sharp and your sticks taped and whatnot" Lester explained. "It also seems he's been promoted to act as your tour guide".

We were moved into Dwyer's Forrest Hotel on West 49th, between 8th and Broadway, a mere half block from the Garden. Apparently, Big Bill Dwyer and his family occupied the entire upper floor.

The front desk clerk confirmed there were a dozen speakeasies within a four-block radius hidden behind innocent and non-descript store fronts. He suggested we try the Green Door, which was very nearly part of the Garden itself and popular with the actors and writers in the area, especially after games.

The busboys bragged about the other tenants of the Forrest as we rode the elevator. I was excited to learn the famous writer of gangsters, Damon Runyon, inventor of such colorful characters as Good Time Charlie, Nathan Detroit, Harry the Horse, and Benny Southstreet was our new neighbor. His stories were found even in the far reaches of Canada. He and his wife live in the building.

It wasn't long before we shared the elevator with Mrs. Dwyer and their teenage daughter. Mrs. Dwyer was polite, and somewhat over-dressed, as if trying a little too hard to impress and be accepted. Their young daughter, Elizabeth, was charming. Alone in our room, Frank commented that in a few years she's going to be strikingly beautiful, but heaven help anyone foolish enough to date the daughter of a gangster.

The Forrest Hotel was elegant and popular. Darkly dressed men came and went frequently. It was easy to imagine business, much of it suspicious, was being conducted under this roof.

The Cook brothers didn't plan to remain at the hotel for long. Bill and Fred had three sisters, nurses all, who were living in a Brooklyn apartment house. The sisters offered to help them, and by extension, us, find fully furnished and affordable apartments once we were settled and had the lay of the land.

We knew about American football and played pickup games. But this spectacle was nothing like the sandlot game we went to weeks ago in Toronto. That game had maybe a hundred spectators on a sandlot. Tens of thousands now surrounded us as we found our seats in Yankee Stadium.

Ching was the only one of us who previously played on a football team. Sam explained the finer points for those few of us who needed a better understanding of the rules.

Sam would lean between us, and enthusiastically use his hands to explain. "It's all Napoleonic tactics. Close formation battles designed to exploit a weakness in the enemy's line or to outflank your opponent."

Having served in the infantry within a trench mortar outfit during the Great War Ching was especially fascinated to overhear Sam's analogies.

"Mr. Johnson, how did you come by the name "Ching? You're clearly not Asian." Sam asked.

None of us had dared ask him before. I was curious about this myself. The big man laughed and flashed a bright smile.

"Used to go camping and fishing with my pals on the Red Deer River."

"Alberta" he offered as way of explanation when realizing a kid from New York wouldn't have a clue where that river is.

Sam still had a blank expression, trying to hide the fact he had no idea where Alberta was either.

Ching smiled and offered "It's way up northwest in Canada."

"Oh, right." Sam smiled appreciatively.

"We used to hire an old Chinaman to clean the fish and care for our cooking. We loved that guy. We hired him every year until making the hike to the river was too much. That's when I discovered I enjoyed the work. My pals started calling me Ching and my old nickname seemed to die off."

At once several of us asked in choirs "what old nickname?"

"Ivan the Terrible!" he said with a growl for effect.

"Why Ivan"? Sam asked.

Ching laughed. "You ask about Ivan but not 'The Terrible'? I like this kid. Cause that's my real name. Ivan Wilford Johnson" he said proudly.

We learned that Yankee Stadium was the largest of its kind anywhere and was built only three years earlier. It was painted white, and an elegant copper façade hung along the length of the third-deck roofing.

The second and third tiers only stretched down the baselines and came to an abrupt stop well short of the outfield. The stadium was only half built.

I surmised that when baseball and football games were not being played, construction was underway to extend both tiers into the vast reaches of the park. Deep holes for pouring foundations we're surrounded by cranes, scaffolding, earthmoving machines along the baselines where future seating would go.

Sam explained that just over a month ago the Yankees lost the World Series to the St. Louis Cardinals. With disappointment, he shared they lost in the seventh and deciding game right here in front of their hometown fans, despite a home run by the great Ruth himself.

"The Cardinals pitched around the Babe the whole game. The only mistake they made was giving him something over the plate in the third inning. Ruth promptly planted it over the wall in the right-center field. It was the only swing he took all day. The Cardinals walked him four times in the game and the bat otherwise never left his shoulder."

Sam's enthusiasm was infectious.

Bill Cook offered up that he too plays baseball in the offseason and he and Sam fell into a long conversation about the game.

Maybe a couple of the guys might have been a little put off by Sam's exuberance or maybe they didn't like the idea of being around a kid who knew so much. He was no dummy, that was obvious. Excluding his lack of Canadian geography, Sam was especially bright and articulate for a water boy and tour guide.

I was sensitive to the fact that I was the only university educated player on our team. That I had graduated from the University of Manitoba with a degree in economics was not something I shared with the guys. The ribbing would be unrelenting. But considering he was thirteen years younger than Bill and seven years my junior he seemed to otherwise fit right in with our tight group. Several of us took an immediate liking to the kid. He was our new sidekick.

On the subway back to Manhattan, my linemate Paul Thompson got a little disgruntled, as he seemed want to do.

"We're getting screwed guys. I read that Ruth is making $210,000 this coming year for playing out in the boondocks. We're playing in the heart of the city. Our tickets sell for just as much. I'm telling you we're getting taken advantage of by these big city suits. They think we're dumb hicks, but these free tickets are just to keep us from getting wise".

Bunny quickly joked "What are you talking about Paul? Tex and the Colonel are paying me just as much as Ruth. You too, right Frankie?"

"Hell, I'm making more!" Frankie replied.

I chuckled.

Despite the joking, Paul wouldn't let it die. He kept at it until he had a couple other guys riled up too. The flasks with schnapps we had been passing around all game probably wasn't helping, and the atmosphere was getting uncomfortable. I didn't know what to do or say and it looked like Bill was about to speak up when unexpectedly Sam said, "It's just math Sir."

Everyone was shocked that Sam would speak up in such a conversation. My immediate reaction was that he was overstepping his bounds. But he didn't wait for Paul to respond.

"Now I don't know what you're making and it's none of my business. And you're probably right that the front office negotiated deals in their favor. But it isn't realistic to compare your salary to Ruth's."

"Why not? Why should he make so much more than any of us do?" Taffy asked, echoing Paul's argument.

Although Sam was well-built for his age, he was tiny compared to Taffy who stood over six foot and weighed easily two-hundred and twenty-five pounds. Yet Sam didn't retreat. He calmly explained the obvious economic facts while holding onto the hand strap as the subway rattled on.

"Mr. Abel, Madison Square Garden holds what? 15,000 paying fans for a hockey game? The Rangers will play forty-four games, home and away, this season.

"So?" Thompson pressed.

"Well, Yankee Stadium holds some 70,000 people or more, and the Yankees will play 154 games. Tickets at the Garden range from forty cents to four dollars for seats down on the ice. Putting home and away games aside and just to keep the math simple let's say the average price for a ticket at both Yankee Stadium and Madison Square Garden is $1.00. If the Yankees sell just half their seats, they generate over five million dollars not including concessions. Plus, they're adding a lot of seats and building more. If the Rangers sell every single ticket this season, they generate maybe seven hundred thousand dollars. Now I mean no disrespect sir, but Babe Ruth is established as the greatest player in the game, maybe ever. He's single-handedly changing the entire sport. Heck, they're practically building this stadium around him."

The kid didn't need to mention that the Rangers hadn't even seen a puck drop or that no one in this city even knew our names. In less than a minute he defused whatever grumbling Thompson had started and the rest of the subway ride was peaceful.

Still, I don't think Sam made a new friend in Paul.

Chapter Ten
November 16, 1926

Nearly everyone in the locker room had a serious case of nerves. I had barely slept and the tightness in the room was stifling. We were still many hours from the puck drop and I was hoping our morning skate would help us relax.

For the first time, we were finally able to use the Garden ice and I excitedly got a running start as I burst through the gate and strode onto the rink for the very first time.

My skates inexplicably slipped out from underneath me, and I fell to the ice.

"What the heck!" I whispered, mortified, and trying not to draw attention but everyone saw me and got a good laugh. I tried to stand but immediately went right down again. The guys were all bent over laughing hysterically.

I grasped I was the butt of a well-timed practical joke. Sitting on the ice I looked at my skates and discovered a stripe of clear tape on my blades. It was a great prank and served its purpose at breaking the tension for the whole team.

Who was our prankster? I wondered.

As usual Lester was on the ice with us. Billy Boyd practiced with us for the first time. He was a fluid center and Lester had him skating between Thompson and myself. This left Ollie, one of our four experienced professionals with even less ice time.

Those of us on the second line knew we'd only be seeing precious few minutes a game. The seventh skater knew he'd have hardly any ice time unless there was an injury. But like the consummate pro, Ollie accepted the demotion gracefully.

Lester wanted only minimal contact during our practice. He kept stressing that we be fresh for later tonight, but we were anxious to get rid of our remaining debut jitters. Like Louis Armstrong's latest song, many of us had the heebie-jeebies. Not surprising, both Taffy and Ching were up for a fun clean bumping. It helped us release our butterflies.

Boyd, Paul, and I immediately clicked on the second line. I could see that Billy Boyd was a solid defensive center who would help us get the puck out of our zone.

As we headed into the locker room after practice, Lester pulled Hal and Lorne aside for several minutes. This was the news we were waiting for. The room was silent as we got undressed and waited for the decision. Who would be our starting goalie?

I struck a match, lit a cigarette, and opened a noon edition of a paper. I stole a quick peek over my copy of the Daily News and could see both men standing stoically just outside the door with Lester. Several of the guys had towels around their waists but no one wanted to hit the shower just yet. We just sat, waited, and tried to enjoy our smokes.

A small caption caught my attention as I flipped to the rear.

Opening Winter Season
Madison Square Garden
Championship Hockey
World's Champions
Montreal Maroons
vs
New York Rangers
Tonight Nov. 16 8:30pm
Added Attractions

European Skating Ballet
12 Most Beautiful Women
Skaters in Europe
West Point Band, 156 Pieces

I turned the page and found small portrait photos of both Ching and Taffy just above an article that read:

"King ice will rule supreme tonight at the new Garden when the New York Rangers meet the world champion Montreal Maroons in the opening game of the season. The proceeds of this first game are for the benefit of the Grosvenor neighborhood house. The Garden has been transformed into a veritable winter palace and a pretentious program has been arranged for between periods for the entertainment of the hockey patrons including Katie Schmidt's ice ballet. Neither the Rangers nor Maroons were able to indulge in a regular practice game because of the short time available to put the Garden in readiness."

Lester came into the room with both goalies in tow and in typical fashion cut right to the matter.

"Gentlemen, Mr. Winkler will be starting tonight's game. However, since I have not seen either of these fine goalies play outside practice and scrimmages, I feel it is only fair that both be given a chance. Mr. Chabot will be starting our second game. I know it is unorthodox but for a few games I am going to alternate them. They have both worked too hard these past weeks for me to decide without seeing them in game situations. Now, go relax. Eat well and no alcohol before the game. Stay out of the speakeasies. Our game is at 8:30 and I want all of you in this locker room by six-thirty. Later tonight we will celebrate our first win together and the first round is on me!"

Cheers and clapping filled the room.

Bunny and I were the last to get dressed after our morning skate.

We left Harry alone in our locker room. We were talking about positioning as we strolled for the exit down the damp corridor. Sounds echo in those long cement block halls and faint noises coming from the rink caught my attention. I stopped to listen and hushed Bunny to stop talking.

Bunny and I looked at each other when we heard a loud slap immediately followed by a powerful bang that sounded like a puck hitting against the boards. We turned around and moments later came out of the tunnel at center ice.

Before I recognized the lone skater, I heard a completely new sound. It was so distinct I would never forget it. I would be chasing it for much of my career. The noise reverberated and echoed up among the rafters. It was the sound of power.

It was coming from his skates. They cut into the ice so strongly, so loudly, so deeply that I immediately knew I was witnessing a revelation. He moved with a gracefulness and precision I didn't know was possible.

He cut his turns so tightly that he pivoted in place while his body was at an angle that seemed to defy the very laws of gravity. He had looked strong and athletic but now I could see that his thighs were thick like a horse's and his fast-pumping calves like iron engine pistons.

His quick feet were shoulder length apart, knees bent, and his backside was down low. Hips moving dramatically in unison with these legs. His back was bent forward at a forty-five-degree angle, and he'd swooped past us with the puck, low to the ice. His head was up, looking ahead and although he had total control of the puck, he never looked at it.

While crossing center ice he suddenly lifted his stick behind him and straight up over his head. Rotating his hips with a fluid wipe-like motion his hands came down in a large arch. As his blade slapped the puck his right leg kicked out and in the next instance his stick and back leg were parallel to the ice pointing in opposite directions. The puck exploded off the stick and flew from the blue line. It ricocheted off the net's crossbar, making a loud ping.

I had never seen anything like that, but he had already gathered another puck and was preparing to take another blast. This time the puck sailed into the netting. Bunny and I stood in silent awe.

With every change of direction, it seemed his skates cut so deeply that the ice would be permanently marked. He suddenly stopped on a dime, a wave of ice sprayed from his blades and with a series of quick crossovers he picked up another loose puck and was at full speed in the opposite direction. He flew past us again.

"My oh my" I muttered.

"Sweet mother of God, he's…he's…he's…" Bunny's voice trailed off, uncertain how to finish the sentence.

On the eve of our first game, I finished his sentence. "he's… the future."

"Do you think Lester could get him in a sweater for tonight?"

"How old is he? Fifteen? He's just too young. I don't care how talented he is, one solid body check by someone the size of Ching and he wouldn't get up."

"If Ching could land a hit on him, yeah. But I'm not sure he could touch him."

"Jeez, he's not even Canadian."

"Does Lester know about this? We need to find him."

"He already knows" Bunny replied. He motioned with his head for me to look over his shoulder.

Sure enough. The man missed nothing. There was Lester Patrick standing a level above us in the entryway to section 39.

Patrick was beaming as he watched our water boy, Sam Crawford, show us what's possible on the ice.

I strolled into the locker room expecting to be early, but several guys had already arrived. At my locker, I removed my jacket and hung it up. With the clock ticking towards game time, I was once again feeling anxious.

My game sweater was neatly folded and laid with great care on my stool. That was very nice touch by either Harry or Sam I thought. As I loosened my tie, I reached down to pick up the jersey and jumped in surprise.

Laugher suddenly erupted! The sweater was not only completely frozen solid, but it was frozen to the stool. I was bent over laughing at yet another prank.

"Gotcha!" Ching proudly proclaimed, laughing, as he raced over to collect the prop. Bunny handed me my actual dry sweater and stool. Taffy, standing at the door was peeking down the long tunnel and whispered,

"Here comes Raffles".

Ching quicky placed the gag in front of Frankie's locker and everyone went back to their places. All of us, now in on the joke, awaited the next victim.

An hour later, the Garden's Public Relation suits, Johnny Bruno and Dick Blythe were holding court with the New York beat writers outside our locker room. We spoke with the writers during a luncheon yesterday. We gave them quotes and posed for pictures on the ice.

Now they stood outside our door presumably waiting for a pre-game quote from Lester. Despite Ching's earlier ice breakers, we drank our sodas and smoked to settle our growing nerves. Our Chesterfields, Camels, and Lucky Strikes didn't help. Bill was relaxed and reassuring as he made his way around the room. Reminding us how hard we had worked and how important it was to show these New Yorkers how our sport was played.

The waiting was excruciating, and I began a letter to Marie to help pass the time. My plan was to finish it after the game and report the results.

My dearest Marie,

We play our first game tonight and I wish you were here to share it with me. This day has already been remarkable. After a sloppy practice, Bunny Cook and I were leaving the Garden when we heard noises coming from the rink...

Bunny and I had peppered Sam with rapid-fire questions when he came off the ice. "Where did you learn to skate like that?" "What's that shot called?" "Doesn't your stick break?" "Has Lester signed you to a deal yet?" "Are you old enough to sign a contract?"

We were finally able to get him to share with us that he was raised up the Hudson River. He claimed that he finished with school early and was hoping to play at university but had to wait a year. In the meantime, he got this job with the Rangers. Lester had already raised the possibility of helping him get into a university.

"Do you also work on a farm?" I asked curiously because Sam frequently smelt like he spent time around horses.

Sam seemed offended at the question. I apologized and blamed my terrible sense of smell after being in locker rooms much of my life.

The weather got worse as the day wore on. A drenching rain had been falling since the afternoon and we could hear it even in the bowels of the Garden. Harry wandered the room making nervous small talk while Sam finished putting a last-minute edge to Frankie's blades.

Anxious to get on the ice I stood fidgeting in my own well-worn skates and re-taped my stick for the second time this day. Our uniforms looked sharp. Our blue socks with red and white stripes matched our sweaters. Our tan pants were held up by suspenders. I pulled on my jersey with pride, the number 9 on my back. My elbow pads were strapped on over the sweater.

We could now hear the West Point Band playing to get the crowd riled up.

Lester entered the room and clapped his hands together. "Gentlemen, shall we go play some hockey?" He didn't have to ask twice. I grabbed my padded leather gloves, pulled them up over my forearms and made for the door with my stick in hand. We marched in unison past the few reporters down the tunnel. We could hear the crowd rustling above us.

A garden employee held the door open and clapped our shoulders with a "good luck boys" and "give'm hell" as we filed past.

As we took the ice, I looked up at the large clock at center ice. The time read 8:37. The West Point Band, all 156 pieces, escorted us on a parade around the rink. We smiled, nodded, and waved as the audience got their first look at us.

I was a long way from Manitoba.

The crowd was still filing in, but it was obvious we'd have a full house despite the sour conditions outside and not having big name players. In the upper levels it appeared the men were dressed in their everyday suits and hats but down low near the ice I was surprised that many of spectators were wearing formal evening wear. Men were in tuxedos and top hats. Women wore evening gowns and jewelry. There were more women throughout the Garden than I might have anticipated.

Montreal, in their maroon sweaters with a large white M came out of the tunnel with their own band led by an eight-foot-tall giant in kilts, red coat and big bearskin hat. It was quiet a spectacle.

We took several laps and I felt better as the air rushed past my face. We stood near the blue line and took turns with practice shots to get Hal warmed up.

Out of the corner of my eye, I caught Bunny trying to bring his stick up over his head and arch it down. I burst out laughing when he lost his balance on the follow-through and the puck dribbled harmlessly off his stick. With all the players on the ice the crowd didn't seem to notice Bunny go down, but I decided to wait before experimenting with Sam's new shot. Bunny looked at me and shrugged his shoulders; sheepishly embarrassed at having fallen on his backside minutes into our debut.

If Sam took that shot in an actual game, it could kill the goalie if it struck his face. It made no sense to try and perfect this long-arched slap. The league would quickly ban the shot. I had no doubt.

The West Point band took a section halfway up the stands behind our goal and kept the music going. The Garden was several degrees warmer, and the ice was softer then in our earlier morning skate. It had a slushy feel and thin pools of water were noticeable after the ice crew put down water. If the puck hit one of these wet spots it would stop dead. The rink would need a little more time to fully freeze over.

The ever present thick blue cloud of cigar and cigarette smoke was hovering over the rink.

Lester called us to the bench and introduced us to the game's referee, Lou Marsh. He explained that Marsh, a powerful stocky man, was a Toronto sports editor when not refereeing.

"Welcome to the National Hockey League. I'm gonna let you boys play but keep your sticks down. If things get too bloody, I'm throwing you from the game. Good luck to ya." And off he skated to the Maroons' bench, presumably to give the same speech.

"All right let's get everyone out there" Lester said.

We all stood on the ice, facing both the US and Canadian flags as the West Point band played *The Star-Spangled Banner*. The Maroon's band had the honor of playing *God Save the King*.

I got off the ice and took a seat on the bench with Reg, Ollie, Paul, and my new center Billy Boyd.

Tall and lean, Lester paced behind us. It struck me that even a legend like Lester Patrick could be nervous. Harry and Sam stood in each corner of the bench, ready to assist us with any equipment issues that might arise. Nothing separated us from the fans behind our bench. Chicken wire in the defensive zones were all that protected the fans sitting down on the ice.

Sitting alone a few rows up behind us was Lorne Chabot. Of all the players on the team, I still knew the least about both Lorne and Hal. Both goalies continued to keep some distance from us. I smiled and nodded to him, which he acknowledged back.

The loudspeaker announced, "joining us on the ice for the ceremonial faceoff is moving-picture actress and screen artist Lois Moran." The crowd roared. The band played another tune.

Bill Cook escorted and supported the extremely attractive blond to center ice where she was met by referee Marsh, Frankie, and the Maroons' center Nels Stewart. The two players took their ceremonial face-off positions, and she gracefully dropped the puck.

The two players gently tapped their blades on the small disk and Frankie reached down and retrieved the puck. The actress shuffled her feet as she made her way off the ice with the assistance of Bill.

With the ceremony over it was time to begin.

Marsh ordered the two centers back to the faceoff circle as the wingers and defensemen took their positions.

The ref looked back at both goalies to make sure they were ready. Each nodded back.

The Garden suddenly got very quiet.

March dropped the puck.

Our first game was underway.

Frankie won the first faceoff decisively and got the puck to Bill on the right side. Bill raced for and gained the blueline. The Maroons' left winger Babe Siebert swatted the puck off Bill's stick simultaneous to Marsh ringing his bell. He called offsides on Bunny. He had jumped over the blue line before the puck.

Another faceoff resulted in another Boucher win. I saw the Maroon's center, Stewart, give Frankie a nasty slash across the wrist. But the ref's eyes followed the puck as it went back to Taffy this time.

We gained the zone and both Bill and Bunny got off shots on their veteran goaltender Clint Benedict before the Maroons were able to get the puck safely out. The play, back and forth, up, and down the ice, quickly took an increasingly physical tone. The world champion Maroons rapidly grew frustrated that we weren't proving to be the pushovers and bumpkins the Canadian dailies had been claiming.

It must have been obvious to all in the Garden that Montreal had decided to intimidate us, and it wasn't long before my blood was boiling. Stewart chose a new, bigger target. As the puck rolled behind our net, he and Ching crashed hard into the boards as they fought for the puck. But while our defensemen's stick went for the puck Stewart's hooked Ching above his left eye. Feeling the warm blood pouring down his face, Ching tackled Stewart and slammed him to the ice. The Garden erupted in cheers and awes. Marsh separated the two and tossed them both for roughing, two minute each. Ching had to leave the ice with Harry to get stitched up.

The offsetting penalties allowed Mackey, our reserve defenseman to see his first ice time. With Ching Johnson off the ice for repairs, Montreal pressed even harder to score the first goal, but Hal turned away shot after shot.

Sitting on the bench the speed of the game was far faster than I imagined, and the checks were more powerful and violent. This was the professional league and every play, every decision, every pass was happening much faster than I was accustomed. My anxiety grew. Although I had found my stride in practices and scrimmages, this was a different animal.

I watched as their defensemen, Reg Noble, got caught behind the play and slashed Taffy on the back of this knee. Again, the penalty was missed. Getting up from the ice I thought Taffy would retaliate. His face was a mask of rage and pain. But to my utter amazement he kept his position and cool. That is until he saw Ching return to our bench with a white bandage over his eyebrow.

At his first opportunity Taffy skated toward our bench "you ready?" he asked Ching who yelled "Yeh!"

The moment Noble touched the puck, Taffy, with a smile that lit up Broadway, left his position and checked him hard into the boards. The two dropped their gloves and started swinging. The crowd, used to boxing matches in this building, leap to their feet fully entertained. Abel eventually dropped Noble to the ice and Marsh stepped in. The penalty box was seeing plenty of visitors.

The play only got more violent. Maroon defenseman Dunc Munro viciously slashed Bunny on the forearm but Marsh saw this one and we had a man advantage. Bunny came off holding his arm. I froze. I heard Lester's voice "Let's go Mr. Murdoch, keep your head in the game lad." I jumped over the board onto the ice for my first professional shift.

Behind our own net, Ching sent the puck up the boards to me. Somehow, I didn't muff the pass. I skated with the puck out of our zone, feeling as though with each stride I would fall flat on my face. I hit Frankie at center ice with a sharp pass just as I was blindsided. The air was violently expelled from my lungs. I was seeing stars and flashes of light even before my body hit the ice.

I rolled on my said, gasping for breath and could see Frankie take the puck wide up the right side. Bill Cook crossed behind him and turned up center ice towards the net. Frankie was just about to get the pass off to Bill, who had a wide-open shot, when a Maroon's defensemen mauled him. The play evaporated. Our first period, twenty minutes, ended right there.

The crowd had seen seven penalties, five stitches above Ching's eye, and no goals. I imagined that Tex Rickard and Colonel Hammonds were as satisfied with our first period efforts as we were. But I seriously doubted I belonged at this level.

As we came off the ice and headed down the corridor to our locker room, we passed a line of young female skaters. They were the advertised European ballet skaters, and the crowd would be entertained between periods. After such a grueling round of men slashing and hitting each other senseless, the crowd would find these gals a more pleasant sight for the eyes.

We popped open our sodas and several of us lit up our smokes. I had only skated for seconds at the end of the period. I was promptly put on my bum and got my clocktower rung. I had hardly worked up a sweat.

Harry and Sam attended to Ching and Bunny while the others loosened their skates and caught a few minutes rest.

Lester burst into the room "Gentlemen, good first but we need to stay disciplined and play our game. Taffy, good job holding back and waiting for Ching to return. Bill, Frank, Bun, you guys just keep up the pressure in front. Keep taking shots. The biscuit will go in the basket for us, you can be sure of that. Mr. Murdoch, good shift. You and the second line will see more action this period so be ready. Gentlemen, be smart and stay away from the penalties in our offensive zone. Hal, you did not see many shots because Mr. Johnson and Mr. Abel are shutting these guys down before they can get a shot off. But be ready. They are angry and frustrated and will come out strong."

"Good shift?" I thought? I was pulverized and flattened. The game was too fast for me.

It seemed like no time at all before we were heading back down the corridor to the ice. The Garden crew had cleaned the loose ice with their big push scrapers and once again the ballet stepped aside as we marched passed. The girls wished us luck in accents that ranged from Swedish, French, and maybe Austrian. It was Paul Thompson who asked, "So where can we find you gals after the game?" The girls giggled as Harry yelled at Paul to keep moving.

As the game resumed the temperature at ice level was easily in the seventies. The blue smoky haze, which had only grown in thickness with each puff from the many thousands of paying customers, had now descended to ice level.

The second period picked up where the first ended. Winger Punch Broadbent was sent off for a vicious blow to the back of Bill Cook's head just two minutes in. Bill seemed fine and the boys had a couple quality chances. But as we didn't score with the man advantage Lester sent out our checking line. Billy, Paul, and I went right to work throwing our bodies at anyone in a maroon sweater. This I thought I can do, assuming I can catch them.

Our job was to play strong defensive minded hockey and to physically punish their players as much as possible in the limited time Lester gives us. And should we find ourselves with a scoring opportunity, all the better. The three of us are not large or intimidating. But we are quick, or so I thought before the game started. We know how to check. I understood Paul's frustration with our not getting more ice time. But there was no disputing that Bill, Frank, and Bunny were something very special. Not yet halfway through the game I felt our starters were playing even with the world champions.

The Maroons couldn't get through our formation, and they started playing a riskier brand of hockey. They dropped the puck back to their defenseman Munro on the blueline. With Taffy and Ching engaged with the forwards, Munro skated deep in the zone towards our net. This can be an effective tactic, but it leaves only one defenseman back to guard against a quick counterattack should they lose the puck. And that's exactly what happened.

Munro took a good shot on net, but it rebounded hard off Hal's leg pad right out to Thompson's stick. With Munro out of position I immediately recognized the opportunity and turned up ice, skating hard and yelling Paul's name the whole way. The other Maroons' defenseman, Noble, was racing to cover me. Paul saw me open at center ice and sent me a long pass across the width of the rink. It wasn't a perfect pass and I had to slow my stride to receive it. I knew that pause would give Noble a chance to catch me. Once I had the puck, I took off as fast as I could. I felt Noble just behind me and he started whacking at my arms with his stick. I ignored him and stayed focused on their goalie Benedict. He was squared up and I thought I could beat him low on the glove side.

I was about to shoot when Noble, in an act of desperation, hooked me down from behind. I slide hard into Benedict and the two of us ended up in the back of the net. Marsh rang his bell and did his best to pull us from the goal. I was enraged at Noble, and I'm sure the fans way up in the cheap seats could hear my colorful language. But Marsh had already sent him to the penalty box by the time I was untangled. Lester yelled for a line change, and I skated off continuing my verbal tirade at Noble. By the time I reached the bench I knew he had made the only play he could in that situation. Any one of us would have done the same.

Sam handed me a tin cup of water and I gulped it down. Our first line was back out for yet another man advantage. I looked up just in time to see Bill feed Bunny with a beautiful pass that Bun shot just wide of the net. Benedict had dropped his weight in the wrong direction and Bunny's side of the net was wide open. The puck couldn't have missed by more than an inch and everyone in the building leapt to their feet with a collective "AWE!" It was the best chance of the game thus far for either team. I could see Bunny cursing himself at the missed opportunity.

It's a terrible feeling to know you had more time, perhaps another second, to place the shot right where it's needed. But in front of the net, when that puck reaches your twig, you may only have a hairsbreadth to get that shot off before a defenseman puts you on your backside or the goalie recovers. In this instance, and only in hindsight, I'm sure Bunny realized that he had more time to put the puck in the net.

The man advantage expired, and the Maroons went on a relentless attack. For a few minutes everyone in the building sensed the game was swinging in Montreal's favor. But in those moments of doubt, the Garden began to fall in love with our defensive pair.

Ching and Taffy were in their glory and showed no signs of panic.

They would wait at our blue line, stick at the ready. Taffy wore a fierce grin that would intimidate a grizzly and Ching, far scarier with that crazed maniacal smile. They waited for their prey. Few Maroons got by them unscathed and those that did were denied quality opportunities. Hal made every save, but he wasn't being tested.

Taffy would very effectively get his large body in front of the attacking forward and tie him up or force him to the boards. Ching, with blood seeping through the bandage above his eye was taking a different approach. When he tried to wipe the blood away from his eye it smeared across his face. A kind of war paint. Even the spectators in the farthest seats could see the bright red blood on one side of his face. Ching would hip-check, tackle, and pound anyone with a puck. Eventually he would flip someone feet over head. That inevitable outcome was intimidating for our opponents. The crowd roared approval at every knockdown and anticipated the next big hit. They loved him.

With under two minutes left in the second period the Cook brothers found themselves racing up ice, successfully eluding their checkers. Bunny broke free and had an excellent shot on Benedict. In making a nice save the goalie landed hard against the pipes and the puck bounced harmlessly deep into the corner. Bun bounced over quickly, again beating the Maroons' defenseman and recovered his own rebound. He spun and passed the puck to his brother, firmly planted in front of the net.

Benedict was still down on the ice and struggling to get back on his feet. But it was too late.

Bunny's pass was right on Bill's blade.

Bill lifted the puck into the net.

The red light went on.

The crowd erupted.

Those of us on the bench hugged each other widely in celebration. I felt Lester's hand on my shoulder, and I looked back at his broad smile. He stood above us roaring his loud belly laugh. He looked so happy and proud.

When it became clear that their goalie Clint Benedict had been hurt on the play and needed help off the ice the crowd respectfully quieted down. A gash had opened on the goalie's scalp and blood was streaming down his face. It was likely he hit it on the iron crossbar of the net. As he skated off the ice, the game would be delayed while he was patched up in the visitor's locker room. There were still ninety seconds to play of the second period and the Maroons didn't carry an extra goalie. We would all have to wait until he was patched up.

Our first line skated over to our bench. We congratulated our Captain, the stoic Bill Cook, on scoring the Ranger's first ever goal.

Sam stood on the bench behind us. Facing the spectators, he started encouragingly waving his arms and pleading "Come on! Let's hear it for Bill Cook!" he shouted.

A few spectators responded but most were distracted during the stoppage in play. Sam didn't stop. He kept encouraging the crowd to make noise.

This was an unexpected moment of awkwardness. The spectators in front starred with blank expressions and we players squirmed uncomfortably. But Sam didn't back down and he yelled again. Lester looked very uncomfortable. I saw Harry moving in Sam's direction with a furious expression that might have given Ching or Taffy pause. It seemed the whole arena was suddenly silent but for Sam. Once again, he chanted "Let's go Rangers!"

My line mate Paul, no fan of Sam's said "fucking arse" loud enough to be heard by all on the bench.

Suddenly, Lorne Chabot, just a few rows back stood up and started clapping. He yelled back, "Let's go Rangers!"

He and Sam repeated themselves in unison this time. A few of the men and women around him, in black tie and gowns stood and did the same. Suddenly it was contagious. Within seconds the entire section was chanting our name in unison. Looking around, people were standing throughout the whole Garden cheering widely. It was the first time I had experienced such a connectedness with a crowd. Sam was the conductor of an orchestra. Harry stood behind him, ready to yank him off the bench but even he could see that something special had just happened. I'm not sure Sam expected the response. The spark he lit had caught hold and was now a blazing fire with all the fuel it needed to sustain itself indefinitely.

Bunny, leaning over the railing said what all of us were thinking "boys, I think we have fans."

The drinks flowed freely after the game. True to his word, Lester bought the first round. But after that I don't think they cost any of us a cent. Strangers were buying us drinks all night.

It wasn't long before I was feeling the effects. Like most of the speakeasies we explored since our arrival in Manhattan, the *Green Door* wasn't large or well-lit, but it was gay and exciting.

Ching was proving to be our guide in this regard. Not only did he love the hunt to find them, but he also mysteriously secured the secret phrase to gain entry. This establishment was clearly the most popular gin-joint just outside the Garden. I sensed it was going to be our go-to spot after a win.

The music was lively, and the dancing was a jitterbug of energy.

It was full of actors and actresses high after their evening's performance. Businessmen and their wives, or as I suspect their girlfriends and mistresses spilled out from the shows and our game to enjoy a drink and cigar. We were being introduced to local politicians and uniformed policemen, off duty or not, who could say, but it didn't matter.

The beat reporters were huddled together in a corner; no doubt comparing notes for tomorrow's editions and finishing their beers before heading home to their typewriters with the quotes they needed.

Bill, our lone goal scorer of the night, was at the bar in conversation with a tall, slender, brown haired man wearing glasses. Bill waved me over. "Murray, this is Damon Runyon. He and his wife, Ellen, are at our hotel."

I was starstruck. Damon Runyon.

"Hello Mr. Runyon, I hope you'll write a good article about us tonight." I remembered the busboys from our hotel said he lived in our building. I knew he was a sportswriter of the highest caliber. He worked for Hurst, but quickly corrected me.

"Actually Mr. Murdoch, I cover boxing and baseball. We were in attendance only as spectators and very much enjoyed the performance, especially as Mr. Cook put the 'biscuit in the basket'. Ahh, here's my ever-loving doll now."

Emerging from the powder room was an attractive slender woman in pink dress and matching cloche hat pulled down over her ears. Her white gloves went up to her elbows. Ellen was introduced as Runyon lit her cigarette. The next two drinks were spent listening to Runyon share his passion for gambling and Broadway. It was all very intoxicating, and my head was starting to spin just a little off axis.

Keeping the party flowing was our new best friend; tall and burly, ringmaster and bartender, Mikey Lossi. Mikey looked like he could put on a pair of skates and join us on a whim. If my glass was empty, he'd hand me a new drink without being asked. He would simply point to the customer who graciously put it on their tab.

Single women abound and they were not shy about introducing themselves. Only a few minutes would pass before a new friend would pass out shots and toast our performance. I rarely knew what I was drinking. Paul was talking to three young gals while Taffy, Bun, Reg, and Ollie looked on in envy.

People just kept handing me shots.

Ching, with a fresh bandage above his eye and Frankie, with ice wrapped in a towel nursing his wrist, held court together at the bar telling jokes to a circle of cops. Mikey stood behind the bar making sure the cops were topped off.

I was making my way to join them, always appreciative of a laugh, when a blonde wearing a forest green turban and broach suddenly stepped in my path. "Got a light?" she asked innocently. Pulling out a box of matches I lit her cigarette and then reached for one of my own. My head was swimming pretty good. She was maybe twenty, nice curves and American. She exhaled slowly and smiled. "My name's Ginger, my friends tell me you play hockey for the new team."

The swing band was loud, and I had to lean in closer to hear over the music.

"That's right" I replied. "I'm Murray, Murray Murdoch."

"You have such a cute accent." She said giggling. "You must be from Canada."

"Yes, Manitoba"

"Mana…? Oh sugar that you're Canadian is enough. So, you're new to the city, aren't you?"

Her neck was so slender. "Yeah, we've only been here a few days. Where are you from? You don't sound like a New Yorker."

"I arrived last year, from Kansas. Nothing but farms and dirt there. I want to be an actress. I'm going to be a Broadway star" she said dramatically for effect.

"And how's that going? Are you on stage?" I asked enthusiastically.

"Not yet, but soon. I'm just waiting for my big break."

"So how do you pay the bills waiting for that big break? `

"I make twenty dollars a week selling dresses at Macy's" she boasted proudly. Ginger put both hands on her hips, showing off her dreamy cream-colored dress.

I wasn't hearing much at that moment beyond the music and Ginger's voice, which included smoke escaping her delicate red lips. A voluptuous girl was standing in front of me, in Manhattan, flirting with me. I knew this wasn't good, but it was intoxicating.

"I was at the game tonight but fear I don't know a thing about hockey. What are the rules?" she asked naively.

"To score more goals than the other team." I replied, trying to be witty. I laughed but I knew I was too drunk to be it funny. I hoped she was well-oiled with drinks, but she at least pretended to laugh with me.

"I could guess as much silly Mr. Murdoch. No, I mean the rules. Referees stop the action sometimes, and I don't know why."

"Those are probably offsides calls. You saw the two blue lines separating the ice into thirds? The attacking team must get the puck over the blue line before their bodies can enter that zone."

Lifting her delicate wrist so that her forearm was parallel to the floor I asked her to imagine her arm was the blue line. Pretending my glass was the puck and my left hand the skater, mimicking a skating motion with my fingers I demonstrated "If a player goes over the blue line ahead of the puck it's called offsides."

To which she immediately responded, "and if the puck enters the zone first you move in to score, right?"

Her comment caught me off guard and I was flustered. I wasn't so drunk as to not catch her meaning. I tried to steer the conversation to safer ground. "And if the defensive players get the puck out of that zone, the attacking team has to retreat back over the blue line before trying again."

"We don't want any retreating tonight, do we Murray?"

Damn, she doesn't miss a shot to score.

She seemed to relish this awkward moment as she took another sensual drag on her cigarette. "I understand. I will enjoy the game so much more. I would just love to show you the sights" she said as she put her delicate fingers on my wrist.

My faithful resolve to Marie, which was resolute when I stepped inside this establishment ninety minutes earlier, was evaporating with dangerous ease. I leaned closer still and was mighty tempted to whisper words I would certainly regret for all my life when "I'm happily married" thankfully came out instead.

At that moment I felt a hand on my shoulder.

Frankie yelled over the music, "Come on buddy, we need to get Sam back to the Forrest. He just threw up in the toilet."

"It was nice meeting you Ginger. Good luck with your singing career." I offered, breathing a sigh of relief.

"Come on Murray, I need your help with the kid."

As I was being led away, I glanced back over my shoulder, and she had a look of exasperation as I read her lips "it's acting, not singing." Before Frankie and I got to the bathroom she was probably already striking up a conversation with Paul Thompson.

"This place is a dangerous lair Raffles."

"Yes, it is Murray."

Frankie and I found Sam sitting on a stool; eye's closed, drool on his chin, his body leaning against the wall. We each grabbed an arm and hoisted him on our shoulders. He was in far worse sharp than us.

Sam rolled his head and half opened his eyes, "Let's go Rangers" he slurred proudly.

Frankie and I smiled at each other and said in unison "Let's go Rangers".

"Come on Sam, you're sleeping this off on my couch tonight" I offered. The three of us stepped out into the cool November air that greeted us on 50th Street and we made our way to Big Bill Dwyer's Forrest Hotel barely a block away.

"We've gotta have each other's back here Murray" Frank stated. Even drunk I understood his meaning.

"You got mine, I got yours."

I added "my oh my, this is only the first game."

Sam muttered "Let's go Rangers."

Chapter Eleven
November 17 - 20, 1926

I finished the letter I started.

When their goalie finally returned, we closed out the remaining seconds of the period. Even with the crowd behind us, the third period was a heavyweight prize-fight, Marie. In the end, it was our defense that won the day for us. Ching and Taffy kept to their positions and hit anyone coming over the line. Who would have believed we rookie Rangers beat the World Champion Maroons of Montreal in our first game.

My play was nothing memorable. I got more ice time as the game went on, but I was very outmatched. The pace is like nothing I've ever experienced. At times I felt like I was standing still on the ice while everyone else was racing past. Lester seemed happy enough with my play after the game, but I suspect that was only because we won. When we start piling up losses, he'll have to make changes. Marie, I really think I'm the weakest player on the team and wouldn't be at all surprised if Lester trades me (although I'm not sure he'd get more than a bag of pucks in return).

I told you about our center-man, Frank Boucher and that he is the team's gentleman. Well, a Maroon player had been mucking with Frankie the whole game. Late in the third period, Frank finally had all he could take and pushed back. Suddenly the two of them were swinging their sticks at each other. The crowd went nuts. Each got clipped in the face, blood was drawn, and the sticks and gloves were dropped. Frankie got knocked down but bounced right back up and gave as every bit as good as *he got. By now everyone from both teams joined in a near free-for-all shindig. Frankie told me after the game, with his eye swelling and his knuckles all blooded that his arms were like lead weights. But he went toe-to-toe and made us all proud. They both got five minutes and were fined $15.00 after the game!*

The final was 1-0. The beat writers were in grand spirits and people were buying us drinks all night. Later tonight we are taking the train north. We return to Toronto to face the St. Pats Saturday night!

I miss you more than I can express Marie. I've been talking to some of the other guys who are married. We think it is time to start planning for our wives to join us. Marie, I know the idea of coming to New York is scary. But the hotel is only a very short distance from the Garden. We are learning our way around. It's an amazing city Marie and I've only seen a tiny portion of it. We are right in the heart of the famous Broadway theater district. I know my time here might be short and for that reason I think you should come sooner rather than later. This might be the only opportunity we'll ever have to be in this city together. I need you here with me. Please think about it. We are on the road for nearly two weeks with games in Pittsburgh and Montreal after Toronto. I won't get your letters until I return. Wish us luck!

Your loving husband,

Murray

When Sam agreed to travel with the team, he never imagined doing so hung over. He was suffering mightily from last night's post game festivity. Most of us were feeling the aftereffects of a good time, but this was his first. He took the relentless ribbing in good humor while trying to find a quiet space to curl up and sleep. Not an easy task on a rollicking train.

We were also finding amusement in the final editions of the newspapers as we pulled out Grand Central. I recited with gusto an article by Paul Gallico called "Meet Johnson and Abel".

"The pastime was reintroduced to New York by a new team known as the Rangers, and on that team are two large beefy gentlemen whom the crowd took to its heart immediately and who, I predict will be the two most popular hockey players in New York this year. Their names are Ching Johnson and Taffy Abel, and they are defense men. Are they tough? Are they good? Can they play? Myomy! Wait till you see those two boys in action."

The nine-paragraph column was accompanied by two hand drawings by the author. The first was a caricature of both Abel and Johnson. They were portrayed as nearly identical smiling, hulking bruisers with hugely broad shoulders. It would have been impossible to know which was which if Gallico hadn't added their names.

The second cartoon showed one of the two, again it was impossible to tell which of them was being portrayed, hacking through laid out opponents. Passing the paper around with much laughter we formed a consensus that the drawing was intended to be Taffy.

A separate article by W.J. Macbeth of the New York Herald Tribune entitled "Local Hockey Sextets Away on Long Trips" talked of our need, and the Americans, to vacate the Garden and play a series of road games.

"Hockey fans of New York will have to take their hockey through the newspapers, until after the annual horse show and upcoming six-day bicycle race in the Garden. The Rangers will make their headquarters at Toronto."

Each of the papers had a whole article about our win against the Maroons and we devoured them. Collectively, they touted the unexpectedness of our beating the world champions, our solid defense, Bill's goal and Frankie's fight. Sitting next to me was Hal Winkler and I couldn't help but notice that little was mentioned about our goalie. Our first game was a shutout after all. He appeared uncomfortable as he was reading a copy of the Herald.

"What's wrong Hal?" I quietly asked.

He leaned towards me "did you look at the box score?"

"Sure" I replied. Truth is I proudly searched out my name listed under the spares.

He folded the paper and held it for me to read again.

"So who's this Shabotsky and Rocco listed on our team?" he whispered.

I looked at the small print of the box score more carefully and I could see that Hal was right.

"Typos?" I suggested.

But Bill said the same mistakes were in his copy of the Times. By now, everyone with a paper was flipping through the pages to find the box score. But in each, Lorne Chabot, who was a healthy scratch and Ollie Reinikka were oddly misspelled.

I didn't think much of it. I just assumed the writers were every bit as drunk as we were.

Our return to Toronto after little more than a week seemed weird. We did not return to the Ravina Gardens but instead prepared for our game against the St. Pats on their ice in the Arena Garden.

The St. Pats had not yet returned from their first game in Chicago and Lester, knowing that we had the ice for the whole day, intended to take advantage. He ordered everyone to lace up, including himself, Harry, and Sam.

Lester's idea of practice, after the normal warm-ups and drills, was effectively a game situation scrimmage with a specific area of attention. Usually this was done on "half ice" but today we were going full out. Sometimes the focus was on passing, or gaining the offensive zone, or shoring up our defense. Lester always preached that defense was the key to our being successful. He was confident that our forwards would score. What he wanted to prevent were the 6 – 5 loses.

We sat on the bench and absorbed his blackboard lessons as he drew x's and o's with a little snub of white chalk.

"Gentlemen, puck possession means we have got it and they do not. The more time the puck is in their defensive zone the less it is in ours. Sloppy turnovers will provide them with scoring opportunities. When we do lose possession our first line of defense is not our big gorillas, but our fleet footed forwards. You will chase down their attackers and pester them and pressure them from behind. You will force them into making panicked and unwise passes, or better yet, steal the puck from their back pockets."

This was a new type of strategy Lester called 'back-checking' and it was not without tradeoff. Traditionally the attackers were solely offensive minded and conserved their energies otherwise. Here, Lester was asking for a whole different mindset. A two-way forward. This meant a lot more skating and exhaustion. But the benefits were also exciting.

A team approach to defense meant fewer scoring opportunities for them. But fatigue would be a factor and Lester made it clear that more frequent line changes were the solution. This could only mean more ice time for the second line and thus Paul, who was always moaning about his time, got on board with the strategy right away.

More importantly, Bill and the first line were fully behind Lester's approach.

Lester summed it up at start our practice session. "Puck possession, pressure from behind, solid defense at our blue line and finally, strong goaltending. I want Murdoch, Boyd and Thompson paired up with Johnson and Abel. Chabot, you are in their net. Bun, Raffles, and Bill, our "bread line" as the press seems to be referring to you, will be with Mackey and Reinikka. Winkler, you are in goal for them. We will be skating full ice gentlemen so Harry, Sam and I will gladly relieve any of you that needs a rest.

It was just us in the whole arena. All of us skating on the beautiful clean sheet of ice together.

There was no ceremonial face-off. Lester just tossed a puck to the other end of the ice and yelled "skate hard and I want to see solid team defense. Go, go, go."

We hopped over the boards and Reg Mackey skated to the far end, scooped up the puck and skated up ice.

After a good half hour of skating, Boyd, seeing both Mackey and Reinikka in defensive positions in front of him, dumped the pass back to me. I skated up the left side. Unexpectedly my stick was slashed from behind and the puck was suddenly on the end of someone else's. I spun to see the number five turning hard in the opposition direction. Bill Cook had snuck up behind me and stolen my puck, or 'picked my pocket', just as Lester had instructed. I was humbled.

I could hear Lester from over on the bench yelling "Yes! That's the way Bill!"

A few moments later Sam jumped over the boards to give Bill a breather.

The kid skated well and held his own, even getting a few shots off but he wasn't demonstrating the kind of speed and skills I had witnessed earlier in the week.

Lester and Harry also took turns on the ice as others needed a short rest.

Lester, who played professionally as a defenseman back in the day, held his own and moved well. Although not as quick as he was in his youth, he could move the puck.

Harry, our traveling secretary, equipment manager and stitcher of both jerseys and skin, was a boxer and clearly not a skater. What he lacked in skill he made up for in good humor. The ice was not his friend, and he spent much time falling on it. We were all decent sports but he lacked basic skating skills. But even if none of us pressured him, his backside usually found the ice the moment the puck found his stick. He would growl and curse to the heavens. But he never made excuses of any sort. He'd just struggle back on his feet and resume play. That alone was enough to earn our respect.

We had been pushing ourselves hard and I finally took my turn to suck some oxygen on the bench. My legs felt like lead weights, but I knew I'd only need a few minutes to recuperate. The rest gave me an opportunity to watch Sam.

I reminded myself that he is only fifteen and skating on the ice with professionals for the first time. Sam seemed comfortable and relaxed. He was "seeing the ice". He knew where people were and more importantly, anticipated their next move and put the puck right where they were headed. His passes were crisp and landed right on the receiver's blade.

Bunny came to the bench gasping for air. Between deep breathes he commented "the kid's good….but he's not skating…like the other day."

"He's doing fine. He's young after all. And it's the day after his first hangover." I offered in his defense. Bunny was sucking hard for air.

"Hey, maybe we should cut down on the smoking?" I wondered out loud.

Bunny gave me an incredulous look. "What the hell are you talking about?! The smokes help open our airways." He protested.

I agreed and sprung over the boards as Paul yelled out for a change.

Two days later, Bill Cook scored off a beautiful assist by Frankie seventeen minutes into the first period against the St. Pats. In frustration, John Ross Roach, their goalie swung his stick at Bill as he passed the net. Our Captain went right after Roach and a long donnybrook ensued to the amusement of the paying customers.

Order was eventually restored but the hostility was evident. Coming into the new season, Toronto was already a struggling franchise. They were running out of money and selling star players, like Babe Dye a couple weeks earlier, for cash. They were desperate to get the season off to a strong start, but they played poorly in their first game against the Black Hawks.

Now down by a goal to a rookie club, in front of their home fans, they pressed harder. The harder they pressed the dumber they got with their plays and penalties. Conversely Lester kept us focused.

Their winger Ace Bailey sent the puck down along the boards behind our net. Ching got to the puck first, looked up and had room to skate.

Our first line was spread out wide and skating north. Ching could have passed to any one of them. Bill, Frankie, and Bun were all finding open ice. But he had a head of steam and took the puck right through center ice and into the zone himself. Neither defender seemed the least interesting in engaging our big brawling hulk and just kept backing up in anticipation of his passing the puck off. From the bench I imagined Ching asking himself, "Why pass the puck if they're giving up a lane to the net!"

He skated practically right at their goalie's doorstep and wristed the shot past Roach on the stick side. From one end of the ice to the other, Ching was never touched.

A chorus of boos rung down from the rafters towards their own players.

With six minutes left in the second period, Lester sent Paul, Boyd, and I out for the ensuing faceoff.

Ace Bailey skated into our zone and made a beautiful cross ice pass to Carson on my side. I tapped Carson's stick just as he got the shot off and Lorne was forced to make a good save. But there was a rebound in front and Bailey, who had crashed the net, was in position to score an easy goal. To the amazement of all, Chabot made a tremendous second save while spread out on the ice.

Again, the crowd voiced its frustration.

Getting to his feet, Lorne, with the puck in his glove noticed the referee didn't ring the bell to stop play. The St. Pats forwards were idle, as if time had been called. Lorne looked up ice and our eyes locked.

With my back to the boards, I made several crossovers to get my momentum going and turned on the speed. Lorne dropped the puck to the ice and using his stick, passed it straight ahead where I caught it on my blade before crossing the red line at center ice.

Their defensemen Corbeau and Brydge had not been fooled though.

Corbeau stayed with me, while Brydge backed up into position. I was going to need to beat them both. Corbeau was on my left side, trying to force me off the puck while I kept it wide to my right. As I'm a left-handed shot this meant the puck needed to stay on my backhand while my left arm was crossed over my body. He kept leaning into me as we crossed the blue line into their zone, and I knew Brydge was going to stop retreating and stand me up. They had played their defensive roles perfectly and I was caught in a closing vice. Neither Boyd nor Thompson were in position to receive a pass yet.

With nothing to lose, I waited for that moment when Brydge would stop his backwards direction, spring forward and engage me. Just as that happened, I made a quick motion with my body to the right as if I were changing my direction and taking the puck wider. Predictably this caused Brydge's right foot to crossover his left and put him ever so briefly in a position of not being able to change direction back again.

I put my shoulder down and leaned hard into Corbeau on my left side. I just kept pumping my legs and somehow the gambit paid off. I split the two defensemen, brought the puck back across to my forehand, looked up briefly to find an open spot of net and shot as hard as I could.

I watched as the puck sailed into the back of the netting for my first NHL goal. Not a minute had passed since Ching had scored and we were now leading by three.

The next evening, I purchased two copies of the local daily paper and clipped out the article. I mailed one copy to my parents. The other I mailed to Marie along with a letter I wrote on the train.

RANGERS DEFEAT
TORONTO ST. PATS
BY 5 TO 1 SCORE

Toronto, Ont., Nov. 20 – The New York Rangers showed Toronto some neat hockey tonight when they defeated the local St. Patrick club, 5- 1. It was the Rangers second win of the season and enabled them to tie Boston for the National league lead.

Bunny Cook was the leading goal getter for the Rangers, counting twice. Bill Cook got one, as did Johnson and Murdoch. The Rangers outplayed the Irish throughout, and only in the last period did the St. Patrick team get near Chabot, who played a great game in the nets for the winners.

Ching Johnson starred on the defense. The Cook brothers also stood up well. Bill Carson got the lone Irish goal and was the best Toronto man.

The Rangers had plenty of condition and they proved better in their combined efforts than their opponents. It was a typical pro hockey game, with both sides making plenty of trips to the penalty box.

Dear Marie,

As you can see from the press clipping, we won our second game, and I scored my first goal. It was a great return to Toronto, and we are now on our way to Pittsburgh after changing trains in Buffalo.

I have written you so many letters telling you of my teammates and I realize you still have no idea what they look like. As you see in the article there are small head shots of Bill Cook and Ching Johnson, only their names are switched! Ching is not the handsome one. There, now at least you know what three of us Rangers look like. I hope you still remember my face.

While this Toronto writer got Chabot's name correctly, the New York papers still call him "Shabotsky" or "Chabotsky" and all the box scores incorrectly listed Reinikka as 'Rocco'. We are all getting rather suspicious, and Lester has sent back a telegram to our team publicist asking for them to be corrected going forward. Lester thinks our P.R. guy Johnny Bruno is playing a stupid game of "press agentry" making our French-Canadian goalie appeal to the large Jewish population in the city. The same seems to be happening with Ollie. Apparently, there aren't enough Finnish in the city, so Bruno is going after the Italians, hoping they will come see their very own "Rocco".

After our long practice on the 18th Frankie had a shock when we stepped into our Toronto hotel. His lovely wife Ag surprised him! She took the train down from Ottawa all by herself. You never saw a husband and wife so excited to embrace! The whole team stood there and watched them kiss, but when several moments passed, we started to get a little uncomfortable. Bunny coughed into his hand and said "get a room" when it suddenly dawned on me what her presence meant.

I was the one sharing a room with Frankie! I ran upstairs and grabbed my trunk and toothbrush. Fortunately for me, Lester had a room to himself, and we shared his bed. I admit, it's a little awkward sleeping with the manager and the next morning, in front of the whole team, he threatened to cut me from the Rangers if I kept taking his blanket! Well, forgive me but Lester Patrick snores like a horse and I told everyone so! But for the fact that I was so tired after that long practice I doubt I would have gotten any sleep at all. And sure enough, for all our joking and jocularity our next two nights as roommates proved difficult to say the least and I am very tired as I write you. Frankie however had been dancing on cloud 9. Ag watched her husband play as Lester was able to get a good seat for her. Although Frankie didn't score, he played very well and registered an assist on the first goal and set up several others. I often looked up to see her clapping in a sea of very unhappy Toronto fans.

It was very difficult on them both when Frank put her on the train back to Ottawa earlier this morning. He is sitting at a table writing a long letter to her now. He looks heartbroken but they've made arrangements for her to move to Manhattan in just a few weeks.

It seems very far away but on December 15th we are in Chicago. After we return, we're home for a couple weeks but for one game. We can be together over the holidays. Please consider taking the train from Winnipeg and meeting me in Chicago. I miss you and long to hold you.

I signed my letter, made out the envelope and then set about trying to cheer up Frankie.

Chapter Twelve

November 22 - 27, 1926

We arrived in Pittsburgh tired from the overnight train after our game. We had a full day practice and the team enjoyed dinner at the Oyster House in Market Square. From there we drifted from one speakeasy to the next. At one joint I noticed Taffy seemed withdrawn from the rest of the guys and assumed he was fatigued.

We were back at practice on Tuesday the 23rd. Harry didn't lace up, but Lester and Sam did everything with us.

Sam was starting to show his real skills. His turns were tight and low, really using his edges and generating power. Making a sharp pivot his skates were so far outside his center of gravity I thought he would fall. I couldn't comprehend the physics behind the centrifugal force that slingshot him forward. On turns to his right he would use only his left hand to control his stick and the puck would follow as if magnetized, while his free right hand would skim along the surface of the ice with the grace of a speed skater going around a turn. That his skating and stick handling skills were on par, if not better than most of us, was now becoming evident.

But he still seemed unwilling to let it loose in scrimmage. I was convinced that he had a whole other level of play in him. He played to fit in with us. He was no showboater. Guys were comfortable passing him the puck, except for Paul who was the least likely guy on our team to pass to anyone. But we weren't seeing the full range of his true gift. I was sure of it.

Hal Winkler started our third game and gave up a soft goal ten minutes in. We played poorly for two periods. The referee, Dave Ritchie, let the rough stuff get out of hand. He only rung the bell on Ching for a two-minute tripping call in the first period and no penalties were called on either team in the second. It was a vicious game with frequent spearing and slashing to the body and head. Harry was kept plenty busy patching us up quick. Sam would hold the light in position and pass Harry instruments as needed. Sam was getting a crash course in battle-field sutures.

Pittsburgh wore God-awful, bright yellow sweaters with 'Pirates' scripted above a large letter 'P' on the front, and yellow socks with two thin horizontal black stripes.

Lester gave us a good locker room rally before the start of the third, and we got back to playing our style of hockey. But it wasn't enough. Hal gave up a goal by Herb Drury five minutes into the period. Both our lines fought hard to score but we couldn't find the back of the net. Despite our furious efforts the game ended 2-0 and their goalie Roy Worters recorded the first shutout against our team.

No one was happy as we loaded our gear onto the overnight train to Toronto and then to Montreal. By morning, we'd be back in Canada.

Lorne was starting in his hometown.

Lorne Chabot no doubt came to Connie Smythe's attention after helping the Port Arthur Bearcats win the Allan Cup two consecutive years. Lorne was fiercely proud of his French-Canadian heritage and his family, friends and neighbors purchased tickets for our game against the Canadians.

From the moment Howie Morenz and Auréle Joliat stepped on the ice their presence was felt and the crowd roared admiration.

Morenz, the "Stratford Streak", was arguably the greatest hockey player of this generation. A center with lightning speed and a nose for the back of the net; we knew he was going to be tough on us.

Joliat, the “Little Giant” provided a one-two punch in their lineup we hadn’t yet seen. Only 5’7” and 136 pounds, Joliat was the reason the Canadiens won the cup two years ago.

This wasn’t just a test for our defense, but for Bill Cook. Bill was the lead scorer on our team and the comparisons between Morenz and Cook were inevitable.

Lorne Chabot wasn’t the only one reuniting with family at the rink. Frankie’s older brother Bill Boucher was on the ice skating against us. He was Montreal’s second line right-winger. The family resemblance was unmistakable and wondered if his whole family looked like bankers.

We got a surprisingly nice ovation as our starters were introduced to the crowd. Although two years old, the Montreal Forum was new to the Canadiens, having only played their first game here nine days earlier.

Located at the northeast corner of Atwater and Saint Catherine Street, the arena, with some nine-thousand seats filled with surprisingly respectful fans. It was also the home of the Maroons.

The Canadiens wore a classic red sweater with blue and white horizontal bands. An “H” sat inside a larger “C” emblem on their chest. The “H” was for hockey and the “C” Canadiens.

The speed of the first period was tremendous. Both teams raced up and down the ice at an unsustainable pace. Lester called for changes at nearly every stoppage of play. Billy Boyd, taking a shift for Bill Cook, went right after Morenz and the two were quickly escorted to the penalty box for two minutes by Cooper Smeaton, our referee for today’s festivities.

Lorne was kept busy as he was facing more shots than we were putting on their rookie goalie, George Hainsworth.

Lester had stressed before the game that Hainsworth was untested and under tremendous pressure as he was replacing the legendary goalie, Georges Vézina. Vézina had played 327 consecutive regular season games and a further 39 playoff games, literally every game since the birth of their franchise in 1910. He won them two Stanley Cups before leaving early during a game in 1925 due to illness. Shortly thereafter Vézina was diagnosed with tuberculosis and died this past March.

I truly couldn't begin to imagine how anyone could play in so many consecutive games in such a brutal sport. It was unfathomable. I was impressed I was playing in our fourth straight game.

Thus far the young goalie Hainsworth, wearing the traditional wool capie on his head, seemed to be coping with the pressure of replacing a legend. He was turning away everything we threw at him.

Boyd and Morenz weren't out of the penalty box but for a couple minutes before our Captain Bill Cook and Auréle Joliat found themselves battling for the puck in the corner. Both were free with the high elbows. I'm not sure who got popped in the face first, but both dropped their gloves and were throwing fists in short order. Each had a solid hold on the other's sweater so there was no retreat. The two just pummeled each other unrelentingly until Joliat finally dropped to one knee. Bill was furious and I could tell he wanted to keep hitting him but stopped.

I was taking a shift for Bunny and on the ice. By the time Bill's fight was winding down, the rest of us were just getting started. Art Gagne and I matched up, and we were both tasting blood before peace was restored. As we separated, I could see that Frankie and his brother Billy were wrestling, but neither threw any real punches at the other.

Bill and Joliat both went off for five minutes and moments later Taffy was called for tripping. I looked up at the clock. With two minutes and five seconds remaining, the Canadiens had 5 on 4 advantage till the end of the period. Lester sent Thompson and Boyd, to join me to kill the penalty with Ching.

"Murdoch, I want you back on defense with me" Johnson ordered. I nodded and dropped into position for the faceoff right in front of Lorne in our defensive zone. I was no defenseman and Ching's choosing me to pair up with him caught me by surprise. Didn't he realize that we were facing Howie Morenz? I kept expecting to hear Lester's voice booming from the bench ordering me to switch up with Thompson. But he just stood there seemingly content.

Referee Smeaton dropped the puck and Morenz skillfully tipped the puck forward. Quick as lightning he squirmed between Thompson and Boyd to pick up the puck mere feet in front of the net and instantly took a wrist shot. My oh my, he's too fast.

Lorne blocked the shot and Ching, seeing Morenz anticipate the rebound, sprung like a coil. He lifted Morenz with a body blow and drove him to the ice. I got to the loose puck, picked up my head and shot it out of the zone. The Canadiens retreated and regrouped to attack again.

Billy Boucher, Frank's brother, came up the right side with the puck and just before he felt Ching's wrath, he sent the puck deep behind our net. Morenz anticipated this, and I stayed with him as he raced down the left side. We got to the puck together and battled against the boards.

Neither of us yielded as we put our weight into each other. The fans were only inches away from my face, cheering Morenz on in French. I remembered the elbows he and Bill Cook exchanged earlier so I tried to position myself to prevent his getting a clean shot. But that didn't stop the great Morenz who had a full bag of tricks. He couldn't get his elbow up, so he suddenly slid the shaft of his stick and the butt caught me square under the jaw. I felt my teeth crunch together awkwardly. That was all he needed. Suddenly he was spinning away from me with the puck.

But I tied him up long enough. The second Morenz spun around he was greeted by the freight train that is our Ching!

Morenz compressed into the boards right next to me. I could hear the air literally pressed out of his lungs as Ching's shoulder was determined to put him through the boards, right into the stunned crowd. The rows of spectators instructively jerked backwards in self-protection, so convinced that their hero was about to unceremoniously join them in the third row.

Morenz slumped to the ice as his teammates came to start another brawl. Ching and I fought back. The other Rangers jumped in. The whole time I could hear Ching laughing.

The second period picked up right where the first ended, with Ching Johnson dominating the game. The Canadiens controlled the puck in our zone and got a couple shots off on Chabot. Lorne caught a wrist shot in his glove and tossed it behind the net. Ching picked it up and realized the Canadiens were failing to pressure him right away. He took off up the ice. He got through the forwards easily enough, faked out one defender and plowed right past the other before ripping a shot their goalie Hainsworth couldn't stop. We now had a 1-0 lead.

But towards the end of the period a bizarre confluence of events occurred. Frankie's brother Bill brought the puck into the zone while the Canadiens were getting a change. It seemed harmless enough. He was skating up center ice and was attempting to split Ching and Taffy. Not a single skater had yet accomplished this feat and sitting on the bench I commented "good luck with that". I'm sure Frank's brother intended to simply dump the puck deep and skate off for a change himself.

But somehow Ching and Taffy got their signals crossed; each thinking the other was going to engage him at the blue line. Billy Boucher, sensing the mental lapse shot forward. Taffy and Ching, both caught on their heels, responded at the same moment, and thrust their sticks at Boucher's feet as he skated through them. Both sticks caught his blades and Boucher went flying face first onto the ice.

The ref's bell rung, and he pulled our two defensemen aside. Ching and Taffy protested but were both sent off to the penalty box for two minutes. Smeaton skated over to our bench to address Lester, who was irate. But Smeaton just kept repeating himself. "Lester, I'm sorry but I have to call them both for tripping." After a few choice words, Lester sent out our only other defenseman Reg Mackey, who mere moments later took a hooking penalty himself. It was a penalty for sure and the ref had no choice.

We were suddenly left with only two skaters on the ice, against their five.

This was most unusual.

We quickly gathered at the bench while Smeaton settled matters in the penalty box and the scorer's table. It was inconceivable we could escape the next two minutes without the Canadiens tying the score.

Lester saw that Bill Cook was winded. He and Joliat had been battling each other without mercy.

"Bill, take a breather. Bunny and Frank, you two will kill this penalty. But get a change at your first safe opportunity after one minute." Lester's orders were received without complaint or hesitation. Bill lifted himself over the boards and accepted a tin cup of water from Sam.

Frankie lined up for the faceoff in our defensive zone. Bunny positioned himself close to the net, careful not to block Lorne's view. As soon as the puck was dropped their center Morenz physically tied up Frankie. It was a set play.

The puck just sat on the ice untouched, and Art Gagne immediately scooped it up and shot at the net. Lorne blocked the shot, and it ricocheted in the corner. Frankie got loose from Morenz.

Frank and Bun didn't chase after the puck, instead positioning themselves in front of our net. Uncontested, Joliat skated with the puck behind our net and sent a pass to their defenseman Herb Gardiner, who quickly passed it across to his partner Albert Leduc. He skated towards the net and sent a quick pass to Morenz, but Bunny was able to poke-check the puck off his stick for a moment.

Morenz regrouped and feed the puck to Joliat who took a hard shot that Frankie blocked with his leg.

Frank dropped to the ice in pain.

Morenz recovered the puck and tried to power his way to the net, but Bunny put his shoulder into him and kept whacking at his stick. The puck came loose and Frankie, back on his skates, sent the puck out of the zone but only barely.

The Canadiens had to retreat but neither Frankie nor Bun had enough time for a safe change and had to stay on the ice.

Montreal returned to our zone with no opposition to stop them. Gagne to Joliat to Gardiner to Leduc to Morenz. Uncontested, the puck was freely passed back and forth constantly tempting Cook and Boucher to leave their defensive position.

Leduc charged the net and Bun was forced to stand him up with his elbows and stick. The attack failed but Gagne quickly recovered the puck and took a quick shot. Lorne stopped it again but there was a rebound and everyone crashed on the net in a wild flurry.

In the confusion Bun, Frankie and Lorne were slashed and hacked at with sticks. But the puck did not go in the net and Lorne sent it harmlessly in the corner.

I stole a quick glance at the penalty clock; a full minute and twenty seconds remained on the first of the three penalties. The Canadiens were growing more desperate, and the crowd was growing increasingly impatient.

Morenz dug the puck out of the corner and drove straight for the net. Bun positioned himself to block his advance, but Morenz lowered his shoulder as if he was prepared to bull his way through. But just before the impact, Morenz shuffled a pass to the wide-open Joliat who released the shot as quickly as he received it.

I gasped, sure that Montreal had finally scored. To the utter amazement of everyone in the building our Lorne Chabot threw out his right leg and blocked the shot.

Frankie was able to reach the rebound first, skated two full strides and shot the puck out of the zone just before he was body checked by Gagne. Frankie fell hard to the ice and had trouble getting to his feet. He was bleeding from somewhere inside his mouth and spat blood onto the ice.

Lester was screaming for him to come to the bench for a line change. So desperate were we that our coach was willing to allow one utterly exhausted skater to be all that stood between a full squad of skaters while we got an injured one off the ice for fresh legs. I could see that Bill Cook was ready to leap over the boards to his brother's defense.

But Frankie couldn't do it. He couldn't make it to the bench. And the Canadiens were on the attack yet again. A full minute remained.

The Canadiens kept the puck to the perimeter with crisp quick passes while the great Howie Morenz set himself up in front of the net. He was pushing and shoving Bunny and Frankie while waiting for the inevitable rebound.

With each pass the Canadiens skated closer and closer, ready to spring their attack. The crowd was screaming "Tirer! Tirer! Shoot! Shoot!"

Gagne took a quick shot that hit the blade of Lorne's skate. Morenz gave Frankie a hard elbow in the gut and pounced for the puck, but Bunny swung his stick and just knocked the puck off to the side. Leduc swooped in and took a shot.

Save by Chabot. Rebound and Morenz shot.

Save again. Frankie spun and fired the puck out, but Gagne stopped it at the blue line and staked right for the net.

Everyone crashed the net, and I was livid as I watched my friends getting speared and slashed with such viciousness. Someone shot and missed the net. The crowd was in a screaming frenzy and those in the first few rows were shaking the chicken wire fence.

Sam screamed "six seconds!"

Joliat skated out from the pack, spun, and whipped another shot. It ricocheted off Bunny's ankle and hit the metal post of the goal making a loud ping. The shot was fired hard enough that the blow to Bunny's ankle collapsed him to the ice.

The dual penalty over, Ching and Taffy sprung from the penalty box and raced to the rescue.

With the puck near the net, they each picked a target and threw their bodies at anyone in a Canadien's sweater. Our two defensemen were in a rage and heaven help anyone in their path.

Taffy slammed Joliat to the ice with such force that I didn't know if he'd get up. Lorne was able to fall on the loose puck and the referee was quick to blow the whistle.

Bunny Cook and Frankie Boucher were barely able to skate to the bench. As they approached, we slapped our sticks in unison over the boards. Blood was streaming from Frankie's lip and Bunny's ankle was such that he could barely put pressure on it. Bunny was leaning on Frank as they drifted to our bench. Both were deeply bruised and battered beneath their pads.

Those Canadiens would not soon forget the colors of our Rangers Blue. I had never seen a five-on-two so valiantly, and successfully defended. Apparently neither had the fans. Starting with the rows directly behind our bench but quickly spreading like a match tossed on gasoline, the citizens of Montreal stood and clapped in honor of the display they had just witnessed.

Bunny even exacted a measure of revenge when late in the third period he scored to make the score 2-0, which is how it ended. And as we exited the ice, the fans once again stood and gave the visiting team an ovation.

Our record was now a respectable 3 wins and one loss as we boarded the train back to New York.

Chapter Thirteen
February 1994

"I see you brought your gear like I asked."

"I did, but I honestly didn't think you were serious Murray."

I smile and I reach down to untie my boots and start the ritual of putting on my skates.

Mark Messier, Captain of the New York Rangers, perhaps the greatest leader in all professional sports smiles back, only now realizing I'm not bluffing. We're going for one last skate together. He follows my lead and starts to lace up.

I know this is an ask. Although he hides it, Mark's tired and banged up. It took some real audacity to invite him, in the middle of his fifteenth grueling season, to go for a skate on a frozen pond.

In the late sixties and mid-seventies, Marie and I visited Mark's parents Mary-Jean and Doug. Once in St. Albert and again years later in Edmonton. Mark's dad, Doug, was a schoolteacher and minor league hockey player himself. Tough as nails. On both our visits, Doug and I found ourselves with his boys on the ice. We would drill holes and drop lines to fish, then play hockey and wait to catch dinner while we passed the puck around. Mark and his older brother Paul could both skate and clearly had tremendous potential at a young age.

The second time I skated with Mark, he was a young teenager in Edmonton. I immediately knew he had the gift. Mark had an edge. A no holds-barred, no quarter given nor expected, bad-ass attitude to his game. He got that from his father.

Years later, when Mark and Wayne Gretzky were teammates on

the Edmonton Oilers, I saw the unrealized magic that could have been, had only Bill Cook and Sam Crawford played together. Mark and Wayne were like brothers. Born only a week apart.

But at 31, Bill was twice Sam's age. Fate intervened long before age played a factor.

"You know Mark, your playing style and leadership has always reminded me of my Captain, Bill Cook."

"That is a compliment. Bill Cook was truly a great player. In my opinion, the greatest Captain in Rangers' history and yet he's hardly mentioned today. I don't think most fans even know his name. Vic Hadfield, Harry Howell, Andy Bathgate were good Captains, but their time wearing the "C" was brief by comparison. Bill was the first and won the Rangers' two Cups. But for some reason he's been forgotten. He and his brother, and the others, Lester, Ching, and Boucher just aren't spoken about enough, if ever. It's truly an honor to follow them, and you, nearly seventy years later." Mark adds.

"It breaks my heart that none of them are remembered. I watch the games now on TV. I see all the fans wearing player jerseys. Your number 11 is the most popular by far these days. MESSIER in capital letters on the back, with a "C" on the front. Heck, I saw a kid out here earlier copying your celebration move."

"I don't have a celebration move." Mark says defensively with a guilty smile.

"No? The whole arms raised, the smile that lights up a city block. No, that's your signature. Mark, you do everything with purpose."

I continue. "I always prayed that one day you would wear the Ranger colors and we'd have that in common. It's good to see Leetch, Graves and Richter jerseys throughout the Garden. Beukeboom and Kocur are fan favorites and I see plenty of their jerseys too. So many European players now. I struggle to pronounce their names sometimes" I laugh. "Nemchinov, Karpovtsev, Kovalev, Zubov." I struggle but know that I've pronounced them passably enough. "That's the biggest change to the game you know. Yes, forward passing in the offensive zone really opened the game in '29, the red line in '43. That was all Frank Boucher, did you know that?" I asked.

"No, I know the center became the head coach and eventually GM. I didn't realize he also rewrote the rule book." Mark confessed.

"There have been so many other changes that have improved the game. Icing in '37. Goalie masks and the evolution of equipment, the roster sizes, the training, video, nutrition, longer seasons, multiple playoff rounds, airplane travel and expansion." I rattle off a list as they come to mind. "The game has changed so much, but at its heart, it's the same. 'Putting the biscuit in the basket'. But now, the league has the best players on the planet playing together. That's been the most pleasant change in my opinion. It's a special team you've got this season Mark. You and I both know how fleeting this window is. It sure would be nice to see the Rangers lift the Cup again before I'm gone. You don't mind accommodating an old man, do you?"

We both share a chuckle. But I know this is weighting on Mark and I immediately regret making the joke. It's been 54 years since the Rangers last won the Cup. New York traded for him to accomplish one purpose. To win the Stanley Cup after a five-decade's long draught. That's a heavy weight for any one man to shoulder.

In his first season with the Rangers, Mark guided them to the best record in the league and won the Hart trophy as the Most Valuable Player. But the team lost in the second round of the playoffs.

Last season, the Rangers failed to even make the post season. That was the first time in Mark's whole career that happened. The doubters, the naysayers, the sportswriters, and radio pundits who had never played a game in their lives were all quick to claim the window has passed and that Mark is past his prime. Several called for him to be traded for prospects and rebuild again.

But this season he has the team back in first place. They have a chemistry and talent to make another run. But the deeper we go into the season the greater the pressure. For most people, this would be crippling. While Mark is not 'most people', he is human.

"The trading deadline is fast approaching, and I know Neil is going to be aggressive. I've been talking with him and stressing the need for guys with playoff experience and grit." Mark confided.

I know that Neil is Neil Smith, the Rangers' General Manager. "Who's on your list?" I ask.

"Dream list? MacTavish and Glenn Anderson. I played with both in Edmonton. There's also a big fella on Chicago I like. Clutch player. A third line winger. I suspect he plays a little like you played Murray. His name is Matteau."

I shift the subject, "It would be nice to turn on the TV and watch a game and see just a few fans wearing the numbers and names of players past. I don't ever see Jean Ratelle's 19 worn. Or Gump Worsley, Brad Park, Andy Bathgate. Occasionally I see Rod Gilbert's 7. That's nice."

"Or Ching's 3, Taffy's 4, Bill's 5, Fred's 6, Frank's 7, or…your 9." Mark said softly, knowing that I would be touched that he remembered our numbers.

"Yes, that would be a great honor. No one wants to feel forgotten Mark. While you remind me of Bill Cook, there was someone Wayne Gretzky reminded me of.

"Woo, that's rare high praise. There aren't many who compared to the "great one". Mark replied.

"The world never got to see him play and I'm the only one left that remembers him at all. Let's get on the ice. I need to tell you about a kid named Sam."

Chapter Fourteen
November 30, 1926

A cigarette hangs from my smiling lips as I re-read Marie's letter. I'm sitting on my stool with skates laced as we all wait for Harry to give us the signal to head out onto the ice.

My darling husband,

You're a nincompoop. If you're reading this letter that means you're still in New York and haven't been traded. For the record, I'm sure Mr. Patrick could get at least two bags of pucks for you.

Murray, I've been watching you skate since we were kids. I developed a crush on you watching you skate on a frozen pond before we even knew each other's names. It wasn't because you were the best player. I'm not sure you've ever been the "star" player on any team. I was attracted to you because you play with more heart than anyone I've ever seen. There is something about how you play, a grinding, never quit, fight, fight, fight for the puck while never losing your good senses that makes you just about the most valuable player on every team you've ever played for. You aren't the most talented, or the fastest or the strongest or the best fighter. You do all those things extremely well, but if you're on this team, it's because Mr. Patrick knows your heart.

At thirteen years old, I remember thinking, "his heart is big enough to love me."

The game will slow down for you. You'll get a little bit faster. You'll find your stride. Have half as much faith in yourself as I have in you. Now go shoot that puck and score that goal.

And yes, I'm coming down to be with you.

Love,

Marie

"Damn!" I steal a quick look at the clock through the blue smoke at the Garden. Chicago's Mickey MacKay put one past our goalie Hal at 3:56 into the game.

He took the shot before Taffy could engage him and the shot probably should have been stopped from that distance by Hal.

Minutes later Bunny mixed it up with their defenseman Gord Frazer after a hard check. Both were sent to the box. Bun went off hollowing mad, throwing his stick into the box, and swearing a few choice words at Frazer. Our games are not for young children.

But penalties like this often light a fire. After exiting the box Bunny was still hopping mad. He immediately pounced on a loose puck in the natural zone, picked up steam and shot a bullet past Frazer just as the defenseman drifted in front of their goalie Lehman, blocking his vision for just a moment. The shot was fast enough that a moment was all Bun needed to get it into the net and tie the score.

Bunny slowly coasted back to center ice, jawing it up with Frazer.

Now Dick Irvin and Duke Dukowski started in with Abel and all three went to the box. But even with a man-advantage we couldn't score, and the first period ended tied.

To start the second period Mickey MacKay made two powerful solo runs but both efforts ran into the crushing pinch of Abel and Johnson. Taffy rarely showed the ferociousness that struck abject fear that Ching employed so effectively. Taffy wanted to stop you. Ching wanted to terrify you.

Off the ice, Taffy was prone to occasional melancholy moods, especially after a couple drinks. But he was generally just a happy-go-lucky teammate who loved to play cards and laugh. As we walked down the tunnel to start the period, I could hear Taffy quietly singing to himself, as he often did.

"…strolling through the park one day,
In the merry, merry month of May,
I was taken by surprise,
By a pair of laughing eyes,
While strolling through the park one day."

This balance of styles between Ching and Taffy worked like two comedians playing off each other. The straight man sets up the funny guy to deliver the punch line.

Skaters with any common sense were intimidated just enough by Ching's sledgehammer that it influenced their stride toward the softer obstacle. But it was an equal dead-end. True, it was like skating into an unmovable pillow, but few could get past the surprisingly quick and well positioned Taffy Abel.

Bill intercepted the puck in our defensive zone and started up ice. He quickly maneuvered past George Hay, froze MacKay at center ice, did a fake on Irvin at the blue line, skated up the boards and just flat out beat Fraser with his speed and then put his shoulder down as Bob Trappe engaged. Like a bull, Bill leaned into Trappe and kept pumping his skates across the front of the net, forcing their goalie to drop. From left of the net, Bill let loose and lifted the puck. The red light flashed. He scored at 3:03.

It was the prettiest goal of the early season. The crowd and our bench exploded at the display of total dominance. We slammed our sticks against the boards in celebration. Bill engaged and beat every player on the Hawks to score. Our crowd chanted Bill's name and a spontaneous chorus of "Let's go Rangers" rang down from the upper tier.

Sam was celebrating like the rest of us but something about his expression caught my attention. I watched as his gaze quickly returned to the ice. He glanced to the far end of the ice, where the play began, and his eyes darted along the route Bill Cook took up ice to the visitor's goal. I suspected Sam had just replayed Bill Cook's spectacular run up the ice in his mind. And just like that, his private moment was over, and Sam was refilling cups with water for the guys.

When backchecking, Bill and Bunny would force an opposing skater towards Frank, who loved to play with a long stick and poke the puck away from opposing players. This led to frequent turnovers and much frustration for those not wearing Ranger's blue.

This was exactly the strategy that produced our third goal. After Frank forced a turnover, Bun and Frank came down hard on Lehman, rapidly passing the puck back and forth to each other. Cook took the shot at close range and was blocked by Lehman. But the rebound was right there for Frank to bury.

When Irwin was called for roughing, Lester put me on the man-advantage to give Frank a breather.

Bill shifted to center, Bun on his left and I took the right wing. We won the faceoff and Bill pushed the puck up ice. We quickly gained the zone. Bill sent it to me. I took it deep into the corner and sent it to Bunny along the boards. He sent it back to our defenseman Taffy. Taffy sent it across to Ching like a string along the blueline. Ching, just as fast and tight, sent it right back to Taffy. Taffy skated towards the net, looking for an opening, but not finding it, and then passed across an open gap to me on the other side. I quickly redirected the puck to Bill who took a quick hard shot.

Rebound.

I got to it, but not having an angle to shoot I sent it across to Bun. The crowd was going wild, on their feet in a screaming tizzy.

Bun passed to Bill who looped behind the net and passed it right back to his brother crashing the net.

Another shot on goal, blocked. Bill sent the reboard back to Ching who immediately shot from the blue line.

Blocked by Trappe, another rebound.

Again, the passing was crisp and fast. Giving the Black Hawks no time to breath. I got to the puck and looking for an open man found Bunny. Like a trap tightening we closed in and sprung.

Bun shot. The puck was loose in front. Bill, Bun, and I were all fighting frantically for the puck and getting manhandled, slashed, and crosschecked, by Fraser, Trappe, MacKay, and Lehman. At that moment, Taffy crashed himself into the mallee. We all fell on top of one another. I heard Bill grunt.

The puck was somewhere under the pile and the ref had no choice but to ring the bell. The crowd roared in disapproval. Someone was laying on top of me. I was on top of others. I was pulled off; gloves were dropped, and fists were thrown. Bill still on the ice trying to remove himself from the fray but in obvious pain. I pushed the opposing players away to give him room. Order was restored, and we helped Bill to his skates.

He strode gingerly to the bench, where Harry could address his right ankle. Sam handed us tin cups of water while the ref sorted matters out. Boyd jumped over the boards to take Cook's spot.

Boyd, Bun, and I finished the man-advantage without another real threat.

With three minutes left Bill Cook rejoined the action and contributed a good run on Chicago's net, but their goalie Lehman smothered the puck.

Lehman said something impolite to Bill, but it was the swinging of his stick at Bill's right ankle that caught his ire. Bill shoved Lehman backwards into the net.

Referee Laflamme ran Bill up and sent him to the box in a 3-2 game. Maybe not an ideal time for our captain to take an offensive zone penalty but in truth we all would have responded the same.

Babe Dye was one of the best stickmen in the league. He had played several years for the Toronto St. Pats before being sold at the start of the season to Chicago. An option that was equally available to us, but Conn Smythe inexplicably walked away from the opportunity.

Not a big man or overly fast on his skates, his reputation for a quick hard shot was well earned. He was known to send men to the hospital after getting hit by one of his pucks. His shots were so powerful the shaft of his stick would often shatter.

With only two seconds left in the period I cursed Smythe for not signing him when we had the chance.

It wasn't an impressive shot that tied the score, more a garbage goal in front of the net. But Dye tied the game.

Now we were facing our first over-time period of the season. Our home crowd was none too pleased we let a lead slip away with only two seconds left. I'm sure they were expecting to flood out of the Garden and celebrate in the nearby jazz joints.

The bars had a wait because neither team scored in the first ten-minute overtime.

I felt this is where Lester's coaching really shined. Under normal circumstances Lester largely let the first line dictate when they needed a rest. But with Bill's ginger ankle and our top guys being somewhat gassed, Lester was subbing us all in and out during every stoppage.

The Black Hawks were primarily sticking with their top line.

But by rotating Boyd, Thompson, and myself for the Bread line, it was helping us all keep our legs fresh. By contrast, the Hawks were dragging, and the Garden crowd could sense this subtle shift.

Lester sent the second line out to start the next extra over-time period. The Hawks came at us hard, but I anticipated Irvin's next pass. I sprung forward and intercepted the pass at our blue line. Go, go, go!

Racing up ice as a unit the lefty shooting Thompson slide up my left side, and the right-handed Boyd came up opposite. Entering the offensive zone and quickly approaching their defense I passed to Boyd on my right. Boyd was seeing it all happening in front of him. The position of the goalie, where the defensemen were, where Thompson was going to be and my hard pass which found his blade. The puck barely touched his stick before Boyd quickly redirected the puck across ice to Thompson who was now behind both defensemen.

Paul scored the game winner 33 seconds into the period.

Now we could all hit the hidden saloons and celebrate.

Chapter Fifteen

December 4 – 12, 1926

Our next road game against the Detroit Cougars did not in fact take place in Detroit. The financial investors of Detroit were granted an expansion team provided the proposed Olympia Stadium was completed in time. It wasn't.

But the syndicate also invested heavily in purchasing Lester Patrick's old team the Victoria Cougars from the Western Canada Hockey League. The Cougars had won the Stanley Cup the previous season, so the National Hockey League made an exception.

Since Olympia Stadium wasn't finished, their home games were being played in the cold, large barn-like Border Cities Arena just over the Detroit River in Windsor, Ontario.

Once again, Laflamme was the referee, who we kept busy with rough play and hard checks all night. The game was a defensive masterpiece by both teams.

Few players could manufacture scoring opportunities like the Cougars' Russell Oatman and Hobie Kitchen. But tonight, Ching and Taffy were their equal and shut them down. Chabot was every bit as solid as their netminder Hap Holmes.

At 12:30 in period two, the only goal of the game was scored. A quick one-two from Clem Laughlin to Johnny Sheppard. It was just a pretty play.

Both teams played with unrelenting intensity, but Bun, Frank and Bill couldn't find the net. There was no doubt in anyone's mind that our Captain was playing hurt. His ankle still sprained from the previous game.

Our record was now 4-2.

Next were back-to-back games against the Boston Bruins. The first in Boston, the other at our home.

While on the train, perhaps an hour from Boston, Lester called us together for a team meeting in the washroom of our Pullman. It was the only car that could ensure privacy from other passengers, some of whom would no doubt be supporters of our opponents. As the car rattled and rocked Lester gave an honest assessment of our previous game.

"We played strong, with grit, but we were just a step slow. We need more production from our first line. 'Bill, how's the ankle, are you sure you don't need a night off?'"

"I'm good Coach," was our Captain's confident reply. "Harry will tape me up."

It would take more than a bum ankle to get Bill Cook out of the lineup. Besides, after six rough games we all had bumps and bruises. Heck, Ching seemed to have perpetual stitches or a bandage somewhere different on his head with nearly every game.

"Mr. Winkler, you're in our net tonight" Lester added.

There was a knock on the locked door. A passenger needed to use the toilet.

"Just a minute" Lester boomed.

Lester continued. "The Bruins have a rookie defenseman we need to watch for. I've been hearing stuff about him. His nickname is the 'Edmonton Express' and he's prone to violence and drawing blood. He'll be wearing number 2. Last name is Shore."

Another louder knock. We ignored it.

The name Shore sounded familiar to me.

"One last thing. The fans in Boston are…shall we say colorfully engaged and free with their salty dialog. If you allow it, the atmosphere will be distracting. Let's go get two points" Lester concluded our meeting.

There was a line of unruly male passengers impatiently waiting to enter the washroom as we filed out. No one said a word as our hockey team emerged.

As Lester forewarned, 10,000 fans greeted us in unique Boston style, with a shower of profanity and creative language. Located in the South End, the Boston Arena has been home to the Bruins for two years already.

From the opening puck drop we endeavored to show their fans what real speed looked like. Bill and Frank exploded on the first series into their territory and with some quick passes had a quality shot on net that was stopped by their goalie Charles Stewart.

Shortly after, Bill was called for the first penalty of the game, slashing, but we played a tight game of keep-away and stifled Boston's first advantage. The Bruins didn't even get a shot on Winkler before Bill was back on the ice.

Now it was Bunny's turn to find peaceful solitude and reflection in the penalty box after getting called for roughing. He inadvertently caused blood to run freely and unnaturally from Harry "Pee Wee" Oliver's nose.

Lester sent in our second line to kill the penalty.

Frustrated with their first failed attempt, and probably angered by the blood stain on the ice, the Bruins attacked with vigor. Winkler stood firm. Shoulders, sticks and elbows were allowed to find unprotected spots in our armor.

The fans were loving every uncalled slash to the back of our legs and stick butt to our ribs.

Ching recovered a loose puck and sent it up along the boards to me. I could sense a Bruin's defenseman racing towards me. Just as the puck reached my blade I was hit with the force of train. Hammered into the boards, face pushed into the chicken wire, I tried to jump back into the play. The Bruin's player was all over me. I struggled with him for the puck and to gasp for air when his stick come across my face. Hard and with intent.

I felt my lower lip open and tasted the blood instantly.

Now he crosschecked me again, and not the professional love-tap to let an opposing player know you're there and mean business. I mean the kind that tries to break bones and end careers.

I fell to the ice hard, and the player purposefully kicked at my leg with his skate blade. But for my shin guard, the blade would have sliced my leg open. Still, I felt the blow intensely and feared he was close to breaking the bone.

I saw number 2 skate away with the puck towards the net. "What the hell!" I muttered. This was the guy Lester warned us about. Shore.

I waited a heartbeat for the ref to call a penalty. Nothing.

"Welcome to Boston ya dumb fuck" I heard one fan yell. My mangled mouth smiled. Blood pooled on the ice as I rolled onto my hands and knees.

There was now a scrum in front of the net. Total chaos. Ching and Taffy were in full battle mode, trying to protect our goalie.

I jumped up and pushed off towards the action.

In front of the net, I could see bodies in both jerseys were falling and crawling over one another to stand back up. Sticks we're poking for the loose puck. I could see Shore was throwing his body and hacking at my guys with no restraint. He wasn't just slashing; he was chopping at them like his stick was an axe! Where the heck was the ref? I raced toward the action.

Shore looked so familiar. I picked up speed. They need me!

Winkler dropped on the puck to cover it up, but Shore was continuing to whack away with his stick. He was cropping at Hal. Literally chopping. He had no regard. The ref finally rang his bell, but Shore didn't stop. I had never seen the like. Hal was curled up to protect himself and keep the puck covered. Ching and Taffy were both tied up and couldn't come to his rescue in time. I was the only one close enough.

Faster, faster. Get there!

I threw myself as hard as I could into Shore's back just before he took another hack.

I couldn't see what part of his body smashed into the metal crossbar of the net, but I hoped it was his ugly mug.

I landed with all my weight onto his body with every intent to put him through the sheet of ice. The net was now off its mooring and slid back against the boards. No one stopped. Squirming, swearing, wrestling, punching. Fists trying to find their target. Eventually, I was pulled off.

It was Ching. He had a look on his face; equal parts surprised delight, pride and shock.

Harry and I went into the locker room so he could stitch me up. Blood covered the front of my sweater. He handed me a tin of water and I rinsed my mouth. I spit the red water into a pail a few times. Harry felt around my mouth with his raw finger to test the integrity of my teeth and jaw. We were both amazed they seemed intact. I jumped up on the trainer's table and settled back. There was a lightbulb hanging from a cord above. Harry had me hold it at just the right angle so he had some decent light to work with. I felt him manipulating my lip and placing it generally back into position. My throbbing lip felt twice it's normal size.

He stepped away and grabbed his kit. I watched him carefully tread a fish-hooked needle. I was feeling surprisingly relaxed and marveled that this bruiser of a guy, who was so clumsy on the ice, could thread a needle on the first try.

With the needle in his right hand, he held the separated sections of my lips together with the fingers of his left, trying his best to get them aligned.

Suddenly the guys were streaming into the room.

The first period ended.

Bill walked over, limping, stole a glance, and patted my shoulder just as Harry was pressing the needle to my lip, "good job kid". Harry cursed.

Harry pressed the point through the front and back of the skin to make the first stitch. He pulled tautly.

Frankie and Bunny leaned over me to get a close look at the action. "Get out of my light" growled Harry. Both moved their heads even closer. Sam approached, surveyed the situation, and took the light from me. He adjusted it to help Harry.

Another stitch.

Ching and Taffy entered my vision. Now Harry, Sam, Frankie, Bun and our two defensemen were all staring down at my repair job. Six heads, not two feet from my face.

Ching leaned in closer and pointed "Harry, pull that together tighter there. No, there. Yes, better. We don't want his wife upset with you Harry."

"I'm trying but my fingers are slipping on the blood." Harry paused and told me to rinse and spit again while he poured water over his hands and dried them in a nearby towel.

He was back to it now, the bleeding reduced, poke in, poke out, pull taut. He kept repeating this action as his five assistants supervised his work with general approval. Poke, poke, pull taut. "Just about done Murray."

"How's my iron-man Harry? I heard Lester's voice approaching. Bunny and Taffy backed away and now Lester was getting a good look.

"He's ready to go back in Lester" Harry said with confidence as his scissors cut the thread.

I felt Lester's hand on my throbbing chin, turning my face side to side to inspect Harry's work. "Damn if he's not ever better looking."

Halfway through the second, it was Taffy who gathered the puck after a failed Bruin's campaign. Gathering steam up ice, Taffy moved fluidly, keeping the puck away from their defensive skaters, Sprague Cleghorn and Lionel Hitchman. He penetrated their zone and shot from the right side, beating Stewart from far range to score.

Goal!

In a tight 1-0 game, the play got even more physical as it got later in the third period. Shore, who's face looked like he just gone eight rounds with Dempsey, was even more agitating or dangerous. Getting a better look at him I recalled he and I briefly skated against each other when I was in Manitoba. I think he was kicked off a team for being too vicious.

With four minutes left in the game, Boston sent all five of their skaters to crash the net. Desperate, violent play ensured, but no goals. Hal held strong. We won.

We were now 5-2 on the season and looking forward to a rematch against Boston on our home ice on Sunday.

The Sunday Times gave hockey encouraging real estate. Nearly a whole page, devoted to the sport, including photos of players on visiting Boston and Ottawa teams. The standings showed us with ten points and atop the American Group. But Ottawa, who we had not yet faced were the only undefeated team and stood atop the International Group with seventeen points.

The article read, "In the pro ranks there will be a game at Madison Square Garden tonight between the New York Rangers and the strong Boston sextet, and another on Tuesday night between the New York Americans and Ottawa, a great team that has made hockey history for several seasons."

"A big crowd is expected to see tonight's program…led by the redoubtable Sprague Cleghorn. The Rangers, one of the three new teams to join the National Hockey League this year, got away to a flying start, and by very clean-cut play have jumped into the lead in the American division of the league. Tonight's game should bristle with action. The Bruins were beaten, 1-0, by the Rangers in Boston on Tuesday night and will be out for revenge".

I was interested in the assessment of the Senators a couple paragraphs further down.

"The Senators are undoubtedly a wonderful hockey combination, probably the most consistent winners that ever skated out on the ice. They have been to every Stanley Cup play-off since 1918 and have won the world's trophy three times. In winning form they are an extremely hard combination for any team to beat…."

"Damn" I snapped. My lace broke. "Hey Sam, can you toss me a new lace?" We were tightly packed into our warm locker room.

"Eight eyelets or ten?" he asked.

"Twelve" I replied.

"hmmm" he replied and vanished into the storage room.

"You're going to want a pair of new skates one of these days Murray" Paul Thompson suggested.

"Someday Paul, but not today." I answered as I removed the old lace from my skate.

"Your lip looks like it's healing well."

"Yeah, it's been five days. Harry said he wants to wait a few more days before taking the stitches out." I shared.

"Murray, these are the longest we've got. Sorry." Sam explained. He tossed them across the room.

I pulled one of the waxed white laces out of the wrapper and held it up. It looked a little short. I laced them up and realized I would have to skip the top two eyelets if I was going to have any chance of tying them reliably.

With both skates now on, I stood up and realized it felt odd having them tied up at different heights. So, I took the lace out of the top two eyelets on the other skate and wrapped the extra length once around my ankle. Both skates were the same now. I stood again and flexed my knees forward. Manageable.

A large, well-dressed crowd was filing into the Garden as we took our warmups on one end of the ice. The Bruins on the other. Pee Wee Oliver's nose was still noticeably bruised. Eddie Shore still looked ugly. Stewart was in net again and tonight was Lorne's turn. I saw Lester and Boston's manager, Art Ross talking with folded arms like old friends.

Just like the previous game, we had a quick rush to get the festivities started. Bun skated with the puck up the boards and almost got as far as the net before being forced to shoot. Stewart made a good stop on a hard shot.

Moments later Bill and Frankie reentered the zone and put on a passing clinic for all in attendance. But this time it was the strong defensive positioning by Cleghorn and Hitchman that stopped the attack.

Gravity was tipping the ice in our favor as we kept the puck in enemy territory and pressed the assault. Again, Bill found Frank on a beautiful pass and a quality shot was turned away. The home crowd was letting the Bruins know this was our house.

Harry Oliver skated the puck out of their zone and coughed it up at center ice. Ching stepped up and attacked with a crazed grin. But again, Stewart made the save.

Like the previous game, it grew more rugged with each passing minute.

Boston's Cleghorn and our Billy Boyd got tangled up as competitors do and both were sent to the box for two minutes. Roughing was the call.

Oliver, Jimmy Herbert and Percy Galbraith staged a coordinated fierce attack. Ching and Taffy were well positioned but the Bruins were capable of some impressive passing of their own.

With crisp passing an offensive squad can slowly wear down a defense and eventually draw someone out of position. Taffy thought he could intercept a pass, he didn't, and that slight misstep allowed Herbert to blast the puck at Chabot unimpeded.

But Lorne blocked the shot, and everyone joined in the fight for the loose puck. A wild melee took shape, and no one seemed to know quite where the puck was. Boston was screaming it went into the net, but the ref signaled no goal.

Jimmy Herbert lost his temper and used some salty language, as people from Boston are wanting to do, and he was fined ten dollars by the ref right on the spot.

The first period would see no scoring and we withdrew to our locker room to regroup. No one had to say anything, but it was now our third game without any scoring from our first line. Bun and Frankie were pressing, trying to overcompensate for Bill's still tender ankle, which just slowed him a step. Bill calmly reassured his linemates the goals would come with time.

We had just too much talent for us to panic. Chabot was playing brilliantly in net. Ching and Taffy were the best defensive pairing that I had seen in the early season thus far. And our checking line and subs were all pulling our weight and contributing where we could. Bill was right, the goals would come.

The second period started with another passing clinic by the Bread line. But several attacks produced no goals.

Johnson was called for another roughing penalty and moments latter Herbert also went to the box. The crowd was deeply worried when Shore and Oliver combined on penetrating attacks of their own.

Just as Johnson came out of the box a scrum was developing in front of our net. Ching immediately joined the fray, and although his efforts may have prevented a goal, he took another penalty and found himself in the doghouse for the third time. He had only been on the ice for a few seconds before getting into trouble, again. I watched him growing increasingly friendly with the now familiar fans behind the penalty box.

I knew two truths about Ching Johnson. When he was on the ice, everyone knew it. And whether on the ice, the box, the locker-room, on a train or in a bar, he was enjoying life.

Cleghorn, never seemed to tire, now attacked, and took a foolish offensive zone penalty. Just as Johnson's penalty was expiring yet another melee was taking form in front of our net. Once again, Johnson skated right into the donnybrook, only this time he emerged with the puck on the end of his stick and skated north. Although a few players were still piled in front of our net behind the play, Ching still had to get through Shore and Hitchman.

He was like a bull and charged. Instead of taking them wide he decided to go right down their gullet. As they moved to pincer him in the middle of the ice, he tossed the puck just past them both. Without breaking stride, he put his shoulders down and caught them both just at that moment when they were each deciding whether to chase after the puck.

He was through, off-balance, but through. He caught up to the puck and in one motion fired right into the net. The shot beat Stewart and Ching fell forward onto his stomach and slid, just missing the net, and crashed hard into the boards behind.

The goal light flashed.

I held my breath, unnecessarily. Ching leaped up and started celebrating. I probably should have been more worried about the boards.

Not to be outdone, Shore and Herbert combined on some impressive passing and Shore found an opening on the left side of the net. The period would end in a tie. Shore clearly had skills and wasn't just an animal.

The crowd loved the end-to-end action. The tension only continued to build through a scoreless third period.

Johnson and the Cook boys combined in a thrilling attack, but Stewart stood his ground and turned every shot away. Cleghorn and Johnson got tied up together in a dance and both were again sent to box. It was Cleghorn's third and Johnson's fourth of the game.

Time expired on the third period, and for the second home game in a row our fans were treated to bonus over-time hockey.

To start the overtime frame, Boston's rookie defenseman Eddie Shore once again gave the Garden a scare. He jumped on the attack as his team was crossing the blueline. He found the puck on his blade, and he put a powerful quick shot on Chabot. The shot was blocked but Shore got to his own rebound and came around the back of the net. Hugging the net tightly, as he emerged from behind it, he backhanded another shot.

He whacked at a third attempt.

But again, Chabot made the stop. So Shore took a whack at our goalie instead. Ching took great exception. They gave each other a few shoves and within seconds were dropping their gloves to the delight of the Garden. The two wrestled each other into the boards, taking shots where they could. Shore would not back down despite Ching's size advantage. Ching plays a hard, intimidating violent game but he's not intentionally trying to cripple. The same could not be said for our experience with Shore. Ching had enough and decided to end it. With a firm grip on Shore's sweater, Ching landed an uppercut and another quick jab and followed Shore to the ice.

The ref was pulling Ching off when I heard one of our spectators in the front row scream through the chicken wire fencing at Shore.

"This is New York you cocksucker!" To which his wife or girlfriend slapped him on the shoulder. I smiled.

Boston had nothing on us.

Both Shore and Ching were escorted to the penalty box. I wondered if Ching fancied one of the well-dressed ladies just behind the box because this was now his fifth banishment of the game. Along with his earlier goal, he was giving the fans their money's worth. He had indeed quickly become the fan favorite here at the Garden.

Seven minutes into the period, our checking line was sent back onto the ice. Boston won the ensuing face-off and pressed their attack. I sensed that Galbraith was about to pass, and I reacted instinctively.

Just as he released the puck, I sprung forward.

My intent was only to break up the play and get it out of our zone. But I had anticipated perfectly and suddenly found the puck moving in my favor with open ice.

A lot of open ice.

I turned on the speed and practically tripped I was so excited. I put my head down and just pushed off each skate as fast as I could muster without losing control of the puck or falling flat on my face. I knew that my teammates were all behind me and there was no one to pass to. I had a true breakaway.

I felt the Bruins right on my heels, their sticks about to hack at the back of my legs or hook my skates out from under me.

But that didn't happen, and I was suddenly closing in on Stewart.

I leaned on my left skate and gave Stewart the appearance I was going to shoot forehand, just as Ching had scored earlier. I saw an opening on Stewart's right side. Their goalie bit and shifted to block my anticipated shot.

I pulled hard across to my opposite side, shifted everything to my right skate edge, trusted it, and backhanded the puck just a heartbeat before losing any angle.

Goal!

My god, I just scored the game winning goal!

My guys were hugging me in no time, the crowd was ecstatic. They were cheering my name "Murdoch, Murdoch, Murdoch".

My oh my, I wish Marie were here to witness this moment.

Even for a late Sunday night, we had no trouble celebrating. Church was many hours ago for those who attend, and work was still a few hours ahead. The speakeasies around the Garden and just off Broadway were doing a booming business. The theatre crowd and performers mixed with the hockey fans and players.

Damon Runyon was waiting with a drink for me in hand as I entered to celebrate. Lester and Bill huddled with the beat reporters to make sure they had what they needed. Bill was rarely quoted himself, and often called one of us over to chat with the writers. Everyone was in gay spirits after our great win. Tonight's band was really jumping, and I wished Marie was here to swing. I leaned against the bar rail and found Taffy nursing a beer.

"Great game tonight Taf" and I clicked my glass against his. I could instantly tell he had slipped into his gloomy mood.

"You too Murray, that was a beautiful goal." He offered.

"Hey, is everything ok buddy? You seem a little down. Let's talk."

"I'm good. I'm going to turn in early."

Moments later he finished his beer and quietly slipped out.

The rest of us celebrated into the wee hours.

Thankfully, Lester gave us an off day on Monday. Hungover I forced myself to join Bun for a very late breakfast. I was learning that walking with Fred around the city was an adventure in adorable frustration. The kind of patience I imagined required for raising a rambunctious child.

My hands buried deep in the pockets of my charcoal wool coat and my wide-brimmed fedora blocking the brisk wind, we were discussing the game as we walked down 8th to his favorite corner diner.

"I swear Bun, I thought I was going to fall flat on my face without anyone touching me. I still don't understand…"

A passing couple were staring at me oddly.

"…how I got a pure breakaway. Runyon was buying me drinks all night and…"

Another weird look from a passing gentleman.

I turned to Bunny and stopped.

He was nowhere in sight. I was talking to myself which explained the looks. I wasn't completely surprised; this had happened before. Bunny was easily distracted.

I started retracing my steps, peeking in each store as I went by.

Then I remembered the Sporting Goods store on the previous block. Sure enough, looking in the window I spotted him in the fishing section. He saw me. With a big smile, he held up a tackle box for my approval.

I smiled back and nodded yes. It was just Bunny's way.

"Wait, what? You and Bill are moving to Brooklyn already?"

"Yep. Frank and Ag too." Bun replied as he bit into the pork sausage.

"What?!? Brooklyn? We barely know our way around here. How the heck are you going to live in Brooklyn? Where is Brooklyn?" I was dumbfounded. "And your mom is coming too?" I sipped my black coffee.

"Yep, you know our sisters have been living there together in the Flatbush section. Nurses. Their apartment house has some vacancies and there are other furnished apartments nearby. Bill, Frank, and I have been talking about getting our families down here but the area around the Garden is more for the single life. Our mom is coming down with our wives. Bill and Claire have a two-year-old. Maria and I want to start a family soon." Bun added shyly.

Bun's fork cut into the stack of pancakes dripping with maple syrup.

"And Frank is moving there too?"

"Yep, as is his mom apparently. He and Ag have a newborn you know. He just found a furnished place for $125 a month. The grandmothers will watch the kids. It's perfect."

The Bill, Frank and Bun line was truly unbreakable.

Scooping scrambled eggs into the corner of my buttered toast I wondered, "And how will you get back and forth? Isn't Brooklyn far?"

"Easy subway commute. The A and C lines take us right from Eighth to Brooklyn. Easy. Most of the wives are making the move down after we return from Chicago."

"Yeah, Marie is taking the train from Winnipeg and meeting us in Chicago. She'll ride back with us and stay with me at the Forrest until we're back in Chicago again on January 1st. But I don't think she's ready to stay and live here yet. We want to be together for Christmas. All our games are local except for one game in Ottawa on the 23rd so we'll have some time together. I just figured we'd all be staying at the Forrest a while longer."

I was feeling embarrassed. Besides our team trip to Yankee Stadium, and leaving Manhattan to play in other cities, I'd barely been on the subway more than a few blocks from the Garden. The older guys were thinking long game.

"You need to come out to Brooklyn with us Murray. Let's keep the team as tight as possible."

"Hey bun, is everything ok with Taffy?"

"I think so, he seems to have brief funks. Most of the time he's so easy-go-lucky."

"Yeah, most of the time." I replied.

Chapter Sixteen

December 14 – 17, 1926

I arrived at Penn Station for our overnight to Chicago. A few of the guys were already waiting and killing time. Paul and Frank were reading the paper. Bunny was getting a coffee. Bill was getting a shoeshine.

I looked at my own worn shoes and concluded they desperately needed a dime shine.

I've always polished them myself, but I never thought to bring a brush, can of polish and a buffing cloth with me to New York. The neglect was apparent.

Shoeshines were common at the train stations, and on countless corners around the city. On the street you could find poor kids with a self-made wooden box, angled to comfortably rest the patron's foot. The customer might sit on a bench or just stand. The shiner would kneel right on the sidewalk.

In the station, it was a more professional operation. A mahogany platform was constructed. Bill was sitting in one of five comfortable leather chairs secured to the top of two big steps up. Metal footrests were bolted into the bottom step. This allowed the shiner, still typically a poor kid, to at least stand up while working.

I climbed up and sat next to Bill who appeared very relaxed.

"First shine Murray?"

"Yeah, my puppies need it." I replied as I was happy to wait my turn.

"It's a bit of an indulgence, but you'll be grateful. You'll see." Bill explained.

A black boy, perhaps thirteen, had just finished polishing and was now buffing Bill's boots.

We talked about Bill's farm in Saskatchewan. Following the War, he was given a land grant in Lac Vert, which he shared with his brother Bunny.

"What do you grow?" I asked.

"We don't, we're ranchers. Cattle. I got some local hands running the place. I go there to get away. Also, some good fishing up there."

"I'll bet, Bun told me you were both raised in Kingston, Ontario. That's a long way from Saskatchewan but I suppose the Canadian Government doesn't give away prime real-estate."

"Yeah, that's true. We learned to skate right on the Rideau Canal in Kingston. Did you know we have another still younger brother nicknamed Bud?"

"Your family has three son's named Bill, Bun and Bud?" I teased.

"Well, technically our parents named us William, Frederick, and Alexander but yeah. And we all play hockey." He chuckled.

Bunny had shared in confidence that Bill enlisted with the Canadian Expeditionary Force in 1915 and served two years in France where he took part in the Somme offensive and the brutal battles for both Vimy Ridge and Hill 70. There was another year on the Belgian front where he saw action at the second battle of Ypers. After the war end, instead of being sent home, he was sent to Russia for eight months to secure munitions as part of the allied intervention in their civil war. He finally came home in 1919.

Ranching, hockey and raising a family were his occupations now.

Bunny, eight years younger avoided all this carnage and followed his older brother from team to team, to the ranch, and right to the Rangers.

Bill handed the young man ten cents for the shine and another ten for a tip. Bill whispered to me as he got up, "his only income is on the tip. The owner of the shine station pockets the rest."

The young man's livelihood depended solely on gratuities.

The shiner started by positioning my feet on the footrests and untying my laces. He pulled my pant legs up and carefully tucked them into my socks.

I found his methodical process instantly absorbing. The kid's trade was well practiced and precise.

He pulled open a hidden draw filled with all his tools and polish. He used a well-worn brush, and I was surprised at how much of his strokes I could feel through the leather of my shoes. Skating daily, my feet are in a natural state of soreness such that I don't even notice. But his brush strokes felt lovely, and I understood why Bill was so relaxed when I sat next to him. Minutes later, during the polishing stage, it felt even better. Bill was right, this was an indulgence I was going to repeat.

After paying my tab and leaving a generous tip, I strolled over and sat next to Taffy.

"You really gotta treat yourself. Forget about your shoes, your feet will love you for it." I suggested.

He glanced up from his paper, looked over at the young man and said "No, that's not for me." For such an easy-going chap his face was way too serious.

There was something about the way he said it that reminded me of the time he refused help from the busboys when we first arrived in Manhattan.

Maybe it's the money? I wondered.

"Let me treat you. It's my gift." I insisted.

"No thank you."

"Taffy, please tell me it's not because the kid is black, is it?" I was hoping this wasn't Taffy's reasoning.

He flashed me a glance that beheld anger but just as quickly returned to his paper.

"No, yes, but not in the way you think. I'm just not comfortable with it, ok? I have no problem with the color of his skin. Let's just drop it. It's none of your business." He snarled.

After waking the next morning, I entered the wash car to relieve myself and get cleaned up. We would be arriving in Chicago in three hours. Ching had just finished shaving and I waited as he wiped down the sink.

We chatted and agreed to meet in the food car. He kindly left me a folded towel on the edge of the counter. Bill and Frank entered and waited their turn behind me. Ching hung around as we all talked, and I lathered my face and shaved. I rinsed off, grabbed the towel, and dried my face.

"What the hell," I muttered. I looked in the mirror. My face was covered with white foam. The towel was filled with shaving cream. I spun and Ching was bent over laughing at his prank.

Entering the food car, I was greeted by the bright sun outside the eastern facing windows. The light reflecting off the snow along our route was nearly blinding.

I was starving.

Harry, Sam, and Lester were sitting together. Harry had just been served his usual eggs and ham. It was an appetizing plate until he suddenly started drowning the eggs in ketchup. It was a lot of ketchup. Sam, Lester, and I exchanged a quick amused glance.

Lester coughed and wryly commented "My, Harry, your eggs do look…lovely."

Harry, never sure how to speak with his boss, blurted out "your eggs look lovely too, Lester." Again, the three of us shared an amused glance. Lester had ordered two hard boiled eggs. They were sitting in front of him in their unbroken shells.

We never tired of Harry.

Our trainer had all the hallmarks of a man who spent too many years in the boxing ring. Short, square of stature, a mangled nose, prominent cauliflower ears and not much brain matter between them. Words were a daily struggle for Harry. Simple conversations could go sideways. Once in our Toronto training camp, a player who didn't make the team showed Harry a small blister that had burst on his foot.

"Say, Harry, for something so trivial this really hurts. Can you help me wrap it?" the player asked.

Immediately grabbing his medical bag, probably the same one he only recently used with me, a very serious Harry snapped back, "of course it's trivial. It's bleedin' ain't it?" Words were a struggle for Harry but he had a heart of gold.

Harry had one vice. He loved to bet on the horses. One of Sam's many responsibilities was to run back and forth to the Forrest to place Harry's bets and occasionally to collect his winnings. Harry loved it when he won.

That breakfast was just about the only good highlight of our trip to Chicago. Although we did discovered Sam could stitch.

Located between South Madison and Wabash Avenue, and just blocks due west of Soldier Field, the Chicago Colosseum had an impressive castle-like façade which surrounded an enormous multi-use hanger. Chicago was famous for hosting the Republican convention in this building. The Colosseum had a beautiful metal lattice arch structure along the roof line with enormous sky windows that allowed for both fresh air and natural sunlight during our earlier warm up. The thick smokey haze that was so dominate in the Garden was absent here.

It was in this vast structure that we suffered our first blowout. A rough 6-2 loss to the same Black Hawks team we beat at the Garden in overtime. We were never in this game.

Dick Irvin scored the first goal and beat Winkler less than five minutes into the game. Hay added another score after an even prettier pass from Cully Wilson. Cully had skated the full length of the ice before making that pass against my checking line. Our line isn't expected to score, but we are expected to prevent the other team from scoring. I think this was the first goal a pure line of Thompson, Boyd and Murray had given up all season. It was just sloppiness on our part.

Lester yanked us off the ice and Bill Cook responded. We had some action going in front of their net and just as a pile up was starting to develop Bill emerged with the puck. He skated backwards a few feet, spun and just let one fly past Lehman. It was Bill's first goal in a while. Although we were now only down by one goal, the Black Hawks wasted no time.

Merely a minute later, similar frantic action was taking place in front of our net. Winkler poked the puck away but sent it right to Irvin who shuffled it to Mickey Mackay who added the third goal of the period.

I've never seen Lester so angry. He wasn't swearing or yelling but I could feel the anger just emanating from him. None of us wanted to let the old silver fox down.

But let him down we did.

To the delight of the fans, the second period saw an early massive brawl in front of our net. When the fire finally died out two of our players needed medical attention. The combat began when Hal took a stick to his face. His lip below his nose had split open. It needed stitches. Ching also took a blow coming to his goalie's defense and his eyebrow needed to be sutured too.

The game was briefly paused while Harry, Hal and Ching retreated into the locker room. Harry just started to work on Ching, but the ref came into the locker room and insisted Hal had to be worked on first.

Lester and Harry were both furious.

"Mr. Patrick, you know every trick and I can only hold up the game for your goalie. The Black Hawks insisted I come in here and sure enough your trainer is working on Ching. Once your goalie is repaired, I must restart the clock" explained the ref. "you'll have to be without your defenseman while your trainer stitches Ching up after."

To which Ching replied, "It's ok Lester, let the kid stitch me up. He's been watching Harry."

It turns out that Sam's stitches were better than Harry's.

We quickly gave up a Baby Dye rifle shot from about thirty feet and Irving then scored their fifth goal from directly in front of the net on a pass from Rabbit McVeigh.

Mickey Mackay registered Chicago's sixth goal in the third. We were all furious and disappointed with our play. But we didn't quit. We just went to work and kept putting shots on net.

We used a four-man attack, leaving poor Taffy to defend alone. Ching was able get a pass to Bill who drew Hugh Lehman out of position and notched his second of the game. But there was nothing to be proud of in our shellacking.

I imagine the team had a long-subdued train ride back to Manhattan. But Lester gave me special permission to take a later train.

The Great Western arrived in Chicago's Grand Central on the morning of the 16th and Marie stepped out of the car. A conductor helped her down the steps onto the platform. I ran the length of three cars, weaving between disembarking passengers, and wrapped my arms around her. Her excitement was palpable. This was the furthest she's traveled and her first time away from Canadian soil. We kissed and held each other for several minutes as passengers walked around us.

"Murray, what the devil happened to your lip?!?"

"Oh, it's better now, the stitches came out a few days ago. We can kiss, but please be gentle" I said with a smile. Marie gave me a wry look, trying to decide if she was ok with the new feature on my face. Her kiss was anything but gentle.

We gathered her trunk, and I tipped a porter to see that it was put on the afternoon train to New York, the Shenandoah. The guys had left earlier this morning on the Columbian.

Marie and I would arrive back in New York early Friday morning. Along the overnight route, we enjoyed an elegant dinner in the food car; salmon for Marie and a T-bone for me, with several martinis and shared cigarettes. As the sun set, and this time of year it sets early, we retired to our private sleeper berth.

It was a joy to see the city through Marie's fresh eyes. Even after a short six weeks I had started taking Manhattan for granted and suddenly it was new again. Marie noticed and commented on seemingly every sight, smell, and sound and we were only just out of Penn Station's great hall.

Sam had been kind enough to meet us at the terminal and arrange to get her trunk back to the Forrest. Sam's charm and disarming nature made Marie feel instantly welcome. Sam happily explained that the Cook families arrived from Toronto only two hours earlier.

"Mr. Rickard wanted to let you both know he has a special seating section set aside for the ladies for every game moving forward. Mrs. Murdoch, your name is on a list at a special entrance, and you never need to show a ticket. You are welcome at every game." Sam explained.

Sam and I loaded the luggage into a carriage, and thanking him, explained "It's a nice day. Marie and I are going to walk back to the hotel. We'll catch you later."

"Oh Murray, Sam is adorable. If he doesn't have a girlfriend, I need to fix him up!"

I took Marie to Herald Square and her eyes lit up at the sight of Macy's. She insisted on at least poking her head inside. Certain that I would lose her for the day I reassured her that we would return soon. But she insisted.

Ninety minutes later, carrying two Macy's bags we linked arms and strolled up 6th Ave. We walked through Bryant Park and turned up 5th.

She wanted to stop in every store. The Christmas decorations and displays captivated and amused her. While New York in mid-December is a bitterly cold and windy city by most American standards, for a young woman right off the train from Winnipeg it was a most pleasant and warm welcome. Her eyes went wide at the sight of the towering cathedral.

"Is that St. Patrick's? I've never seen the like…" she said in awe.

We stepped inside the massive wood doors and tried to absorb the scale. Somehow it was even grander than Grand Central. The incense was powerful and even on a Friday, barely noon, there was music that lifted the soul.

"Murray, they could fit twenty of the Saint Boniface in here, maybe more."

As we emerged back onto Fifth it had started to snow. Big, fluffy flakes.

"I want to see more." Marie proclaimed. She turned to me with a smile that had just witnessed a new, previously only imagined world. I held her hand. She had never looked more beautiful.

"Let's get lost" I offered, smiling.

Chapter Seventeen

December 19, 1926

My ears were undeniably more sensitive to the sounds within the Garden now that several of our wives are in attendance. There was always some guy up in the rafters with a bullhorn yelling at us to "shoot the puck" which I thought was amusing. Now, every time I heard something inappropriate, I looked up at Marie and the other ladies for a reaction. But they were talking amongst themselves and were barely paying attention to the action on the ice, or the vulgarity.

I couldn't blame them. The first period of the game was uneventful.

Four minutes into the second period I was on the ice with Frank and Bill; giving Bun a breather. Frankie controlled the puck and skated north, weaving, and avoiding Detroit's players. I followed him close behind.

The crowd sensed a play developing as we penetrated their defense. Suddenly Frank let fly a hard wrist shot. Holmes blocked it, but the rebound came out further than he wanted.

I only needed a slight adjustment, and it was my turn to rip a hard shot as soon as the puck found my stick. This time, Holmes couldn't stop it. Goal!

Celebrating with my mates I stole a quick glace and found Marie, Ag, Claire and the other wives cheering wildly. I chuckled, wondering if Marie saw me score.

As we approached the final two minutes in the third period, the crowd of well-dressed New Yorkers were tasting victory and yelling "Let's

Go Rangers" in harmony. But Hobie Kitchen came in hard and got behind Taffy. Ching denied him a path to the front of the net, so he chose to circle behind it. Hugging it tightly, Winkler had to drop to prevent his coming around and finding an easy wraparound opportunity. But instead, Kitchen looked up and found Jack Shepard barreling toward the net. Hobie put the pass right on Shepard's blade and with one minute and twenty-nine seconds from victory, tied the score.

We headed into our third consecutive over-time game at the Garden, but unlike the previous two victories this game ended tied 1-1 after an additional twenty minutes.

Marie and the other gals were completely amused as we approached our destination. The store front was a nondescript haberdashery, obviously closed on a late Sunday night. But just to the side of the hat shop's large windows was an equally nondescript, battered steel door that pedestrians walked past unnoticed every day.

This door was a gateway to Casablanca.

It only required a secret phrase to enter. To no one's surprise, Ching was the only one of us who had access to the daily changing code. Having scored the only goal tonight he bestowed the honor to me. He whispered it into my ear.

I knocked. Moments passed and the ladies started getting nervous, worried a passing police officer would get suspicious. But the guys knew the routine. Finally, the door cracked open, revealing only darkness and a voice. "What?"

Now I shined for the second time this evening.

"The baker has no friends but the fat man" I said, smiling back at our pack and I noticed Ching chuckling to himself.

The door opened just wide enough for us to squeeze through one at a time. We entered a long, weaving, barely lit hall. We went down steps into the basement and could hear music and laughter. A curtain parted. Light and smoke enveloped us. The party had already started. We would catch up.

The speakeasy was filled with the usual cast of characters consisting of actors, actresses, directors, playwriters, reporters, writers and now hockey players. Runyon raised a glass to us as we entered. Mikey was behind the bar and rang the bell at our arrival. Although we only tied the game, the patrons raised their glasses and cheered us.

There were rotating customers, the audience members of both stage and game, different every day. But some were regulars, their faces becoming more familiar. Everyone was drinking, smoking, talking, or dancing to the jazz band in the corner. The unmarried Rangers mingled with their fans and the drinks flowed.

Returning from the bar with whiskies, I found Marie leaning against the wall and chatting it up with Ching. She took a drag on her cigarette, leaned into Ching's ear, and whispered something I couldn't make out. He smiled at her comment, and then looked at me and his smiled broadened even wider. As he drifted away, he shared "she's a smart one, smarter than you Mr. Murdoch. And a hell of a lot prettier."

"What was that?" I asked with amused curiosity.

"Oh nothing, I was just informing Mr. Johnson that while I was born on a farm I wasn't born yesterday".

"And I was?"

"Oh Murray, I love your innocence. You're an easy mark my love. It's no wonder you're the brunt of so many practical jokes."

"I'm savvy enough". I protested.

"You are? Hmm. Murray, you come to this speakeasy regularly, right?" she asked.

"Often, yeah. Very often. So?"

"And you said Ching is the only one who has the super top-secret passwords to enter whenever you do pop in?"

"Yeah, I have no idea how he knows them, but he gets us in every time."

"So, you think that this joice joint is going to deny professional hockey players, who play in an arena just yards away, from becoming regulars because they don't know a password? You don't think by now that the fella at the door doesn't recognize you all?"

"I just know that we need a password and Ching has the inside connection."

"Ching Johnson, the same prankster you've been writing to me about for weeks?"

"Yeah, I don't…oh…oh gosh," laughing,

"Ching just makes it up?" I asked.

She tilted her head and gave me a knowing smirk.

I spun around and found Ching on the other side of the bar with a few reporters including Seabury Lawrence of the Times. We made eye contact and he put his finger to his smiling lips, signaling me to keep the secret.

I smiled back and tipped my drink to him. Prankster indeed. I sheepishly turned back to Marie, "you're right, I'm an easy mark."

She leaned up and kissed my cheek. “I love you just the same. But for the record, I figured that out on my first visit here, you dimwit.”

Chapter Eighteen

February 1994

"My great-aunt Marie was a firecracker." Mark acknowledged with pride.

"More than you can imagine, Mark. She was the greatest love of my life. Her first visit to New York changed everything. It opened her world, our world, and it wasn't long before she wasn't content with only Manhattan. She quickly grew to love traveling and exploring." I explained.

"I remember growing up hearing about your adventures to Europe, Latin America and Africa." Mark said as he pushed off onto the ice.

He took a few gentle strides. Pond ice is dramatically different than cut ice on a pro-rink. But we both grew up on ponds and backyard rinks. This was not a difficult adjustment.

"She had a natural aptitude for language, did you know that about her? Music too. But when we traveled, she would put great effort into communicating in the native tongue. For me, that was a struggle. I was much better with numbers. But she loved to learn the language of whatever country we were in. I gravitated towards photography and documenting our trips."

I took a puck out of my pocket and tossed it on the ice. My stick blade corralled it, and I took several strides. My movements were not quick, but I felt a grace that belied my age.

"You're still amazingly spry, Murray. Please, for the love of God don't fall and break your hip. Joan will fly up here and beat me senseless." Mark pleaded, knowing my daughter, now in her late sixties, would do just that.

I took a gentle turn using crossovers, lifting one skate and placing over the other and pushing off using the inside edge of the blade. The puck stayed right where it belonged, on the end of my stick. As I made the full circle I passed the puck sharply to Mark, who received it without looking.

We ventured into the center of the pond and the surrounding activity.

I was not at all surprised that several people on the ice, adults and children stopped skating and were watching the two of us gliding across the surface as gracefully as the hawk was soaring on the airstream above us.

Seeing an old man skating was unusual enough. That I still had skills and could move the puck might have caused a few to pause and stare for a moment or two. But Mark; that was different. In the three years since coming to the Rangers, he had become a celebrity, and his social activities around the city were nearly as well documented by the papers as his game-winning goals.

Although he was wearing a stylish black beanie and sunglasses, he was still recognizable. Two young kids skated our way and fell in with us. Mark passed one of them the puck. She received it and sent it right back to him. He then sent it to the other boy. He fumbled with it slightly but kept control. I tapped my stick on the ice, a universal signal to pass me the puck. I could tell he was hesitant because of my age. I tapped it again, reassuring him. I took the pass and made a tight circle before passing it back to Mark. Our group was growing rapidly as others joined us.

My oh my, what a beautiful day this is. The forked road in my life was taken that day Connie Smythe took that wad of bills out of his pocket and offered me a contract. Marie always knew I never signed the contract for the money. She knew I couldn't give up these moments of magic that have blessed my long life.

Chapter Nineteen

December 20 – 25, 1926

Our bare feet sank into the sand as the cold waves barely reached us. My pants were rolled up to my knees. Marie held her dress and long wool coat up to keep them from getting soaked by the spray.

We had to remove out hats or they would have blown away.

Our hair and scarves blew and whipped wild in the breeze.

The scent of brine and salt were both rancid and smoothing.

The incomprehensibly ferocious waves were our introduction to the earth's true authority.

The sensation of being pulled out was unexpected and unsettling.

But we stood our ground. Holding hands without saying a word.

At the edge of the world.

Trying to absorb…Infinity.

We took the train to Coney Island for 5 cents each. A boardwalk ran parallel to the shoreline, and we saw an advertisement for something called the 'Cyclone' coming in the summer. It was a contraption of some sort called a 'rollercoaster'. Marie used its thrilling promise as an excuse to return. I wondered if we'd still be living in New York in 1927. We split a frankfurter at the only open restaurant called Nathan's. It was so unexpectedly good that we each got our own and experimented with the different condiments.

"I don't know about the Cyclone, but this is a good reason to come back!" I commented as I sipped my root beer.

We came here, at our first opportunity, in the dead of winter, because neither of us had ever seen an ocean.

Now we stood before it, alone on the shoreline but for the seagulls and sandpipers.

Feeling both connected to the universe and utterly insignificant.

We held each other's hand in silence.

We couldn't explain our scoring drought. Bill, Frank, and Bun were dominating on the ice. Fast, crisp passing, receiving, and shooting often. The biscuit just wasn't finding the back of the basket as Lester called it. Yet, Lester's confidence never waned.

Although we had lost to the Pittsburg Pirates 0-2 in our third game of the season, they had struggled mightily since. Now we were facing them on our home ice.

Well into the first period of a scoreless game Lester, the constant strategist, put in our second line. Paul Thompson, never shy about asking for more ice-time, always played with a fire in his belly. I've come to like Paul despite his occasional surliness towards Sam. Usually affable and game for a fun time, he was a talented winger. He hailed from and played in Calgary before coming to the Rangers. On many teams he might indeed be a starter but here he was stuck behind Bill Cook.

Paul never wasted a second of the precious ice time he was granted and that probably contributed to his lack of passing. Once he had the puck on his stick, he wanted to do something with it. This was usually considered selfish play and Paul was developing a bad reputation. Teams were no doubt seeing his default was to carry the puck and played him as such. Lester would often explain to Paul that if he passed more often, he would see better results. He was too predictable and one dimensional. Paul was just talented enough that he could gain the zone, but his shots were not usually threatening. Defenses could cut down his preferred angles without having to worry about his beating them with a dangerous pass. But Paul's predictably was not solely a liability.

It also meant his teammates knew what to expect.

And Billy Boyd was nothing, if not a smart player. He was one of the older guys on our team. A mature, private, no-nonsense guy. He knew how to read a play and position himself accordingly.

Thompson found the puck and started skating north. I was a few steps ahead of him at center ice and was tapping my stick on the ice for him to see that I was open. But he just kept skating with enough skill to get around guys and gain ground, but he was being steered wide towards the boards. He took a shot on net and the Pirates goalie Roy Worters made the save.

But Boyd anticipated all this. As the puck deflected off the goalie's pad Billy was able to bury it before Worters could reposition himself. We scored at 13:36 into the game. Although that would prove to be the deciding goal of the game, we suffered two devastating injuries.

Ollie Reinikka, who even started referring to himself as "Rocco", found himself emerging from a scrum in front of their net with a deep nasty cut just below his left eyebrow. The blood was flowing unabated, and he left a long trail on the ice as he skated to the bench. Harry was already reaching for his medical bag. I heard Ollie curse that a skate blade caught him square in the face.

In the second period, Taffy and Ching were doing their act, shutting down the Pirates line of Hib Milks, Harold Darragh and Ty Arbour. It was a nondescript shift, and none of us really recalled how or when it happened.

Ching rode Arbour into the boards. He also planted a few two-handed checks and the usual bump and grind on guys. But none were Ching's trademark crowd rousing, thundering body blows that shook the Garden's foundation.

As soon as the puck safely cleared the zone, Ching skated right to the bench holding his arm. He motioned for Reg Mackey to jump over the boards and take his spot. The expression on Ching's face was blank. This scared me because even when blood would be streaming down his forehead, he'd be grinning his happy-to-be-here smile. But this expression struck me as Ching trying to hide his pain or fear.

Without saying a word Ching and Harry headed straight back to the locker room.

Between periods they were behind a closed door.

Ching returned to the ice and started the third period but only lasted one shift before pulling himself out.

We now sat atop the American Group in first place with fifteen points. Our next game in two nights would be in Ottawa against the International Group's first place Senators with twenty points.

While crawling into bed I confided to Marie that considering our impressive record I was feeling rather gloomy after this win. Our first line wasn't scoring, and Ollie and Ching were surely going to miss some time.

Marie said I was asleep the moment my head hit the pillow. But I awoke in the morning feeling I had tossed and turned all night.

An hour outside Ottawa, we commandeered the train's washroom car for our team meeting. Lester got right to it.

"I'm sure you're all aware that Mr. Johnson rudely and inconveniently broke his collar bone two nights ago. Damn inconsiderate if you ask me." Lester, shaking his head with that wry smile of his. Ching, standing beside him with his arm in a sling, tried to humorously shrug his shoulders but instantly winced in pain.

"Consequently, he will be helping me on the bench while it heals. Mr. Johnson will not be enjoying a paid vacation. Mr. Reinikka will also need time to recover from being maliciously kicked in the face with a hockey skate. The doctors are concerned the injury may be more serious than first thought. We do not play the Pirates again until early February and we do not know who committed this dastardly deed. I trust you will remind the Pirates that this beautiful and gentlemanly sport of ours does not tolerate knives to the face." Everyone in the washroom car nodded agreement.

Lester continued "This has forced our first roster move. I have signed a defenseman from the Detroit Greyhounds. His name is Stan Brown. He will be assisting Mr. Abel and Mr. Mackey in Mr. Johnson's absence. He has won two Allen Cups, and he's a graduate of the University of Toronto where he played hockey. I'm sorry Mr. Murdoch but you will no longer be the only college graduate on the team."

Lester continued, "I was able to sign Mr. Brown as a free agent and asked him to join us in Ottawa."

"Now gentlemen, before we discuss the formattable Senators of Ottawa, there has been a change in our travel plans" Lester continued. "Because of some so-called chilly weather hitting Canada we will not be staying in a hotel tonight but instead taking the train back early. Our sleeping car will be waiting at the station and leaving for New York at 3:25 in the morning. I am told by the good railway conductors that the temperature will be about thirty-five degrees below zero. They seem to feel that water may freeze at that balmy temperature. When you return to the train, having no doubt spent a night drinking beer in Mr. Boucher's hometown, a few of you with weak bladders may need to use the facilities. This very wash car will be closed as the water lines will be frozen. You have been asked to use the pails which will be hung outside the car."

To which Ching worriedly asked, "but Lester, what if we need to take a crap?"

"Dress warmly and use the toilets in the station itself Mr. Johnson. Please try not to drink the city dry tonight fellas and leave some beer for your fellow countrymen. Have fun and do not miss the train."

There was the inevitable knock on the washroom door.

"Now, those Senators…" Lester continued, "our Mr. Boucher will have the privilege of playing against his other brother, Buck..."

The Ottawa Auditorium was rather small, and intimate compared to the other arenas we had visited. It looked like it might hold only seven or eight thousand seats with some room for standing. The ice was also oddly shaped. The boards were shaped with the same continuous curve behind the net typically seen on a runner's track. The whole rink was oval shaped, instead of the standardized curved corners with flat boards behind the net.

The Senators themselves wore their traditional barber-shop sweaters and socks with repeating red, white, and black horizontal stripes. Each player had a stitched twelve-inch square patch on their backs with their number in black. As sweaters went, they were traditional, so I liked them.

We all knew this game had special meaning for Frankie. Not only was he playing against one of his older brothers, but he was also playing against his hockey idol Frank Nighbor. Nighbor, already a ten-year veteran of the NHL, played with a style that Frank freely admitted he emulated. A clean player having won the Lady Byng trophy the last two years, Nighbor's name was also already on the Stanley Cup four times. He perfected the poke check style that few other centers beside Frank have been able to master. Both played with a defensive emphasis at center ice and used their speed to take the puck away from the attacking player. Ching repeatedly said one of the primary reasons our defensive pair was so respected was due to Frank doing so much of their work before the attacker ever got into our zone.

Now Frankie was facing Frank Nighbor for the opening face-off while his brother Buck, was positioned on defense. Paired with King Clancy, Lester warned us that this defensive duo could make scoring sparse. Their wingers were no slouches either. Cy Denneny was positioned on the left-side. Lester had warned our goalie Hal that Cy played with a curved blade. He was prone to lifting the puck when shooting and Hal needed to be on guard for headshots.

On the right wing was Hooley Smith who wore a leather jockey helmet after having suffered a serious head injury last year. I couldn't recall ever seeing a player wear a helmet during a game.

In all, our first-year squad was facing a team that had won the Stanley Cup three times over the last six years and a starting lineup of future Hall of Famers.

The referee Cooper Smeaton dropped the puck.

We didn't like to party after a loss. But this hard-fought battle held no shame. With our train hours from leaving there was little else to do in Ottawa at night. Across the river in Hull, we found Frankie's friends just as he arranged. They greeted us at a small hidden tavern with kegs of Canadian ale, live music and all the cold cuts a hungry hockey team could consume.

The Senators scored one goal six minutes into the game. Nighbor got through our defense and connected on a beautiful pass to Denneny. Denneny didn't need any fancy tricks as he was well positioned and shot hard and fast. Winkler didn't have a chance. Both teams played at an unrelenting pace with hard backchecking. The centers for both teams put on a poke checking clinic. Abel and Mackay saw most of the action, but our new skater, Stan Brown got several minutes and looked solid. He's got a totally different style than the physical play of Ching and Abel. Agile and quick, Stan played a smart and positional approach that cuts down on the good angles. When he found the puck on his stick, he made crisp passes up to our wingers instead of trying to skate with the puck himself. A 0-1 loss to the mighty Senators was barely a loss.

Around 2:45 in the morning Frankie started us on our caroling hike back to the station. As dangerously freezing as it was, we hardly felt a thing after all that beer and food. Hitting the head in the station first, Bill advised us not to wake Lester as we climbed on board to our berths. We all wished each other a Merry Cheer as it was now the 24th of December. Our first Christmas Eve together.

Our group was the last to arrive at Bill and Claire's new place in Flatbush. Ching & Ellen, Marie and I only found the building because Sam helped us navigate our way. The welcome smell of fresh baked ham greeted us as we walked through the door.

"Merry Christmas" said a cheerful Bill Cook as he took our heavy jackets and hats. He showed us into the living room where we found the rest of the team already enjoying the spiked eggnog. Lester stood to welcome us. Bunny and Frank immediately started taking drink orders. The sounds of Christmas carols played softly on the phonograph. Lester introduced us to his two sons.

"This is Lynn, he's fourteen and Muzz, eleven. Their mother is in the kitchen, I'll introduce you when she comes out."

Marie and Ellen made a beeline to help the other wives with the food.

I peeked into the hectic kitchen and knew well enough to keep out.

Ollie was the only one not here as he returned home to Alberta for treatment on his eye.

Frank's wife Ag walked into the room with their six-month-old son Earl. We gathered around to ooh and ogle as we passed the happy baby from one tough character to the next. It seemed there wasn't a man on our team without a soft side.

Ag, relieved for the break, playfully collapsed into the couch and accepted a light from Stan, bending over with a match to her cigarette.

Lorne and Hal were talking goalie talk with drinks in the corner.

Claire poked out of the kitchen and announced that dinner would be served in fifteen minutes. I sat down at the table with Bill, Frank, and Bun as they were talking strategy. Bun had a new trick he wanted to try, and he was drawing it out on a napkin. Sam perked up at the prospect of a new scheme.

"As I come up with the puck, the defenseman is going to be focused on my hips, right? He wants to direct me towards the boards or hit me."

"Or hit you into the boards" I joke.

"Exactly!" Bun continued with barely contained enthusiasm. "So, Frankie, you fall a few strides, maybe ten feet, right behind me. I'm going to keep skating hard like I'm driving towards the net, and when the defenseman commits, I'm going to give him what he wants, and I'll drift slightly off towards the boards and get him tangled up. But…"

Bun starts to chuckle with excitement at his own punchline.

"…I'm going to leave the puck behind for Frankie! At that moment, Frankie will have a clear line to the net! It'll only create a moment of confusion, but a moment is all we need. If the other defenseman steps up than Bill is open for the pass! If we're lucky the goalie will lose track of the puck in that moment too. It can't miss!"

Bill and Frankie, now accustomed to Bun's creative X's and O's agreed to run through it at tomorrow's practice. Marie and Claire began to bring large bowls of mashed potatoes, string beans, corn, carrots and steaming hot biscuits to the table. We stubbed out our cigarettes and got out of their way.

The "table" was several folding tables placed together with mismatched table clothes surrounded by a mishmash of equally diverse chairs, stools, benches. Somehow, they were able to gather enough plates, glasses, and silverware to feed an entire hockey team and its extended family. It was going to be a tight fit, but we all squeezed in. Twelve players, Lester and his family, Harry, Sam, five wives, two moms and two of Bill and Bun's three sisters as one was working the Christmas shift.

Bill walked in with a massive plater of sliced ham.

I noticed Marie's expression, as she watched with utter awe at the unchoreographed dance that followed. The other women quickly caught on too.

All the guys began passing bowls, plates, spoons, spirits, jelled cranberry, butter dishes and the like around and across the makeshift table with a precision, sharpness, anticipation, and coordination that must have seemed practiced and rehearsed. Guys were putting food on their wives' plate, each other's plates, as well as their own. We were buttering each other's biscuits. Not a kernel of corn was spilled, not a drop of wine hit the table clothes. Within seconds, every plate was stacked. After months of being together, we could communicate nearly telepathically.

But to the women at the table, it must have seemed almost supernatural.

Before anyone took a bite, Bill stood to speak.

"Let us hold hands."

He stood silent for a few brief moments and then continued.

"Take this moment. Look around at our new family. Recognize the gift we have been given."

Lorne was sitting directly across from me, and we locked eyes and nodded. I caught Frank and Ching and Lester. I held Marie's hand on my left and Hal on my right. We squeezed our hands knowingly. We all felt the moment.

Bill continued. "Now, let us pray. Thank you, lord, for the blessing on this bountiful table before us. Thank you for bringing this collection of fine men and women together. Although, I suppose Connie Smythe deserves some credit for that" he said with a chuckle that we all shared. "As we celebrate the birth of Christ, let us recognize the new life we have here too. Our newborn miracles." Bill nodded to his own child and Frank and Ag's baby.

He continued, "we have also given birth to something else. This team. The New York Rangers. We have begun something while so many teams across the north and west are unable to stay in operation. Let us give thanks to Tex Rickard and Colonel Hammond for giving us this opportunity to build a foundation. A foundation built on pride and determination. A foundation that will become a tradition for those that follow us. May this new team outlive us all. To the Rangers of New York." We all raised our glasses and repeated his cry. "The Rangers of New York".

Bill kept his glass raised and looked to our goalie Lorne Chabot.

"Mr. Shabotsky, as our press men insist that you are Jewish, would you like to add anything?

Lorne raised his glass, looked around the table with a big smile and proclaimed "L'chaim!"

"L'chaim!" we repeated.

After we cleared the dishes and stacked all the dry plates and pans, Lester called us into the living room. He was standing in the middle of the room and behind him were two hockey bags.

"Gentlemen, I have a letter here from Mr. Rickard that he asked me to read tonight. It is brief and in usual Tex style, right to the point." Lester unfolded the letter, cleared his throat, and began.

"Rangers, I am pleased with our start. Carry on. Merry Christmas. Tex"

Lester chuckled and continued with his own thoughts.

"We are all far from home and trying to establish roots here in the concrete and steel of this still unfamiliar metropolis. Claire and Bill, thank you for opening your abode to us tonight and making us all feel at home. Mr. Rickard is accurate. We are off to a good start, but the hard work has only begun. We have only played our first twelve games. God willing, we will be playing deep into April for Lord Stanley's Cup. Tex agreed we should look good while we're doing all that." Lester reached down and unzipped the first bag.

He pulled out a beautiful wool and suede, blue and tan varsity jacket with a felt Rangers' logo on the left breast. Lester looked at the name stitched inside. "Mr. Westerby, would you kindly come forward?"

Harry didn't know how to respond. He was utterly befuddled, but at our collective urging, he slowly rose from the couch.

"Mr. Westerby, everyone one of us is an equal and integral part of this team and key to the success of our future endeavors." Lester slipped it on him. "Seems to fit like a glove". We clapped.

Harry was beaming. As he sat back on the couch, I heard him whisper to Ching's wife Ellen "do you know what integral means?"

Lester continued "Mr. Brown, as the newest Ranger, I am sorry to say that your jacket has only been ordered. But rest assured, you will have it before this winter is over. Clarence, you are next. Come forth Mr. Abel".

Lester proceeded to gift each of us a team jacket, each with our name and number stitched inside. We clapped at each turn.

"Sam, you're last but not least" our youngest member stood and was presented with a jacket that was at least two sizes too large. Sam looked inside for his name, and I noticed his expression change, from pride to confusion, ever so slightly.

Lester quickly interjected, "do not worry Sam, you will grow into this. Gentleman, I saved Sam for the end because he has arranged for some of us to visit an upstate orphanage on January 3rd. We need two volunteers to join him in a good cause…

"I'm in" Ching raised his good arm before Lester could finish.

"Me too" I volunteered. Marie was riding back to Chicago with us on January 1st and I would be suddenly alone again.

During our morning practice we carved out time to experiment with Bun's "drop pass". Stan played the defensive role and pretended he didn't know what was about to happen. His job was to play the position naturally and not anticipate the trick play.

But equal parts near tragedy and comedy ensued on the very first attempt.

The first line took the puck into the zone. Bun had the puck and just as planned raced towards the net anticipating the defensive response. Frankie trailed the play, nonchalantly steering himself a few paces behind Bunny.

Just as Stan was engaging the winger, Bun left the puck behind and pretended it was still on his stick. Frank instantly had the puck and readied his quick and precise wrist shot.

But in that heartbeat, Bun did what Bun was fond of doing. He was being a bonehead.

Instead of following his own plan and allowing Stan to direct him towards the boards, Bun wanted to watch the play develop. So, he unexpectedly bent over and looked backward between his legs without drifting out of the shooting zone.

Just as Frank was about to rip the puck he looked up and caught sight of Bun's upside head right where the puck was about to be shot.

Frank aborted the shot by jerking up so violently that he lost his balance and fell backwards. He wasn't so much shaken by the fall, as he was by the thought of the puck's path leading right to Bun's face. He was convinced it would've been a kill shot. We never saw Frank so shook up. Bun kept apologizing. We agreed to run the drill again but with Bill responsibly playing the role of dropping the puck.

The play had potential under the right circumstances.

After practice, Bill went around the locker room and took up a collection. He quietly explained the front office bean-counters didn't approve Sam's jacket. Lester didn't know until the Christmas party when he was handing out the jackets. He didn't want Sam to feel left out, so Lester used Ollie's jacket. That was why Sam looked confused when he saw the name inside was Reinikka. Lester and Bill spoke and agreed on a team collection so that Sam could have his own.

Chapter Twenty

February 1994

"I respect how Bill Cook and Lester kept finding ways to turn negatives and adversity into a 'team building' experience" Mark acknowledged. "I doubt they were familiar with that term, but they instinctively kept striving to unite the team and recognize everyone's role as crucial to success. Including your trainer and water boy. This Harry sounds like a real character".

"He was. He cared about every detail. He treated our sweaters with the utmost respect. During the off season, he refused to put them in storage. At the end of every season, he would have them shipped to his home in Toronto where he would ensure they were cared for and not get moldy."

"Harry retired in '46 and we lost touch with him after a few years."

"I understand he was a heck of a boxer in his time." Mark replied.

"You know, it's funny, I only ever saw him throw one punch. But one was all he needed."

Chapter Twenty-One
December 26, 1926

This was our most anticipated game of the early season, and whoever made the schedule did us a real Christmas kindness. While we were technically playing an away game, we didn't have to travel any further than the visitors' locker room in our very own arena.

New York hockey fans were excited for this first match up between the newly formed Rangers and the established Americans. Every local paper had some variation of a headline in the sports section that read…

"Two New York Sixes Will Meet Tonight"
"Rangers and Americans Expected to Stage Bitter Battle"

"Babe Ruth is here" Harry casually informed us as the especially raucous crowd awaited the 8:30 start. "Standing room only tonight boys". We could literally feel the fans above us sending a tremor through the building.

"Embrace this energy fellas and get used to it." Bill informed us. "As the season progresses into the playoffs this will only be magnified. This is an early season taste of what awaits us."

Ching, dressed in a brown suit, spoke next, "Stan, since this is your first game here at the Garden, we have a tradition where the new guy leads us all out on the ice. It's a great honor. Welcome to the Garden."

Stan was beaming.

I had no idea what Ching was talking about. A "tradition"? This is our sixth game at the Garden. What tradition? Knowing Ching, something was up, and I kept quiet.

Stan led us down the hall. The noise was truly intimidating.

Ching opened the door to the ice and told Stan "Go out there and make a big loop around the whole rink."

"But aren't the Amerks warming up on their end?" Stan protested as he looked out at the ice.

"No, it's fine. I'll send the guys out one at time to follow you. It's important to go slow and wave to the fans. Stop behind the American's net and. make those fans feel welcome."

I was trying not to crackup.

Stan burst through the door and dutifully did as he was instructed. Within seconds, he was on the opposite end of the ice, waving to the crowd, slowly weaving between the opposing players, and trying to avoid their warmup shots.

The crowd started to see the humor and laugh.

Stan looked around, confused.

The American's were now having a good chuckle too.

Ching held the rest of us in the tunnel and Stan started laughing hysterically at the practical joke.

"He's going to fit in just fine." Ching announced.

It was clear the Garden was filled with fans of both teams. We were equally cheered and hearing colorfully profane laced jeers.

We went through our warmup routine, and I glanced to find Marie and the other gals. They were in their section, clapping wildly and waving Ranger pennants.

I noticed a commotion in the seats halfway up center ice behind our benches. The Bambino was making his way to his seat.

The American's were wearing their patriotic sweaters. Red, white, and blue invoking the American flag with little white stars on their chest and shoulders. Each player had his name stitched across their back. I had never seen this before and wondered why they would do that. Could their fans not remember their number?

I recognized the familiar last names of Burch, Conacher, Reise and Green. I followed them in the same local papers, articles written by the same reporters who did double duty in covering us both. We read about our rival Amerks regularly. Although we had not yet faced each other we knew them as well as any other team in the league. Their record on the early season was 6-6 while we had gotten off to a 7-4-1 start. But with the indispensable Ching sidelined we knew our defense was vulnerable.

The Amerks felt that same because they revealed their strategy from the first drop of the puck. They unrelentingly attacked our defense. Abel and Mackay held firm in front of Lorne. Stan would rotate in and out to keep them rested.

While Taffy was perhaps the perfect complement to Ching's style, he was not a leading man on his own. Instead of playing his own style, Taffy was trying to play more aggressively like Ching. It often left him slightly out of position and Lorne was forced to make one impressive save after another.

Bill, Frank, and Bun were not skating ideally either. While they were getting shots on Jack Forbes it was their Captain Bill Burch, and not our Captain Bill Cook who scored the first goal at 11:51. With that goal the Amerks' fans found the courage to raise the level of noise and involvement.

While I rarely paid attention to the fans, there was one irritating Amerks fan who was roaming around being a loudmouth. For much of the first period he positioned himself right behind our bench and wouldn't shut up. We did our best to ignore him, but I'd be lying if I said he wasn't a distraction. He was unrelenting. Right after the first goal by Burch he repositioned himself in the aisle behind Lorne and the verbal abuse got ugly.

Because of our crack publicity men, the city of New York mostly knew Lorne Chabot only as Shabotsky, or Chabotsky. The papers in other cities used the correct spelling of Chabot, but not here. For our own home games this didn't seem to have any impact beyond selling more tickets to Jewish fans. But now, for the first time Lorne was hearing anti-sematic slurs from this one obnoxious fan.

To start the second period the fan moved with Lorne to the other end of the rink and kept calling him "jewboy", "Christ-killer" and "hymie". Thirty seconds into the period Lionel Conacher got past Taffy and scored their team's second goal. It was a quality goal, no doubt, but all Lorne could hear were derogatory curses coming from this one guy. Regrettably, this guy seemed to be emboldening a few others. Not many, but like a virus, the hate spread to a few others.

Lester and Ching were both yelling from the bench for Lorne to shake it off and keep his head in the game.

Lorne skated out from the net to regroup as the ref Dave Ritchie took the puck to center ice for a face off. Lorne skated behind the net and whacked his stick at the chicken-wire as he passed this one bum. The guy flinched but this only seemed to encourage him. It was the worst mistake Lorne could make. Now this lout knew he was getting under Lorne's skin and that Lorne couldn't physically reach him.

I didn't get a sense anyone on the American's were proud of this fan's tactics, it riled the rest of us up. The game got increasingly chippy and violent. Bill Cook and Lionel Conacher took major penalties for fighting and the inner-city, inner-arena rivalry was rapidly building. By the time Bill Burch scored the third and fourth goals, still in the second period, we outright despised these guys. Taffy was embarrassed and lead the way by throwing the body and elbows harder. Bill, Bun, and rest of us followed suit.

Stan Brown got things started for us. He settled the puck down behind our net and seeing a lane started up the left side. He could have passed but kept pushing forward and penetrated their zone. He used a little head fake and backhanded the puck past their goalie Forbes for our first goal.

A few minutes later, Taffy got the same opportunity and scored. With the score now 4-2 things settled down into a more competitive back and forth.

Starting the third period we switched sides once again and so did this one fan. He started right up with the anti-sematic cursing again as we came out of the tunnel.

I'd had enough.

I took a detour behind our net and pretended I needed a little warmup. I skated by him slowly and got a good look at his face. I made sure he saw me looking at him.

He responded predictably.

"What? What you gonna do Jew lover?"

I calmly stopped in front of him. Most of the fans weren't even back in their seats. Others weren't paying attention anyway.

I showed no sign of anger or annoyance. I just smiled, and placidly leaned my shoulder against the chicken wire like I was just having a normal conversation with any fan before the start of hotly contested third period. Which of course, never happens.

"Hey buddy" I said. He couldn't resist.

He came just close enough. I had ever so subtly placed the top of my stick against the wire, knowing the shaft would fit through the mesh. I gave it quick hard upward jerk.

The butt of my stick caught him square on his bulbous nose. It exploded. He fell backwards, blood streaming through his fat fingers covering his face. He cursed and squirmed on the steps.

I didn't stay to watch. I withdrew my stick from the wire and skated off. Lorne must have watched and tapped me with his stick as I passed on my way to the bench.

The young rookie Normie Himes, truly an outstanding stickhandler, scored one more goal for the Americans and we lost 5-2. But we gave New York a rivalry to get excited about.

In the locker room, Bill stood with his head hung low and his arms on his hips. He had pulled off his sweater but his should pads were still on. We all knew when Bill had something on his mind and wanted to speak. He didn't have to ask for our attention.

He spoke softly.

"These last few games, we're not finding our stride. Ching and Ollie being out of the lineup hurts, but we can't use that as an excuse. Every facet of our game needs to tighten up. We've got the Senators here in two nights and we're not ready. We lost to a .500 team tonight. We lost 1-0 in Ottawa three nights ago against a great team. We barely beat Pittsburgh, a terrible club on our home ice. We skated to a tie against Detroit and before that we got spanked in Chicago." Bill paused for effect.

"No drinking till we get this turned around. I know our ladies are waiting for us right now and they're looking forward to some swing music. But no. No more drinking or partying until we've found our stride and start winning games again."

The room silently nodded. Bill sat back down, and no one said a word. We just proceeded to get out of our wet gear and absorb Bill's words. He was right. No one in the room would disagree or argue. The team needed to come first. Teetotalers until we've turned this around.

A booming voice entered the room like a thunderclap.

"Your captain is probably right, but I always prefer to drink more, especially when things are going badly." His belly laugh filled the room. He was larger than life and every person in the room recognized him instantaneously.

He was wearing a double-breasted dark suit and tie, with polished black and white wingtips. He looked to be about thirty and had a large sixty-cent cigar clenched and hidden behind his left hand. His presence seemed to electrify the very air with a current.

"I just shook hands with tonight's victors, and I have to say they look pretty beat up. I don't think they're looking forward to your next boxing bout". He started with Bill and then went around the room and shook hands with each of us in turn. Asking our names. Making a quick joke.

The Babe took a few extra moments with Lorne, who had a rough night. The two spoke quietly to each other and I couldn't hear them, but Lorne's head was shaking in agreement.

When Ruth got to Taffy, he commented how they were both similarly shaped "superior athletic specimens. The Greek gods themselves modeled us after heavy beer drinking lumberjacks". He assured Taffy how much New Yorkers appreciated his efforts. It clearly made Taffy feel better to laugh after a rough game.

Then he arrived at my stool.

We shock hands and his cigar clenched lefthand rested on my shoulder. Loud enough for my teammates to hear he said, "I would've popped that loud-mouth bigot too, but I would've drawn too much attention. I could never get away with that but I'm glad you did. That was alright what you did." He graced me with a generous smile. I don't think I'll ever forget the smell of his cigar or the beer on his breath.

Fifteen minutes after the Babe left, we were showered and getting dressed when one of the Garden workers stuck his head into our locker room. "Hey guys, there's a problem outside. I think it's your gals."

We bolted for the door, some dripping wet and wearing only a towel around their waist. Many of us barefoot and partially dressed. All of us trying to squeeze through the door at once. We ran down the tunnel and burst through the metal door to the outside where our wives and friends had taken to waiting for us.

There was tense commotion. A rowdy group of intoxicated fans were popping off. I saw Marie and a few of the wives furiously yelling at some of the drunken idiots.

Sam was standing in front of Marie and the women, his lip bleeding and holding his gut. One guy was in Sam's face. Sam held his ground. We all moved as one but suddenly Harry came out of nowhere. He moved like lightening.

He jumped in front of Sam and popped the guy one time. His punch to the guy's chin was so fast I barely saw it happen. The guy on the receiving end crumpled to the pavement. The other fools backed a step. We all got between them and the gals.

Lorne took one step forward. After a long night of hearing slurs and giving up goals he was in no mood for bullshit.

"I suggest you pick up your friend and leave." He growled.

Lorne is a big, strong guy. But there's always one fool in a drunken group who doesn't know when to keep his mouth shut and follow good advice. This was no exception.

"Hey, it's the kike goalie."

Marie burst through the line and slapped the guy hard across the face. I rushed forward but as the guy motioned to swing, Lorne hit him with a combination one-two.

That was it. The mob was running away, and it was over.

Standing beside Lorne, and watching them skedaddle, I asked rhetorically, "that felt good, didn't it?"

"Yeah. Yeah, it really did." And he smiled.

"Ruth gave me a pat on the back" I told Marie as we sat at Ellen's corner diner sharing a late-night apple tart and chocolate milk shake. We were decompressing from a crazy night. The game, meeting The Babe and the street fight. Marie rested her right hand on a bowl of ice. It was sore from slapping that drunk.

Before the tart arrived, Marie explained. As the ladies were waiting, this group of Amerks fans saw one of the Ranger pennants they were holding. The men were drunk and started yapping. At first the women just ignored them but, when it escalated, the ladies made for the door. A couple of these hooligans blocked their retreat, and it was getting scary.

"Sam came running down the street and jumped in. He yelled 'leave the women alone, backoff. Trust me, you fellas don't want this kinda trouble."

"But these punks were riled up. He sucker-punched Sam in the stomach. As you saw, the guy was quite bigger. Sam kept his cool and warned them again to leave but he clocked Sam across the jaw. Then a posse of Rangers burst through the door." She could laugh now at the sight of us in towels and half-naked. "My gosh those had to be the dumbest group of drunks ever."

"I loved when Harry put his arm around Sam's shoulder and said "come on kid. Let's get you some ice for that lip."

But first Marie, then each of the women in turn planted a kiss on Sam's other cheek. His face was swelling on one side and covered with the lipstick marks on the other.

"Imagine, Babe Ruth himself" Marie continued. "I'm glad you took care of that loudmouth in the stands. Who would have ever imagined that meeting with Connie Smythe at the Fort Garry Hotel would have led to all this? It's so exciting Murray."

"I really love it here. Much more than I imagined." She added.

I reached across the table and gently took her sore hand, as the other hand was busy scooping another piece of pie. "Just stay here. You don't have to return. We'll find a flat."

"Oh, I'm moving here right away. But I need to get my mom and sister settled, and I need to close the house properly. I'll pack to remain through April or May. I'm not sure I'm ready for New York in the summer. Oh, I don't know, that Coney Island sure did look fun, didn't it? I'll join you and the guys on the train back to Chicago in a few days and get to Winnipeg from there just as we planned. I'll make my way back to New York by mid-January."

"That'll give me a couple weeks to find us a place here in Manhattan."

We were tempted of course, to start looking for a furnished apartment in Flatbush near the Cooks' and Boucher's. But their priority centered around raising a new family and Brooklyn held obvious appeal. It was quieter and kids could play outside.

As Marie and I had not yet started a family, her love of Broadway and the surrounding shopping, restaurants, music, and nightlife, got us thinking we'd be staying closer to the action. A few of the other guys found smaller places a couple blocks just west towards Hell's Kitchen, which had a rough reputation as the name implied. They were single and happy to pay only about $60 per month for a furnished place. Ching and Ellen may have found a place on 57th street for $130 a month. I decided to look around there and work north towards the park.

Chapter Twenty-Two

December 28, 1926 – January 1, 1927

Lester had an uncanny knack for finding talent.

Stan Brown emerged from a scrum in front of our net and skated the length of the ice. But he lost control of the puck and Ottawa's goalie Alec Connell aggressively came out of the net to bat it away. At which point most defenseman would circle back and resume their position.

But Connell didn't get solid wood on it and Stan sensed an opportunity as the puck trickled away. He chased after the puck, scooped it up and whipped himself around the back of the net. Connell wasn't back in position and the Senator's defensemen were caught out of position. Stan made the backhanded goal look rather easy and less than five minutes into the first we were up a goal.

Nearing the end of this period, Thompson, Boyd, and I were taking a shift. I didn't see the penalty, but referee Ritchie stopped play and sent Hooley Smith to the box for roughing. That's when I caught slight of Billy Boyd half bent over and holding his mouth.

I rushed over. He was holding his cupped gloved hand under his chin to catch the blood and I could see at least one tooth in his palm. The blood was seeping between his fingers and leaving a trail on the ice. Paul and I helped him off and I watched Harry walk him to the locker room.

The period ended moments later and it wasn't unusual to find Harry doing his best needlework and embroidery as we entered the locker room. But it was strange to hear him cursing. Sam was assisting but Harry was flustered so we knew it was no joking matter. We gave them space to work. Lester however walked over to assess the situation.

"One tooth was knocked out right out" Harry explained "but a second tooth is shattered upward, stabbing into his gums. It's a mess and can't see anything with the bleeding. It won't stop. He's in pain. This was going to need real surgery."

Lester leaned closer to Harry, and they whispered together. I could see Harry nodding his head yes.

"Doctor Brown," Lester shouted across the room. "I wonder if you might consult with us on this patient."

All our heads turned in unison towards Stan, who had just calmly removed his sweater and walked in his skates gingerly over to the medical table.

Bun leaned over to me and asked, "did he say Doctor?"

"Yeah." I admitted in confusion. Lester mentioned that Stan went to the University of Toronto. It felt like Stan had been our teammate for weeks, but it was just five nights ago that he met us on that cold night in Ottawa. He fit right in with all of us. He was a particularly handsome dark-haired fella, average height, and strong lean build. Maybe a 150 pounds. Between the holiday party, practice and this being our third game in the short span I never asked him what he studied.

Stan had gone and washed his hands and returned to examine Billy's mouth. He asked Sam to position the light closer and requested to see Harry's medical equipment. We only had a few minutes between periods to drink a pop, enjoy a smoke and dry off a little. Of course, we also needed to discuss strategy and make mid-game adjustments. Especially against Ottawa. But by now the whole team was standing as close as we could to watch.

Stan grabbed the smallest forceps and had Harry pour what appeared to be alcohol over them. Stan started probing around. Within seconds he removed a piece of tooth and placed it on a steel tray. Then another, and another. He paused from working in Billy's mouth and assembled the tooth pieces together with his fingers. He explained there was more still to pull but that he had gotten the biggest pieces. At Stan's request, Harry got some needle and thread ready. Stan put in a few quick stitches. Sam watched every move and appreciated the skilled technique.

Dave Ritchie came into our locker room and asked "are you guys coming? The Senators are on the ice already."

All of us scurried to throw our sweaters and elbow pads back on. We grabbed our gloves, sticks, and headed out. Stan and Billy were right behind us. On the bench Stan confessed that he graduated with a Doctorate in Dental Medicine.

Our first line put on intense pressure with the man advantage but couldn't score. Billy Boyd went out with us on the second line and was no doubt in some pain, but his play didn't seem bothered.

Seven and a half minutes into the second, Hec Kilrea got a pass from Frankie's brother Buck and beat Hal Winkler.

With less than four minutes in the period, Doctor Brown made a sharp smart pass to Bill Cook near the Ottawa net and Bill put a quick shot right between Connell's legs.

Between the second and third periods we were once again mesmerized watching Stan take even smaller pieces of tooth out of Boyd's upper gum. He used a scalpel to open a section of the gum to get a better look inside. He then did another examination of the tooth puzzle. Satisfied, he did a quick stitch job and promised Billy he'd finish up properly after the game. It looked like he lost at least two teeth, and another seemed wobbly.

Dental distractions aside, we had a 2-1 lead going late into the third period and we were feeling the pressure of a close game. We played well throughout, but the Senators were skating with confidence. The fans were certainly getting their money's worth of back-and-forth action. But I suspect they too recognized that Ottawa was undeniably just a cut above us. Thirteen minutes into the period we had a wonderful ruckus going on in front of their goalie Connell, with bodies falling and flying. Everyone sensed we were going to score when it was Kilrea's turn to calmly emerge from the mass of tangled bodies and attack up ice. At just the last moment he passed across ice to winger Alex Smith who was crashing towards the left side of the net and tied the game.

While this late goal was treating the Garden to yet another over-time game, it was bitter knowing we were so close to ending the game with a win.

It was Senator Frank Finnegan who scored the game-winner three minutes into OT.

In what could only be described as the hockey gods being asleep, substitute Jack Adams stole the puck off Doctor Stan Brown's stick and made a pass to the veteran Finnigan who knew how to end the contest quickly.

Otherwise, Stan finished the game with a goal, an assist, and a surgery. Tonight's star player regardless.

True to Bill Cook's edict, I'm not aware that anyone drank a drop of alcohol since our loss to the Americans. And here it was, New Year's Eve. We were on the overnight sleeper to Chicago. The rollicking dinner car was a crowded celebration of drunk passengers mixed with a very sober but still jocular hockey team.

Even Marie respected Bill's order, which certainly wasn't intended to include her. Harry was the only member of our team who grumbled at all. He couldn't understand why the ban included him. Bill explained.

"Harry, you are welcome to drink yourself drunk as a skunk and wet yourself. Your drinking will not impact the outcome of the next game. You're right. But you will be drinking alone and when is that ever fun? This is a team Harry, and you're an important part of that team. The guys know you hate this. Maybe your misery makes them find a little something extra to help us win the next game."

Marie and I parted at Union Station. Her train to Winnipeg was leaving shortly and I tipped the bellhop well to make sure she was escorted, and her bags were transferred. It wasn't fun saying goodbye.

We were headed right to the Chicago Coliseum for our practice skate.

When we arrived in the visitors' locker-room, we were delighted to find Ollie Reinikka there to greet us. Ollie was always a very reserved and quiet gent. He was still bruised and swollen but the doctor had given him the okay to resume work. His eyeball was red inside with blood, and he had a red scar through his eyebrow. I wondered if this was such a good idea and questioned if Ollie's doctor knew his profession was ice hockey.

But we were happy to have him back. Of course, Lester already knew that Ollie would be meeting us here. But in typical Lester fashion, he didn't ruin the surprise during our early morning washroom meeting on the train.

Sam was really feeling it at practice. The kid was something to watch and his confidence kept growing. Today he was explosive. His ability to carry the puck and pivot at full speed were unparalleled. There was no use denying his talent. But for his age and size, his skills were rival to anyone in the league. Frank and Bun were generally considered the fastest skaters on our team. Bill, Paul, and I were probably in a close second tier. The five of us were fast by NHL standards. Sam was faster.

And he was proving it time and again today.

Sam took position as defenseman. When Sam felt like stretching his legs, he could run the length of the ice practically at will. We all tried to catch him and failed. He played his options. If he was feeling pressure, he would make a beautiful crisp pass. If he could find a lane, or make one, he would take the puck deep and shoot it. I noticed that while he was taking plenty of shots he wasn't scoring much. The puck would typically be caught by our goalie. On one such shot on net I had an epiphany. He wasn't trying to score. He was literally aiming for the inside of the goalie's glove!

His speed was such that even if he penetrated deep into the offensive zone, he could still get back in time to play defensively.

Thompson gathered a loose puck and attacked. Racing up ice he saw Sam skating backwards, easily matching Paul stride for stride.

Paul tried a fake move to the right and quickly cut to the left. Sam didn't fall for it. Frustrated, Paul spun, tried to go wide, but couldn't shake Sam. Paul twisted and turned, put his shoulder into Sam and tried to push his way past. He couldn't. Sam was a wall. Since the start of the season Sam had put on a little muscle and bulk.

I could hear Paul cursing.

He gave Sam a quick slash to the shin. Sam chopped right back. Paul swung harder and within a heartbeat the two were tangled up and wrestling.

We broke it right up. Sam was calm throughout and to Paul's credit the brief incident was over, and practice resumed.

We went to our hotel to wash up and eat a good meal. The food in Chicago seemed to be especially good on our previous visit and this meal of fried chicken and cheesy macaroni did nothing to convince us otherwise. We then retired to our rooms for our afternoon nap.

An hour later we'd waken and have another lite bite. A peanut butter and jelly sandwich always sat well with me before a game.

Together, we'd put on our team jackets and head to the Coliseum two hours before the 8:30 start. This rhythm gave us plenty of time to digest our food and hit the head. We would use the time to tape our sticks. A process that I suspected would always be sacred to hockey players before every game.

The game started with Babe Dye showing the same spunk and energy as Sam did in practice. He wasn't a big man, but his skill was impressive, and he was all over the ice. But Dye was something of a lone one-man crew tonight.

Billy, Paul, and I were barely on the ice for our first shift when Stan once again skated up with the puck and put a quality shot on Lehman that found the back of the net. It was Brown's third goal since joining us a week ago. Incredible.

Two minutes later Taffy scored his third goal of the season. Eighteen minutes into the period Frankie Boucher poke checked the puck off Irvin's stick and turned on the speed. Frank's awareness on the ice was remarkable. He seemed to have eyes in the back of his head.

Bunny was racing behind him and yelled "now!" just as Frank was engaging the Blackhawk's defensive line. Frank played it perfect. He pretended to take a quick wrist shot and immediately put his body directly in the line of sight of poor Gord Fraser. Fraser played the body and not the puck as all defensemen are taught and stood Frank up. But Frank had left the puck for Bunny coming up behind.

Now Bunny had a clear lane to skate the last few strides towards the net. Lehman, caught off guard, committed and dropped one leg to the ice. It was an easy move for Bunny to skate past him and flick the puck into the net. This was Bunny's fifth goal of the season but his first using this 'drop pass' strategy he drew up on a Christmas napkin.

The increasingly frustrated and stymied Hawks only continued to rack up penalties now that we were up by three.

Babe Dye went hard after Frank. The refs know Frank is the cleanest player in the whole league and except for one fighting penalty in our first game he has otherwise refused to drop his gloves. Dye was sent off to cool down for two minutes.

No sooner had that advantage ended that Mickey Mackay took a run at Stan. A moment later Mickey took a swing at Lorne's wrist. He was called for slashing and sent to the box. But I had enough.

I looked at Lester and he nodded. I called the closest winger to the bench, which happened to be Bun. I jumped over the boards and surveyed the available options. Bob Trapp was their biggest defenseman and no stranger to penalties. When you're looking to send a message, find the meanest, biggest, ugliest guy available.

As the play developed, I skated alongside him and may have said something about his mother meeting me after the game. We dropped our gloves at the same moment and fists flew. We each got in a few good shots. The ref untangled us as our arms got tired and the crowd showed their appreciation. The message was sent, don't go after our players if you don't like the score, just play better.

With both of us in the box cooling down, Bill Cook found his stride and ripped one last beautiful goal. The Hawks would take one more penalty but that would be the only way they got on the official scorer's sheet tonight.

Lorne had a 4-0 win.

After the impressive win, Bill lifted our prohibition, and we made our way to a local underground tavern just before midnight. Chicago was reputed to have as many as 3,000 speakeasys but we heard there was a place called the Green Door on North Orleans Street. Off we went. Sure enough, we found a green wooden door and we were directed down to the basement. Tobacco smoke, jazz music, the odor of whiskey and beer, and the heat of bodies seemed to intensify with every step. Bill bought the first round of beers as we toasted the first day of 1927.

A couple rounds later Bunny approached with three mugs of beer. "Hey, Murray, Taffy seems a little outta sorts tonight, no?"

I took one of the mugs from him and looked around the crowded room.

"Yeah, and he played well. I don't get it. He's off sitting by himself at the bar. Let go cheer him up."

We approached and placed the spare beer on the bar. Clicking our three glasses together we sat for a bit and watched the lively action. Couples were doing the Charleston as the musicians played.

We talked about the game and the moment from each contest that haunts each of us after. We laugh about it, but every hockey player experiences this feeling of a missed opportunity, even after a strong win. There are too many split-second decisions in every game to make the right choice or the perfect execution on every one of them.

"If only I had..." is typically how the line begins. Followed by... "made a better pass or received that puck at center ice on the breakout or lifted that shot another inch over the goalie's glove." Each of us ends every game with at least one moment of guilt, where we know we could've made a better choice.

When Bunny excused himself to find the head, Taffy and I watched the swaying and twirling couples dancing. Taffy leaned over and confessed "I'm just living a lie, Murray. Every minute of every day, my life is lie. Tell Bunny I said thank you for the beer. I'll see you guys on the train in the morning."

He threw some change on the bar and left.

Chapter Twenty-Three
January 3, 1927

An Imperial red chasse and black retractable roof was waiting for us at the Tarrytown station. Our train ride up the Hudson offered a beautiful view of the Palisades, and the cliffs were still visible on the far side of the river as we climbed into the carriage. Our driver took us up a steep street through the heart of the village. The vehicle seemed to struggle at times with our weight.

Shops selling shoes, sundries, and hardware lined both sides of the bustling street. A red bricked Music Hall stood proudly near the crown of the town and looked out over the wide river. We continued upward for a few minutes and turned down a dirt lane which led to a tired looking stone mansion. This was the orphanage.

Neither Ching nor I were sure how to address the clergyman that approached our vehicle as we pulled up. No one at the Garden provided any instructions beyond the time and station. No helpful hints on what to say or how to act. How to fill the time or what to do. Sam just said to bring my skates, stick and bag of pucks. Ching took his skates but with his arm still healing he didn't bring his stick. Sam brought both.

The priest was dressed in a black suit and white collar. He was older, perhaps in his fifties, with neatly combed silver hair. Suddenly this all felt very formal and serious. Ching and I were wearing our team jackets and they seemed very out of place.

Suddenly anxious, I jumped out of the automobile and extended my hand. "I'm Murray Murdoch and this is Ching, umm, sorry, Ivan Johnson and Sam Crawford. We are here representing the New York Rangers."

I immediately felt foolish and stiff. I could hear Ching chuckling.

The priest disarmingly used both hands to shake mine. "Why hello Mr. Murdoch and welcome. I'm Father Sabastian. Our boys are very excited to meet actual professional hockey players. And merely showing up and spending some time with the boys is incredibly appreciated."

He had a warm, welcoming smile but it was his accent that caught my attention. "Do you mind if I call you Murray? I saw you score a game winning goal a few weeks back at the Garden. I was very excited to hear you would be joining us today." He now looked at Ching.

"And hello, I hope my calling you Ching is ok Mr. Johnson? I am a huge fan. The boys here all know you as Ching or Ivan the Terrible."

"Sure," we both replied in unison.

"Quebec?" I asked.

"Oui" he smiled. "I grew up in Saint-Augustin-de-Desmaures. Very near the river."

He didn't have to say more. It was implied that he too skated.

"We read about your exploits the day after every game in the papers", Father Sabastian explained.

"Shall we go inside and show you our home?"

The tour was emotional. The home was clean but aging. We were shown a section for the babies and the very young. Three nuns were feeding, changing, and caring for perhaps ten infants. We came to a few classrooms with age-appropriate desks. Finger paintings adored some walls. Maps, and multiplication tables others. Being Sunday, the classrooms were empty of students. At the other end of the house, as far as possible from the babies, were two dormitory rooms with a large comfortable living area between them. Each sleeping area held perhaps a dozen beds. One for early teenagers, younger kids in the other.

But the once elegant home was slowly falling into disrepair. Water damage from previous leaks and peeling paint were visible in a few places despite their best efforts to keep up repairs. The funds were dwindling explained Father Sabastian. The home would be closing within the decade as the State was transitioning to foster care and away from orphanages. The home operated for years as part of the 'Orphan Train' system. The goal was to first get these abandoned or dangerously unsupervised kids out of the city, housed, fed, educated, and playing in the countryside while awaiting adoption throughout the country, or the rarer outcome of being reunited with parents who had turned their lives around. If adoption never came, the goal was to teach them life skills and trades like farming, carpentry, painting, plumbing, mending, and sewing cloths, and shoe repair before they aged out around fifteen. Some join the military. Father Sabastian explained that most of the home repairs were done by the older boys, and that much of the food was grown on the grounds.

The kids were in the cafeteria eating their lunch and anxiously waiting for us. Their excitement when we appeared was electric. Their eyes widened; their mouths gasped. They surrounded us and were mesmerized by the sight of our jackets. Child, after child just wanted to show me something they had made or owned. A beat-up baseball, a crayon-colored drawing, a carved wooden figure of an animal.

This was breaking my heart.

Father Sabastian did his best to encourage the kids to finish their lunches, so I sat at one table while Ching took another.

I thought of the great Babe Ruth in our locker room just a few days ago. He was reputed to have grown up in similar circumstances. A Catholic orphanage. Perhaps something very much like this. He walked around our locker room and introduced himself to each of us. One of the most famous athletes alive and he made time for each of us. He didn't just walk in the room, say a few words and leave. No, he made a personal connection with each of us. That's how it's done.

I looked around my table. I was sitting with eight kids.

"Hey, it's nice to meet you. My name is Murray. I'm from Canada. I play hockey for the New York Rangers.

I turned to the first kid on my left "what's your name?" I asked.

"Luke," he answered and then paused, "I don't know where I'm from."

My heart was still breaking, but I now had a plan that included each child feeling seen and heard.

When lunch was over and the tables were cleared, I asked the whole room "hey, who wants to go skating?"

Sam informed us in advance that the home had a large pond on the far side of the property. It was frozen, and the kids loved to skate on it. Now I understand why Sam encouraged us to bring our skates.

It started snowing heavily while we were inside. We all walked together along the path, the snow crunching beneath our boots. I can see the pond through the trees just ahead.

The trees are leafless, and the sky is white. The wintry air reminds me of home. Clean and crisp in the lungs as I breathe deeply.

The kids are so excited. I quickly lace up and then help them. They don't have enough skates for everyone so they will take turns on the ice. The skates they do have are the kind that attach blades onto the bottom of their shoes with leather straps and buckles. They are not sturdy under the best circumstances. But they allow the kids to glide and play. There are a few actual hockey sticks but most of the kids are playing with a home-made version of two pieces of wood nailed together or tree limbs that just happen to have a natural hockey stick shape. Those don't take especially long to break.

Father Sabastian has donned his own skates and joins us now that most of the kids are on the ice. Sam and Ching have their skates on too. The four of us, each in our own way are showing the kids how to push off their skates and use their edges. Their strapped-on blades won't allow them to execute any of these drills, but they are having fun. Some are frustrated, who isn't when learning something new, but no one is giving up. Father Sabastian clearly has some skills and a genuine love of the sport that I recognize and respect. He moves well, especially for his age.

We start just passing and chasing the puck with the kids. The best way to learn is just to do. It isn't too long before some kids take a rest and share their skates with another kid, allowing everyone a go. Like growing up anywhere in Canada, there are no clocks on the pond. We'll play until it's too dark, or Father Sabastian tells us to stop. My money is on the sun.

The heavy snow is making the day magical.

By now Ching is pretending he's a silly ref. The kids are loving him. He's just a big playful kid himself.

I notice there is one child who is really attached to Ching. He can barely stand on skates and Ching is holding his hand. That kid just doesn't want to let go. I make eye contact with Ching. He looks down at the kid and back at me. Ching always has a smile. But I've never seen his eyes like this before. This is the real Ivan Johnson.

Not so terrible after all. In fact, he's a beautiful soul.

The kids are really slowing down now so Sam and I start finding each other with the puck. The kids are endlessly entertained at our passing while skating at speed. To them it seems like magic, as if the puck is attached to an invisible string that goes like a magnate between our two sticks. Sam and I are just playing catch. We goof around. We go wide and hit each other from a hundred feet apart and close the gap. Tapping it rapid action fire back and forth when we are only eight feet apart. The puck is moving so fast I doubt the kids can even see it.

Ching dumps the whole bag of probably twenty pucks on the ice. They fall randomly and all land within a twelve to fifteen-foot radius. Sam corrals one puck with his stick and I take another. We are both skating through and around the other pucks, twisting and turning rapidly around them and each other, without ever touching another puck or crashing into each other.

We are putting on a clinic for these kids, showing them how we can control the puck on the end of our sticks. I notice Sam looking up at the kids and smiling at them as he's skating around and avoiding the pucks. He's not even looking down. I've got to steal a glance here and there. Heck, he's putting on a clinic for me too.

The kids laugh hysterically when we start showing them that we can skate backwards as well as forwards. Sam and I flip between back and forth, and I skate towards the kids and stop hard spraying their legs with an ice and snow shower. I'm starting to feel my legs burn and figure it's time to slow down. There's no topping the ice spray. Every kid loves that.

But Sam isn't feeling tired yet. He motions that we start doing figure eights with the puck. We are demonstrating tight circles. Sam and I are pushing each other now. Who can go faster, lower, tighter? Sam and I are each skating our own figure eight doing crossovers that put us on our inside edges and our bodies at angles that seemingly defy gravity. It's a clockwise direction immediately followed by counterclockwise. My lungs and legs are burning. But he smiles at me as we pass each other and starts making that noise with his skates. I can get close to that noise if I really focus and push with all my might. I'm leaning into my edges hard. Really hard. Any player in the league would be impressed. The burn is intense. It seems effortless for Sam.

I'm a pale imitation but I keep going.

Sam is doing something else altogether…new. Something powerfully violent. He's not only going faster, but the noise is echoing across the pond. His blades are carving the ice. No, he's not just carving the ice, he's carving INTO the ice. He's slicing it, and it's screaming in pain. My lungs are about to explode.

I happily concede this. I slow up and like Ching, Father Sabastian, and the kids, we watch Sam turn it on. He continues this figure eight motion, while controlling the puck, until he's left a deep scar in the ice. We are all cheering him on, and he suddenly graces the kids with another hard stop, sending a shower of ice and snow that goes over their heads to great applause. Ching and I share a look of awe.

We've made a bunch of hockey fans for life.

We made sure each kid had a hockey puck when we left. Ching,

Sam, and I signed my hockey stick and presented it to Father Sabastian and the school.

I thought about Marie on the train back to Manhattan. About how fortunate our future kids would be. About how few of these kids would have a future like the Babe. The day broke my heart.

Chapter Twenty-Four

February 1994

"This was the same pond you skated on all those years ago." Messier stated.

"Sam skated those figure eights right here, probably this very spot." I replied.

The two of us stood on the ice, side-by-side.

"Can I ask about Ching?" Mark asked. "It seems like he was a pretty special guy."

"He was the best. A dear friend for life and one of the greatest teammates a guy could have," I pause.

"Ivan and I played eleven seasons together. He played one season at the end with the Americans, but he knew it was time to retire in '38. He coached for a few years in the lower leagues. He tried being a ref but actually body-checked a player who was misbehaving."

We laugh.

"He quickly decided refereeing was not for him. He was inducted into the Hockey Hall of Fame in '58. I was there for the ceremony, as were some of the guys. After his career in hockey was over, he moved to Washington, DC and worked construction. He retired in Silver Springs, Maryland. Marie and I visited him and Ellen once a year. He had some nice fishing holes. Their two children, Geraldine and James were very close to our Joan. It wasn't long before he and Ellen were blessed with four grandchildren. He had one great-grandchild when he died in 1979. He was 81 when we lost him."

I pull off one of my gloves and I wipe my eyes.

Chapter Twenty-Five
January 6 - 11, 1927

The Montreal Canadiens lost to the American's two nights earlier. Now, in our first game of 1927 at the Garden we were paired up against the same visiting Canadiens. The game was raising money for the Cathedral of St. John the Divine, and it was a thinner crowd than usual of maybe 9,000. We usually drew better on a Thursday night. Neither team had scored, and it looked like we were headed to another over-time treat for those lucky spectators when Stan Brown scored a beauty against their goalie Hainsworth with under two minutes in regulation. The next day the press reported that Shabotsky pitched another shut out for us.

Sunday night Lester came into the locker room and tapped his clipboard against a stall to get our attention.

"Fellas, when we face the Cougars in two hours, please note that they've had some roster moves. Their Captain Art Duncan is back and playing well on defense. They also traded Frank Frederickson to Boston, and they got Duke Keats and Frank Briden in return. These are two solid forwards, and we know that Keats can really move at Center. Frank Foyston is also back from injury and will probably be their starting winger. Holmes is in goal."

"Ching is our only regular still out. Lorne is in goal again tonight."

"We all read the papers and see the standings. Detroit is struggling and tied in last place. Do not fall into a false sense of confidence. This is essentially the same Vancouver Cougars team as last season, and they made it to the Stanley Cup playoffs. I know how good they are because I was their coach last season. We've played them twice now. They beat us 1-0 in Detroit. We skated to a 1-1 tie here at the Garden."

"Mr. Abel, can you kindly tell us how many goals we've scored against the Cougars this season?"

Taffy's mind often appeared to wonder. It seemed he could only concentrate while on the ice. Lester liked to joke 'only God knows what's going on in that cavern' and he would give Taffy these comical questions just to try and keep his attention.

"Uhm, what were the scores again boss?" Taffy sheepishly asked.

"Correct Mr. Abel. The answer is one goal. I am certain we can do better Gentleman. Harry, what have you got?"

As the season progressed Lester had been giving Harry more and more responsibility as our travel secretary.

"Tomorrow, we're getting on the 5:44pm sleeper train to Montreal. It's a good fifteen-hour ride. Eat your breakfast in the dining car as we'll go straight to the Forum and practice."

There was nothing to do now but sharpen my skates and tape my sticks. Sam was available at the sharpener, so I took my old skates over and handed them to him. I leaned against the work bench and lit up a smoke.

"The other day was swell Sam. Those kids at the orphanage seemed to know you a little. Do you volunteer there?" I asked.

"I live nearby, so I've spent time on that ice. I've gotten to know some of the kids."

"I spoke with Lester about our visit and how the kids don't have sticks or real skates. He spoke with the front office about asking the manufacturers to donate children's equipment to the orphanage. It sounds like the team may cover some of the costs if necessary. The gear may not arrive before the ice melts, but they'll have it for next winter."

"That's the bee's knees!" Sam exclaimed, genuinely excited.

He methodically placed my black Alfred leather skates into the Berghman clamps mounted to the bench and positioned the sharpening stone over my blades. He slowly slid the sharpener back and forth by hand.

"Is there a story with these skates Murray? I've noticed you seem especially attached to them. They've been repaired a few times. It looks like you replaced the steel plates and blades. You've popped a few eyelets because you've had some of them restitched and reenforced. It probably would have been cheaper and certainly easier to just replace them." Sam observed.

I liked that Sam called me Murray. He would never dream of speaking to Bill or Ching as anything other than Mr. Cook and Mr. Johnson. But he was at ease calling me Murray.

"They were a gift from my parents when I left for university." I explained. "My parents were very poor when I was growing up in Alberta. Life was hard for them. Our town, Edgerton, was typical of rural Canada. Maybe we had a couple hundred residents, one of them being my future wife. One schoolhouse. My dad Walter worked the fields from before sunrise to sunset. When he'd get home, he'd often fall asleep right after eating if not at the table itself. Mom got whatever small jobs she could, often mending clothes or helping farmers with their ledgers. Mom was always good with numbers, and I guess that's why I got my degree in Economics."

"My parents were very proud that I went to college. They had to work many hours to afford those skates. Gifts weren't in our budget and the truth is they were an old, outdated model even when they purchased them new. I suppose I'll do everything I can to keep using them until they just disintegrate."

Sam had stopped sharpening and was just listening to this. I explained, "My parents are still alive, and about once a week I've been mailing them clippings from our games."

"What about your family Sam? Do you have any siblings?" I inquire.

He leans back over the skates and brushes a fingernail up the side of one blade edge. A sliver of nail is left behind indicating this edge is ready. Sam checks each edge in several places to make certain there are no dull spots or nicks.

"No, but I'll make sure your skates are well cared for Murray."

"What about your plans Sam? You mentioned that you were going to a university next year?"

"Yeah, it looks like I may play hockey at Yale. Lester has been helping me set that up. He says that's the best way for me to mature as an American player. I hope to play professionally when I'm ready." He offered.

"I can't imagine that isn't in your future Sam. You're the most gifted skater I've ever seen. What are you going to study at Yale?" I asked.

"Don't know. Just focusing on hockey, I guess."

I'm reminded that Sam is just fifteen, and what I'm about to tell him won't be absorbed. But I give him some unsolicited wisdom anyway. Maybe it'll plant a seed.

"Sam, I hope you don't mind some advice. Just focusing on hockey would be a mistake. You need a backup plan. An injury can end my career. Heck, I can get hurt tonight and never play again. I never imagined I'd play professionally like this. It wasn't my plan. I only have a one-year contract and when this is over, I may need to return to Winnipeg with Marie. I'll have prospects because of my degree. I'm confident I'll be able to support my family. You're a bright kid Sam. In fact, you're smarter than most adults I know. If you're at Yale take advantage and get a good education. You've already proven you can suture wounds. Maybe medicine is an area you can explore."

He's finished with my skates and hands them back to me with a smile, but I sense I have touched a nerve somewhere. I thank him and head back to my stool as I pass Paul, taking his skates to be sharpened next.

I watch from a distance as Paul hands them to Sam without a word. Sam goes right to work. Sharpening them with every bit of attention he put into mine. When the first skate is finished, he hands it back for Paul to inspect.

Paul examines it carefully. Then unexpectedly I hear him compliment Sam.

"You do the best job of anyone I've ever met at sharpening my skates Sam. Thank you."

"You're welcome Mr. Thompson."

"Sam, can I ask you a question?"

"Sure."

"How do you generate that power in your stride? Were you just born with this God-given gift?"

"I assure you; God has paid little attention to my life thus far." Sam paused and continued. "But like you, I started young. Had a good teacher and had a lot of time to practice on the ice. Some of what I do is just self-taught."

I walked back towards Sam's workbench. I wanted to hear this too.

"When you push off with your skate you do two things differently than me." Sam explained. First, your skate is pushed straight back. Second, you drag your toe just a little after the push. That costs you."

Paul considered this in silence. As did I. "I understand about the toe drag. But if you don't push straight back, where are you pushing?" Paul asked the same question I would have.

Sam demonstrated with the other skate. "It's somewhat counterintuitive but I push outwards and make a crescent shaped push backwards. Then I immediately lift my back skate so there's zero drag."

"But that doesn't make sense. It would take longer to drive your legs like that, no?" Paul wondered.

"True, but the power generated is far more efficient and powerful. Honestly, I discovered it by trial and error. If you like, we can work on it together."

"I would be grateful. Call me Paul, ok?"

Seconds into the game, Bun put a powerful blast on Holmes. The goalie blocked it, but he felt that shot. Our guys are flying out there. Detroit seems flatfooted and it's not long before Bun has another strong shot that is again blocked.

The ice is tilted in our favor and our crowd is loud and excited. There were more fans here this evening and chants of "Let's go Rangers" rain down from the rafters.

Laughlin and Duncan both took separate lazy penalties, and our bread line had early advantages to put on the pressure. Although we haven't scored, Bun, Frank and Bill have already been skating hard and intensely deep in their zone.

Eight minutes into the period Lester gives them a breather and our second line jumps out. My legs feet good. I'm lining guys up and dropping them. The crowd stands and yells with each hit.

The Cougars can't get the puck to stay on their sticks and suddenly there's a loose puck. I race for it and get there before Keats. He's whacking at my stick and legs but I'm moving pretty good up ice and pull away. I get over the blueline into their zone and sense Paul coming down hard on the right side. I know where he is going be. I make solid eye contact with their goalie Holmes. Without looking I slide the puck across the ice to Paul who hammers it past Holmes at 9:11.

After their breather, and up by a goal, our first line is unrelenting. With three minutes left in the period Bunny found another gear. Racing towards the net he was pushing through their porous defense and put the puck right between their goalies' legs.

Holmes was furious. I'm not sure who he was angry at, Bunny, his swiss cheese defensemen or himself. But he put on a display of cursing and slamming his stick repeatedly against the posts.

Less than a minute later Bill Cook had penetration. He shot and Holmes blocked the first shot. But their goalie jumped out of the net to try and recover the loose puck. Bill beat him to it, but with the wide-open net and no pressure he took a couple strides and put the puck right towards the net for an easy goal.

But Holmes, in frustration intentionally flung his stick across the ice and deflected the puck before it went in. The entire arena went wild. Everyone, especially Lester, was screaming at the illegal play. All our outrage was unnecessary because referee Billy Bell was already skating to the scorer's box to record that he was assessing a penalty to the Cougars and awarding us a goal to be rightfully credited to our captain.

The second period saw no developments until nearly fifteen minutes in when Bill Cook once again came hard towards their net and at the last second passed to Frank on the opposite side. Frank made the score four to nothing and each member of our first line was now on the scoresheet with a goal.

Finally, with nearly four minutes in the final frame, Frank Foyston beat Lorne. The crowd dispersed with a 4-1 final score and Lorne, who was proving to be the superior of our two goalies, was deprived of his second consecutive shutout.

I arrived at Grand Central early, grabbed a cup of joe and a couple of papers. A few of the guys were doing the same and we found benches to sit while we waited to board. We were reading the sports sections and enjoying a butt when I noticed the front page of Bunny's paper across from me. It was just a quick flash, but I caught 'Montreal' in the bold highline. Seeing as we were boarding a train to Montreal I turned to my own front page of the Times.

"77 CHILDREN DIE IN TEN-MINUTE PANIC AS FIRE STARTS IN MONTREAL THEATRE; ALL SUFFOCATED IN JAM ON STAIRWAY."

"Oh god, hey fellas, front page."

The article was a nightmare. "Five Feet from Safety." The Times had a long list of their names. I scanned their ages. The oldest was 16, the youngest was five. Most of the girls and boys were between 7 and 11.

Bill Cook read that the theater was called the Laurier Palace and that it was located on St. Catherine Street.

"The Montreal Forum is also on St. Catherine" Lester noted somberly.

When we arrived, the city was in deep mourning. There was some discussion of canceling our game but ultimately it was decided to play. Lester asked Harry if he could quickly fashion something respectful and he tied strips of black cloth around each of our left arms.

There was a moment of silence before the game. The Maroon's were noticeably shaken and during the Anthems we stood on one blue line together. Our heads bowed. The crowd was thin.

From the puck drop we could see that the Maroon's didn't want to be on the ice. Six minutes in Doc Brown scored a solo goal. A few minutes later he scored again, this time off a strong pass from Frank. The Maroon's head coach Eddie Gerard made the unusual move of taking all his starters off the ice, except for Benedict in goal. He replaced them with the second line guys. With seconds left in the period Bill Cook had no trouble scoring untouched as he skated the full length of the ice.

During intermission Lester advised us to not let our guard down. Neither team scored in the second period, but the play was turning decidedly nasty. Noble and Taffy were both sent to the penalty box twice. The first time was for roughing and the second for fighting. Siebert, Oatman and Stewart were given timeouts for being too free with their sticks and elbows.

None of us were sure how to handle this situation. We knew the Maroon's didn't want to play and it wasn't our fault that the game wasn't rescheduled. As sportsmen we didn't want to disrespect them by running up the score while they were down, but nor were we willing to be their punching bags. The tenor resumed a more normal pace when five minutes into the three period their second line scored on Lorne.

Lorne Chabot refocused and blocked the next few shots when he came out of the net to recover a dangerous rebound. As he was dashing for the puck, he and Montreal's Dunc Munro collided hard. Lorne went down and lay motionless. Feeling it was a cheap shot, Taffy went after Munro. Referee Lou Marsh only sent Taffy to the box which angered us all.

Lester and Harry rushed onto the ice to treat Lorne, who still hadn't moved. Lester was giving Marsh an earful at the same time. Several minutes passed as Lorne was finally sitting up and slowly helped to his feet.

When play resumed, Phillips scored another goal and suddenly, with ten minutes to play the score was only 3-2 in our favor.

Lester sent our second line out to shut them down and as we were leaping over the boards, I felt his hand on my shoulder.

"Murray, you've got Stewart. White on rice." I nodded that I understood.

Their best player was Nels Stewart, and I knew they would keep feeding him the puck. He was just over six foot and at 200 pounds played an inside game. He wasn't a fast skater, but he was strong and smart. He could see the ice, anticipate the play, and position himself where he could do the most damage. He had three inches and a good 25 pounds on me. It was my job to shadow him and keep myself positioned between him and the puck. White on rice.

Boyd, Thompson, and I threw our shoulders at every maroon sweater that either had the puck, had just touched the puck or was a moment away from touching the puck. Our goal was to support Lorne and not allow quality shots on net. Our rotating defense of Abel, Brown and Mackey kept sending the puck to the other end of the ice to a steady chorus of boos.

This was a boring tactic none of us were fond of, but it would kill time and frustrate them. They would bring the puck out of their defensive zone, and we would engage and disrupt them at center ice.

We killed minutes with this strategy before Siebert gained penetration. This is when I needed to account for Stewart who I spotted racing to position himself in front of the net. Taffy would no doubt harass him from behind and I would do everything possible to prevent the puck from reaching him. The weakness would be when another player shoots on net. Unless Lorne could control it on the first shot it would lead to some sort of rebound situation and a scrum in front. This is where Stewart's size and strength was most dangerous.

This was the very plan the Maroons were now attempting to execute. Siebert passed the puck back to Kitchen who sent it across to Broadbent. Broadbent put a quick shot on net. Lorne made the save but couldn't corral the puck. Stewart was moving for the rebound and Taffy had no choice. He cross-checked Stewart and the two went down. Marsh rang the bell and sent Abel off for two minutes.

Taffy made the only play possible but now we were in bigger trouble. The Maroon's had a man advantage, and the crowd was now fully reengaged.

The ensuring face-off was in our zone to Chabot's left. Stewart went to the net, and I paired up against him as Brown, Thompson, and Boyd fended off the others. I was putting my shoulder and weight into Stewart. He would ignore me until he needed space, then he would shove me away hard.

There was a shot and rebound. This was it. I put my stick under his and lifted both off the ice a few inches. My jaw was introduced to his elbow pad, and I heard the tune of chin music. But I kept his stick away from the puck until Lorne could send it into the corner.

With this he stabbed the butt of his stick into the side of my ribs. The pain took the air out of my lungs. Broadbent reached the puck first and sent it behind the net to Siebert who was waiting. Siebert redirected the puck in front of the net.

I put my shoulder into Stewart and pumped my feet to push him off. This brought just enough time for Doc Brown to clear the puck and send it all the way to the opposition end of the ice. But as the Maroons were retreating Stewart turned, raised both hands on his stick and cross-checked me across the chest with his full weight. I went flying backwards onto the ice. He skated away. No bell from Marsh, who probably didn't see the penalty as he was following the puck. This happened behind the play.

I could hear Lorne talking to me as I lay on the ice. "Taffy is out of the box in ten seconds."

"Thank god" I said as I crawled to my hands and knees to get back on my feet while still gasping for air.

I saw Taffy come back on the ice and we were back at full strength with only two minutes and thirty seconds to play.

Again, the Maroons attacked and Paul Thompson poke-checked the puck off Seibert's stick. They had to regroup. We positioned ourselves as they came into our zone.

I skated right alongside Stewart, who by now was tired of seeing my face. He whacked me hard in the ankle with his stick. I grunted in pain. I whacked back but it hardly had any force behind it. I heard him chuckle. I could barely put weight on my skate.

Someone sent the puck his way. I deflected it with the same skate he had just bruised. I felt the shock travel up my shin bone. I spun and slapped the puck away, but it was stopped at the blue line. Their defenseman Munro was taking a long shot on net. Stan Brown stopped the shot with his stick but couldn't control it. Stewart sprung for the puck, attempting a shot at close range.

Taffy was responding but I knew he would be forced to take another penalty. Instinctively I put my stick blade around Stewart's ankle and yanked hard. He went right down.

Marsh rang the bell and called me for tripping. I limped to the box, knowing I was of no further use on the ice tonight. I gambled that a fresh Taffy Abel would hold the line for another ninety seconds.

He and the guys did. The game ended 3-2 and our record was now 11-6-1.

After the game, Lester himself handed me three bags of ice for my ankle, ribs, and jaw.

His pat on my back meant everything.

Chapter Twenty-Six
January 12 – 18, 1927

I woke in my berth, sore everywhere. I usually slept deeply on the train. Between the sound of the wheels on the rail and the steady rollicking of the cabin, I'm out like a light. But this had been an uncomfortable and restless night.

I moved quietly, careful not to wake Frank who was still in the berth above me. My feet rested on the cold floor. I liked bunking with Frank. In addition to being a swell guy, he didn't snore.

I rubbed my jaw. It was painful to the touch, but the stubble confirmed I needed a shave. Lifting the left side of my white tank top revealed the anticipated large bruise that was already multiple deep shades of purple along my ribs. Continuing my self-evaluation downward, my right ankle had another deep bruise, but the swelling wasn't nearly as bad as I expected. Rather gingerly, I stood and tested it. Tolerable was my verdict.

I have apartments to look at later today when we arrive back in Manhattan, and we play the Toronto St. Pats tomorrow night at the Garden.

Taffy scored with just over two minutes left in the first period. It was a fast-paced contest and Lorne, now in his third straight game was once again steady between the pipes. His getting his bell-rung two nights earlier seemed to leave no lasting repercussions.

Unfortunately, the same couldn't be said for Ollie who was now missing his third straight contest since trying to return. After two games of limited ice time, he confessed to Harry and Lester that his vision was blurry in the one eye. It was agreed he wouldn't dress until he was better.

Our one goal lead lasted until six minutes into the third when the Toronto winger Happy Day intercepted an ill-advised pass. He turned it around quick and made us pay for our mistake. Neither team allowed another goal for the evening. We played the rest of the third period, and two ten-minute overtime frames. The night ended 1-1.

The blizzard was the largest of the season with temperatures just above zero. The wind was harsh, and the icy snow was whipping horizontally. No doubt the city would be blanketed in a beautiful white crystal once the storm passed. But for now, this was a cold blast even by Canadian standards. Marie and the Black Hawks arrived on the same train, and they both accompanied this storm all the way from Chicago.

I met her at the station, but we didn't return to the Forrest. I had a surprise prepared.

She stepped out of the checker cab smiled at the sight of the building on 89th street.

I found a nicely furnished corner apartment five blocks east of Central Park on the 5th floor. This part of town would set me back $88 a month but I wanted to give Marie access to everything. Museums, shopping, restaurants and of course the park itself. It was larger than my room at the Forrest Hotel. Here we had a small kitchen, comfortable living room, nook for a dining table and a bedroom. Granted the bathroom was tiny but the building had its own doorman. All that mattered to me was that Marie was happy.

12,000 fans filled the Garden for our Sunday night matchup. The blue haze of smoke was as thick as I'd ever seen it. Marie was reunited with the other wives and together they were holding court and paying not a lick of attention to the game itself. As cold as it was outside, it was another warm contest inside. The pace was furious, and the Hawks came to play.

The forward lines on both teams were testing the goalies. Lorne turned away Babe Dye's line repeatedly. We broke the ice late in the period when our Bread line got into their zone with speed and precision. Frank passed to Bun on his left and Bunny immediately tapped it right back. Frank now went to his right side and Bill faked a pass back. Their goalie Lehman committed and drifted out of position just enough for our captain to take advantage and score.

Five minutes into the second period Bill Cook was called for a roughing penalty. The line of Dye, Irvin and McKay crashed our net but could not beat Lorne. Just as the two-minute penalty expired, Taffy was able to recover the puck and find space. Bill flew out of the penalty box at mid ice, behind all their players and held his stick up high. Taffy spotted him immediately and sent a beautiful pass that found its target. Bill received the puck right on his blade. The Hawk's defensive pair of Fraser and Trappe had no chance of catching Bill.

Cook raced towards the net, picked his spot, and didn't miss. The first two goals of the game belonged to Bill Cook.

Lester decided now was the time to put our second line out. Paul Thompson was noticeably improving as the season progressed. The youngest skater on our roster, he was beginning to understand his role. He was slowly recognizing the advantages of passing more during our limited ice-time.

He carried it into their zone and the defense cut down his angles. But instead of forcing the issue, he skated behind their net. As he came around the backside he looked up, surveyed the ice, and found me crashing on the left side. A few weeks early he wouldn't have looked. But now, he saw I was open and sent me the puck. My hungry stick blade was on the ice. Once I felt the puck make contact, I instantly gave a quick wrist shot. The score was now three to zero.

Lester rewarded us and left us out to play. Billy Boyd won the face off at center ice and tapped the puck forward. I happened to be heading in the right direction as Referee Marsh dropped the puck and it found my stick. I took three or four fast strides up ice. Fraser and Trappe backed up and gave me space as I entered their zone. Trappe was now moving to engage me. I took a long hard shot towards the net. Somehow, Lehman misjudged it and the red light flashed, signaling another goal. I just scored two goals, ten seconds apart. I had never done that before and was as flabbergasted as anyone in the building.

Everyone on our bench was laughing and congratulating me. Ching was especially beside himself. He hated working the bench in a suit and missed being on the ice. I was certain his laughter could be heard in the top seats. The fans were all standing and certainly enjoyed the display. I knew Marie would fib to me later and claim to have seen both goalies.

Three minutes later, Rabbit McVeigh scored the Hawk's first goal. A minute after that, Dye scored with only fourteen seconds left in the period and suddenly the score was 4-2.

Lester took control of the locker room during intermission and re-emphasized our game plan. "Settle down Gentleman and focus on playing defense. Lorne played a superior two periods in net and one of their goals was on the man advantage. We play our game for twenty more minutes."

Unfortunately, Rabbit McVeigh wasn't in our locker room listening to Lester's calming words. Rabbit wasted no time and scored 37 seconds into the third period.

We needed to stop the bleeding and Bill figured the surest way to disrupt their momentum is to reduce the ice to four-on-four skaters. Bill took back-to-back penalties but made sure that a Hawk player was also in the box. This had the desired effect and when Bill came out of the box, Bun took a turn agitating Trappe and the two went off for another two. This was working until Taffy decided to help. Apparently, Taffy didn't fully understand this strategy required a level of salesmanship to convince the referee that players on both teams needed a time-out.

Now with eleven minutes to play, the Hawks had a man advantage. Exactly the scenario we didn't want. Babe Dye went right to work and scored. The game was now 4-4.

Bill Cook and I had each scored two goals for the Rangers. McVeigh and Dye had each scored two for Chicago.

Minutes ticked off the clock and it appeared we were heading to another over-time frame at the Garden. Lester sent out our second line in the final two minutes to prevent them from scoring. Thompson, Boyd, and I had developed into a skilled line that could be counted on to shut down other teams.

But we could flip the switch when warranted.

I won the puck along the boards in our zone and looked up for a quick breakout pass. Everyone was covered. I took off as Chicago's defense was well positioned to intercept a pass. I continued to have a lane, so I picked up speed through the neutral zone. Their centerman Irvin now had me lined up and he was about to piledrive me into the boards when I spun and evaded his attack. He slammed hard, and perhaps somewhat embarrassingly into the boards. I did not stop to see if he was ok.

I was back at full speed but still had no passing options. I could see a path and I went for it. As Fraser engaged me, I put my right shoulder down and drove hard with my skates. I kept the puck on my stick using only my left hand, while my right pushed off Fraser. Just as I was getting past him, I put both hands back on my stick and shifted my focus to Lehman's position in net. He seemed enormous and I couldn't see even one square of the white netting behind him. I needed something, and I suddenly stopped hard and sprayed him in the chest with ice. It wasn't dramatic but it was just enough to put the puck through his legs. With ninety seconds left in the game I had just put us ahead with my third goal of the game!

Harry produced a case of cold beer that he kept hidden somewhere for special occasions as we celebrated our victory. Lester called for everyone's attention. "Gentlemen, Mr. Murdoch has now given our loyal followers two dramatic game-winning goals here at the Garden this season." The team clapped and hollered. Dark brown bottles of beer were handed out and passed around.

Lester continued "Mr. Westerby, were you able to recover the memento as I requested?"

"Sam has it, Mr. Patrick." Harry beamed.

"Excellent, Sam would you be so kind? I will also need a roll of white hockey tape and pen."

Sam, at the ready, produced both. He also had the puck from the winning shot.

We all watched, almost in a hypnotic trance, as Lester carefully wrapped a strip of white tape around the circumference of the black puck and wrote on it with the pen.

He worked in deep concentration, and it was mesmerizing. The room was silent.

"So" he began, "in recognition, I present this to our Mr. Murdoch." He walked over to my stool. I stood.

"You can see on this game puck, which Sam was thoughtful enough to collect from referee Marsh as the game ended, I have written 'First Ranger player to score three goals in a single game. Murray Murdoch, January 16, 1927. Madison Sq. Garden.'"

As the celebration died down, we showered, dressed, and filed out. As I was leaving, I noticed Lester pull Hal Winkler aside. They went into his office and closed the door.

Lester informed us at our practice the next day, but several of us had already read the small Associated Press blurb reported in the papers.

Boston Six Buys Winkler

Boston, Jan 17 (AP) – Hal Winkler, goalie of the New York Rangers National League Hockey team, has been purchased outright by President Charles Adams of the Boston Bruins and will don a Boston uniform against his old team in the Bruins-Rangers game here tomorrow night.

The hockey gods love irony. Officially now our goalie, Lorne Chabot played his worst game of the year against Hal, in his new Bruins sweater. Boston beat us 7-3 in Bean town. Just to remind me that three goals in a game isn't anything to brag about, the Bruin's star center Frank Fredrickson scored four.

Chapter Twenty-Seven
January 20, 1927

Two nights later we walked into our locker room at the Garden and found a black cat with a white spot on its face.

"What's a cat doing in here?" Raffles asked as he bent down to pet it.

"I found her outside. She lives here now." Harry explained as he was folding towels.

"Actually, I'm allergic to cats." Thompson protested.

"Too bad. Her name is Ranger." Harry stated matter of fact.

Now on our home ice, the Bruins attempted to pick up where they left off two nights earlier. Frederickson, Oliver, and Galbraith kept up a fierce attack and had great success getting past Abel and Brown, but Chabot held the line this time.

Lorne was incredibly upset with himself after the last game, especially as we were facing Hal Winkler. Lorne wanted to reassure Lester that the right goalie was awarded the job.

Ching's absence could be hidden for only so long. Dr. Brown was a tremendous find and had been filling in superbly. Abel shouldered much of the physical demands vacated by Ching's long injury, but the burden was physically draining. Mackey was giving his best in support. But none of the three had the same impact as Ching Johnson.

Lester criticized the forwards for not backchecking hard enough. His expectations were the highest in the league and no team backchecked like the Rangers. We were solidly in first place in the American division and if we wanted to remain there, we knew both forward lines needed to play stronger defense.

But our agreeing with Lester was not the same as executing it on the ice.

Our nemesis Eddie Shore carried the puck up the boards. Bunny didn't pursue him hard enough. Shore put a couple quick moves on Abel, but Brown cut down his angle so the Bruins defenseman evaded traffic and skated behind the net. Neither Brown nor Abel could respond fast enough, and Shore had all the speed he needed to score on a wraparound goal five minutes into the game.

Nearly seven minutes into the second period Herb Oliver beat Chabot to run the score 2-0. We had only around 7,000 fans on the cold, damp Thursday night and they drew increasingly quiet. The usual energy in the Garden was dissipating fast.

Besides a healthy Ching, no one could get a crowd riled up like Eddie Shore. Everyone in the Garden knew he played with a particular ferociousness. In the second period he found another scoring opportunity, but it turned into something ugly. To anyone with eyes, Shore blatantly shot the puck at Lorne's unprotected face.

The puck caught him square on the chin. Keeping his wits, Lorne covered the puck and prevented a goal even before the blood started flowing. From the bench we could see where the puck hit him, and watched as this skin opened and blood slowly made its appearance. With play stopped he calmly skated right to the bench. Harry put a towel on the cut and wiped it for a clean look.

"It'll need stitches." He told Lester and tonight's ref Billy O'Hara.

The two, and Sam, went back to the locker room and returned not fifteen minutes later. Lorne's stitches were evident, and he refused to put a bandage over them. He felt the white square would only encourage Shore to take target practice.

In the meantime, Shore did himself and his Bruins no favors. The Garden crowd roared to life and Shore was lucky to be on this side of the chicken wire fencing. A few fans behind the visitor's bench threw objects at him and more than a few patrons offered to meet him in the alleyway after the game. But we needed to play this game, and that meant we had him all to ourselves.

Lester sent our second line out as the game resumed after the medical break.

Pee Wee Oliver and I took our ready positions next to each and waited for the puck to drop. He leaned over and asked, "is that cat hair all over your sweater?"

The crowd went into a tizzy every time a Ranger hit Shore. There was no denying, Shore was a tough S.O.B. Ever since our first game against Boston, Eddie and I seemed to have a personal animosity that ran deep. Now I had every opportunity and incentive to shadow him.

Meanwhile, Lorne went back to work and squared up. He was blocking everything, and the crowd thundered its appreciation.

The game was getting late into the third period, and we were still down two goals. Billy Boyd carried the puck into their zone and feed a pass to Paul. We crashed the net together. Our former mate, Hal stopped Paul's first shot and Billy found a rebound that was also stopped. This was now a prolonged scrum in front of Winkler. It was not only an excellent scoring opportunity, but it also allowed us to corner Shore in close quarters. We were all whacking at the loose puck. Shore strode for the puck, and I stood him up just as I kicked the puck back towards Paul. My balance wasn't strong. Shore shoved me hard down to the ice. I got right back into the action and positioned my leg behind his and using my arm flipped him backwards. He landed hard on his back, and he swung his stick at my ribs. He connected with my still healing memento from Montreal.

The puck bounced out towards Taffy. With bodies all over the ice, and others pushing and shoving in front of the net, Abel stopped the puck, paused, and took a hard shot that was lifted just enough to find the back of the net. As we celebrated the goal Taffy whispered to me "I was aiming for Shore. If I missed him, I figured I'd score. A win either way."

Still down by one goal Lester sent the first line back out. The Garden faithful screamed with every shot we put on net. Suddenly, Dr. Brown found the puck and started his attack run. But Shore had him in his sights and lined him up. We yelled helplessly. From the bench we watched as Shore took a run at Stan and put his shoulder into him. Stan never saw him coming and went flying hard into the boards. His body was rolling on the ice in obvious agony. Abel immediately started to go after Shore, but Bill Cook intervened as Bunny went after Shore instead. The Cooks both knew we couldn't afford to lose another defenseman at this critical moment. The game was again stopped as Stan gasped for air and was eventually helped off the ice. He was badly shaken and dizzy.

Shore and Bun were both sent to the box for two minutes for fighting.

It took us until we were deep in the third period to finally get going and we were now dominating and controlling the action. But the clock was ticking, and we had only two minutes left.

Frank started the play with a poke check that Bill Cook scooped up. Bill attacked, found open ice, and saw Frank now coming hard down the ice. Bill put a quick fake move on Shore, got around him and hit

Frank in stride. Frank immediately let the puck fly and tied the score with only a minute thirty left in the game.

The crowd was now overjoyed. A fan threw his hat onto the ice. Another followed. Now a storm of hats and paper were raining down from the rafters. The crowd loved that we not only tied the score, but that Bill beat Eddie Shore to get the puck to Frank.

It took a while for the Garden crew to clear the ice. We played two over-time periods and neither team could score. But our fans went home happy, if hatless.

Although the game was over much later than usual, several of us first helped Stan Brown, who was not feeling well at all, back to his room at the Forrest across the street. Once he was settled, we met the others and our wives back at the Green Door for a late, late-night capper.

Lorne was already at the bar and chatting with several of the local reporters from the Tribune, the Herald, the Sun, the News and Times. Now he had a small white bandage taped on his square chin to cover the stitches.

For many weeks Lorne expressed to these same reporters how annoyed he was at Bruno and Blythe's ruse. Changing his name, and Ollie's, to attract more ticket sales was ridiculous. Lester complained too, but only took the fight so far. Lester was uncomfortable with the whole situation but didn't want to interfere with how the company ran its business operations any more than he wanted the company to interfere with how he ran the team hockey operations.

All season Lorne kept his distance from the reporters as they were obviously taking their orders from the Garden's publicity men. They knew it was a stupid ploy, but the papers needed the Garden and access to sell papers. But the landscape was changing. The Rangers were in first place, ticket sales were strong and surpassing their rival Americans for the heart of New York. With out-of-town papers accurately filing articles that were printed in the New York papers using Chabot for away games, it was beyond awkward that for home games those same papers claimed his name as either Shabotsky or Chabotsky.

With Winkler now in Boston, Lorne was our only goalie. Game after game, players and reporters ended up at the same bar. While the reporters were always working and hoping for a good quote, friendships had started to form. Reporters grew to respect the players rapidly and the whole charade was getting too personal.

It was especially ugly during the last Rangers vs. Amerks game, and our two teams were scheduled to face off again in three nights. We all noticed the box score and articles the next day used Chabot. This silliness was finally past.

Chapter Twenty-Eight
January 23 - 24, 1927

I had never seen the Garden so packed. Every seat was sold, and we were told that thousands waited in the sleet for the chance to find standing room inside. There must be over 18,000 fans tonight for our second game against the American's. This time we were the home team. The papers had heavily promoted the game as a family affair. Brothers Bill and Bun Cook would be facing the Green brothers, Red and Shorty.

When we last played the Americans, the day after Christmas nearly a month ago, they beat us 5-2. In the time since, we certainly had the better record. But our defense is now in shambles. Abel and Mackey were our only two healthy players to guard the blueline. Ching has missed six weeks while his collarbone heals. Stan has been more than a swell find, but he's now shaken. He'll lace up tonight, but we all know that he's not right since bring steamrolled by Shore.

Ching is close to returning to practice, but he can't help us today. Lester asked Frank to emphasize his poke-checking talents and the wings to back-check deeper than usual. Our patchwork defense puts more pressure on Lorne, but he seems eager to shoulder the burden.

I watched Bill Cook huddle up with Frank and Bun in the moments before the game started. From the moment Lou Marsh, our frequent Garden ref, dropped the puck Bill sprinted forward and cut across the ice. Frank won the face-off and popped the puck forward right where Bill was headed. Bill could really turn on the speed and he did so now. As Bill and his brother crisscrossed, and Bun was now coming up the right side. Bill got behind Conacher on defense and took a quick, hard shot. Forbes blocked it, but the rebound came right out to the crashing Bun Cook who buried the puck nine seconds into the game. Just as Bill drew it up.

Our Captain was a firm believer that we could play a better defensive game when we had a lead. He made sure it happened on the opening drive.

The goal had another unforeseen advantage. The Americans had been in New York a full year before us and should have built up a strong following. The crowd in the first game was decidedly mixed. But not tonight. The raucous celebration was wildly in our favor and sent a clear message to our rivals. This is our house. This is our city now.

Every player on our team was contributing to the defensive game. Taffy was thrilling the crowd with solid hits and cutting down angles. He was probably playing his best game of the season. Likewise, Frank was playing a selfless defensive game and shutting down the advancing Americans long before getting in shooting range. He was like having a third defenseman. But both squads were playing at a fierce pace and the Americans were still getting plenty of shots. Lorne stopped them all and was covering rebounds. At 6'1" Lorne filled a big portion of the net. These last few weeks Lorne was finding his groove. Opponents couldn't find openings or weak spots. He was taking over the ice.

Nine minutes into the second period, Taffy had the puck and decided to go for a stroll. He simply isn't our fastest, nor fanciest skater. But he's a big guy with good hands. He skated up the length of the ice, keeping his body between the Americans and the puck. Finally, from thirty feet out he took a rip and Forbes failed to block the shot. Another goal.

In the closing minutes the Americans pressed hard, but Lorne stood firm. The Garden crowd started chanting "Chabot, Chabot, Chabot" after every impressive save. The whole team appreciated the irony. The game ended 2-0.

Marie was enjoying a martini after the game, and she raised her voice so I could hear her over the club's music.

"I think you could have a new rival heartthrob on the team." She waited for me to light her cigarette before explaining further, no doubt amusing herself at my confused expression.

She nodded across the room where Lorne could be seen laughing with Bill and Bunny. Mikey was pouring him a drink from behind the bar.

"I've rarely seen Lorne without, well, a dour expression." She explained and I knew she was right. Lorne often looked sad. This just seemed to be his natural expression and because he was frequently aloof from the team, as goalies often are, he went somewhat unnoticed. But tonight, hearing his name being chanted, he couldn't help but crack a wide smile. Marie was right, it was a whole different look for him.

Marie went on teasing me, "With that stylishly full head of black hair, those dark eyes, that solid frame. Gosh, add a smile to that square jaw and he's suddenly a movie star. You better step up your game Mr. Murdoch or you might lose your spot as the team heartthrob".

"Stop it. I am hardly a heartthrob. I'm sure Paul is the most handsome guy on the team, by far." I protested playfully.

"He also knows he's good-looking. Murray, you play on a hockey team. You guys are hardly easy on the eyes. I just said your goalie, the guy who gets hit in the face with the puck, is surprisingly fetching when he smiles. It's all relative so accept the compliment. Besides, all the other wives agree with me. Come on handsome, it's time for us to go home." She added with a sly smile.

Walking arm and arm to the subway I shared my concern for Taffy.

"I don't know how to describe it, except that he has these bouts with some internal struggle. I don't know what to do for him, or even if I should."

"Well, why shouldn't you try?" Marie asked.

"It seems to be something personal. Some deep…guilt. What if he tells me something I can't unhear? What if he confesses that he's done something horrible to another person? A terrible crime perhaps. What do I do then?" I asked.

Marie stopped walking and looked me square. "Mr. Murdoch, Taffy is your teammate and your friend. You haven't known him long but in a sense you're brothers in arms. If he is struggling, do for him what you'd hope someone would do for you or me."

I had just washed up after our practice skate on Monday. I was adjusting my tie and combed my hair when Lester called for me from his office.

I entered to find Lester behind his desk, flanked by Ching in a suit. Bill Cook and Frank Boucher, were freshly dressed and standing to the side. These were our team leaders, and the sober mood filed me with dread. They seemed to be having a deep conversation. "Mr. Murdoch, please close the door." Lester asked.

Something about his tone caused an instant pit in my stomach. Oh gosh, am I being cut? My heart raced. No, no way. I'm working so hard. I love this too much. Am I being traded? How do I tell Marie?

He leaned forward and rested his elbows on his desk. He motioned me to sit in the empty chair. He began, "We have a tough decision to make. The team is playing strong and we're in first place in our division. We're heading for the playoffs, which are a completely different game, and this team doesn't yet have the experience needed. Our defense is thin. We all know this, and our opponents know this. Ching will soon return to practice. He might even be ready to return before the season ends." Lester somberly offered.

Ching now spoke "but even when I get back in the lineup. My shoulder isn't going to be ready to play my physical style. I'm going to be a paper tiger. They may be intimidated by my presence at first. But they will be watching and testing me. Teams will figure out that I can't hit like before."

Lester continued "I've been searching for another defenseman. They are not easy to find as you might imagine. We were very fortunate with Stan Brown, but he has not been the same since that hit by Eddie Shore. I've spoken with Toronto about a kid named Leo Bourgault they have sitting on their bench. He just turned 23, he's from Sturgeon Falls. He's scrappy but not a large intimidating fellow. He doesn't get much ice time with the Saint Pats and he's being wasted there. He plays a solid defensive game like Brown but without the scoring.

My heart sank, they want to trade me to Toronto for this guy, I thought.

"Murray" Lester ask.

"Oh gosh, he just called me Murray! He never does that.

"We've asked you in here because we think you're a bright young man with good judgement. So, we want to ask you. Do you think Ollie will be able to recover and contribute? If I purchase this kid Leo's contract, I will need a roster spot once Mr. Johnson returns to the ice."

"Wait, you aren't trading me?" I blurted out.

They glanced at each other and laughed.

Bill spoke up. "No, Murray, you aren't being traded. We're asking for your opinion. We all like Ollie and he has experience we need down the stretch. But you skate with him often in practice. Can he make it back? A simple yes or no is all we need."

I suddenly realized the gravity of the question. I was being asked if one of my teammates, a friend, should be cut to make room for another player we were desperate to add. A lot of thoughts flashed all at once about Ollie, most prominently the unfairness of his plight. Ollie and I were often paired up against each other in practice. Sweet guy, and not a negative bone in his body. But his vision was deeply compromised and showed no sign of improving soon. I was often skating around him with ease, and he missed a lot of passes. There was only one answer.

I met Lester's eyes. "No, he won't. We need help on defense. Buy the rights to this kid and when Ching is ready to return, it would make sense to release Ollie."

Lester allowed for a thoughtful pause. "Thank you, Mr. Murdoch. You may yet make a fine head coach when your playing days are done, hopefully many years from now."

With that, the meeting ended.

Marie and I hosted our first dinner at the new apartment. We invited the Johnsons. Ellen and Ching are always up for a fun evening. To my surprise Marie also invited Sam. She wanted to thank him for stepping up and protecting her and the other ladies.

A few days ago, Marie spotted Sam outside the Garden coming from the direction of the Forrest Hotel. He had probably been running

Harry's bet for the next horse race somewhere down south.

When she extended the dinner invitation, she was utterly charmed by his reaction. It seemed that he had never imagined being invited to a real dinner with adults. He accepted and asked one question.

"Can I bring a date?"

Marie spent days preparing and reading recipes and articles. She took the evening very seriously and wanted it to be memorable.

Ching and Ellen arrived first. Marie gave them a quick tour as I made gin and tonics. Our music collection was a modest three albums, recently purchased, and the phonograph that was furnished with the apartment was our first. We were enjoying our smokes when the bell rang. Marie got up to answer it.

Sam stood in the doorway, dressed in his usual attire but cleaned up nice. His shirt, usually hanging out from beneath his vest was tucked in. His collar buttoned to the top. His hair was neatly combed, and he held a bouquet of flowers for Marie.

Ching, Ellen, and I stood to greet him. His date entered first. I could feel Ching giving me a quick elbow. It was Big Bill Dyer's daughter. We knew her from our time at the Forrest.

Behind them, in the hall was a "chaperone". He made sure we saw him standing in the background in his double-breasted dark suit and fedora. His coat was neatly slung over his arm. Marie asked him if he preferred to come inside but stated he would wait outside the door.

Oh Sam, what have you gotten yourself into I thought.

I strode over and welcomed them both.

"Elizabeth, it's a delight to see you again.

I never saw Sam so excited to eat. Marie made a special dish called Linguine alle Vongole. We knew next to nothing about Sam's family but clearly, he had never eaten anything in a garlic and oil sauce in his life. Nor had he ever eaten clams.

His eyes were as big as saucers, and he leaned over his plate trying to manipulate the pasta from his dish to his mouth. He was twilling it on his fork, and it kept falling off. As the conversation turned to shopping, a topic that occupied Elizabeth and our gals attention, I silently gave Sam a subtle nudge. I showed him how, using my large spoon against the end of the fork I could better control the pasta.

It was a trick an old man once taught me while at university when Marie and I were dating. I was slurping up the spaghetti, probably getting sauce all over my shirt, when I heard a light taping from the table across from me. It was an old man, eating with his wife. He performed the same, silent, tutorial I now passed on to Sam. Sam immediately picked up on my cue.

Sam was fascinated to find a bowl Marie set on the table specifically for our empty clam shells. He was keeping track of how many we each deposited there. But when Marie offered him a second, and a third helping he immediately accepted and relished every bite. Dipping every morsal of sauce up with his bread.

Elizabeth was a delight. She spoke of Sam's thoughtfulness. The night of our game against her father's team she was sick in bed. Her parents were in the Garden but as soon as the game ended Sam rushed over to the hotel and left a bowl of chicken noodle soup from the corner diner at the front desk for her. It was on his way back to the Garden he discovered the punks harassing Marie, Ellen, and the other gals.

Marie and Ellen made it a point to offer their unwavering gratitude to Sam for his chivalry and bravery.

Despite my initial concern of having a mobster standing outside our door and what the neighbors might think, it was a beautiful evening.

Chapter Twenty-Nine
February 6 -9, 1927

Four months into the season we all developed routines. On Sunday mornings, Marie and I loved to stay in bed. Eventually one of us would get around to making coffee, and breakfast. We'd read the papers together. She had taken over the clipping duties for our weekly letter to my parents.

In the two weeks since our win against the Americans, we played three games. The headlines told the story.

Montreal, January 28, 1927

Rangers Six Beat Canadiens, 3-2

Goal by Bill Cook in 3d Period Wins for New Yorkers Before 9,500 in Montreal.

This was the new kid, Bourgault's first game for us and he proudly went right to work and earned the first penalty of the game for roughing.

WINDSOR, Ontario, January 29, 1927

Boyd's Two Goals Win for Rangers, Beat Detroit Cougars.

Chabot in Fine Form, Allows No Goals.

New York February 1, 1927

Ranger Six Here Tonight

The New York Rangers, fresh off two road wins will meet the Canadiens at Madison Square Garden. Ching Johnson, star defense man, whose collarbone was broken over six weeks ago engaged in a full skate with the team yesterday. He may get into the lineup tonight.

Ching did practice with us, but he did not play in the game. He and Lester decided to wait a few more days.

New York, February 2, 1927

Rangers Downed in OT Game Lose 1-0.

Defensive Masterpiece. Chabot stops 52 shots.

And today's highline.

New York, February 6, 1927

Rangers Play Pittsburgh Tonight

Johnson To See Action

It was against the Pirates that Ching broke his collar bone and Ollie's eye was damaged. I was excited to play tonight. I think we all were. It was time for a little payback.

I emerged from the subway station at 50th street and 8th Ave and spotted Taffy heading into the diner for a pregame meal. I looked at my watch and had plenty of time.

"Hey Taffy, mind some company?" I asked as I approached his booth.

We ordered our usual lite fare and coffees.

"How are your mom and sister back in Michigan? Any chance

they will come to New York?" I asked.

"They are ok. But no, I don't see them making it here."

"I know you've been struggling at times, and I have no idea why. It's not my business, but I'm told it sometimes helps just to talk. You can tell me anything. You have my word; I will never share anything you say to me in confidence. Not even with Marie."

Taffy listened and stirred his coffee. His metal spoon clinking along the ceramic cup.

"It means more than you can know Murray. I appreciate the offer. Bill and Ching have both said similar. Murray, it's not anything I can talk about. Not now, maybe not ever. You're gonna have to take my word for that."

Ching arrived to lace up for his first game in seven weeks. The normal locker room chatter made the space feel alive. Taffy was petting a purring Ranger in the locker next to Ching's. We were all focused on our pregame routine.

But that was just a cover.

Ching pulled off his suit jacket and hung it up.

Only the hook and jacket fell of the wall.

He went to sit down on his stool.

Only to find it was three inches lower than he remembered.

He landed with a soft thud on his backside.

"Ha! Someone cut the legs down, cute. Very funny."

Everyone in the room went about their business.

He continued to dress.

Ching pulled his skate onto his foot and rolled his eyes.

He cracked a smile and slowly pulled it back off. His foot was covered in whipped cream.

"Ok, one of you wise guys got me again. I know it was you Murdoch."

The room still went about its business just as I went about putting on my own gear.

"Oh, so there's more is there? Not just the one skate?" Ching was now checking inside the other skate, only to find it dry.

He pulled it on and tightened it up.

As he pulled both ends of the laces they snapped. The room erupted in laughter.

He dropped his head and chuckled.

Sam walked over and handed him a new lace.

I walked over and leaned down behind him and whispered "better check the bottom of your skates for tape too. Welcome back big man. We've missed you."

The payback was just starting.

Thirty minutes before gametime I grabbed tape off my locker shelf and realized I needed a fresh roll. I headed to the storage room and found Sam sharpening a pair of skates.

"Hey Sam, how's tricks?"

"The bee's knees sir."

He didn't fool me. "Is something wrong Sam?"

He stopped sharpening. "Elizabeth's a real tomato Murray. I'm not in her class."

“Are her parents giving you a hard time? I asked.

“No, not exactly, they are very protective of her, and we don’t go anywhere without an escort. But I haven’t been exposed to the…worldly stuff she has. She’s traveled. She’s eaten at fancy restaurants. She has nice outfits. I’ve never seen her wear the same dress more than twice. I only have two sets of clothes Murray. I’m not in her class. She deserves better.”

“Sam, there is one better. If the class differences are a problem for her let that be her decision. Don’t take yourself out of the game. If she likes you, like you like her, she’ll work through those differences. Just don’t ruffle her father.”

Lester started Abel and Brown. Reg Mackey was a healthy scratch and given the night off. He was dressed in a suit and helping on the bench to coach the defensive squad much as Ching had been doing these last couple months.

Ching Johnson and Leo Bourgault were paired together and would form a second defensive line. It was expected that Ching would see limited action and ease his way back.

Bun, Frankie, and Bill started the game and there was aggressive play on both ends of the ice, but thus far no stoppage in play. Bill sent a breakout pass to Bun who broke free and skated up ice. The crowd of 14,000 rose in excitement. Bun slowed as he approached the Pirates net. He was bobbing and weaving, looking for an open hole and trying to get Worters to commit. When none of that produced a result, he shot anyway. Unfortunately, he shot the puck right into Worters’ breadbasket and it would’ve been the easiest block of the night. Worters didn’t have to move or even raise his glove. The crowd roared at the lost opportunity. Bun veered off, cursing himself at the lost chance. The puck dropped to the ice, and everyone expected Worters to stick it away or pass it to one of his own players.

But he somehow lost sight of the puck and frantically started looking around for it, even though it was right by his skate. It was in a blind spot, an anxious feeling every hockey player experiences.

I held my breath. His own skate tapped it behind him, and he caught a glimpse of it sliding behind him. He flung his body around and reached with his gloved hand, but it was too late. Lou Marsh was right there, and the red light signaled a goal.

Bun stood there watching as all this happened ten feet in front of him. He looked to us on the bench and shrugged his shoulders, proud of himself in that adorable way Bunny could make you laugh.

The first line came to the bench. Sam and Bunny had a good chuckle at the fluke goal. Lester sent our second line out for the faceoff, and I could hear Lester yell his familiar "Let's go boys, let's go."

For the next two minutes I hit everyone in a Pirates sweater. I rode Ty Arbour into the boards as he tried to advance the puck up the side. I put my shoulder into Hib Milks as we raced each other for the puck. I knocked the wind out of Johnny McKinnon when he tried to skate with his head down.

I wasn't the only Ranger having fun.

Taffy put his shoulder into a hard check on Harold Darragh and Boyd found another opportunity to pound Arbour. The Ranger's faithful fans had not forgotten that game here at the Garden before Christmas when Ching was injured, and Ollie's eye was cut. They roared and leaped to their feet with each clean hit.

The Pirates Ty Arbour advanced the puck, barely avoiding Boyd and made it into our zone. Just as Taffy laid him out, Arbour passed the puck to the rushing defenseman McKinnon. Doc Brown had him lined up, but Doc seemed to pull up at the last moment and just swept his stick at the puck. The contact was ineffective.

I was already racing to support and cut off McKinnon's path, but I was too late. His shot beat Lorne on the stick side and the score was tied.

Lester used this opportunity, halfway into the first period to make another change. He sent out Ching to give Brown a rest. It was obvious to all of us that Stan was hesitant to make physical contact.

The crowd once again had another reason to stand and cheer.

The thunder and reverberation throughout the Garden were like nothing I ever felt or heard. As Ching sprinted out to his position for the faceoff our eyes caught, and I could see his emotion. The man hadn't played in nearly two months and recently, after a few drinks, he predicted the crowd wouldn't make much notice of his return. I told him he was wrong and now the deafening proof was raining down on him. He flashed that menacing smile of his and somehow the crowd got louder still.

I skated over to referee Marsh and asked him a silly question just so Ching could bask in the adoration for a few moments more.

Marsh understood and he and I discussed the proper season for growing blueberries for a bit.

Game on.

Boyd won the faceoff back to Taffy. Taffy instantly sent it across to Ching who decided to test his legs. He went right into their zone and shot. He missed the net, but the crowd didn't care.

A few minutes later the Pirates were staging an attack. Ching found a target and started to mix it up. They traded blows and Marsh sent them both to the box. Just as the penalty ended, Ching jumped on the ice and the puck quickly found him. Another rush and again he missed the net just as the first period came to an end. But it was obvious to all, Ching was the still the dominating force on the ice.

Six minutes into the second period, Raffles executed his trademarked poke-check and took the puck away from Hib Milks. Frank recovered the loose puck and spun to avoid a McKinnon hit. He then outraced the remaining defenseman and gently swept the puck past Worters to score.

With a 2-1 lead we went into our defensive mood. Lester was rotating the pairs of Abel and Brown for Johnson and Bourgeault every few minutes to keep them all fresh. Chabot was still seeing shots but nothing he couldn't handle. Our second line saw plenty of action and we earned our paycheck as the checking line. The Pirates left the Garden feeling especially manhandled as the final bell rung.

In the locker room after the game, as we celebrated a good win, Harry and Sam tended to Ching. He needed ice for his shoulder. The pain and discomfort were as bad as feared. During the excitement of the game, with adrenaline flowing, Ching could land the blows. But after the game? He was in pain. We knew this wasn't workable. Stan Brown also wasn't right. That hit he took from Shore was nearly two weeks ago, and he still complained of headaches and sluggishness. We've all seen a dramatic change in his game. He's trying to play technical and cut down angles. He's poke-checking. But he's not playing physical and hitting bodies like he had been. He's avoiding physical contact, and he hasn't scored once since the hit. We need the new guy Leo to step up. Lorne and Taffy are continuing to carry the team defensively.

Chapter Thirty

February 1994

The kids have now formed one large hockey game. There must two dozen kids, teens and even a couple of dads chasing the puck. The chance to play in front of Mark is too great a temptation. He and I are floating around the center of the game, occasionally snatching a pass, and sending it to the kids who aren't fast or strong enough to win the puck on their own.

I imagine these kids will not forget this afternoon.

"Did Taffy ever tell you his secret?" Mark asked just as he skated a few strides and redirected the puck to a young boy.

"Not directly, no, but I did learn it. True to his word, he never spoke of it to anyone in the league or any teammates. It must have been a terrible burden, not being true to himself for so many years. But he was right, the league and society were not ready. At best, it would have been the end of his career. At worst, he would have been in real physical danger."

I certainly have Mark's full attention now.

I continued, "Only after his mother's funeral in 1939, some five years after his final season of playing, he spoke to the local reporter in Michigan. Taffy announced he was Native America."

Mark's expression is shock. The implications quickly being calculated.

"You're telling me, that Taffy Abel was the first to break the NHL's color barrier?"

"Perhaps, we can't prove that he was the first, but it seems likely.

What we do know for a fact is that Taffy was the first Indigenous Olympic hockey player and flagbearer for the United States in 1924. We know for certain that Taffy was the first Native America to play for the New York Rangers."

"Why isn't he considered the first in the NHL?" Mark asks. "What about Willie O'Ree and Fred Sasakamoose?"

"Sasakamoose was certainly the first Native Canadian with treaty status to be recognized in 1953. Willie O'Ree was the first black to break the color barrier in 1958."

"Taffy hid his identity from nearly everyone his whole life. It seems extremely likely that Taffy was secretly the first in 1926. But it's possible others hid their identity for the same reasons. To be recognized as an Indian in the early 1900's was a dead end. Remember, this is many years before Jackie Robinson broke the color barrier in 1947 with the Brooklyn Dodgers. Jim Thorpe, two-time Olympic gold medalist and professional athlete was the exception, not the rule."

"Taffy's dad was white and a traveling lumber salesman. But his mother was full Canadian Chippewa. They were married in the United States and Taffy and his sister were both born in Michigan, as US citizens. They raised their kids in Sault Ste. Marie and passed them off as white. To do otherwise would have meant the kids would have been taken and sent to brutal boarding schools that would have forcibly assimilated them to white culture."

"His dad died when Taffy was twenty. He had to support his mother and sister. Taffy had no choice but to continually hide his heritage. Otherwise, he would not have been chosen for the US Olympic squad. Connie Smythe would not have signed him to a contract. If he acknowledged his heritage while he was playing, someone in the league office would have forced him out of the league. Lester would have supported Taffy, but I don't know how the front office would have reacted. I know there were racist players on other teams that would have hurt him. At some point, a spectator would have attacked him outside the rink."

"Taffy didn't want to live with that fear. Nor did he want to live a lie. But he had a family to protect and support. He had eight productive years in the NHL and played the last few years in Chicago. When he retired from hockey, he operated a tourist hotel called 'Taffy's lodge' back home. The depression became worse, and he turned to drinking to cope. He kept the secret."

"At 38, upon his mother's passing, he finally embraced his legacy and spoke to the reporter."

"We had been seeing each other regularly. First when he was playing with the Chicago Blackhawks and we were opponents. Later, the Rangers would bring us back for reunions and ceremonies at the Garden. At one Ranger event, with prohibition now long over, and Taffy being free, we sat together in a bar with windows. Taffy explained he was never comfortable asking other minorities to carry his bags, shin his shoes, or fold his sheets in hotel rooms."

"The league wanted nothing to do with the announcement and ignored it for decades. Even retrospectively, they made no effort to recognize Taffy. He was invited to fewer, and fewer functions. He lived to the age of 64. He died in Sault Ste. Marie, on the American side."

"Honestly, I didn't know this." Mark confessed. "How is that possible? Taffy Abel won two Stanley Cups and an Olympic Silver Medal. How has history forgotten?"

Chapter Thirty-One
February 9 – 17, 1927

We gathered at Grand Central for the start of our three-game road trip that would take nearly a week. We scratched our heads at the league schedule maker. We were heading to Toronto for a game tomorrow. Then to Pittsburgh for a Saturday match-up and inexplicably, we would then have to pass right back through Toronto for a game in Ottawa on Wednesday. But the backtracking bickering was quickly replaced with a new and unexpected distraction.

A most disappointing distraction. Every one of us understands the importance of promptly arriving and catching the train. All professional sports teams have two unbreakable rules. Never gamble on your sport, and never be late. Arrive hours early if you must. But never be late and never miss a train. These are unforgivable sins. The kind of sin that gets a person traded or fired.

The train won't wait if one of us is running late. Our gear was loaded, and everyone arrived on time.

But Sam wasn't here.

Lester calmly read his newspaper and would occasionally lift his eyes to catch the time on the large wall clock. The minutes ticking away. He and Harry had huddled thirty minutes earlier, and Harry sent word to the front office at the Garden. The reply came back that there was no word from Sam.

The conductor announced the final boarding call.

Lester folded his paper and without saying a word got up and walked to the train. We followed. The train pulled out, without Sam

Crawford.

Toronto was without their starting center and leading goal scorer, Bill Carson. But eleven minutes into the game their young winger Butch Keeling put a hard shot on Chabot. Lorne made a spectacular save and deserved a better outcome, but the rebound went right to defenseman Bert McCaffrey's stick. Lorne never had a chance.

Two minutes later Bill Brydge simply poked the puck past our goalie during a scrum in front of the net. The puck had been bouncing around in heavy, tight traffic and everyone was swatting at it.

We went into the locker room down by two. Lester and Bill implored us to tighten up our play defensively and the goals would come.

My line started the second period with this strategy in mind. For the next several minutes the St. Pats didn't get a single shot on net, whereas we had the puck down their end of the ice and kept the pressure on their goalie John Roach.

Leo Bourgault was getting plenty of ice time in this period against his former mates and making the case their coach Charles Querrie committed a mistake in selling him to Lester. Leo was easy to like and immediately fit in.

He was a true sportsman and shared our love of fishing. He also had passion for hunting and golf. Being from Sturgeon Falls near the North Bay and Lake Nipissing meant he was from wilderness country. Physically, he was chiseled without an ounce of fat. Hunting moose and cutting pulp wood while living in a tent during the off-season will do that, I imagined.

Leo went right after their best player Ace Bailey. They dropped their gloves and after a few fisticuffs went to the box.

We heard from the local press our old 'friend' Conn Smythe was making a play to become the owner of the St. Pats. We saw him sitting behind Toronto's bench at the start of the game and while I found his presence irksome a few of us also felt some appreciation for his bringing our team together. Our attempt to say hello and wish him well was barely acknowledged.

That we were losing in front of him now seemed to provide us with an added spark. Taffy, Leo, and Ching were taking turns being an impenetrable wall in front of Lorne. We played tight and patient, knowing our opportunities to strike would come.

Seven minutes into the second period that time arrived. Frank Boucher, at center, pulled his trademark poke check at their blue line and turned the play around in a flash. His quick shot was right on target and forced Roach to extend his full reach to block the shot. Block it he did, beautifully. But like Lorne earlier on a similar play, Roach deserved a better outcome. The rebound was gift wrapped for Bill Cook, who was perfectly positioned. With Roach spread on the ice, Bill calmly lifted the puck over him and found the back of the net.

Although we were still down by a goal, we were now controlling the game. Boyd, Thompson, and I went out following Bill's goal and continued to take the wind out of the Pats, denying them any momentum while giving our first line a chance to harvest their energy.

You can't take your eyes off Bunny because he'll surprise you. For the whole game and well into the third period, his older brother Bill and Frank were drawing all the attention. Bun had played an almost invisible game without a single shot on net.

Now the puck was loose along the boards right in front of our bench. He scooped it up and stopped with control right in front of me. He was inches away really, his back to me and the boards. I could see him perusing the ice, looking for an outlet pass.

I was seeing the ice too. "You've got time Bun. No one is on you."

He calmly replied, "and I've got a lane so I'm going to put this biscuit in the basket myself".

He took off like his namesake. He flew into their zone and spun one way and then the other to avoid their defenseman Brydge. Two Pats players swarmed on him and somehow, he shook them off. He drifted in close to the net, never panicked, and just found a hole.

The game was now tied.

Ten minutes later, Bill was carrying the puck at center ice. He knew Frank was on his left and he put the pass just out in front so Frank could keep skating at full speed and receive it. I've come to pity any defense that had to face Bill Cook, Frank Boucher and Bunny Cook flying at them with the puck. In two strides, Frankie was in their zone.

He backhanded a pass to Bun. The puck barely touched Bunny's stick before he fired and put us ahead for the win.

No one said a word about Sam, but I looked for him as our train pulled into Pittsburgh. Whatever his reason for missing our trip to Toronto, he had time to meet us in Pittsburgh. The train fare would have to come out of his own pocket, but it was the only chance he had to save his job and prove to Lester how badly he cared. Everything was on the line for him. His job, his opportunity to attend Yale. My oh my, what was he thinking?

But there was no sign of him on the platform, inside the station, at Duquesne Gardens for our morning skate or at our hotel. Sam was not here. Later I pulled Harry aside and asked if there had been any word from Sam at all. Angrily, Harry said there had not and that he would strangle the kid himself.

Ching and Abel started the game together for the first time in over two months. There was just no denying they had a chemistry and their styles complimented each other.

Lester was doing a masterful job of rotating our defenseman. Ching played the first three minutes of the game, got warmed up, hit a couple guys, and then took a rest. Lester was intent on transitioning Ching into the lineup more but there was no reason to risk further injury. At this point in the season, we were clearly bound for the playoffs.

Mackey and Brown were the defensive pairing at the four-minute mark when the Pirates scored. Harold Darragh attacked down the right side and shot. Lorne blocked it and tried to send the puck away using his stick. But Hib Milks picked it off and quickly shot and scored.

Two minutes into the second period Taffy emerged with the puck and skated up ice. Frank dropped back to cover Taffy's defensive position. Abel carried it through center ice and was pleased to find Bill Cook supporting him. Abel presented as if he was about to shoot but instead passed to his right. Charlie Langlois, the Pittsburgh defenseman stretched out to block the pass, but Bill skated to the puck, easily got around Langlois and beat Worters.

Bill was talking to Taffy as they skated back for the face-off circle. I could envision Bill's mind at work and sure enough, not two minutes later, Abel and Bill were at it again and scored on an almost identical play.

Our 2-1 score held firm until, with only minutes left in the game, Darragh took a long shot from nearly center ice. It was not a serious attempt to score. He just wanted to get the puck deep and try to gain the zone. Lorne played it cleanly and sent it harmlessly into corner. The red light never went on.

But the ref rang his bell and signaled goal.

We were all dumbfounded. The puck never went into the net, and no one committed any penalty that would have awarded the Pirates a goal. The referee just messed up and stood firm that he saw the puck go over the line. Lester and Lorne protested and made their case. But once the ref makes the call, there is no recourse. Suddenly, the game was tied, and we were headed for overtime.

Having scored two goals already, Bill decided that we'd played enough hockey. He attacked with his brother and sent the puck across the ice. Bun took a few more strides with the puck and sent it right back across to his brother. Bill did the same and sent it back again. It was as if there weren't defenders on the ice. Worters was having to shift his whole body from one side of the net to the opposite with increasing speed. The closer the Cook brothers approached the less time the goalie had to react. One last rapid-fire back, and Bill just ripped the shot past Worters. That ended the contest.

The talk before our morning skate concerned the announcement in the local Ottawa papers that Connie Smythe pulled it off. He raised $160,000 and purchased controlling interest in the Toronto St. Patrick Hockey Club. He now owned the players, the franchise, and all assets of the last place team. His first act was to announce the team had a new name. The Toronto Maple Leafs.

"Hey, Harry, when do we play Toronto next?" I asked.

He pulled out his black binder and flipped a few pages. He seemed equally curious. "One week from today. At the Garden." Looking down the schedule he further stated, "It's the last time we'll see them this season."

"All right fellas, let's get our heads in this game tonight." Bill Cook snapped. "We've got three other games to worry about before Toronto and our attention needs to be on Ottawa tonight. We've played them twice and lost both games. They're the only team with a better record than us and the only team we haven't solved yet. Standings and points aside, they are simply the best team in the whole league. Who can tell me about our previous games? What can we learn?"

Frank replied. "We lost the first game 0-1 in Ottawa."

"And a few nights later we lost in overtime 2-3 at the Garden" Ching immediately added.

Lester added "Their team is healthy. All their starters are playing. Mr. Boucher will once again be playing against one of his many brothers. So, let's talk about match ups."

The 6,000 paying customers in the Ottawa Auditorium witnessed a brisk back and forth. Lorne was peppered with a half dozen shots in the first couple of minutes.

Leo Bourgault took a hard hack at the puck from the blue line. It sailed in the air towards their net but rang loudly off the cross bar. The sound echoed in the small arena.

Nine minutes into the contest, Frank Finnigan found the loose puck in our zone and beat Lorne at close range.

We were awarded a goal toward the end of the period when Frank's brother Georges, the Senator's Captain, inexplicably tossed his stick at Bill Cook. Bill was skating with the puck and was about to shoot when Georges let his stick go. The stick did in fact knock the puck away from Bill. It was a strange action because Georges must have known that the referee, Cooper Smeaton would award us a goal on the infraction and take away his goalie's chance of making a save.

The score was now tied at one heading into the second period, which saw long carries from Bill Cook and King Clancy, but both were fruitless. Frank and Ching teamed up on a powerful attack, but Frank's shot went wide.

Shortly after, Frank nearly had a breakaway but Kilrea, in a full out effort, caught up and swatted the puck away. Kilrea immediately fell to the ice, taking Frank with him. Unfortunately, Bill Cook was too close behind and couldn't avoid the unexpected pileup. He twisted himself to try and avoid hurting Frank but landed awkwardly and was slow to get up. He glided slowly to the bench for assistance. Billy Boyd was at the ready and jumped right into the action.

I admired the effort shown by Hec Kilrea on the play. Kilrea's extra effort might have saved a goal. It was symbolic of the commitment everyone on the Senators displayed on every shift. We needed to learn from this and emulate it. Bill was right, their experience, which we lacked, was the subtle difference.

In the second period, Ching and Hooley Smith, Ottawa's top enforcer, had been exchanging elbows for a few shifts. But the ref just happened to witness Ching connecting with Smith's chin as Hooley fell to the ice. The ref sent Ching off.

Our penalty killing squad of Abel, Bourgault, Frank and Billy Boyd brilliantly stymied their attacks. But just as the penalty was ending, Leo was called for tripping. It wasn't a bad penalty; the Senators were in our zone, but his stick got caught between some legs. It happens.

Unfortunately, the Senators forward line of Clancy, Denneny, and Smith could be every bit as talented in the passing department as our top line. They played a little tic-tac, when suddenly Cy Denneny scored.

Our captain was still not ready to return from the earlier collision and Lester sent Paul and I out to join Boyd. We were fresh, and the tempo picked up.

In the natural zone, Paul barely beat Denneny to the puck and sent me a quick pass. I had a lane and took off. Georges Boucher and King Clancy were both positioning themselves to block my progress. I took the puck wide so that Frank's brother had to chase me. I could sense Billy Boyd racing to fill that void. But I needed to get the puck through Georges. I gave a quick reverse twist and generated just enough distance between us to let me pass. I hit Billy without his breaking stride. The puck found him on the fly, maybe five feet in front of the net. Billy only had to deflect the puck to get it past Connell. For the second time in the game, we had tied the score.

2-2.

The punch for punch continued but neither team could get past either goalie in the third period or two intense extra periods of overtime. The game ended in a tie. We took great satisfaction that we didn't lose to Ottawa and that we earned another point in the standings. Our three-game road trip ended with two wins against the St. Pats and Pirates, plus a tie with the Senators.

We traveled from Ottawa back to Manhattan on Wednesday and enjoyed a lite morning practice on Thursday in preparation for our game against the Maroons later that night. I inquired about Sam with the receptionist at the front office. She had not heard anything from him.

Something wasn't right. It had now been eight or nine days since anyone had seen or heard from Sam. Something was wrong. He had been utterly responsible and dependable these past four months. Lester had helped him set up Yale. The kid has a promising future. It made no sense that he would just vanish without word. I forced myself to remember that he's only fifteen and that I know precious little about him.

Chapter Thirty-Two
February 17, 1927

We lost Doc Brown. He was on the receiving end of a clean check. He was barely able to get himself off the ice before he started throwing up in the tunnel.

Nels Stewart scored the first goal almost four minutes into the game. With sixteen seconds left in the first, their defenseman Red Dutton beat Lorne to make it two to nothing.

Ching and I had a great chance in the second. He sent me a pass that I slapped right into the net, but ref Lou Marsh signaled off-sides. We all thought it was a horrible call and the crowd agreed. Regardless, the goal was disallowed.

There was no score in the second and our forwards were having a hard time penetrating their defense. Dunc Munro was especially tough on Bill and Frank both. Our second line was having far better success against their defense. Nine and a half minutes into the third, Paul and I put on a good rush, and his goal did count. If my earlier goal had been allowed the score would now be tied. But it wasn't, and two minutes later Merlyn Phillips emerged from a scrum with the puck and put it past Chabot.

With thirty seconds left in the game Stewart scored yet again and the final was 4 to 1.

Despite the disappointing score, the crowd of eight thousand saw an entertaining contest. Fighting hard for a playoff spot, the Maroons came to play. There were multiple fights and hard hits throughout the game. Bunny and Siebert mixed it up at center ice in the first. That fight went for several blows before both guys tired. Bill Cook and Red Dutton followed with a bout that drew blood from both. Punch Broadbent and I found some minor and insignificant reason to throw fists at each other right after my goal was waved off.

Ching had several crowd-pleasing checks but was paying a price. Leo Bourgault continued taking a lot of the rough stuff off Ching's mighty but still wounded shoulder. Yet Ching can't help himself and he probably threw one too many hits.

After the game, Lester confirmed we didn't play badly. A couple tough breaks and a bad bounce. The hockey gods felt the need to humble us after our successful road trip.

A Thursday night at the Green Door was always lively and crowded. The joint was swinging, and it was so warm most everyone had beads of sweat on their foreheads. Along with our martinis, Mikey kindly gave me a bowl of ice to soak my hand. Truth is I could have used ice in a towel for my jaw too. Harry Broadbent's nickname was 'Punch', probably for a good reason.

Marie and I found a table and we were soon joined by both the Boucher's and the Johnson's. Frank and Ag, and Ching and Ellen had drinks in hand.

"How's the shoulder?" I asked Ching.

"Not so good. I fear I might miss another game or two" he replied.

Lester and Harry made their way over. We made room for two more.

It was odd for them to both be in the club. Harry usually had a lot of work in the locker room after a game. Without Sam's help that would only be worse tonight. Lester would only occasionally join us for a whiskey and cigar. He would give the beat reporters a quote before calling it an early night. The topic was inevitable, but I was caught off-guard when Harry brought it up right away.

"I'm worried about the kid. I think something bad happened" he said with concern in his voice.

I leaned back in my chair. My own concerns were vindicated. Nobody had really talked about Sam in the last week while we were away. With our game against the Maroons now over it was time to address his unexplained absence. I looked around the table and caught Ching and Frank's look of shared concern. I suddenly remembered that Frank was a former detective for the Mounties.

Marie spoke up "ok, what do we know? Where does he live?"

Lester offered, "I checked with the front office. We have an address in Dobbs Ferry. There is no telephone at that address, but I already sent a telegram from Ottawa four days ago."

Lester pulled out a piece of paper from his suit jacket pocket. He unfolded a copy of the Western Union telegram. He handed it to Marie.

She turned the yellow parchment and read.

February 13 1927 Ottawa Station to Sam Crawford 191 Broadway Dobbs Ferry New York

Report status to front office immediately

Team concerned

Lester Patrick

Lester continued, "We haven't received a reply. I followed up with the local telegraph office. Fortunately, the person I corresponded with is a Ranger fan. He claims the owner of the house told the Western

Union agent to tack it to the door of an adjacent horse stable."

"A horse stable?" I added. I recalled how Sam often smelt like he lived on a farm.

Bill and Bun Cook had drifted over and were trying to pick up the conversation. I noticed Boyd and Reg were standing at the bar looking our way. I only now realized that Lorne, Taffy, and Paul were drinking at a table directly behind us and clearly straining to hear over the dancing and jazz. The whole team was concerned.

Mikey served a fresh round of drinks and hovered around.

Frank spoke up "we need to go there and see for ourselves."

"Agreed, it's not far" offered Ching.

Lester confirmed what we were all already thinking "tomorrow is an off day. No practice."

"I'll go" I offered.

"I'll go with you" Frank stated.

"I'm coming too" declared Ching.

"Ok, but three is enough. Let's not freak the kid out or make him feel worse with the whole team pounding on his door." Lester suggested.

"There is likely a perfectly reasonable explanation for all this." Ag suggested.

"Let's meet at Grand Central at 9. We'll take the local to Dobbs Ferry and find the kid." I offered.

Harry spoke again for only the second time "if you find the kid and he's fine, strangle him for me." Harry stood and walked out of the bar.

Marie and I left shortly after and caught the subway uptown. We looked at each other and I asked, "what do you think?"

"Ag is right. It's premature to panic and there is likely an explanation. He could be sick or injured and can't get to the telegram office. Maybe a family member took ill, and he had to rush home. Wherever 'home' is. We might want to consider approaching Elisabeth to see what she knows."

"He's a bit of a mystery, isn't he?" I asked.

She stared at me, and I could see the worry in her face. "He's a good kid Murray. He's responsible and mature for his age. He should have found a way to communicate with someone by now. Get up there tomorrow and find him."

Chapter Thirty-Three

February 18 -19, 1927

As we stepped off the train onto the Dobbs Ferry platform, I looked to Ching with a powerful sense of deja vu.

"Is this the same town we got off with Sam last month?" Ching asked.

"No, but it sure feels similar. I think the Tarrytown station is just the next stop or two." I responded. I looked out over the frozen Hudson. The palisades were closer and loomed larger from this angle.

Two taxis we're parked in front. We approached the drivers who were standing together enjoying a smoke.

"We're looking for 191 Broadway." Frank inquired.

"Sure, it's only up the street a bit mate." the first driver replied.

In unison, Frank, Ching, and I looked up the steep hillside. We looked at each other, and finally back at the driver. "We'd appreciate the lift." Frank concluded.

A few minutes later we stood in front of Sam's address. The main house, very close to the street, appeared to be an old cottage set atop an embankment. The view from this height provided yet another panoramic vista of the river and the sheer cliffs on the opposite bank. The river was flowing rapidly and had massive chucks of ice. The shallow areas along the shore appeared frozen.

Below the main house, was indeed a stable. It was merely six feet from the dirt road. This was the same Broadway that traveled all the way to Times Square, but the contrast couldn't be more profound.

The yellow Western Union telegram Lester sent from Ottawa was still tacked to the door. It flapped in the chilly wind. Frank knocked. No response. He tried the door, but it was locked.

I walked up the stone steps to the main house and knocked. The taxi driver told us that a widow named Walker lived here. I could hear her shuffling towards the door and once open, she appeared to be barely five feet, wrinkled with oily white hair. She was wrapped in a shawl. There was a kindness to her. I realized she probably wasn't as old as she looked.

"Hello, can I help you?" she asked with the hint of an Irish brogue.

Frank and Ching were standing behind me. We must look like three police detectives standing on her doorstep. But she didn't seem concerned in the least.

"Good morning, ma'am. We're sorry to trouble you. My name is Murray. This is Frank and Ivan. Mrs. Walker, we work with Sam Crawford. We're his friends. Is he home?"

"Oh, that young man is so popular these days." Her face lite up with a smile. "He's been away. He travels all over the country you know, and he's sometimes gone for days at time. Would you gentleman like to come in for a spot of tea?" she asked.

"Yes ma'am, that would be most gracious of you. We stepped inside, out from the cold. Ching closed the door behind him. The inside had a peaked ceiling. A wood burning stove was roaring in the cooking area to warm the house. It was hot and we removed our long wool jackets. She set right to boiling water. We sat at her table as she proceeded to put out old cups and saucers with small chips around the edges.

I noticed her pile of wood for the stove was getting low.

"Ma'am, can I ask you how long it's been since you've seen or spoken with Sam yourself?" Frank inquired.

"Oh, it's been several days. He travels all over the country you know." She repeated.

"Yes ma'am. We do know. We travel with Sam for work. He's a friend and we haven't heard from him in a bit. We are getting concerned. You said, he's popular. Have other's been asking about him too?" Frank continued.

"Yes, the telegram man came by. I told him to tack it to Sam's door." She answered.

"So, Sam lives in the stable?" Franked confirmed.

"Oh yes, he needed a place. My horses died a couple years ago so when I learned he needed a room I told the church he could stay here. In return he helps me carry the wood and keep the place up. He's a sweet young man." The water reached a boil and she moved to fill our cups.

"Have you seen Sam in the last week?" Frank tried again.

"No, he's been traveling. It's a long trip this time."

"Does he have any family that you know of?" I asked.

"Oh, I don't believe so. But he works with good people now. He travels all over the country. He even goes to Canada. Can you imagine that?"

"After we finish our wonderful tea, would you mind if we look inside Sam's room? Do you have a spare key?"

She gave us a concerned look, obviously uncomfortable with my request."

Ching reached out with his good arm and put his hand on hers.

"Ma'am, Sam is our friend. We are only trying to find him to make sure he's ok. I promise, we won't take anything."

She got up and walked to the cupboard where she opened a ceramic jar and dug around inside. She handed the key to Ching.

"Mrs. Walker, do you keep your wood out back?" I asked.

"Yes, under a tarp."

"Let us bring some in for you ma'am." I nodded to Frank. Together, the two of us made several trips outside to bring in a quarter cord while Ching asked more questions.

As we opened the door, the smell hit us.

Horses once lived here.

The room was dark and just large enough for two stalls, the half wall separating the horses was now removed. The names of the former resident's, Nixon and Trot, were painted in black on tin plates nailed to the wood wall boards. Sam's room was until recently, a stable.

The room had three small windows. A separate small room held a makeshift kitchen with a wood stove and toilet. There was a pile of wood.

The room had been given electricity and basic plumbing. Wires ran along the wall and ceiling to a single bulb with a pull string. A bed was in the corner. A desk and dresser in the other. Before Frank pulled the string to turn on the light, I could see the walls allowed shafts of sun light to beam through the planks. When it stormed, the walls would not prevent some wind and snow from coming into the room. The floor was a hard packed dirt. Even if the stable had been regularly cleaned, the soil was no doubt infused with years of manure and urine. This was a rough way for a fifteen-year-old to live.

Sam had little belongings. One set of neatly folded clothes were in the dresser. Frank went through the drawers carefully and found a shoe box with $107 dollars in cash. Money he likely saved from his wages with the Rangers.

A duffle bag he used to travel with the team lied empty on the side of the desk. Also on the desk were a stack of dogeared books that included The Great Gatsby, Riders of the Purple Age, and Burroughs' Tarzan of the Apes. The Mysterious Affair at Styles by Agatha Christie sat at the top of the pile.

A novel called The Sun Also Rises rested on his bed. Based on the folded corner, Sam was up to page 42.

There were no letters from family. No photos of parents or siblings. A shovel leaned against the wall by the door, presumably for snow. A mirror hung from the wall on a nail.

The only item that definitively tied Sam to this space was a typed sheet of our schedule. It was the same copy Harry passed out every week to each of us that covered games, practices, and travel details. Sam used a pencil to check off the games and practice dates. I noticed he marked the score for each game as well. He handwrote "2-1 W" after our February 6th game against the Pirates. The 7th was a late afternoon skate. I remember he skated with us and there was his checkmark after that date too.

The whole team was off on the 8th so we could spend time with our families before the week-long road trip to Toronto, Pittsburgh, and Ottawa. There was nothing checked after our practice on the 7th.

Ching broke the silence, "This is a dead end."

"Yes and no" Frank replied. We're no closer to finding Sam. But it's likely that whatever happened occurred on the 8th or possibly the 9th. More likely the 8th. Our train to Toronto left on the ninth and he doesn't have it checked and his bag isn't packed. The wood stove is stone cold. There is a water valve, so the pipes don't burst when it gets too cold. If he had been on his way to the Grand Central to meet us, he likely would have turned it off. It's fortunate we've had an unseasonably warm February otherwise I suspect we'd have walked into a flooded mess. His cash and clothes are here, so it isn't a planned trip. I don't think he ran away with a pretty gal to get married."

That was certainly a thought that had dawned on Marie. The facts here seemed to indicate that he and Elizabeth had not run off.

"So, what's our next step?" I asked.

"We split up and knock on the neighbors' doors and ask if they've seen Sam. Then I'm afraid, we need to visit the local police station and make inquires. We can file a missing person's report. We can contact all the local hospitals and see if they have any patients around that date. We'll have to check the town paper for any stories, and we should run a posting asking about Sam.

With only one goalie, Lester put on the spare pads for practice so we could skate full ice. He was surprisingly spry for an old man in the net, and we loved peppering him with shots.

After our fast-paced practice on Saturday afternoon, we gathered in the locker room to compare notes on our efforts to find Sam. As we untied our skates, we explained that the few neighbors we spoke with were for the most part pleasant but unhelpful. Some were aware of Sam staying at the old stable but had never spoken with him. They had simply noticed him coming and going but none could recall seeing him in the last week or so.

The station master at the train stop was more familiar with Sam and shared our concern. He often enjoyed chatting with Sam while waiting for the train. With his skates often slung over his shoulder and stick in hand it was an easy conversation starter. He promised to speak with the train conductors as Sam was a regular rider. But the station master couldn't recall seeing Sam in the last many days either.

The Dobbs Ferry police were helpful, especially once they learned that Frank was once on the force himself. The clerk and officer on-duty kindly double-checked their logs while we were there. It's a small, quiet village with the occasional car accident or intoxicated local who needed to sleep it off. Neither could recall or find anything in the last couple weeks that would tie to Sam's having gone missing. They filed the appropriate paperwork and assured us that they would check with the other river towns and the local hospitals.

"I called the station house today and spoke with the same clerk" Frank informed us. Reading off his notes, Frank went on. "In the last two weeks the hospitals don't have any record of a Sam Crawford or any unidentified 15-year-old males. The hospital in Dobbs Ferry had a 10-year-old drowning victim and a sixteen-year-old with an appendicitis. The police were certain they knew the family of the kid who needed the surgery and that he didn't fit Sam's description. There are more teen-age males in the Yonkers hospital, but all were identified, and none matched Sam's description. The police went up the line as far as Peekskill. Same story. Patients, yes. But none that were named Sam Crawford or were otherwise unidentified or without families." Frank concluded.

"Marie and I were able to contact the local paper. They claim there was nothing in the news that fit our concern. We placed a missing person notice and it'll run in the town paper every day. No replies thus far" I finished.

The room was quiet. The guys continued to remove their gear and pads.

"Why was he living in a stable? Where was his family?" Bill Cook inquired.

"His landlady thought he had no family. The local police didn't know anything about a Crawford family."

There was silence and a palpable disappointment that our effort didn't produce more answers.

Lester, still in goalie pads, looked at Harry to wrap it up.

"Arrive back here at 10am tomorrow. We'll do a review for the Bruins game. We skate for two hours at 11. Break, lunch, nap and our game is at 8:30. Be back here by 6:30 at the latest."

Chapter Thirty-Four
February 20-21, 1927

After our morning skate it was determined that we'd be without both Ching and Stan tonight. Abel, Leo, and Reg would have to hold our blue line.

Every game against Boston was physical and tonight was no exception. Eddie Shore was not usually in the starting line-up, but coach Art Ross would employ him like a special weapon. Ross would pull any one of his starters at any time and put Shore in with a specific target. Shore would chase after Bill Cook until eventually Bill would get tired of his agitation. The two would drop their gloves and serve time in the box. Only we were losing a critical rook for a pawn. So, Lester would counter by putting our second line out before Shore could get to Bill. This partly explained why Shore and I developed an increasingly adversarial relationship. Ever since our first game in Boston months ago, he and I traded blows with little regard to consequence.

Ten minutes into the first period this very scene played out again. Boston was pressuring Chabot and our defense. We all collapsed towards the net and the crowd roared at the pushing and shoving. I tied up Shore and he caught me with an elbow to my ribs. I gave him a solid illegal cross check the ref didn't call, and he then tried to trip me with his stick.

But while I was keeping Shore's attention on me, Paul Thompson came out of the chaos with the puck on his stick. He headed north and Shore tried to chase. I chopped my stick against Shore's stick so hard that mine broke right in half, and his flew out of his hands. He chased after his stick and reached down to pick it up. I dropped my broken end to the ice and with both hands pushed him hard as he was leaning over to retrieve it. Cursing he went down, and I made no effort to avoid landing with my elbow on his ribs. We tussled as I heard the clanging of the bell. I figured the referee Cooper Smeaton had called me for a penalty but when I looked, he was signaling a goal.

Paul had taken advantage and scored. The crowd was loving the scene. Paul and the guys were celebrating a goal on one end while Eddie Shore and I wrestled on the ice at the other. Smeaton had to skate back down to separate us.

Four minutes later, Frederickson took a pass from Oliver and put it past Lorne to tie the score at one each.

Frank won the second period faceoff back to Taffy. Bun, Frankie, and Bill all moved ahead, and each tried to find open ice with an eye over their shoulders anticipating a pass. The entire Bruins team retreated into a defensive posture.

With no pressure on him, Taffy sent a sharp pass across to his partner Leo. Every pass forces the opponents to adjust their stride, and this can create openings. Leo patiently held the puck as he took one stride forward and then sent a no look pass right back to Taffy. The puck landed right on Taffy's blade, and he already saw where a now open Frank was headed. He redirected the puck and hit our center at full speed cutting across the ice.

Frank put his shoulder down and cut between forwards, Frederickson and Oliver. That left the two defensemen, Hitchman and Coutu. Frank looked to his right and left, both Cook brothers were in position and coming hard, but the glance was just a faint to prompt indecision for just a heartbeat between the Bruins defenders. Their stutter was barely noticeable, but it was all Frank needed.

He shot forward and split between them. He now focused on our old teammate, Hal Winkler. Surprisingly, Hal aggressively came out of the net to cut down Frank's options. Against most players, this play would probably work. But Frank is just too skilled and cool. He took the puck wide, barely cleared Hal and swept the puck right into the net from about ten feet out.

2 – 1.

Bill Cook's goal near the end of the period wasn't nearly as technically pretty but it counted all the same. Paul Thompson carried the puck into the zone and spotted Bill. Paul's reputation of not passing was behind him and he sent a beautiful saucer pass through the air. The pass sailed just over the Bruin's blades, but Bill knocked it down with his stick. It barely landed on the ice before Bill let the shot go. Hal had no chance.

The game ended 3-1. Considering our depleted defensive squad, we were all in an especially celebratory mood as we streamed into the locker room. Our sweaters came off as dark bottles of unlabeled ale were passed out by Ching. I dropped my shoulder pads and reached for my Chesterfields. We clicked bottles and Lester came into the room smiling "well done Gentlemen, well done."

Harry had enough on his plate, so I didn't want to bother him about replacing my broken stick. I went into the storage room and started looking through the inventory of spares.

This room was usually Sam's domain. Metal cabinets held tape, laces, and all the extra gear we might need in an emergency. As were the medical supplies. Extra sweaters were in a box on the floor. The workbench Sam used to sharpen our skates and make repairs ran along one wall.

In the opposite corner was a military cot used by either Sam or Harry on various occasions when it was just too late to travel home. Our locker-room mascot, Ranger, took ownership of the bed and was curled up on a blanket. Next to the cot was a wooden chair.

Laying over the chair were Sam's shoulder pads. His shin guards, girdle and elbow pads were neatly laid out to air dry. We all stack our gear to dry between games and practices. With a tight schedule like ours they never dried out completely. We often put on our gear, wet and recking of sweat. I paused to look at Sam's gear. I felt a tingle envelop my body.

With my cigarette in my mouth, I walked out of the room over to Frank. I quietly sat down next to him and took a sip from my bottle. I was deep in contemplation when he noticed my composure and asked, "what's up Murray?"

I paused before posing the question. "When we were in Sam's place, going through his stuff. Did you see any hockey gear?"

Frank considered the question before answering, "No. But I don't keep my gear at home. Ag would literally kill me. We all keep our gear here."

"Right, we all do. We keep everything here. But the station conductor told us that Sam often had his skates and stick."

Frank took this in.

I turned my head to look at him.

"So where are Sam's skates?" I asked, "because they aren't here, and they weren't in his apartment either."

Marie and I laid in bed considering this potential clue.

"This is nonsense, the police need to be doing more. We're hockey players. We're not coppers." I complained.

"Your right, they need to be doing more, but in fairness, they don't have much to go on either. And not to be disagreeable, but one of you 'hockey players' was an actual detective." Marie responded. "It seems no one is going to care as much about Sam as this team. It sounds like he has no one else."

"Bill said something the other day. It's stuck with me. I feel like we're missing something. Why was Sam living there, in those conditions? If his family died, like the landlady thought, where were they from and how did Sam end up there?"

We held each other, deep in thought. We both started to drift off.

Suddenly I blurted out "church!"

I bolted upright. "She said, she told 'the church he could stay.'" I practically leapt out of bed. "How did three of us miss that?" I asked incredulously.

"Seriously how did we miss that?" I demanded of Frank and Ching the next day, my anger spilling out.

"Easy Murray" Ching warned.

We stood in section 102, closest to our locker room. Although I called them out here to talk privately, my raised voiced echoed over the Garden ice and the surrounding empty seats.

"Jeez, Frank, you're an actual detective! How did you not catch that?!" I went on.

I knew I was hotter than they deserved but I couldn't help himself. It was fourteen days since we last saw Sam.

"Murray, I was a Mountie." Frank shot back, his temper now up too. "I rode a fucking horse. I was nineteen years old and held the rank of detective for four months before going off to play hockey. I mostly tracked down moonshines and opium dens. I never said I was Sherlock Holmes."

"You're no Hercule Poirot either, that's for sure." I snapped.

We moved to get in each other's faces.

Ching immediately got between us.

I had never seen Frank this upset, and I knew I went too far.

I sat down in the closest seat feeling utterly defeated. After a few minutes of pacing so did Frank and Ching.

We sat together in silence. Each of us calming down. I felt scared. I'm sure they did too.

"I'm sorry guys. I really am. I'm scared for Sam. It's not fair to take it out on you."

"That's right, it's not. Take it out on the Maple Leafs tomorrow night." Ching said with a smirk.

"Which church do you think she meant?" Frank asked. "Sam never spoke about religion at all."

"We'll go back and ask her, but it must be a local church? Right?" I responded. "Even in a small town, there must be three or four. Not too many for us to check out."

"But when?" Ching asked. "We practice today, and we have a morning skate and game tomorrow."

I pulled out a copy of our schedule from my pocket. We're gone pretty much from the 28th until March 18th. "We only have one day off between now and our longest road trip of the season. This Friday, February 25."

I exited the Garden after practice on 49th. I turned towards 8th when I heard my name.

It took me a moment to recognize that it was our bartender Mikey Lossi. I had never seen him outside of the Green Door. He was leaning against the brick wall, seemingly waiting for me.

"Hey Mikey, how's it?" I asked.

"Murray, the boss would like to speak with you."

"The boss? I don't understand Mikey." I said smiling but was quickly getting suspicious. "I thought you were the boss?"

"Come on, Big Bill wants a word. He told me to bring you up."

"Wait, Mr. Dwyer owns the speakeasy?"

"Big Bill has many business interests in this area. Including the clubs."

We walked down the street and entered the Forrest. It had been a few weeks since my last visit. I exchanged pleasant enough greetings with the doorman and bellhops. One of whom operated the elevator to the penthouse. My stomach was in knots. With Mikey in the elevator there was none of the usual banter and gossip from the bellhop.

I stepped out. Mikey remained in the elevator as the doors closed.

I expected the penthouse to be more ostentatious. Instead, it was a humble home. I heard Big Bill Dwyer's voice from my right. Through a door I saw him getting up from behind a wooden desk in his office.

"Mr. Murdoch, thank you for making time for me."

I was tempted to ask if I had a choice but held my tongue. Instead, we greeted each other warmly and sat. I declined the offer of a drink, although I really needed one.

"I'm hoping we can help each other Mr. Murdoch. I understand you have a missing water boy?"

"Yes, Sam Crawford. He's been missing over two weeks and we're all quite concerned."

"His disappearance is a problem for me as well."

"I'm confused Mr. Dwyer. May I ask how Mr. Crawford's disappearance affects you?"

"Please call me Bill, I hope it's ok if I call you Murray. Good. I take it you aren't a father?"

"No, I'm not."

"Well, as you know, I am. And my daughter is refusing to speak with me because she's convinced, I made Sam leave. She's distraught. I know you and your wife entertained them recently. Sam didn't write her a letter explaining his intentions to leave or say goodbye. She was under the impression he had traveled with the team. But he never appeared when you returned from your road trip. Mikey overheard you and the guys talking at the club that he's vanished. Until we find Sam, my daughter is unhappy, and my life is a living hell here at home."

"You were ok with Sam and Elizabeth dating?"

"Murray, no father of a fifteen year is ok with his daughter dating. If she were dating a young Charles Lindbergh or Lou Gehrig, I wouldn't be happy. But I met Sam on several occasions, and he struck me as a bright, ambitious, trustworthy lad. A go-getter, but not a hustler, like me if you get my drift. Elizabeth could do worse for a first crush. Her mother and I made sure they were never alone. I've already put out word through all my associations around this part of the city to look out for Sam. Lots of young men that fit his description so no solid leads yet."

"Murray, I have many interests, but despite my daughter's suspicions and my reputation, I am not a violent man. I abhor violence and it is not good for business. I assure you; I had no roll in Sam's disappearance. Now, what can you tell me so that I may help?"

Chapter Thirty-Five
February 22, 1927

Toronto took the ice with new threads. Gone were the beautiful green sweaters with 'Toronto St. Pats' across the chest. Instead, they wore a generic white sweater with a large green maple leaf symbol stitched on the chest. 'TORONTO' was in much smaller letters arched beneath the leaf. Even their green socks were replaced with white. They struck me as a hasty and uninspiring replacement. I hoped they might do better next season.

I was still uncertain what to make of Connie Smythe. The rumor was he parlayed what the Rangers owed him and gambled it all and kept winning. He used that newly amassed fortune to purchase the Toronto franchise. Bill, Bun, Frank, and I crossed paths with him in the hall before the game. We made an honest attempt to congratulate him on the purchase. He seemed indifferent and aloof, especially with me. It was as if he was unable to comprehend how I made the team. He acted like he had someplace more important to be. Perhaps he did.

In contrast, we all worship Lester Patrick. We respect him as the manager and a man. Lester never felt it was a risk to connect with each of us personally, to know us and our families. A person always knows where they stand with Lester. This only strengthened our loyalty. We would go to war for that man.

Yet, it couldn't be denied, that Smythe formed the core of this team from nothing. Months after his departure and all the unnecessary tension, screaming and baiting I have a somewhat different perspective. He had a blank slate and a lot of pressure to sign big names. Perhaps he couldn't coach worth a lick, and I'm still not sure he's even a hockey guy. But he personally selected each of us. We fit together like the pieces of a puzzle. That wasn't by accident. He saw our talent and potential. Had he remained, who can say who he would have ultimately selected. I'm certain I would not have made the cut.

Now, all these months later, in our first season, we're solidly in first place of our division and clearly the second-best team in all the NHL. We're headed to the playoffs. While Lester knew how to nurture and mold us into a winning team it was Smythe who assembled the main roster. I respect his ability to spot talent.

Apparently, Connie Smythe now saw talent in Butch Keeling. The young forward was elevated to their starting lineup and joined their star, Ace Bailey and veteran, Bert McCaffery. Those three were giving Lorne Chabot fits to start the game. Taffy and Leo did all they could to stop their attacks, but Lester was forced to put our second line out to help defensively in the first period.

Fortunately, on the other end of the ice their goalie, John Ross Roach, was seeing action too. Roach plays with a more acrobatic style than any goalie in the league and he needed every flop, stretch, and kick to keep our shots out of his net.

Suddenly, their first line created some time and space. Taffy has the experience to stay positioned but Leo is still wet behind the ears, and it wasn't long before he took the bait and lunged to block a pass. With that one brief misstep their top scorer Bailey swept in and shuffled the puck past Lorne.

Between periods, Ching took Leo aside and spoke with him about positioning. It was killing Ching not to be on the ice again, but he was very involved on the bench. Often yelling out advice and warnings in his brown wool suit.

Neither team scored in the second period, although our first line had ample chances. Roach made fifteen saves in the first period and seventeen more in the second. The score could have been tied when Frank and Bill broke through their lines, but Bill shot just wide. I could hear Bill curse all the way from the bench.

Early in the third period, Roach blocked a shot and covered the puck. The ref stopped play and called for a face-off to the right of the net. Frank won and the puck headed Bun's way. Bunny rushed forward, beating the Leafs player to the puck, and gave it a flip towards the net that Roach failed to stop. The score was tied.

Frank won the proceeding faceoff at center ice and again Bunny found himself with the puck and gained speed. He faked a shot and instead sent the puck across the ice to his brother who did not miss the net a second time. Within 13 seconds, the Cook family had scored two goals and put us ahead.

But we still had seventeen minutes and thirty seconds to kill. For much of that remaining time, Billy Boyd and I were paired with Frank at center. We played a very defensive minded style, attempting to keep the puck away from them as much as possible. We back-checked, poke checked and hit every white sweater with the puck. Those few shots that did make it to Lorne were blocked and cleared.

As we reached the final minute of play, our fans were on their feet in wild applause. The Leafs attacked and Frank knocked the puck off Bailey's stick. I got to it and sent it to the far end of the ice to kill more of the quickly expiring time. The kid Butch Keeling raced after the puck and scooped it up behind their net. He looked up for a pass, but we had everyone covered. Instead, he raced up center ice. He evaded Frank's long reach and stayed clear of Boyd. I caught him and our shoulders pushed against each other as I swatted at the puck. But he did a good job of keeping it just beyond my reach. Leo and Taffy were now racing to provide support. With seconds left in the game he took a desperate wrist shot. The puck flew, and Lorne had a clean look at it. But the shot barely clipped Taffy's shin pad on the approach and deflected just enough. The crowd let out collective gasp as the red light flashed.

Exasperated, I glanced up at the clock. Only twenty seconds remained. Now, we were headed to another overtime game knowing the fault was ours for letting a clean victory slip through our fingers.

For eight minutes the action in the extra frame was frantic. The crowd seemed to be on their feet the whole time as both teams raced up and down the ice. But Ace Bailey intercepted a tipped pass and was off to the races. He scored to win the game 3-2.

There was a lite drizzle as Marie and I left the Garden. A group of players from the Leafs were standing around, enjoying a smoke, and seemingly trying to get their bearing. I tipped my hat as I passed, and Butch Keeling approached.

"Hey, good luck in the playoffs" he offered.

"Thanks, nice goal in the closing seconds. I thought we had you." I lit Marie's cigarette and my own.

"Any recommendations on where we should hit tonight? How do we find these speakeasies we all hear about?"

"They aren't hard to find. There are dozens around here." I looked around and spotted a small group of couples. "They probably just left a late show on Broadway and are looking to keep the night going.

Follow them" I offered. "They're probably headed to a joint now."

The other players thanked me; Ace Bailey was among them.

"It must be a dream." Keeling offered.

"What's that?" I asked, genuinely.

"Playing here. In New York. Every team in the league can't wait to come here and play you guys. No other city is this exciting. I would love to play here someday."

I took this in and replied. "You guys have a fun time tonight. There's no partying for us after that loss, but you guys earned it. See you guys' next season."

"Oh, when you knock on the door to the bar, it will only open a crack at first. Just tell the bouncer, 'The fat man has no friend but the baker.' That'll get you inside." I added.

"Thanks" Keeling replied. I could hear him repeating the phrase to his buds. I smiled and Marie silently elbowed me in the ribs.

As we walked away, heading to the subway it hit me again how lucky I was to be playing on this team. In this city. With Marie and with these guys. The lights, the sounds and smells, the people. The energy. No place else could compare.

"I ran into Mr. Smythe during the game." Marie informed me.

"I didn't know that. Did you talk?" I asked.

"Briefly, he pretended not to remember me. But I know he did."

"People don't forget Marie Heinrich Murdoch once they've meet you, Darling."

"Darn right, anyway, I thanked him for all the pantyhose".

Chapter Thirty-Six

February 1994

Mark is signing autographs for the kids. He keeps sharpies in his coat for just such occasions. He's a pro. He signs their hats, sticks, pucks, just about anything. It's all spontaneous and genuine. It's pure adoration and gratitude from the kids. He gets down on one knee to autograph a few skates. The girl wearing his Ranger jersey got it signed. We are close enough that several parents risked slipping on the ice to join us.

Mark keeps telling the kids they should get my signature, too. He insists it's more valuable. It is certainly rarer. Even the parents have no idea who I am.

"Seriously kids, how many of you know who Lou Gehrig was?"

Nearly all of the kids raise their hands, and all the parents did.

One kid blurts out "He was the Iron-Man."

Mark gently corrects him "Very close, he was called the Iron Horse. And he set the Major League Baseball record for most consecutive games played."

Another kid volunteers the sacred number of "2,130! Next year Cal Ripken will break that record if he doesn't get hurt."

"That's right. It's a pretty big deal, right? Well, this is Murray Murdoch, he was the Iron Horse of hockey and he and Lou Gehrig knew each other well. Their playing careers in New York overlapped. Mr. Murdoch is a hockey legend and one of the original Rangers. He doubted he'd even make the team that first season. But when he retired from the Rangers 11 seasons later, he played in every single game. Like Gehrig, that record stood for a long time. Can you imagine how hard it must be to play 11 years of professional hockey and never miss a game? You really should get his autograph." Mark insisted.

Several kids asked for my autograph at Mark's prompting and that felt good. When Mark explained I was an original Ranger, I expected him to add "the last" to that title.

Old and forgotten. That I can live with. But lonely, that's the kicker. I haven't just lost all my mates.

I lost my dad in '52 at a solid 77 years. But my mom, Jane, lived to the age of 102. Lost her in 1980. Not hard to figure where I get my longevity.

I never imagined my mother would outlive my beloved, but she did. By six years. The heartbreak is still intolerable. It is twenty years now that I've been without Marie. I've never been particularly religious. But since her passing, not a day has gone without my silently praying it would be my last and that we might be reunited in some afterlife I doubt exists.

We had returned to our home in New Haven after an extended trip to Florence, Italy. It was late and we had a long day of travel. We agreed to unpack our bags the following day. After our culinary adventures and wine tours we took comfort in ordering a pizza and pouring two cold beers for ourselves. We sat in front of the television together and watched All in the Family. By 8:30 Marie was nodding off and it was time for bed.

She put on her most comfortable nightgown. I stripped down to my boxers and white tank top. We stood in front of the bathroom sink brushing our teeth, playfully jostling for space at the facet. Two seventy-year old's, never more in love with each other and life.

We crawled under the sheets and kissed each other. We both laid on our left side, as usual, and I snuggled up and spooned her tight. My arm around her waist. My knees behind hers. I whispered "I love you" but she was already asleep. Within moments, I joined her in peaceful slumber.

I awoke hours later, both of us, in the same position, but knowing instantly something was horribly wrong.

Marie had passed in her sleep, without so much as a stir or gasp.

I feel a tug on my arm. A young boy is asking me if I'd sign his stick. Mark stands behind him, looking at me with concern. "Are you ok, Murray? You vanished on us for a moment."

Chapter Thirty-Seven
February 24 -1927

The Garden made a huge deal of tonight's game against the Senators. That two first place teams in their respective divisions were playing each other was all the excuse the PR suits needed. During our morning skate, workers in the Garden were busy hanging bunting and flags representing both countries. Harry warned us to be prepared for a sideshow. There would be military bands and dignitaries. Whenever politicians were in front of a crowd there would no doubt be speeches. This meant we'd be standing around, in our skates, waiting endlessly for the pomp to end so that we could play hockey.

Even our morning skate was slightly delayed because they were still getting the ice ready after last night's bout between Delaney and Maloney. It never ceased to amaze me how Tex packed this arena nearly every night. If it wasn't hockey, or a full night of boxing it was a circus, bike race or political rally. That the building could be transformed so quickly was a daily marvel.

I read in the paper earlier today that a Madison Square Garden Club had been established. This was exclusive to the wealthy local members of finance and industry. They were given their own private entrance at the Garden and had open access to any event in the Garden along with a special seating area. They were all expected to attend tonight.

Far more importantly than any of that, Ching would be lacing up and available to skate tonight. Lester insisted his playing time would be very restricted but having him back on the bench in skates again, instead of standing behind it in wingtips, was welcome news.

We waited in the tunnel to take the ice as the West Point marching band performed in formation in the center the arena. The lower level appeared to be filled with military brass from both the United States and Canada. Women wore colorful gowns and cloaks. Men, if not in full-dress uniform, wore tuxedos. Eventually we were let onto the ice so that we could stand for both national anthems. The last time this level of pomp occurred was opening night.

The Senators took position across from us. But Harry was right, and the local politicians all had to hear themselves speak first. This really was taking forever, and my feet were getting rather sore just standing around; first in the tunnel and now here on the ice.

Bun started to noticeably rock from one skate to the other. I heard Bill, the older more mature brother, whisper with some annoyance to his younger sibling "what are you doing?"

"It keeps my feet from cramping up and getting sore." Bun replied. "You should try it". Truth is all our feet were sore, and we were all bored. Over hearing this, Taffy started swaying and within seconds everyone on the team was shifting from one skate to the other, including Bill. It wasn't long before we were in unison, gently swaying from one skate to the other. We all hid our chuckling as no one in the audience sensed we were goofing around. They didn't know better. They probably just assumed this was what professional hockey players did. I stole a glace over at Lester and Harry, watching us out of the corner of their eyes. Harry didn't even try to hind his grin, but Lester had looks of feigned exasperation and prideful amusement. I imagined this was the kind of stunt that Lester himself would have delighted in if he was still wearing skates.

I honestly couldn't tell if it was helping my feet or not.

Billy Boyd elbowed me and nodded across the ice. The entire Senators team were mirroring us, each player trying to mask their smiles.

The game was finally ready to start forty minutes late. Paul leaned over to me on the bench as the starters got into position for the opening face-off, and predicted, "with this delayed start you just know this game is going into overtime.'

At the end of three periods neither team had found the back of the net and Thompson's prediction came true. We were headed to overtime. But no goals did not make for a dull game. The action was electric and considering the level of competition between the two best teams in the league, there were surprisingly few penalties.

Dave Ritchie called Leo and Jack Adams for two minutes each for some roughhouse in the first. Alex Smith for tripping in the second period and nothing since. Frank was nearly called for a penalty when he inadvertently hit his brother Georges across the eye with his stick. Frank was allowed to keep playing while his brother went back to the locker room for repair.

King Clancy repeatedly proved he was the fastest skater on the ice tonight. No one on our team was fast enough to catch him in a foot race. I couldn't help but wonder how he and Sam would match up. But our defense of Taffy, Reg, Leo, and Ching were enough to help preserve the shutout.

As overtime started, I noted that uncharacteristically, a third of the seats in the lower level were now empty. Many of the dignitaries and military brass, apparently not being fans of intense fast-paced hockey, had drifted off as the night wore on. But those that stayed got a heck of show, even if the outcome wasn't in our favor.

The young Hec Kilrea covered the length of the ice on his own and slid the puck past Lorne almost six minutes into the fourth period to finally end the contrast.

We played the Senators four times. We had not won a game. We had lost 0-1, 2-3 in OT, tied them 2-2 and now lost again in OT 0-1. Three of our four games went to overtime. As evenly matched as could be, yet decisively tipped in their favor. If we play them again this season it would only be in the Stanley Cup Finals where something would have to change if we wanted a different outcome.

We tapped our sticks on the ice as they skated off with our respect. This was their tenth season in the NHL. I hoped that as a first-year team we were learning from them what it would take to be champions.

Frank and I returned to Dobbs Ferry with Marie, who asked to come in Ching's place. He needed to bow out for increased treatment on his shoulder. It seemed the injury, which had not fully healed, was going to remain a factor for the remainder of the season. Ching could play, but not at the level of intensity he wanted. On any hit the shoulder might go again. He was in constant pain, and he figured, 'heck, if I'm going to be in pain anyway, I might as well play".

With the season winding down, I felt a growing anxiety. Although we were solidly in first place of our division and at no risk of missing the playoffs, we were none the less headed for the playoffs in our first season. That came with its own pressure and rapidly increasing expectations, largely encouraged by the sports writers. Suddenly, we were expected to win the Stanley Cup. Anything less would now be a major disappointment.

Bill and Frank tried their best to prepare us. They kept stressing that playoff hockey and the regular season were two different animals. On a couple of occasions, we'd only experienced a small taste of the impending intensity level. A lack of playoff experience was our Achilles heel. I pointed out we would likely face either the Bruins or the Blackhawks in the semifinals, both fairly new franchises themselves. Bill countered, he wasn't particularly worried about the Hawks, but that this was the third season for the Bruins and that several of their players have actual playoff experience.

Then there was Sam. We had to find answers today because after our next home game we were facing our most intense travel of the season. We would be gone for over two-weeks. It has been eighteen days since we'd last seen him. Whatever trail and potential clues still existed would surely be cold by the time we return.

The same taxi driver took us back to Sam's place. We asked the driver to wait. We found his landlady, Mrs. Walker, to be less coherent on this visit. She now comprehended that Sam's absence was worrisome and she became very emotional. She seemed to be confusing Sam with someone else she had lost. Marie's presence helped and she took the lead.

"Mrs. Walker, can you tell us which church you attend?" Marie asked gently.

"I'm catholic, I go to the church just down the road."

Before leaving we reentered Sam's room and double-checked we didn't just miss his hockey gear on our earlier visit. We hadn't.

Standing in Sam's space hit Marie hard. The dirt floor, tiny windows, the wall boards that allowed multiple streaks of light and no doubt rough weather. It was barely fine shelter for a horse. To know that a young man lived here, and not just any young man, but our sweet gentle Sam, was rough.

The church was indeed within easy walking distance, even with all the hills. However, it was an Episcopalian and not a catholic church that we found.

"Perhaps she attended here because it was the closest", Frank surmised.

We found an organist preparing for a funeral that was to start later in the afternoon. He directed us to the attached rectory where we found Pastor Montgomery.

He poured us coffee in the parlor as we explained our story. He was fascinated to discover we were Canadian hockey players on the new team. He made it abundantly clear that he did not approve of all the fighting, but otherwise he was rather accommodating and more importantly, he had seen our missing person advertisement in the town's paper.

"Yes, Mrs. Walker is a member of our parish. Lovely woman. Good soul. She lost her son in the great war. Her husband, who I did not know, died years before her son. She's all alone."

"So, you invited her to take in a boarder?" Frank inquired.

"No, I didn't. I never suggested that." Pastor Montgomery replied comfortably.

We were shocked. Involuntarily all three of us shifted in our chairs and he immediately sensed our unease with his answer.

"Reverend, she said the church asked her to give this young man room and board. Are you saying it wasn't you?"

"I'm sorry, but it wasn't. I visited her at home perhaps six months ago. I am not aware that the young man was living there then. I suspect he moved in after my visit. I wasn't even aware she had room for a boarder."

"Did she attend any other church in town?" I asked.

"Not that I'm aware of. But perhaps you should check with Monsignor LoRusso with the Roman Catholic Parish? Mrs. Walker is Catholic and perhaps she has more connections with that parish than I am aware."

The three of us looked at each other. No further questions sprung to mind. We all stood up. "Thank you, Reverend, you probably need to get ready for that funeral. We appreciate the time you've given us. Please keep an eye on Mrs. Walker and contact us if you hear anything about Sam Crawford."

"I will, and I will speak with my congregation about him. Perhaps someone knows something helpful. I wish you success in finding your young friend."

The Roman Catholic church, and the two others churches we visited in town produced no results. The police department had nothing further to report either. Their investigation came to a dead end. We spent the entire day chasing our only lead, which originated from a widow who might be suffering from early-stage dementia. We barely said a word on the train back to the city as Marie and I held hands and stared blankly out the window.

Chapter Thirty-Eight
February 27, 1927

The Cooks and Boucher arrived together. Although still early, they were the last to arrive in the visitor's locker room of the Garden. It was our turn to be the away team against our intra-city rivals. The rest of us were already preparing and getting loose. Harry came into the room, looking a bit uncomfortable and tapped a stick against the floor. We settled down. Standing with him was a young man, probably around eighteen, I guess.

"Fellas, this a Mike Hauser. He's from Brooklyn. He's my new assistant. He'll be sharpening your skates and taking care of the equipment duties and all the crap I can't be bothered with. Mike, these are the guys."

That was it. Harry finished and walked back to the storage room.

The new guy, Sam's replacement, was left awkwardly standing in front of a room of half-naked men.

Bill Cook, still fully dressed, stuck out his hand and introduced himself. "Hello Mike, nice to meet you. I'm Bill Cook. We're shorthanded and glad you're with us. Do you know how to sharpen skates?"

"No sir. But I learn quickly, sir. Promise." He said nervously in a heavy Brooklynese accent.

I heard Paul whisper to himself, "I don't want some newbie touching my skates and messing them up."

Bill looked over his shoulder towards Paul. "Come with me Mike, I'll show you how it's done." Bill reached down and grabbed his brother's skates.

"Hey!" Bunny protested, "those are my skates!".

"I know Fred, you don't think I'm going to let the new kid practice on my skates, do you?" he said with a big brother smirk.

Billy Burch won the opening face-off for the Americans in front of a big crowd at the Garden. The puck found their star defenseman, Lionel Conacher, who promptly attacked our zone and took a hard shot on net. The puck went just wide, missing the net altogether and whipped around and up the boards at high speed. Frank swooped in, made a tight U-turn, and corralled the puck as it shot along the boards. He took several strides into the neutral zone and hit Bill Cook with a zinger pass. Conacher wasn't back in position yet and Bill was able to quickly muscle himself past Leo Reise. Bill gave a slight fake and goalie Jake Forbes dropped to protect that side of the net. Bill pulled the puck back and instantly skated across the front of the net and backhanded it into the unprotected side.

Seconds into the game and we had a lead.

The Green brothers, like our Cooks, are the first line wings for the Americans. Red and Shorty, played much in the style of Bill and Bun, although neither was as good. Late in the first period, a non-descript pileup occurred in front of our net. Shorty, all 136 pounds, found himself under a pile of bodies. He continued to play the rest of the period.

As the second period started, we noticed that he did not come out of the locker room.

The score remained 1-0 until four minutes into the second period when our first line put on a show for the crowd. Although both teams were at even strength it seemed like we had a man advantage. I watched with envy from the bench as Frank gained their zone and dropped the puck back to Bunny. Bun immediately sent it over to Bill, drawing the Amerk's team in that direction. Frank set up behind the net. Bill carried it deep and sent the puck around the boards right to Frank. Frank settled the puck, looked up and sent a hard pass between two Americans right to Ching's blade up at the blue line. Ching drew everyone towards him just a couple strides. Once they moved, he slid the puck hard across to Taffy. Taffy, receiving the puck, paused just a heartbeat, as the American's shifted towards him.

By now the Americans felt like they were skating in circles, chasing the puck. Taffy took a step towards the closest American, which caused that player to hesitate. Without pause, Taffy ricocheted the puck off the boards right to Bun who immediately sent it across the ice to his brother. Bill received the puck without taking his eyes off the goalie. Forbes positioned himself, expecting a quick shot. Instead, Bill sent it right back to Bunny on the other side. Bun was all alone at the back door, and it only required a simple redirect to score.

The crowd and our bench went wild with appreciation. It was a brilliant goal.

Paul, Boyd, Reg, Leo, and I all repeatedly banged and slammed our sticks against the boards in applause. Lester was clapping as enthusiastically as I'd ever seen him. On the ice, I saw more than one American shaking his head.

Even without Sam, the crowd chanted "Let's go Rangers" over and over.

As action resumed Lorne looked as calm and confident as ever. Our second line was seeing increased ice time and we were getting as many chances as the first line. Paul came out of a scrum in front of our net with the puck. Our line attacked together with Paul coming up the right side. He looked at both Boyd and me as we crashed their net as a unit. Paul worked so hard all season to change everyone's perception that he was a selfish player. Everyone in the house expected him to pass, and the Americans played it as such. But in a sure sign of his maturity, he now knew when to pass, and when not too. He let it fly and the puck sailed past Forbes for another goal.

A few minutes later, Bill Cook scored another goal to make it four.

Between periods, Lester announced the second line would be getting the majority of ice time in the third. I sat on my stool and as I finished my Coca-Cola, I thought about what kind of player I want to be. Watching the Senators, I witnessed their extra efforts, and how that makes a difference. Up four to nothing, I wanted to try a few things if the opportunities presented.

The Americans came hard. Burch and Green tried their best to prove their own passing skills, but Lorne and our defense stood tall. The Americans hammered us and kept us in our zone more than we wanted. We were having difficulty breaking the puck out against their first unit.

Conacher was suddenly set up to take a hard shot from the blue line. He was my man, the player I was supposed to cover in this situation, but I allowed myself to drift a little too far away from him. He now had time to really put a hard shot on net. 'We're up by four, be smart' flashed in my thoughts.

Just as his stick was connecting with the puck, I kneeled sideways and put my whole body in the path of his blast. Simultaneously, I heard the Garden gasp just as the puck solidly exploded against my right thigh. I felt the muscle scream in agony. I saw stars. My lungs refused to work.

But I had blocked the puck, and it was now laying right in front of me. I scrambled to my feet, my right leg refusing to move normally. Gasping for breath, the puck on my blade, I skated north looking for an outlet pass. But both Boyd and Thompson were behind me trying to catch up. I was passing our bench, and I knew the smart move was to dump the puck deep and skate to the bench for a change. I knew Bunny was ready to jump on the ice at full speed and strength.

But the moment took me. My body felt on fire. Everything slowed down just a little in my mind. I gained their zone, and tried to evade their defenseman when I felt his stick slash against my right leg. That leg immediately collapsed, and my knee landed on the ice. But my left leg kept me steady and straight. Somehow, I was still upright as my right knee slide along the ice. The puck was still sliding along with me, but I couldn't control it from this angle. Instinctively, I dropped my hands halfway down the shaft of my stick, effectively making it half as long. I was gliding on a collision course with the net at nearly full speed. Their goalie Jake Forbes dropped to block me. I lifted the puck and flipped it over him into the net.

But I didn't score. Forbes twisted himself around and snatched the puck out of mid-air with his catcher. My momentum took me crashing into him and the net hard.

I knew this would provoke a requisite fight. Teams can't allow players to crash like this into their goalie without consequence. But while the teams raced to the net, they only half heartily pushed at each other. Forbes lay on top of me, the puck still in his hand never having crossed the line. Our faces inches apart. Uncharacteristically, I spoke to an opposing player.

"That was a darn impressive save there Jake. I have no idea how you did that."

He got to his knees and whispered. "I had to Murray Your play on the other end inspired me."

Paul and Boyd helped me to my feet, still seeing flashing stars in my eyes. My leg was not cooperating, but I was able to hobble towards the bench. The pain was throbbing. Only now did I realize the crowd, split between Ranger and American fans, were cheering our mutual displays with frenzied respect. Both teams were banging their sticks against the boards. The sight of Bill Cook, my captain, hollering and pounding his stick against the boards with such unbridled excitement…for a play that did not produce a goal…wait, is that Sam right behind him cheering? I stopped. No, it's the new guy.

In the locker room, Harry wrapped a big bag of ice around my thigh. Lester and Bill strolled over to my stool. Bill hands me a bottle of beer.

"You get it now Murray. We just need every single player on the team to follow your example and we've got a shot at this." He clicked his bottle to mine and walked back to his changing area.

I looked up at Lester. He stood, towering over me. Hands in his pockets, a slight mischievous expression on his face. "Well done Mister Murdoch. Well done."

The moment I emerged from the locker room Marie threw her arms around me. The other wives and girlfriends were gathered to the side greeting their guys as they came out. But I felt their eyes on us. I whispered into Marie's ear, "I saw him, I saw Sam on the bench for just a moment." She squeezed me harder, and I cried into her hair.

Chapter Thirty-Nine

February 28 – March 5, 1927

I could barely put weight on my right leg as our train pulled out of Penn Station early in the morning. We were headed back to Chicago and then to Montreal. The international six-day bicycle race had transformed Madison Square Garden into a steeply banked indoor velodrome track. We would not play our next game at home until the 13th.

We settled in the dining car. Frank set a deck of cards on the table and let out a happy sigh as the waiter poured our coffees.

Lorne, head buried in the paper, asked "have you guys read the sports section yet? There's a story here about Shorty Green. He's in the hospital in serious condition."

SHORTY GREEN HURT

Star Wingman of Americans Injured in Ranger Game

Dislocated Kidney and Suffering from Shock

"Jeez, when did this happen? Does anyone remember?" Bunny asked aloud. None of us had an answer beyond remembering that he didn't play after the first period.

Lorne continued to read, "it says here he's in Polyclinic Hospital. He dislocated his left kidney and has been suffering from internal hemorrhages. He's conscience and improving but the bleeding continues. He was injured during a mix-up in the first period of the game. A player fell on him during a scrum. He continued to play, but during the intermission he collapsed in the dressing room and was taken home. His condition worsened during the night, and he was rushed to the hospital. Wow! It says his condition was so serious last rites were administered by a priest. Holy smokes."

We all looked at each other.

"I vaguely remember a play involving him in front of my net. But it was nothing noteworthy." Lorne added. It doesn't say which player fell on him or even if it was our team or his own mates.

"I think it was me." Frank said. "I remember getting knocked over and falling on one of their players. It could have been Shorty."

Of course, it would be Frank, I thought to myself. The most sensitive player in the whole league. Frank was unnerved and shaken up a week ago when he inadvertently caused a cut above his brother's eye. His brother made a joke of it. But it really bothered Frank.

"No, I fell on him. I landed on him hard" Bill Cook insisted.

Somehow, I knew that Bill was purposefully lying. He knew Frank took this stuff to heart, and he was absolving him of guilt.

"I was on the ice for that mix-up too. I'm always pushing and cross-checking guys." Ching offered.

"I think I was the second guy that fell on him" Leo offered.

I was impressed at the new guy. Leo has only been with the team a short time and he's already savvy enough to read the play. Frank couldn't bare the blame alone with several of the guys who were also on the ice taking responsibility. I sipped my coffee and gave Bill Cook a glance over the rim of my mug. He held my gaze for just a moment, acknowledging the situation.

"I'll ring the front office and have flowers sent to the hospital from the team." Lester added. "Damn unsetting development."

It was true. This was a rough occupation.

Sometimes, you just encounter a brick wall. We ran into two on our road trip. Against Chicago, Hugh Lehman simply pitched a complete game shutout. We played a solid game at both ends, but we couldn't get the puck past Lehman. Lorne's play couldn't be criticized. As sore as my right leg was, I surprised myself. I skated well and I don't think the Hawks ever suspected I was playing injured. If a player slashed or kneed my right thigh, I would probably have passed out.

Two nights later, our game in Montreal against the Maroons was not all that different. Except, we played five periods of hockey and neither team could squeak the puck past either goalie. Clint Benedict and Lorne Chabot each faced a barrage of shots but they both pitched an extra innings, complete game shutout. Each team settled for one point, in the zero-to-zero contest.

Chapter Forty
March 6 - 1927

With the Garden unavailable to us and a fluke in the scheduling we had nearly a full week of no games. Lester booked rooms at the Peacock hotel in Toronto and rented the dimly lit Ravina Gardens for three hours every day to practice.

Our stay in Toronto allowed us to be reunited with Stan Brown and Ollie Reinikka, both of whom live in or near Toronto. The week of no games also meant we could heal our sore, battered, and bruised bodies. There wasn't a guy on the team who wouldn't benefit from this rest.

To just skate, run drills, practice set plays and formations was a joy. True, the arena was a dive, but having Stan and Ollie back on the ice for practice was welcome. Ollie's season was done. His eye had not fully healed, and his vision in the one eye was blurry. He was still missing or misjudging routine passes. While he was enjoying our company, he was feeling depressed. While the doctor had reassured him it would take time, Ollie was scared it would never fully heal.

Stan felt considerably better and wanted to rejoin the team. His headaches, dizziness, and nausea subsided in home life. He now wanted to test himself on the ice. We all operated under strict no checking rules this whole week.

This week was critical to help Ching too. If we were going to have a real chance, we needed him at full strength during the play-offs. There are only seven more regular season games before the post season and if we can keep our first-place ranking, we'll have a bye for the first round.

Since the Hal Winkler trade, Lester put on the pads and played in goal during practice. He really wasn't half bad and his presence in net kept the week relaxed.

Our evenings were spent as a team. We dined at the same restaurant each night and quickly realized how spoiled we've been living in New York these last five months. One night we went to the theatre to watch the silent film 'The Temptress' with Greta Garbo. While the nightclub scenes of dancing and 'debauchery' were supposedly controversial and risqué, they seemed a pale sanitized version of a typically quiet Tuesday night at the Green Door. We hit the local hot spots and enjoyed the drinks and music. Everything about Toronto had a welcome slower pace we needed at just this point in the season.

On our final day Bill Cook put together a special excursion. He arranged for us to go ice fishing on Lake Simcoe.

We arrived early and chose one of the available wooden shacks out on the frozen lake to store our gear and keep warm. We layered up to protect against the harsh subzero cold. We used a few different sized spud bars to drill our holes. Half of the team was happy with 4" or 5" holes and set bait for yellow perch. The rest of us spent more time making 8" holes so we could try for trout and northern pike.

The water was at depths between 6 feet and 20 feet.

We used jigging rods and Bill did an amazing job with the bait too. We had minnows, maggots, mousies and shiners.

We were all pulling out dinners before long. Ching caught the biggest of the day. A thirty-two-inch pike. Taffy had two impressive crappies, each over twenty inches. I pulled out a 27-inch northern pike. Lester and the guys all pulled out plump sunfish, walleye, and smaller pikes. We had no opportunity to eat them, so they all went back into the ice.

Early Saturday evening, we boarded the train back to Manhattan. Tomorrow we would play the Detroit Cougars at the Garden, before getting on a train to Pittsburgh. Our final seven regular season games would be played over thirteen nights.

We stepped on the ice to find an unusually small crowd of perhaps four thousand. Granted the Detroit Cougars were in last place, but our Sunday night affairs generally produced a better turnout. Our last game at the Garden was February 24th and its now March 13th. I guess they forgot about us during our time away.

Those that did show saw brisk, spirited back and forth action.

In the second period, my line was on the ice when Sheppard, Keats and Foyston created a melee in front of Chabot. Taffy sent the puck away from the net into the corner. Clem Loughlin and I raced after it. We hit shoulder to shoulder. We bounced off each other and both went after the puck again. Our sticks fought for control.

Another Cougar joined the battle and slammed me into the boards from behind. A beautifully dressed woman in an evening gown screamed at the prospect I might land in her lap. The puck was still at my feet. I felt an elbow discover my kidney. The player to my right kneed me in the thigh. I felt that. My thigh was still bruised from the puck blast a week earlier.

Ching joined the fray and pounded the Cougar on my right. This gave me space, I twisted clockwise away from the remaining Cougar. I started skating and I looked up. Thompson had gotten a head start and was already behind the three Cougars who were now racing back. Paul and I read each other. I needed to thread him the puck before he reached the blue line, avoiding the defenders looking to intercept the pass.

I passed the puck as hard as I could. Paul received it without breaking stride. Only the goalie Hap Holmes stood between him and the net.

That was all I saw because the moment after I passed the puck I was blind-sided and sent flying. I lay spinning on the ice, gasping for breath, as I heard the crowd cheer. As the spinning stopped, I was facing a view up ice. I saw Paul celebrating.

Taffy and Ching both helped me up. "Nice pass Murray."

Taffy held up his gloved hand and asked, "how many fingers do you see?"

"Six." I replied jokingly.

On the bench I found myself readjusting much of my gear. My shin pads on both legs were ajar. My right elbow pad was hanging at my wrist. I have no idea who it was that hit me. Our water boy, Mike, handed me a tin cup.

"Thanks, hey, did you see who ran me over?"

"No, I'm sorry. I was watching the player with the puck on the other end." He confessed nervously and I could barely understand his accent.

"It's ok Mike, that's where I was looking too." I replied with a wink.

Shortly after, the six-foot, two-hundred-pound, Art Duncan dropped his gloves and went right after our unsuspecting Captain from behind. Leo Bourgault flew to intercept and tackle the larger Cougar. The two rolled and wrestled before separating, jumping up and squaring off.

Fists in a ready stance, they measured each other up. The crowd was ready for a battle royale. Leo isn't in Duncan's weight class, but he established a solid grip on his opponent's sweater and threw the first punch. Leo's strong and muscular. Duncan felt the blow. But Duncan now had a hold on Leo's collar too and landed three quick bare-knuckled shots with his jackhammer fist. While Leo kept swinging, he was taking more incoming fire than he was getting off. His face was already bloodied when the next punch shattered his nose. We could hear the sickening crack from the bench.

While Duncan went to the penalty box, Leo was allowed to head off to the locker room. He and Henry vanished into the tunnel.

Very late in the third, Taffy twice left his position to try and score. Both times he just missed the net. In a one-goal game, late in the third, his doing this even once didn't make sense. Our priority needed to be defense. We shut them down, we win. But because the Cougars were trying so hard to tie the game, they were poorly positioned defensively. This temptation was too much for Taffy. The second time, his decision cost us.

As he shot wide, the puck whipped around the boards. It was near center ice before a Cougar corralled it. Taffy was still in their zone and way behind the play. They had a five on four. Their shot on net led to a rebound and that produced a messy scrum in front of Lorne. The puck popped out and John Sheppard was the first to it. He spun and let it rip. With all those bodies, there was almost no way Chabot could see the puck.

Sheppard tied the score with less than two minutes in the game. Watching from the bench I thought to myself it was not a smart play on our part.

Neither team scored a goal in overtime and the game ended in a tie. This put us all in a rather sour mood because we now had to race to Penn Station to catch the overnight train to Pittsburgh. We climbed aboard still sweaty and wet, not having had time to shower. Lester informed us that Leo went to the hospital to have his nose reset. He would have to catch another train.

Chapter Forty-One
March 15 -18, 1927

"Gentlemen, the playoff dates have been announced." Lester came into the visitor's locker room with newspaper in hand.

The room hushed right up.

"President Frank Calder and the other NHL officials meet at the Waldorf-Astoria yesterday and announced the Rangers will have a bye for this first round provided Mr. Abel doesn't discover a new way to lose each of our remaining games." Lester paused and gave Taffy a stern glare.

Taffy took the deserved ribbing in stride, and he bought us all a round of drinks to go along with his apology.

"As it stands, Boston and Chicago will play in the first round. We will face the winner April 2 and 4th. First game will be away, and the second game will be at the Garden. Total goals over the two games decide the winner.

In the International division the Ottawa Senators will have the bye. It appears Montreal will be an exciting city as the Maroons play their city rivals, the Canadians.

The Stanley Cup series will start on April 6." Lester concluded reading from the paper.

Bill Cook spoke up. "This is why we've played so hard and taken such a pounding. To get invited to the big dance. You all see how close we are now. Do not ease up. Do not coast. Anything we do wrong now will be magnified in the playoffs. We've only got a few games left to sharpen every aspect of our play and get ready."

Later that night the Pirates never stood a chance. Leo, having had surgery to reconstruct his nose the day before, was in our lineup. His train arriving only an hour before the puck drop, he raced to the rink and laced up. His eyes were black and so swollen he could barely see. Wads of cotton was stuffed up his nasals and he had to breathe through his mouth.

Paul Thompson, getting some first line action scored on a nice pass from Taffy. Less than two minutes later, Taffy attacked but this time he made certain to bury the puck. With five minutes left in the first period, Frank hit Bunny with a pass and Fred quickly made it 3-0.

I was skating with Bunny in the second period. He carried the puck into the zone and sent me a beautiful pass. I wanted to shoot but Worters had good positioning on me. I sent it right back to Bunny who blasted it in for a goal.

A few minutes later, Bill Cook skated unassisted from one end of the ice to the other and scored to put the game out of reach 5-0.

Two nights later our game against the Detroit Cougars in Windsor Ontario was considerably more physical but the outcome was never in doubt. Bill scored the first goal in the first thirty seconds. He then scored the second and final goal. Lorne was brilliant again having back-to-back shutouts and the third in our last four games.

Marie's album collection was rapidly expanding. Our apartment's phonograph was now playing a wide selection of music. I joked that she was wearing a hole in the carpet as she loved playing a steady stream of tunes. Al Jolson, Duke Ellington, Louis Armstrong, Ma Rainey, Bessie Smith, and Eddie Cantor. She had just started 'Rhapsody in Blue' by

Gershwin.

She poured me a 'Bee's Knees'. She had found a reliable source of bathtub gin and loved mixing the lemon juice and honey.

She sat in the chair in front of me.

"Murray, I need to tell you something and please don't be upset. I was safe the whole time."

I sat forward. Completely caught unaware at whatever she was confessing.

"While you've been on the road so much these last two weeks, I went back to Dobbs Ferry to keep searching for Sam."

"Honey?" I paused. I was about to react and chastise her for traveling alone but who was I kidding. Marie was perfectly capable of traveling anywhere by herself.

I smiled "Ok, I get it. Did you find anything? How many trips did you make?" I asked.

"I went nearly every day you were gone. I spoke to everyone again. I spent one whole day at the local paper reading every article for the period he went missing."

She paused.

"I think…I may… have found something. I'm not sure."

I leaned even further forward and sat my drink aside.

"Do you recall, early on, the police said there was a drowning victim."

"Yes, it was a young child, wasn't it? Like ten years old, I think. Very sad. We confirmed it was not Sam."

"Correct, it wasn't. I found a small mention in the paper with three details we didn't know before. That a ten-year-old fell through the ice…while playing hockey."

She hesitated just a second before continuing.

"And I don't think the accident happened in Dobbs Ferry. The article said, 'a neighboring town's lake'. There are three towns on its borders. Hastings, Ardsley and Irvington."

Lastly, "the ten-year old boy was taken to St. John's Riverside Hospital."

I took this all in. "So, I'm guessing you went to the hospital" knowing full well she did.

"Yes, and I spoke with the hospital staff. They were very helpful. Murray, the child didn't die. He was in bad shape, but he survived. When we were told it was a drowning 'victim' we figured that meant he died. He was there for several days, treated and released."

"This is great work, and I'm relived the kid survived. But how do you suspect this connects to Sam?" I wondered.

"You, and Ching went to an orphanage up that way, right?"

"Yes, with Sam…nearby." I added. The hairs on my arms got all tingly.

"Ok, this is bit of a stretch, I know. But it turns out the young child was an orphan at a local boy's home. Murray, you told me you skated on a lake when you visited an orphanage. There are no lakes in Dobbs Ferry, Hastings, Irvington or Ardsley. But there is one in Tarrytown."

I stood up.

Lastly, she added. "The hospital told me the kid was released to a Father Sabastian."

"What? I met Father Sabastian." My mind was frantically trying to put all the pieces together but none of this still explained Sam's disappearance, yet it was too coincidental to be ignored.

"So, this skating accident, it could have happened at the orphanage in Tarrytown?" I asked.

"I wasn't certain, but yeah, I think so" Marie said.

"I could have skated with that young kid. He was probably one of the children we were there to see that day. We need to go and speak with Father Sabastian immediately. Lester gave us the day off tomorrow. Marie, I don't know how this leads to Sam, but you're onto something. I need to put in a call to Frank and Ching."

Chapter Forty-Two
March 19, 1927

The four of us arrived, unannounced at the Boy's Home. One of the older kids answered the door. Being Saturday, they weren't in school. We waited in the foyer only a few minutes before Father Sabastian's familiar figure rushed in.

"Mr. Murdoch, and Mr. Johnson, what a pleasant surprise!"

"Hello again Father." We shook hands. "This is my wife, Marie."

"Mrs. Murdoch, it's my honor to welcome you" they shook hands warmly.

"And this is our center, Frank Boucher".

"Now I am honored again" Sabastian offered sincerely. "Mr. Boucher, truly, I wish we knew you were coming. The equipment the team donated arrived just a couple weeks ago. Sticks and new skates, even pucks. It is all so generous, and the boys can't wait to use it next winter."

"We are happy to help Father, but may we speak privately?"

He looked at us with wonderment "of course, my office is just this way."

Father Sabastian took position behind his desk as Marie and Frank sat in the two wooden chairs directly in front. Ching found an upholstered chair in the corner.

I stood by the window and noticed several of the children running around outside in the mixture of dirty snow and mud.

I have a fear and I pray I'm wrong.

"Father. Are you aware that Sam Crawford is missing?" I asked.

"What? Sam? No. I'm not at all aware. How long has he been gone?" Father's Sabastian whole demeanor became serious. Gone was the gentle smile and replaced with a look of real concern.

"We believe he's been missing since the second week of February" Frank offered.

"What? Today is March 19th. What do you mean missing? Please tell me everything you know." He was up from his seat, both hand on the desk, almost for support.

"Father, forgive me, but respectfully, I have to ask you a question first." I had only shared my suspicion with Marie. I hadn't shared my fear with the guys.

"Sam Crawford was an orphan here, wasn't he?" I asked.

Both Frank and Ching swung their heads sharply in my direction, shocked at my question. But the Father simply held my gaze. He walked over and joined me at the window.

"Yes, Sam was one of our charges since he was a toddler. But Mr. Murdoch, Sam has kept this information private. He has always been deeply ashamed and has never shared this information with anyone outside these walls."

"But when he turned fifteen, he aged out, didn't he?" I asked further.

"Yes, I was able to find a room for him in Dobbs Ferry. It wasn't much, but it's very difficult to find homes for the older kids. We did our best to prepare him to live on his own and find employment."

"So, you were the 'church' that Mrs. Walker said asked to put him up?" Ching surmised.

"I suppose so, yes. I've known Mrs. Walker for many years. I had met her son during the great war. I gave him last rights. When I was assigned here after the war, I checked in on her from time to time."

"What do you know about Sam's family history?" Marie asked.

"Nothing, nothing at all. Sam Crawford isn't even his birth name. He was abandoned and left to our care. I named him myself when he was not yet one year old."

"And you're the person who introduced him to hockey, right?" Ching asked.

"Yes, he took to it so naturally. He seemed at peace on the ice, so I encouraged his passion. Obviously, I enjoy the game myself. We formed a bond, and I nurtured his development. But he got the job with the Rangers all on his own. I suspect he just appeared at the Garden and found ways to make himself useful. Eventually, I suppose someone offered him a job. It was such a thrill for all of us when he appeared with Mr. Murdoch and Mr. Johnson."

"Do you have any idea where he may have gone Father? Frank inquired.

"Absolutely none. His immediate goal after the season was to prepare for Yale. I believe Mr. Lester Patrick was responsible for making that happen."

"Father, I'm not sure what the connection could be, but I don't believe in coincidences. Can you please tell us about the young boy who fell through the ice in February?"

"Of course, Mr. Murdoch, but I don't see a connection."

"Please indulge me."

"Young Luke. He told his teacher, sister Mary that he was not feeling well during class and asked to go lay down. She sent him to bed in his dormitory. When he didn't come to lunch the sister went to check on him. He wasn't in his bed, and it was never slept in. She notified me at once. After a cursory search in the building, we became concerned and suspended class for the older children. While the youngest ones were kept distracted in class, all the rest of us thoroughly searched the building and then the surrounding grounds."

Father Sabastian's voice started to crack. He sat down and continued. "We kept expanding the search and when we reached the lake one of the boys spotted Luke laying on the ice near the center. He was motionless and didn't respond to our yells. We had been on the ice just two days earlier and it was solid. I thought perhaps he had fallen and hit his head. Several of us ran towards him and when we got to within maybe twenty yards, we all heard a loud crack. The ice held, but we all heard it and froze in our tracks."

"I immediately sent everyone back to the shore. Once they were safe, I proceeded slowly. As I got closer, I saw a hole had refrozen perhaps five feet behind him. He had fallen in and pulled himself out before collapsing. I crawled on the ice, trying to distribute my weight as widely as possible. If Luke could break through at his weight, then I certainly could. He was still holding his hockey stick. I remember thinking to myself he might have even used it to prevent his going under or used it to brace himself and pull himself out. I reached for him and pulled but he was frozen against the ice. He had been soaked through. I had to yank several times on his jacket to break the seal. The poor boy was blue, and I couldn't tell if he was breathing at all. I pulled him to shore as fast as I could, but it felt like forever. When I was far enough away from the hole, I had to risk lifting him. One of the sisters had the good sense to call the ambulance as soon as he was spotted, and I could see them arriving. The stick was frozen to his glove, and I'll never forget the sound it made as it was dragged along. I'm pretty sure he was still holding it when they put him in the ambulance."

He paused and took a moment to compose himself. Ching poured him a glass of water from the pitcher on the corner stand. When he was finally ready, he continued.

"I went with Luke to the hospital. It all just seemed to take so bloody long. The guy in the ambulance doubled up blankets over him. We got to St. Johns and the doctors took over. I know they put him in warm blankets and gave him sugar. I don't know what else. I was rather emotional by this point. I was sure the boy was dead. It was touch and go for a few days, but he pulled through."

"Is he still here?" Frank asked.

"No, his hearing was badly affected. We got him transferred to a special facility in Pennsylvania. I'm in touch with them regularly. They say he's making small strides. That's everything I recall. Like I said, not sure how this could be connected to Sam."

"It's a terrible story, what happened to his kid. But I agree. Seems like another dead end as far as Sam is concerned." Ching voiced.

But I suspected otherwise. There was nothing in the father's story to disprove my theory. "Father, is the lake still frozen?"

"Well, it's still covered in ice but it's long past safe. No one has been allowed on it since Luke fell through."

"But it hasn't completely thawed and refrozen." I asked.

"No, it's been thawing slowly, it's pretty wet."

"I'd like to take a look at it." I motioned for the door. We put on our jackets and walked outside and down the path.

The ground was very much a frozen, icy muddy mess. There were signs posted all around to stay off the ice. Father Sabastian explained that since it was the only skating spot in the area the local kids also ventured here. He didn't want anyone on the ice.

As we arrived, we all looked out. It was a beautiful scene. The pond still had a layer of ice, but it had large pools of water scattered throughout. I asked "Father, please point out where you say Luke fell in."

Father Sabastian pointed.

The five us stood. There wasn't much to see on the ice.

But it was there. Faint, and far.

I felt the blood drain away. Marie supported me. Ching and Frank immediately knew something was wrong and rushed to my side. "What happened?" they asked.

I could visualize the whole sequence of events. All the pieces fit like a puzzle. Together we walked over to a fallen tree. Marie and I rested against it. Father Sabastian, Ching, and Frank stood over us, concerned.

"I'm sorry Father. I don't know if we'll ever have definitive proof but..." I stood back up. Regained my composure and broke the hard truth.

"…Luke fell in the ice on February 8th, correct?" I asked.

"Yes, yes. It was February 8th." The Father replied.

"Potentially the same day Sam went missing" Frank acknowledged.

"Wait, that can't be a coincidence." Father Sabastian realized.

"It's not. I'm so sorry Father but I think Sam is dead. I suspect he fell through the ice and didn't come out."

We retreated to Father Sabastian's study. Coffee and hot tea were served. The room was silent. I took one final drag of my cigarette and began.

"Sam didn't run away. His money was still in his apartment. But his hockey gear is missing. His skates, his gloves, and his stick. Father, are there other local ponds between here and Dobbs Ferry?"

He paused to consider this. "No, not really. Like I said earlier, this is where all the kids come to skate."

"And did Sam come here and skate from time to time since moving out?

"Yes, as often as he could, but his schedule with you guys was pretty full. But on a few occasions, he came here to practice. If it was a weekend, he would skate with the kids. But during the week, he would just practice on his own. He would sometimes stay and eat with us and share stories about the team."

Frank chimed in. "So, Sam would take the train up the line from Dobbs to Tarrytown. The conductors said they occasionally saw Sam with his equipment. He walked up here from the train station."

Marie now ventured, "perhaps he walked right past the classroom windows where young Luke, sitting at his desk might have seen Sam heading to the lake. He told the teacher he was sick and snuck out to skate with Sam."

"That's what I'm thinking" I confirmed.

"All this makes sense. But none of this puts Sam on the ice for certain. We need to speak with Luke and only he can confirm it, right?" Ching asked.

"The boy was traumatized by the experience. In the short time he stayed here after the hospital he remained in bed, couldn't hear, and never said more than a word or two. He didn't speak in sentences. He never said anything about Sam." Father Sabastian explained. "But Mr. Murdoch, you saw something down at the pond. Something that convinced you Sam was here that day. May I ask, what did you see?"

I looked at him and recognized how much he cared. How committed he was to these kids. How my next words would break his heart.

"It was his stick. Luke's stick is still on the ice." I explained.

"No, no, no, no. Luke's stick was frozen in his hand. He dragged it as I carried him. His stick isn't on the ice!" Father Sabastian protested, raising his voice.

Marie looked at me. She gave me strength.

"No sir. That was Sam's stick in his frozen hand. We'll never know the exact sequence of what happened. But I'm guessing the two were skating together. Maybe Sam passed Luke the puck and Luke missed it. It kept sliding out deeper into the center. Luke chased it. The ice gave way, and he went in."

I had to stop and take a breath. This was conjecture but I knew in my gut what happened. Even though we didn't know Sam well, we knew his heart and soul. He would never quit.

"Sam went to rescue him. Like you, he knew to lay on the ice and spread his weight out. Maybe the ice gave way, and he went in too. Maybe Luke was under the water and Sam made a hard choice and went in after him. Either way, Sam and Luke were in the water together. Sam gave him his stick to help Luke brace himself out. Sam pushed Luke out of the freezing water. But during all this Sam's skates are filling with water. The leather and metal blades would have felt like lead weights. His clothes would have weighed a lot. His body would be going into shock from the cold. I've fallen through the ice myself as a kid. I'm sure Frank, Ching, and you have too. We hop out right away, but Sam couldn't leave Luke. His muscles would have started to cramp and cease functioning very quickly. His energy was spent on getting Luke out of the water. He only had seconds. And during that time, he chose to save Luke."

"But there was no hockey stick on the ice" Father Sabastian continued to push back. Desperately not wanting me to be right.

"I'm sorry sir. But there was. Only it wasn't a hockey stick. It was just a tree branch."

The room was silent for just a moment.

"UGGGG!" Ching screamed like an animal. The truth finally, conclusively hitting hard.

He remembered. The kids didn't all have hockey sticks. Some used tree limbs as sticks. And there it was. Laying in the center of a frozen pond. Far from any trees. A stick, just the right size.

Marie went to Ching, his face in his hands.

Father Sabastian stared at me.

"The hockey gear that the Rangers donated. It hadn't arrived yet. Most of the younger kids, they were still playing with makeshift sticks." He collapsed into his chair. Resigned, the ugly truth hitting him like the ice itself.

I looked at Frank. He was crying. He was silent for most of this and processing everything that was being said. He understood.

Sam was gone.

Chapter Forty-Three
March 20, 1927

Frank sent word to Lester and Bill when we arrived back in the city. They gathered everyone together before practice. We only have four games in the season left and then playoffs start. But first, everyone has a right to know.

We all stood at center ice in the Garden. Lester and Bill made sure that everyone was indeed there. It wasn't just all the players. Ag, Claire, Ellen, Marie, all the wives and gals. Harry and the new water boy, Mike. Lester called Tex Richard and Colonel Hammonds. They were there too and made it a point to greet everyone. As was the whole front office staff, including the PR guys Johnny Bruno and Dick Blythe. As Bill always preached, the team was every member of the organization, not just the players, but also the secretaries and the accountants. And they were all present.

We also asked Big Bill Dwyer. He came alone and stood with Tex and the Colonel.

Lester stood slightly separate from everyone. His head bowed. I could see he was carrying the weight of our discovery.

The mood was somber. Although Frank hadn't shared the details, everyone knew by now Sam was dead.

Father Sabastian made the journey down and led with a prayer. His strong words, tinged with deep pain, echoed through the cavernous arena.

As planned, Marie stepped forward when Father Sabastian finished. She was no less devastated than any of us. Yet, she somehow found the strength we professional athletes couldn't. She told the story of Sam's sacrifice as we believed it. No mention was made of his being an orphan. Just that he saw a child in trouble and that he responded. That to save the child, Sam risked his life and didn't survive. Our tears fell to the white ice, briefly melted, and froze. Bonded forever.

Then Bill stepped forward. Head bowed, hands in his pockets. As he always does, Bill found the words for all of us.

"Our time with Sam has been cut much too short. Sam was a prodigy. Perhaps the future of this sport. He had a special gift to move this three-inch rubberized black disk precisely where he wanted, while moving at a high rate of speed on thin sharp blades across a sheet of solid ice. All while larger opponents want to slam him into the boards."

"I didn't want this for Sam. He obviously had the talent. And if we're being honest, I suspect we all knew he was already a more skilled player then all of us, and he was only fifteen. He was so darn smart and intelligent. He had such potential to do anything. I wanted a different life for him. This game of such violence and force. Of injury and disappointment. I didn't want that for him."

"But Sam has reminded me this game is so much more. It's grace and fluidity. It's teamwork and trust. It's passion and loyalty. This is a beautiful game. It's a fun game. And Sam exemplified what it is to be a Ranger. Our commitment to each other. Our willingness to sacrifice. Our drive to a singular allusive goal. Sam Crawford will always be a Ranger."

After our private service, Marie and Big Bill walked down the block to the Forrest together and took the elevator up to his residence. While the rest of us began our practice, they knocked on Elizabeth's door.

We prepared for our final game against the Americans. While they were eliminated from the playoffs, having lost their last several games, we were up two games to one in our intracity rivalry. I'm sure they wanted to finish the season tied.

We taped our sticks and sharpened our blades. Harry, as per ritual, entered the locker room and informed us it was time to head out. Earlier Stan Brown opted out, his head not feeling right, and we were down a man.

We all stood and approached the tunnel when Lester emerged from his office. He was fully padded and laced up. He was wearing our blue sweater. With gloves on and stick in hand he said, "let's go hit some bodies. Harry, you're in charge of the bench tonight."

Bill marched right into their zone and opened the game with a quality shot on Forbes that was blocked. But we set the tempo early and it was hard and fast.

Harry had fun shifting players and minutes into the first Lester jumped over the boards to replace Mackay. The bench erupted in laughter when not thirty seconds later ref Smeaton called him for tripping and sent Lester to the penalty box for two minutes.

Leo Bourgault, whose face was still badly bruised, broke up ice. Leo was usually a 'stay at home' defenseman. But today, he had the urge to stretch his legs. He penetrated their zone and made a nice spin move on Roach. He pulled the puck back and let it fly. At fifteen minutes and forty-seven seconds of the first period, Leo scored his first NHL goal.

Harry leaned over the boards and hailed down the ref. Smeaton nodded, retrieved the puck, and brought it over to Harry. Harry handed him a new puck for the face-off. Harry slid the puck into his pocket to give to Leo after the game.

Bill played like a man possessed and he finally scored at the end of the second period. Lester, for his part, was playing just fine when he stayed out of the penalty box. He got into some pushing and shoving in front of our net. Amusingly, the Americans didn't know how to respond. Here was Lester Patrick, a legend, with his silver hair pushing and wrestling guys to the ice. The Amerks finally had enough and decided to respond like Lester was any skater. Nothing made Lester happier. He was smiling and laughing with every exchange.

Lorne faced 28 shots in the period and a full sixty in the game. He only gave up a back-door goal to Bob Connors, a rookie playing his sixth game, in the third. But after that goal, with the Americans within one, we shut them down the rest of the way. The final was 2-1 and we had won three out of our four games with our Garden rivals.

Chapter Forty-Four

March 22 - 26, 1927

For the second time in a week, the poor Pittsburgh Pirates didn't stand a chance. Lester was back coaching behind the bench.

Frank took the puck up the right side, Bill not far behind. Frank shifted his course and headed right for the net but tapped the puck back to Bill who smashed it through for a goal.

Taffy pulled off a nice move to score less than a minute into the second. Even when the Pirates did score, it was on an assist from us. Boyd was serving two minutes for roughing and just as he came out of the penalty box, he intercepted a pass. It looked like a brilliant play for a moment.

But Roger Smith, the Pirates backup defenseman was also in the right place. He knocked the puck from Boyd and skated away. His shot was the only one that Lorne didn't stop.

In the third our Captain just took over. He scored his second and third goals of the game for his second hat trick of the season. The game ended 4-1.

The Garden was packed for our final regular season game tonight against the Chicago Black Hawks. After the game we would need to rush to Grand Central and catch the train to Boston for our last regular season away game tomorrow night.

We had twenty very special guests in attendance. Tex and the Colonel invited the boys from Father Sabastian's home to the game.

Being a Friday, Father Sabastian took along as many youngsters as possible. They were given the full VIP treatment and even got to see our locker room and meet all the players. The guys all really stepped up and made each kid feel special with an autographed souvenir. They were seated in the new Garden Club box with all the wealthy bankers and lawyers. I hoped Father Sabastian could get one of them to help fund the orphanage.

As we were leaving our locker room, Lester announced the entire second team would be starting tonight's game.

Chabot was in net of course but Leo and Stan started on defense. Paul, Billy, and I took the opening face-off. Our referee for the evening Dave Ritchie had a little fun too, telling each of us were to position ourselves.

Regardless of the starting lineup, Bill Cook was still the first to score. He was in the right place for a rebound and simply tapped it in.

Not twenty seconds later, Frank won the ensuing face-off and raced into the zone. He skated behind the net and back out front again hoping to find an open teammate. But when no one got free he spun around and scored himself.

Refusing to be left off the score sheet, Bunny buried the puck with five seconds left in the first period off a nice pass from Stan Brown. But it was how he scored that caught everyone's attention.

As Stan passed to him, Bunny raised his stick up over his shoulder and in one fluid, beautiful, perfectly timed motion, brought it down to coincide with the arrive of the puck. His back leg kicked out as his stick continued its pendulum arch. For one brief moment, the end of his stick was pointing right at its intended target, and his raised back leg were parallel on the same horizontal plain. The puck flew like a bullet. The goalie flinched, practically jumping out of its path as he screamed at Bunny for almost killing him.

It was majestic.

I had only seen it's like, once before, months earlier.

Bunny glided over to me and whispered, "Just like Sam showed us."

There was no scoring in the second, but Ching was sent to the box early in the third for being rude to the Black Hawks. The crowd loved that. But even with the man advantage the Hawks couldn't get past Chabot. In the closing three minutes of the game Bill, Bun and Frank put on one last clinic for the home crowd.

Bill skated up, passed to Bun. Bunny skated with it behind the net and came out the other side, looking up the whole time. He sent it back to his brother who immediately sent it across to Frank who was crashing the net. Raffles redirected it in for the fourth and final goal of the game.

Up 4-0 with less than three minutes, I assumed the well-dressed crowd would begin to exit. But with very few exceptions, they didn't.

When the final bell rung, they collectively stood and kept clapping. I was confused by the spontaneous ovation.

Lester blocked our path to the tunnel and said, "They are not cheering for tonight's win gentleman, they are celebrating the amazing inaugural season you've given this city."

"Come on, follow me." Bill said. He skated onto the ice. The crowd erupted into a tizzy. They were yelling "Let's go Rangers."

We gathered at center ice and looked around us at the crowd. Our first-time together in the Garden flashed in my memory. Ollie and Winkler were now replaced with Leo and Stan. But the core of the team remained largely intact. On that first day in mid-November of 1926, the Garden was empty. Just as it was only days earlier when we gathered in the same spot to mourn Sam.

In only five months, we had built a following of loyal fans and the Garden was alive.

Bill raised his stick high in the air. A salute to the crowd.

We all did the same. Sticks raised high to the crowd. Our way of saying, thank you.

We skated off, cleaned ourselves up and raced to Grand Central to catch the train to Boston.

Lorne skated out to his position and prepared for the opening face-off. The whole team knew we had the hottest goaltender in the league. In our last ten games he'd only given up nine goals and four of those contests were shutouts.

Although our fans and the press viewed the Americans as being our natural rival, on the ice it was indisputably Boston.

I had no greater dislike toward another player than that no-account Shore. Lots of guys played a hard, physical, and intimidating brand. Bill and Ching were two great examples. But Shore inflicted violence under the guise of playing hockey.

Tonight's game against Boston meant nothing regarding the playoff standings, yet it quickly became obvious that Shore's target was our star Bill Cook. Bill was leading the league in scoring, and Shore seemingly wanted to incapacitate our Captain just before the playoffs.

Four minutes into the game Frederickson drew Chabot out of the net on a rush and slipped the puck past him to score the first goal.

Meanwhile, Shore was playing with his elbows and barely seemed concerned with the puck. He was only on the ice when our first line was out. As soon as Bill came to the bench, like he did now, so did Shore.

As I skated by the Bruin's bench, I tried to get under Shore's skin another way.

"Hey Eddie, are you too afraid to skate with me today?"

I spun around as I passed so that I continued to face him even as I skated backwards. Motioning with my gloves for him to come out. He swore back at me. I knew I could keep agitating him and eventually he'd take the bait. The other guys on Boston's bench we're yelling back at me too, defending their teammate. That I understood and respected. But no one on the ice retaliated or provoked me. I took that to mean they were putting on a show. I imagined some of those players might be tired of Shore's antics. He certainly couldn't be a joy in the clubhouse or the bars after.

Oliver scored late in the second and Frank countered with a beauty shortly after. Even though Bill never touched the puck on Frank's goal, Shore blindsided him just the same. Bill, who can protect himself, didn't see Shore, and went down hard. Bill got up quickly but while Shore was dropping his gloves, Bunny slammed hard into Shore.

This prompted fisticuffs with everyone, and it was several minutes before the fire burned itself out and the two refs were able to restore order.

The Boston crowd loved every taunt, shove, and punch.

Ten minutes, thirty seconds into the third, Frank tied the game. Even after the earlier donnybrook, Shore continued to try and remove heads at the neck. He wasn't even pretending to play hockey. He was just trying to hurt us. Ironically, he's a solid skater and would probably be considered one of the more talented guys if he shifted his focus from bare fisted boxing to hockey.

Lester insisted on keeping Ching practically chained to the bench. Ivan wanted to pick Shore up and drop him on his head. But Lester refused to let our defenseman hurt his shoulder further. With Ching recovering, it would normally be Leo's job in these situations to provide protection. But with his nose already badly broken he was also forbidden from mixing it up.

The crowd didn't like it so much when Frank scored yet again, and we took the lead. It was his third goal of the game.

But with just over three minutes remaining Cleghorn tied the game. We threw everything at their net, but an overtime period was soon upon us.

Seven minutes into overtime, Herbert scored and that was it. Our first regular season was over.

Chapter Forty-Five

February 1994

"What was your record when your season ended?" Mark asked.

"We finished with 25 wins, 13 losses and 6 overtime ties. 56 points was the best in our division." I replied.

"We went to the first Chicago vs. Boston game with our gals as spectators. It was incredible to watch from that perspective. It also opened our eyes because even though Lester, Bill and Frank had been preaching to us about the increased pace and intensity, we were shocked to see the actual difference. As were the Hawks because Boston won that first game 6-1. Boston was playing in a whole different gear. It didn't hurt that our old teammate Hal Winkler was outstanding in net for the Bruins. I remember Marie and I sat next to Frank and Ag. Frank was so happy to watch his brother Billy play."

"After that game, our practices took on a new urgency. Lester pushed us harder than ever. We all welcomed it. We spent hours, day after day, at practice working on strategies to tighten our defense even more. The only hiccup was that Billy Boyd wasn't feeling great. He had a nasty sore throat."

"We were at the Green Door when we got word on the score of the second game between the Hawks and Bruins late Thursday night.

"I remember Harry coming into the bar with the telegram. The bartender Mikey quieted down the whole place as if it were about to be raided. The musicians stopped playing. All the regulars gathered around us."

Harry announced, “the game ended tied 4-4. No overtime was played because the winner of the series is determined by goals scored. Boston is the winner of the series on goals, 10-5. We’re traveling to Boston on the 10:30 train tomorrow morning fellas.”

“Oh, and Boyd has scarlet fever and won’t be making the trip.”

“A round of shots were handed out to all of us and we all went home to pack.”

Chapter Forty-Six
April 2, 1927

The morning of our first playoff game, I sat alone sipping my black coffee and dunking my toast into the yellow egg yolk.

Seabury Lawrence filed an article the night before that ran in the Times.

"Rangers On Scene for Bruins Battle"

"Boston, April 1, 1927 - "Bye-bye Blackhawks, bring on the Rangers" is the slogan tonight along Boylston Street and other popular Boston thoroughfares on the eve of the first tilt between the Boston Bruins and the New York Rangers."

"Lester Patrick, manager of the Rangers, made some modest assertions on the arrival here. Patrick, the survivor of many a Stanley Cup playoff, has done brilliantly with his team this season, but sets it in a singular minor key."

"We have only one man on our team, said Patrick, who has ever been in a Stanley Cup play before. This is Frank Boucher, who played twice with the Vancouver Maroons. On the other hand, nine of the Bruins are veterans and should handle themselves well in this series."

"However, I believe the spirit we have been able to develop among our players, their morale, and will to win, even when behind, will bring the Rangers through."

The article went on to mention that Boyd was out of the lineup.

Boyd's absence was a real concern. Lester, Bill, Frank, and Ching had a separate meeting in the dining car to discuss the shuffle. They felt, and I agreed with their choice, that the best option was to move Leo Bourgault up to Boyd's spot at center. The center position is a two-way player, both offense and defense. While Leo lacked the offensive threat, he at least had the speed and defensive skills.

It was Lester's intent to ride Ching and Taffy for as much ice time as they could stand. We had Stan Brown and Reg Mackey to support them when they needed a breather. Lester stressed at every meeting, every practice, and now in the wash car of the train, this first game was about our shutting them down. When the meeting was over Lester asked Paul, Leo, and me to stay behind.

"The three of you have never skated together as a line. This is an unfortunate time to improvise but I know you can make this work. I do not want you to think about scoring. If an opportunity or breakaway presents itself, fine. But otherwise, I want you guys playing smart, defensive, takeaway, keep away, poke-checking, hit every player with the puck, high-speed hockey." Lester stressed.

"Sir, I have a suggestion." I offered, "When we find ourselves in faceoff situations, I propose that Paul take them. Once the action is underway, Paul and Leo can switch positions on the fly."

"I like that, but why not you Mr. Murdoch?" Lester inquired.

"Because Paul is better at winning faceoffs during practice." I replied.

"Mr. Thompson, Mr. Bourgault, do you both feel you can switch positions seamlessly during the action?"

"Yes" Paul replied.

"Yes, Sir. I think that's a good idea sir." Lou agreed. "Truthfully, the last time I tried to win a faceoff I was skating on a pond in Sturgeon Falls. If Paul can help with those, I can handle the defensive responsibilities."

"It's settled than. Thank you, gentleman. Mr. Murdoch, would you stay one more minute?"

The other two left the wash car.

"Murray, play your game and don't let Shore get under your skin. The game isn't about him. I love it when you're on the ice because you're a combination of smarts, discipline, grit, and passion. I never worry about you, and you frequently surprise me. Just play your game and don't allow Shore to distract you."

As we stepped onto the ice in Boston, an unrelenting thunderclap of boos and insults poured down. That was fine, until they started hitting us with balled up programs, buckets of peanuts and popcorn, oranges and apples, and all manner of objects that were within reach.

"Who brings fruit to a hockey game?" Taffy asked as we dodged the projectiles and produce.

The referees Jerry Laflamme and Billy Bell raced over to restore order, but little changed until Laflamme yelled that he wouldn't start the game until the crowd stopped throwing. A few objects were thrown in his direction, but most of the crowd in that section regained control and merely threw obscenities.

As the game got underway, Leo commented "Jeez, I pray there aren't any of our fans in here."

I knew what he meant. If there were any Ranger supporters here, they'd surely get beaten up.

The crowd never appeared to sit down. Thousands must have been admitted without seats in the standing sections. They were admittingly intimidating. Fans down by the ice were pushing and shoving against the chicken wire, their fingers wrapped so tightly around the fence holes I thought they might bleed.

There were no tuxedos and gowns to be found in these seats.

The pace on the ice was furious. Anyone who touched the puck was almost instantaneously checked or slammed against the boards. Those that could find room to take several strides were quickly swallowed up and had to make desperate passes. In the first several minutes there were frequent turnovers and neither team got many shots on either net.

Line changes were happening faster and more frequently too. Normally, changes were made during stoppages in play. But now, we were hopping over the boards on the fly as players were coming to the bench, gasping for breath.

Our shifts were shorter and far more intense, just as we had been warned. We practiced and drilled hard in preparation for these situations, but I felt overwhelmed.

"Left wing!" Bunny yelled as he skated towards the bench. My cue. I jumped over just as he arrived, careful to avoid a 'too many men' penalty. At this pace it would be easy to make that mistake.

Bill was now battling in the far-right corner. Frank, who was getting whacked and pushed in front of their net skated behind it so that Bill had an outlet. Taffy and Ching were both holding their defensive positions. I raced from the bench to fill the void in front of the net. Just as I arrived at the blue line, Bill succeeded in popping the puck back along the boards to Frank.

I skated as fast as I could.

Frank quickly corralled it and looked up, spotted me crashing towards the net. He barely had time to send the pass out front before being pummeled into the boards.

But Frank accomplished his goal, and the puck found me, and I put a quick shot on net. Winkler made a strong save and I cursed out loud, but in that same moment I was knocked senselessly to the ice.

Suddenly the action was heading the other way. Bill and Frank were already chasing the action as Taffy and Ching skated backwards, positioning themselves to defuse the Bruins rush. I got to my feet, my head spinning, desperately trying to catch up with everyone else. By the time I got past center ice, Taffy had successfully sent the puck safely out of our zone. The Bruins had to retreat and regroup. This allowed Bill and Frank to both get a change.

Leo and Paul leaped over the boards and joined me as I was already chasing after the puck. I had only been on the ice fifteen seconds or so ahead of them.

I was pushing hard towards the Bruin with the puck. From this distance my intent was to pressure him into making a hasty pass. I was closing quickly, and he was hesitating, I knew he didn't have an open man. He let the puck go, perhaps hoping for the best, just as I checked him. I bounced off him and spun around. Leo was fighting off two brown and gold jerseys for the puck. The speed was moving so quickly I barely had time to register who the Bruins players were.

Oliver won the puck, and passed to teammate. Paul Thompson was on him immediately. Frederickson tried to send the puck deep, but Taffy intercepted it. He skated out of the zone and again the Bruins retreated as one player pressured Taffy. But Taffy didn't panic, and he created some room to skate. We all turned up ice and pressed the attack, careful not to be called for offsides. Just as Taffy safely crossed the blue line, he sent the puck deep and I chased after it. Cleghorn was ahead of me and reached the puck first. I checked him into the boards and fought for the puck at his feet.

Suddenly, the ref was ringing his bell and calling a penalty. On me? It was a clean check. Then I noticed their centerman Frederickson skating off to the box. He had been called for slashing. The crowd erupted in fury.

We skated to the bench as Lester wanted the fresh A-Line out on the man advantage. The crowd was not settling down. Their rage was nearly berserk.

Leflamme wisely got the game going and the crowd was quicky distracted by the action. The Bruin's defense was barely penetrable during five on five but now with the man advantage we were getting more pressure in their zone.

For the first minute, our front three kept trying for a good lane to shoot but the Bruins were disciplined. Bill Cook now battled for position in front of their net as Bun, Frank, Ching, and Taffy kept trying to penetrate from the perimeter. Our shots were blocked and held by Winkler, denying Bill a juicy loose puck. The fans celebrated every save and cheered widely as the penalty came to an end.

But as the Bruins were now getting the puck out of their zone, much of the crowd did not see Eddie Shore give Bill a wicked cross-check behind the play. The other ref, Bill Bell, saw the blatant crime happen and immediately called a penalty on Shore.

Now the Back Bay spectators were truly out of control. What happened to us in the tunnel earlier now spread throughout the whole arena. Anything that could be thrown was now landing on the ice and in our bench.

Laflamme immediately stopped the game. He tried for a few moments to wave the crowd down, but it was futile. The ice was littered with debris. The fans behind our bench were screaming the game was fixed.

Both teams were sent to their locker rooms until order could be restored and the ice cleared.

We took that time to gather ourselves and settle down.

Forty minutes later, we reemerged, still on the man advantage and again the Bruins masterfully shut down our scoring attempts.

As Fredrickson took the puck up center ice, Frank laid all out and poke-checked the puck off his stick. Fredrickson hit Frank to the ice in retaliation, but Frank, flat on his back still managed to swat the puck away from the Bruin. Rolling over, Frank quickly got to his feet, chased after the puck, gained the zone, and got a shot off. Winkler caught it clean.

Moments later, Taffy was called for roughing and now Boston had an extra man on the ice. Lester sent Stan Brown to join Ching on defense while Leo and I were to handle their attack up front.

It was unrelenting.

Oliver took a hard blast towards Chabot that Stan was able to block with his shin pad. He collapsed to the ice, struggling to get up.

I immediately dropped back and took his defensive position. I yelled to Stan, "take my spot and get to the bench first chance."

Boston passed the puck around, looking for that open lane. Shore parked himself in front of Chabot and took whacks at our goalie. Ching checked him but Shore now whacked at Ching's legs. He was distracting us. Lester was right, play our game and don't focus on Shore.

If Shore doesn't have the puck, he can't hurt us. We had to keep our defensive positions and prevent the Bruins from getting a clean shot. Oliver shot again and I caught it on the blade of my stick cleanly. I skated away from the net, held it as long as I could and sent the puck all the way up ice before getting slammed. The Bruins had to retreat. This bought us a few seconds to regroup.

Stan hobbled to the bench and Reg jumped out. As soon as he reached me, I moved back up to my forward position. Leo had followed the play into center ice and tried to slow Boston as they came at us again.

Hitchman skated towards me with the puck. He was trying to get around me on the outside. I caught him and shouldered him into the boards. Shore, following behind picked up the puck and rushed towards the net. Ching stepped up and smothered Shore's advance. The puck was loose, and I reached it just before Galbraith. He wrestled me for control, but I sent it around the boards and just over the blue line.

Boston had to regroup but the puck didn't go far. They were back within seconds.

Fifteen feet directly in front of me, Hitchman ripped a blast as Shore was crashing the net.

I dropped both knees to the ice like a goalie, trying to use as much of my body to block the flight of the puck. It sailed right at my face. I flinched, prepared for the impact. The bullet hit me square in the left collarbone, not two inches from my chin and throat. My pads didn't cover that spot and I took the full impact. I saw stars but the puck was in front of me. I got up and sent it back down the ice as Hitchman followed up his shot with a check that sent me to the ice. I saw Taffy race out of the box, the kill was over.

Both teams were changing, and I skated to the bench. Better my shoulder than my face I thought.

Harry approached as I gingerly sat on the bench. "You ok Murray? That shot caught you good."

"I'm fine. The pads did their job." I lied. It really was a lie. My shoulder was throbbing in agony. Harry handed me water. The stars were fading now. My god, this is still only the first period. I sat there gasping for air.

Both teams took offsetting penalties next. Bill Cook and Jimmy Herbert were called for fighting. Herbert always seemed like a standup guy and looked like he belonged on a sailing vessel. The four-on-four action opened the ice and cut down on the heavy hitting for the final two minutes of the period.

The second period saw no stop in the high rate of penalties or hard checks. In between periods I had quietly put a bag of ice on my shoulder without drawing attention. But I knew I could barely lift it.

Leo was called for roughing early in the period and Lester kept me on the ice with Paul for the kill. Fortunately, Ching, Taffy and Paul saw most of the action, but my arm worked when needed.

It wasn't until late in the second period that the crowd got its first full taste of the old Ching Johnson.

Hitchman was attacking. Shore trailed behind him. Ching stepped up and engaged Hitchman, steering him towards the boards by the Bruins bench. Ching was able to knock the puck away. Shore closed in to recover it. Ching disengaged from Hitchman and raced Shore to the puck.

Ching got down low and hit Shore in such a way as to physically lift him up and drive him over the boards into the Bruins' bench. Ching deposited him into the laps of his teammates.

Laflamme half-heartedly rung the bell to stop play as Ching was already skating off towards the penalty box. Hitchman and Shore instigated the crowd to a rousing roar.

Lester sent our second line out to close out the period. We did a fine job of shutting down any scoring opportunities and the second ended still scoreless.

Between periods, we were reminded that there would be no overtime period. In the playoffs it was the highest scoring total over both games that determined the winner of the series.

For much of the third, Boston attacked like waves on a beach head. Whereas our strategy was to still hold them scoreless, they threw everything at us. The refs were just letting us play and Boston was taking full advantage with their elbows and slashes. Ching, Taffy, and Lorne just would not bend or break.

First squad battled first squad.

Blood was drawn and flowed on both sides.

From the bench I leapt up and screamed as I saw Shore purposefully kick Ching in the knee with his skate. I had never seen a player do that and I yelled at the refs for not calling a penalty.

Play was stopped allowing Ching to come to the bench for repairs. Stan, who's own leg was still badly bruised, hopped on the ice to take his place.

Harry reached under Ching's girdle and pulled down his sock. On the unprotected side of his knee was a deep dash. Ching removed his shin pad, which provided no protection during this violation. We could all see that it would need stitches, but we didn't have time. The game was still going on with little time remaining. Harry wrapped bandage after bandage around the wound.

"That's enough Harry. Enough. I won't be able to bend me knee if you put more on." Ching yelled at Harry.

His shin pad was strapped back on, and his blood-stained blue sock pulled up. Ching stood and tested his leg on the bench and declared himself ready.

He stood at the rail and waited for the first chance to get back out. Bill Cook sent the puck deep and Stan skated right to the bench. Ching jumped back on. There were now less than three minutes in the game.

The Cook brothers and Frank's normal tic-tac-toe passing had been shut down all game by a defensive wall. Now both teams were trying pure brute strength to force the puck over the goal line. Shoulders were down, bodies were slammed, pushed, practically thrown to the ice.

Thirty seconds remained. Everyone on both benches were standing.

Miraculously, Bill suddenly got one last beautiful shot off, but Winkler stretched full out and made the save with his glove. The ref was about to ring the play dead when Winkler tossed the puck to Cleghorn, who sent the puck out of the zone up along the boards.

Fredrickson broke free racing after the puck when it suddenly took an unfortunate bounce. It seemed to steer itself right to his outstretched stick, and once he had it secured, he rushed into our zone. Ching and Taffy were both all over him, practically dragging him to the ice. There were only a few seconds left.

The crowd, in a wild uncontrolled scream, watched as his wrist shot was calmly blocked by Lorne Chabot, and sent harmlessly into the corner as the final bell rung.

The battle, as it no longer felt like a 'game', was over. Neither team had scored, the winner would now be determined in two days, on our home ice.

The train back to New York looked like a hospital carriage. Harry and the new water boy, Mike, scrambled to find all the ice they could before boarding. Our needs exceeded what ice we could hope to find on the train.

Ching's knee was properly sutured, but now it was bruising. Harry packed it in as much ice as Ching could tolerate.

Stan could barely stand on his own leg and his right shin had a purple golf ball-size lump.

The back of Bill Cook's neck was sore after being cross-checked by Shore early in the game.

At some point Bunny took a stick to the jaw, I never even saw that happen.

Frank had ice on his forearm because of multiple slashes.

I applied a bag of ice to my left shoulder. I could barely lift my arm. Everyone had bumps and bruises that needed ice with a shot of whiskey.

But no one needed ice, or deserved a whole bottle of whiskey, more than our quiet hero, Lorne Chabot. The undisputed star of the game. Our anchor in the storm.

Chapter Forty-Seven
April 4, 1927

I awoke to the smell of bacon and coffee. I rolled over and Marie was already out of bed and making breakfast. My oh my, how I love and adore this woman.

I sit up slowly and swing my legs over the side. I'm wearing a white tank top and the bruise on my shoulder is massive. I slowly rotate my arm up in a wide circle. There is considerable throbbing but at one point, a sharp pain.

There is nothing to be done. We must push through the pain, that is all.

I keep rotating it to loosen up. The worst thing that could happen is if we allow our injuries to stiffen up.

That's why we skated yesterday. It was a lite workout. No hitting. Just skating, shooting, and drills. Lorne was present but he was kept out of the net and didn't face any shots. Lester was happy to stand in his place.

I pulled on a white dress shirt so that Marie doesn't have to stare at my shoulder. I step into our kitchen; Marie is at the stove in her bathrobe. Her hair is already perfect. Mine is anything but.

I walk up behind her, wrap my bad arm around her waist, and with my other hand push her hair aside so I can kiss the back of her slender neck. She goes right on flipping the bacon and frying the eggs like I'm not even there. But I know she's holding back a smile.

"Sit down Mr. Murdoch, conserve your energy." She orders me.

That makes me kiss her neck even more deeply.

She whips around and threatens to poke me with the greasy thongs. "Sit down, I'll pour your coffee. Read your paper." Marie doesn't ask a third time, so I wisely retreat.

"The paper predicts you'll have a new record crowd this evening. The record was set when you played the Americans, at 18,200. Apparently, the Bruins spent the night at the Waldorf Astoria. Tex and the Colonel never set us up in such a swanky joint." She teases.

"I'm sure the player's trashed the place. Just wait until the Bruin's get the bill for the damages." I chuckle.

She slid my plate in front of me and sat down to sip her own coffee.

"It looks like the Ottawa Senators will advance over the Montreal Canadians."

"Yeah, I don't see the Canadians winning. Ottawa is the class of the whole league." I acknowledge as I take a bite of the most delicious bacon.

"The paper talks a little about the money for making the Cup finals. It's a significant amount. That would be nice." She eyes me over her mug.

"I'm sure it would, but the guys never talk about it. It's a motivator, for sure. But we never discuss it." I reply and put the fork into my eggs. I balance a bit of the egg on the corner of my toast and I'm about to bit down when she casually mentions…

"I'm just saying, the extra money would be nice. We will have an extra mouth to feed by next season." As she calmly sips from her mug.

The toast doesn't make it to my mouth.

I fix my stare at her.

"Are you saying? Are you telling me?"

I stand and go around the table and kneel at her side. I look in her eyes and catch my breath. "My oh my, are you knocked up Mrs. Murdoch?"

She leans over and kisses my neck.

It was clear from the outset that this would not be a record-breaking crowd. There were a good 14,000 but not close to the packed house we needed. I would've liked our fans to be just as loud, passionate, and intimidating as Boston's two nights early.

But the whole lower tier was once again dressed in formal wear, fresh from a play. They were rarely standing and never taxing the strength of the chicken-wire fencing.

The seats nearest the ice were filled with Captains of Industry and beautiful dames on their arms. The real noise and passion came from the middle and upper tiers. Those were the fans that really got into it. There were no tuxedoes and gowns up there. The rest of the arena was filled with professionals and laborers, factory workers, teachers, bank tellers, and secretaries. Those were the people who were fully invested in our success. These were the people whose spirits we would lift with a win tonight. The idea of breaking their hearts was not a thought I entertained.

From the tunnel, I watched as Sprague Cleghorn led his team onto the ice. A loud choruses of jeers hit them. The crowd gave us an even louder ovation as we came out. But neither was at the level of intensity as Boston.

Then it dawned on me. How could they know? This was the city's first ever playoff game. This was Boston's third season. Our crowd wasn't prepared or experienced. All the questionable tactics Bruno and Blythe spent on attracting fans, it might have been nice if they spent a little of that energy expressing to our fans the advantages a home crowd could produce.

I chastised myself for getting distracted. This game would be won like every other game. On the ice.

Both refs immediately pulled the team captains together and issued a stern warning that the rough play in the last game would not be tolerated again.

At eight-fifty in the evening, the puck was dropped.

Frank won the face-off and Bunny got the puck. He started the game in unusual fashion. From practically center ice, Bun rifled a long blast that sailed just over Winkler's net by a few feet.

Our guys chased after the puck, and the same intense, hard-hitting action resumed as if a two-day break had never occurred. The crowd was in a tizzy, so fast was the action. Both teams got a couple shots off and both Winkler and Chabot quickly warmed to the pace. Frank was using all his poke-checking skills near center ice to defuse as much of the Bruin's offense as possible.

It was on just such a play that Raffles knocked the puck off Frederickson's stick. The Bruin took offense, grabbed ahold of Frank's sweater, and threw our thief to the ice in the most ungentlemanly manner. Our bench leaped up, the guys on the ice rushed to center ice and much how-do-you-do's took place to the delight of the fans in attendance. But Referee O'Hara already called the penalty, and he escorted Frederickson to the penalty box personally.

This was the situation that we prepared for. Lester stressed we needed to step up our attack on the man advantage.

With their starting centerman in the box, Frank lined up against the less experienced Oliver in the neutral zone. He won the face off back to Ching. Ching held the puck for a moment and one of the Bruin's moved to pressure him while the other three players dropped back into a defensive posture. Once the Bruin got within five feet of Ching, he zipped the puck across the ice to the waiting Taffy Abel.

Taffy immediately turned on his speed and raced into the zone, as did the front line and Ching.

Bill pushed and shoved his way to the front of the net while the other four set up on the parameter. Taffy still controlled the puck and since no one was aggressively pressuring him he skated closer to the net. He ripped a hard shot on goal, but it missed wide by several feet. Winkler barely moved. The puck bounced off the back boards, just as Taffy intended, and ricocheted out to the waiting Bill Cook who didn't waste even a heartbeat slamming it into the net for the first goal of the game.

1-0.

The Garden went nuts. It was a play we practiced endlessly for just such an occasion. We couldn't always count on the bounce off the boards so Bunny was rushing in from the other direction in case Bill couldn't get to it. But Taffy placed it perfectly.

Leo, Paul, Stan, Reg, and I were celebrating together on the bench when I suddenly realized the crowd was throwing programs and papers on the ice in celebration. "No, no, no" we yelled to no avail.

Laflamme immediately halted the game. Neither team had to leave their bench, but there was a delay while the ice was cleared. Whatever momentum we might have just won was just squandered, by our own fans.

Lester was uncharacteristically annoyed. He knew he couldn't show his gruff side to the audience, but we recognized it on the bench. We were all disappointed at the interruption.

We watched as Art Ross, the Bruins' manager was strategizing with his players. Lester implored us to stay disciplined and focused on our game plan. But within moments of the game resuming, the Bruins were within our zone.

Shore was in front of the net trying to get under Ching's skin. He was using his stick aggressively, and I realized that Ching was standing in a way to protect his damaged knee. We were screaming from the bench for the refs to call a penalty on Shore. Ching remained disciplined and merely pushed back. Nothing to draw a penalty, which was clearly Shore's intent.

Getting no response from Ching, Shore turned his attention to Lorne and hit our goalie somewhere in the face with the butt of his stick. The refs didn't call it or see it. With this, Ching had no choice.

He cross-checked Shore backwards. Trying to regain his balance, Shore swung his stick at Ching's face. He only just missed, and Ching immediately tackled him to the ice. Shore tried to throw some punches, but Ching had a superior advantage and threw off his glove and started whaling on Eddie's face. He got in maybe three blows before the refs pulled him off. Both were escorted to the box, but Shore kept antagonizing the crowd with his arms and wearing that arrogant smirk. I wanted to knock his teeth out.

But what concerned me more was that Eddie got what he wanted. He felt he won that. What was the point? Lorne seemed fine. Both players went to the box. And it's Shore's face that's bloodied. It's still five on five because the penalties offset. What was the point I wondered? Is he just psychotic?

The Bruin's front line of Oliver, Galbraith and Fredrickson attacked again. Taffy had help from Stan, but it was only Lorne making solid save after strong save that kept them scoreless. Bunny sent the puck deep into their zone and used the respite to get a line change.

Leo, Paul, and I jumped out. While we had no sustained attack, we held our ground and slowed the Bruin's offense. But the ice felt tilted in their favor, and we were on our heels. We weren't getting the puck out of our zone cleanly, giving them extra opportunities. Lorne, thankfully, was on his game.

Once the penalty ended, we changed lines at our first safe opportunity.

Taffy took off with the puck and carried it into their zone. Frank stayed back to support Ching on defense while Taffy rushed towards the net.

Abel had options. Bunny and Bill were both in position for a pass, but they were also in a good spot for a rebound. Taffy shot hard from about ten feet away. The puck flew over Winkler's left shoulder but hit off the crossbar. The loud, teasing clang rung throughout the arena. The puck careened harmlessly over the net. A fraction lower and it would have been a goal.

We tried to keep the puck in their zone, but inexplicably Billy Stuart, their backup defenseman started mixing it up with Bill Cook. Cook ignored him but Stuart kept whacking the back of Bill's knees with his stick. Bill turned around and shoved him. Stuart immediately dropped his gloves. Bill had no choice but to follow suit. Neither got many blows in before they were both sent off.

Lester sent our line back out again. Same as before, we couldn't penetrate their defense and more of our time was spent defending than attacking.

Seconds into the shift, Shore and Ching were back at it in front of Lorne. I didn't see how it started but Shore punched Ivan in the face with his glove. That's like getting hit with a brick and Ching was in a rage. He dropped his gloves and started swinging. The two got ahold of each other's sweater with one hand and just punched like jackhammers at the other. Everyone jumped in and there was mayhem on the ice until arms finally got tired and the two refs were able to finally get everyone separated.

Ching and Shore joined Cook and Stuart in the box. Two of our star players were off the ice.

But Boston's first line was intact. Oliver, Fredrickson, and Galbraith intended to take full advantage. Although both teams were even in numbers on the ice, we were clearly at a disadvantage.

Hitchman had the puck back at the blue line, took several strides toward the net and shot a rifle. Leo threw his full body to the ice. His slide intersected with the blast and caught him in the ribs. He was slow getting up.

Oliver now had the puck and was trying to go around me. I rode him into the boards and tied him up, trying to kill time. His elbow came up and found the underside of my chin. I tasted blood. We battled for the puck at our feet, and I fought to keep it between my blade and the boards. My left arm was almost useless. I kept my feet wide for balance and strength, and just held on. Another player slammed me from behind. My face was rubbed against the chicken-wire and my shoulder sent a jolt of electricity down my arm. My right ankle was hooked. I felt someone pull hard, and I went down to one knee. I still had the puck against the boards, refusing to give it up. Finally, someone just fell on me. We wrestled and the puck was back in play.

I got to my feet to see Cleghorn put a shot on Lorne. It was blocked and Taffy tried to clear it. But it didn't get out. Hitchman shot again. Paul tried to block it with his body but missed. Lorne made the save but couldn't hold the rebound. Everyone pounced. Suddenly, Lorne and Taffy were both underneath three Bruins. The refs stopped play and Paul, Leo and I were trying to pull bodies off our guys while getting shoved and knocked around ourselves.

Somehow Lorne had kept the puck out of the net.

The first penalty ended, and Lester pulled us off. With our starting forwards back on the ice, Ching's timeout ended mere seconds later. Teams were at full strength now with less than a minute to play in the period.

Cleghorn had the puck and was coming up center ice, right towards Frank. Frank poked at the puck just as Cleghorn shifted his stride. From the bench it seemed as if Cleghorn intended to put his skate as close to Frank's stick blade as he could get. He then took a dive. It was terrible acting. Our bench jumped to our feet, and the crowd protested with rage, but the ref fell for it and called a tripping penalty on Frank.

Boston finished the period with a man advantage that would carry over to the second. Lorne faced fifteen bullets whereas we only put eleven shots on Winkler. The first period saw eight penalties. Somehow, we emerged up by one goal thanks to Bill Cook. But I couldn't shake the feeling we're playing Boston's game and falling prey to their hidden strategy.

As the second period got underway, Shore attacked twice. Taffy impeded the first rush, but Eddie got a shot off regardless. Lorne snatched the second more dangerous shot out of the air, but Shore made sure he clipped our goalie with his shoulder as he passed.

This of course provoked a little prizefighting.

When hockey resumed, Bill Cook took the puck deep, Fredrickson on him. Bill was looking up for an outlet, but neither Frank nor his brother could get open. Suddenly, Fredrickson tripped Bill and fell on top of him. O'Hara sent Fredrickson off.

On the advantage we pressed our attack, desperate to increase our tally. But before we could even get set up in their zone, Shore and Taffy were wrestling. It started behind the play and none of us saw how it started. Shore was sneaky that way. The refs only knew two players were going at it, so both were sent off.

We tried to press the advantage again. The Cooks and Frank quickly gained the zone and started putting pressure on their defense. The crowd was getting to their feet in anticipation of some quality shots. Out of the corner of my eye, and far from the action, I saw Cleghorn take a swing with his stick. The ref stopped play. Ching was hunched over. Blood was dripping on the ice. What the hell is going on here? I wondered.

The ref sent Cleghorn to the box, but Ching had to come to the bench. His nose was cut at the bridge and would need attention. Both our starting defensemen were off the ice. Stan and Reg were on defense now. I looked up at Lester, who was rubbing his chin like he does when in deep thought.

Boston attacked. Galbraith carried the puck up ice into our zone. Reg moved to engage him, and Galbraith slid the puck across the ice to Herbert, who took a quick wrist shot that beat Lorne.

The game was tied. 1-1.

The Bruins weren't even finished celebrating before Shore and Abel were once again fighting as they emerged from the penalty boxes. No one was looking in that direction but the crowd in that section was apoplectic. Whatever happened, they didn't approve. After exchanging a couple blows, Abel and Shore wrestled each other to the ice. We could hear Taffy yelling at Shore, who was again just laughing and smirking.

Harry put a bandage over Ching's nose, but it wasn't a long-term solution. It needed stitches but that would take too long. During the stoppage, Ching jumped on for Reg.

I could hear Harry informing Lester "It's just tape over the cut. Between the blood and sweat, it won't stay. He needs stitches between periods."

"Manage it as best you can Harry. We need him on the ice as much as possible." Lester replied.

Play hadn't resumed a minute before the next stoppage. Now Bunny and Hitchman were fighting. Bunny was trying to avoid a penalty, but Hitchman kept throwing punches. Bunny had no choice. Both went to the box and Lester sent our line back out.

I was trying to keep it all straight. Taffy and Bunny were both in the box. Shore and Hitchman were in the box for Boston. Ching was on the ice but would soon need to come off for more repairs. His nose was bleeding all over the ice. This was just chaos. We couldn't get anything going.

"Damn, is that their intent?" I said to myself as I skated after the puck. I corralled the loose puck and headed north. I was watching as Taffy and Shore came out of the box at the same time. Shore went right after Taffy from behind. He wrestled Taffy to the ice and again play was stopped. Laflamme called them both for roughing. Taffy was so frustrated he had tears in his eyes. He just wanted to get back on the ice. Bunny was screaming at Eddie Shore from the penalty box. Shore just sat and smiled.

Lester was yelling at Laflamme. Laflamme skated past the bench and chastised Art Ross to get his players under control and then did the same with Lester. Lester screamed back that Laflamme should open his damn eyes.

The other ref, O'Hara ordered Ching off the ice to address his nose. Paul took the face-off and won the puck back to Stan. Paul and Leo immediately crisscrossed each other and assumed their proper roles. Stan tried to skate but was quickly under pressure. He sent the puck up the ice blindly. That lead to a sloppy turnover.

Oliver now had control and he passed to Hitchman. Leo raced to engage him, but Hitchman came in fast and ripped a shot. I tried to get in front of the shot with my body, but I was too late. The shot beat Lorne.

2-1 Bruins were up.

My heart sank. Regardless of the circumstances, my line has got to prevent goals. The most important game of the year and we just got scored on. I felt like I was just punched in the stomach.

Lester was ready to get the first line back on the ice and I skated to the bench. I got over the boards and looked into the audience. They were in stunned silence. The Garden was in shock.

I took a quick glance for Marie in the wife's section. Our eyes locked. Even from this distance her eyes told me not to lose hope.

The game was out of control, and it was ugly hockey. The Bruins scored two goals this period, and Ching and Taffy weren't on the ice for either. Frank, Bill, and Bun had all been called for penalties they didn't instigate. They were barely on the ice together as a unit all period. The Bruin's slashed Ching's nose purposefully, which required repairs off the ice. This was Boston's strategy. To keep our star players off the ice as much as possible.

Bunny, just released from the penalty box skated past our bench.

"Boss, Taffy's not at fault. He's not trying to take a penalty. Shore is doing this on purpose." Bunny skated out for the faceoff with Bill and Frank.

I realized, if Bunny is out of the box than the other penalty will be over in just a few seconds. Shore will be back on the ice.

"Lester, let me go out. Call one of them off." Lester looked at me and sensed my certainty. "Call any one of them off quickly, please!" I pleaded. I stood at the boards, ready to leap on.

"Bunny, come back!" yelled Lester. He repeated himself louder.

Bunny looked back, but it was too late. O'Hara dropped the puck.

Frank won the face off cleanly back to Stan.

Shore and Taffy both bolted out of the box. But this time Shore ignored Taffy and had his sights on another target. He raced right for Frank's blindside. Just before he got to Frank, Shore turned around so that he was skating backwards the last few feet before colliding with Frank. Shore was watching the puck but knew full well that he was about to slam into Frank. He made it look like it was an accident. Just an incidental collision. Shore gave Frank a shove after they bounced off each other. Frank pushed him back. That was all Shore needed. He dropped the gloves and squared up. To protect himself, Frank did the same.

The last time Frank got into a fight was our very first game. The irony did not escape me. This was all the proof I needed. Eddie Shore's role today was to cause offsetting penalties to keep our best players off the ice.

Shore threw a punch. Frank took the bait. Both guys swung their fists, and the refs broke it up quick. But the damage was done.

With Frank off the ice, and his defensive skills absent at center ice, the Bruin's gained the zone. Ching was still on the bench, as Harry couldn't stop the bleeding. Within one minute, Oliver tallied another goal for the Bruins.

The score was now 3-1 as the period came to an end. Their strategy, ugly and dishonorable, was working.

Fourteen penalties were called in the second period alone. Shore was responsible and the instigator for most.

We retreated to the locker room. My shoulder was in agony and my arm was nearly useless. The guys were in shock. I looked around the room.

Lorne threw his gloves off in frustration.

Cigarettes were lit with shaking hands.

Frank was struggling to get the top off a coke bottle.

Reg had his face in his hands.

Ching's white towel was soaked in bright red blood. The bleeding wasn't going to stop on its own in time.

Bill ran his hand threw his hair and was gathering his thoughts. He looked rattled.

Bunny was trying to console Taffy.

I could hear Lester down the tunnel yelling at the refs.

I stood in the center of the room.

I paused.

Took a breath.

And spoke.

"Doctor Brown, please help Harry get Ching's nose stitched. I don't care if you put glue on it, stop that bleeding. Guys, their lesser players are taking our top line players off the board. We're down by two goals. We can't score with our top guys in the box. Lorne is standing on his head for us. We have got to ignore them and play our game. I don't care if they slash you or another teammate in the face, you do not retaliate."

I turned around and realized that Lester was standing in the room now, watching me.

“What about Shore?” Taffy pleaded. I could hear the hint of fear in his voice. Taffy hadn’t shown a moment of fear all season. But he had it now. In front of everyone. They all felt it.

I looked Lester in the eye. He gave me a slight nod.

I turned back to Taffy and held his gaze. I was talking directly to Taffy but speaking to everyone in the room.

“Forget Shore. He’s my responsibility this period. You just stay on the ice and play your game. I have a plan.”

I felt a hand on my good shoulder. It was Bill. Our Captain. I suddenly realized that I’ve over stepped. But Bill held tight. He smiled at me.

“Murray is absolutely right fellas. We’ve got to stay on the ice. Ching and Taffy, we need you both to give as much as you can. Brown and Reg will give you breathers but stay on the ice as much as possible. Listen fellas, it doesn’t matter if we lose by two goals or five. Get aggressive and shoot the puck. Take chances. Take risks. Get creative. We’ve got Lorne in net. He’ll hold the line. Murray, tell us what you have in mind.”

The guys were lining up in the tunnel. I snubbed out my butt. Grabbed my gloves and stick. Lester blocked my path.

“Why you, Mr. Murdoch?” was all he asked.

“Because tonight, I’m the most expendable and I’m the only one who can.” I couldn’t meet his eyes. I looked away.

“You could not be more wrong about the first part Mr. Murdoch. But you are correct about the second part. Do not get hurt. We need you next season.”

Frank and Eddie Shore were still in the box to start the third period. There were 20 seconds left on their fighting penalty. I knew what was going to happen the moment Frank stepped out of the box. I needed to time this perfect. Everyone knew their role.

Bill Cook took position for the faceoff with Bunny to his left. Once the penalty is over, Frank would rejoin his mates. Ching and Taffy were at their positions. Our first line would be on the ice together.

Except, I knew Shore wouldn't let that happen.

Bill lost the draw and Frederickson kicked the puck back to Hitchman.

Bunny nonchalantly skated past our bench, and he and I quickly traded places on the fly. No one seemed to notice.

11 seconds.

Hitchman sent the puck deep into our zone. This is perfect I thought. Our team retreated and Ching got to it first. He paused, looked up at the clock and then sent it hard down the length of the ice.

I picked up speed in the opposite direction. I cut into my edges and slingshot myself behind our own net up the boards on the far side. I passed Ching and to everyone in the building it looked perfectly normal.

I could hear the incredible sound of my edges truly carving the ice. The incredible power Sam could generate at will.

3 seconds.

2, 1. The penalty was over.

Shore burst through the door and immediately broke towards Frank's box.

-1

Frank's door was wide open. But Frank didn't come out. Shore froze in total confusion. Frank just stood in the doorway and smiled at Shore.

-2

With every ounce of power and speed I could generate I exploded into Eddie Shore.

The entire arena gasped at the sight and sound of the collision.

It was like a locomotive crashing through a cow standing on the tracks.

For good measure, before the impact, I made sure my eyes were on the puck so it would seem "accidental". But it was anything but. It was totally intentional.

It was by far the hardest I ever checked anyone on open ice. My left shoulder and arm were throbbing. Eddie was rolling on the ice, gasping for oxygen. The refs stopped play.

The crowd erupted.

I stood, expecting the refs to invite me to step into the penalty box, or possibly toss me from the game. But they didn't do either.

They fell for my act, or perhaps the hockey gods felt justice was served.

I skated to our bench and took a seat. It took several minutes before Eddie was eventually helped to his bench by two teammates. One on each arm holding him steady.

Lester leaned over the boards and spoke to the first line.

"Ok fellas, Mr. Murdoch has just taken their biggest weapon off the board. Now, go play and score a goal. Someone else will no doubt try to draw you into taking a penalty. Ignore them."

Suddenly, the action on the ice resembled hockey again. Lightning fast, hard-hitting, with precision passes. Bill, Frank, and Bunny were finding each other, and Winkler was forced to block three quick quality shots.

After several minutes, Art Ross dispatched the rarely used Bill Coutu under the guise of giving Cleghorn a rest. Coutu went after Bill Cook and manhandled our captain to the ice. The crowd was anticipating a fight. But Bill just let the ref escort Coutu to the box. Now we had our man advantage.

Both Taffy and Ching took chances and crashed the net. At times we had all five players in front of their net and Lorne was the lone blue shirt for the length of the ice. The Bruin's defense held.

Time was not on our side.

Halfway into the third, Lester put our second line out. The first line needed a breather, and to regain their legs for the push.

We took the ice knowing that our priority was now to get a goal. After Lorne made yet another stop, I gathered the puck behind our net, looked up and saw Paul in center ice. There were too many players between Paul and me, so I lifted the puck and sent it over everyone's heads. A hundred feet at least. Paul raced to where it was going to land and unfortunately, Hitchman was waiting with an open ice check.

Leo stole it away from Hitchman and got into their zone. For a defenseman with no offensive skills, Leo put a beautiful shot on net, but Winkler made another strong stop.

Fredrickson took several whacks at Leo for the effort. Leo, despite his natural inclination to retaliate, ignored the slashes. Eventually, Fredrickson took it too far and Laflamme finally called a penalty on the Bruin.

Our line came off to give Bill and his squad the best chance to score.

I looked up at the clock.

I knew it wasn't good.

Bill Cook, Ching Johnson, Frank Boucher all took superb chances and put shots on net. Boston took every opportunity to send the puck down the length of the ice to waste time. The crowd gave them hell for doing so, but it was the smart move.

Our guys had to keep regrouping. But we kept attacking. Wave after wave. There was no quitting. Our crowd stood and roared the whole time.

With two minutes left in our season, Bill, Frank, Bun, and Ching drove to the net as Taffy stayed high at the blue line. With every chance, no matter how slim, they put the puck on the net in the hopes of a fortuitous bounce or rebound.

Forty-five seconds.

Oliver chipped the puck out of the zone, and we regrouped for one last rush.

Bill carried the puck and passed over the Frank. Frank tapped it right back to Bill.

Galbraith broke for the bench as Eddie Shore jumped into the fray.

Bill sent it to Ching, who wound up to blast the puck at Winkler. But there was traffic blocking his shot, so he sent the shot across to Bunny who took the shot from his angle.

Shore went right for Bill in front of the net. Cook saw him coming but was trying to deflect the loose puck. With both hands on his stick, Shore rammed Bill from behind. The puck trickled into the corner away from the net. The refs let the clock run. The final seconds ticked off.

The game ended.

Our first season was suddenly…over.

Before Boston could even celebrate, Bill dropped his gloves and went after Shore with a ferociousness I've never seen from him.

The refs raced to separate them, but Bunny, Ching and Taffy impeded their path.

Bill tackled Shore at the waist. They went down to the ice together and Shore tried to roll out from underneath, but Bill wouldn't let him.

Bill landed three hard blows for every one that Shore landed.

Bill pulled his fist back and paused. Perhaps he thought that was enough.

Shore smirked back and threw another punch that landed.

Bill let his fist fly with all his might down on that smirk. Shore's head bounced off the ice. Blood exploded from Eddie's lip.

Bill backed off and got to his feet as Shore spit blood and teeth on the Garden ice.

None of the Bruins really came to Shore's defense. Both teams were on the ice. There was some pushing and holding. But once Bill got off Shore on his own accord, both teams backed off.

The Bruins congratulated themselves and celebrated as we skated back to our bench. The crowd was in stunned disbelief that our season had ended. This was not the script the local papers predicted.

The story book ending of the Rangers playing in the Stanley Cup Finals in their first season was harshly not realized.

It was the Bruins of Boston that would have the honor of facing Ottawa.

The crowd was slowly starting to disperse, and we were about to gather our gear and head to the locker room when Lester held up his hand.

"Gentleman, line up at center ice and wait."

We looked at each other in confusion. But Frank knew the drill.

We skated out and formed a line. The crowd stopped leaving. Confused, they stood and stared.

We were in no particular order, but Bill was in front. I was towards the rear, just in front of Lorne. Harry was on the ice too, just before Lester Patrick, who was last in the line.

When Boston finished congratulating each other they lined up opposite us.

Both team captains, Bill Cook and Sprague Cleghorn skated towards each other and shook hands. They patted each other on the shoulder, said a few words and moved on to the next player in line.

I had never seen this in person but heard and read about the ritual. Just minutes ago, we were battling each other, drawing blood, giving our full measure to defeat the other.

Now we were shaking hands like gentleman. Like sportsmen.

Cleghorn reached me. We shook. I congratulated him and wished him luck. He whispered in my ear "it's an honor to play against you kid. You've got a hell of a future." And he moved on.

I repeated my congratulations and wishes of good luck down the line. Several players had very nice things to say to me in return.

Oliver, Galbraith, Herbert, Hitchman, Frank's brother Billy, Stuart, Fredrickson, Coutu, Meeking. Suddenly, I came face to face with the bloodied Eddie Shore. Neither of us said a word. We simply shook hands and moved onto the next player.

Hal Winkler was next in line. I pulled him tight, gave him a hug and whispered into his ear. "You were a brick wall Hal. Go win and bring the Cup to Boston."

I shook hands with Art Ross…

…and that was it.

The crowd stood and applauded the whole time.

I spotted Marie, standing, clapping with tears of pride, and smiling.

Then I sat on our bench. I looked at the fans filing out. Leaving. In minutes the arena would be empty.

Just as I felt. Completely and utterly empty.

Chapter Forty-Eight

February 1994

Sitting on the wooden bench, looking over the pond, I feel that emptiness again.

"My god Murray, I know that feeling all too well." Messier admitted. "A season that you give everything to, and it ends in bitter heartbreak. The sudden void. The emptiness. In hindsight, you guys must have been so proud. What an amazing time to break into the league. Your original team…Murray, whether any fans or players know it today or not, you guys set the standard for all of us who wear the Ranger colors to follow. There has always been something truly special about playing for this team, and these are the origins of that uniqueness."

"The Ranger colors." I repeated? He just reminded me of something I had long forgotten. I looked away just as tears welled up in my eyes. This day has been harder than I imagined.

"What is it, Murray?" Mark asked concerned. He put his arm around my shoulder.

"You just reminded me of something is all. I remember the team went to dinner the following night at Sardi's. The restaurant had just opened down the street on 44th. Tex and Colonel Hammonds were there. Tex picked up the tab. It was our farewell dinner together. We weren't yet sure who would be back the next season as most of us were signed to one-year deals."

"The next day we were supposed to clear out our lockers. I remember loading up my bag..."

Chapter Forty-Nine

April 6, 1927

My gloves and pads were still damp. I would have to remember to let them air out. My oh my, where is Marie going to let me do that? There's no way I can bring this smelly gear into our apartment. I wondered if our building had roof access. I could lay this all out and let the sun beat them dry. Or the basement. I'll bet there's a furnace down there that'll dry these out.

"Murray, see you next season." Bill and Bunny came over and we said our goodbyes. We gave each other hugs. Most of the guys had gathered their gear and left already. I was one of the last to leave.

I couldn't be sure I would be back. The one season contract I signed with Connie Smythe ended. This hung over me now like a dark cloud. How would Marie and I ever be able to go back to living in Manitoba after falling in love with this city.

In a few days, Marie and I would take the train back north to spend several weeks and much of the hot summer with our families in Canada. Both of us needed the rest. Marie would be starting to show in another month. My body was badly bruised and sore. I needed to spend weeks fishing pike, perch, and walleye. The idea of standing in a hip-deep stream flyfishing, while cold water worked my legs sounded delightful. Bunny promised he would spend a week with us and drop bait.

"Mr. Murdoch," Lester stood in the doorway to his office. "Would you join me for a moment?"

I entered and he poured us both a glass of something strong.

There was a package on his desk. After handing me my drink he put both hands on the box. He leaned over it, almost in pain.

"This arrived a couple weeks ago. I don't know what to do with it." He confessed.

He opened the box. It contained a Ranger jacket, the same varsity style each of us owned and were gifted at Christmas.

I understood.

It was supposed to be Sam's jacket. No doubt, his name was stitched inside.

"I don't know what to do with it Murray." I could hear the great man's voice cracking. "I don't know…". A tear fell on the box, and I knew he was crying.

I came around to his side of the desk and put my arm around his shoulder.

"Your oldest son isn't much younger than Sam." I looked at Lester. "Bring it to a tailor and have them take out the name and stitch in 'Lynn'. Give it to your son Lester, and we'll think of Sam every time we see him wearing it".

I reached for my shot glass.

Lester reached for his.

We tapped them together.

"To Sam, the most talented hockey player I ever saw."

We drank.

Chapter Fifty

February 1994

Mark now had tears in his eyes too.

"I'm sorry Mark. I didn't mean to upset you. At my age, I am burdened with immense gratitude and unbearable sadness in equal measure. Sometimes it comes out. I'm sorry."

"There is no need to apologize Murray. You've lived a truly extraordinary life. When you joined the team, you had no idea if you'd even make the roster. My god, you went on to play left wing for the New York Rangers for eleven years! No matter how banged up, how injured or sick, you played 508 consecutive regular games, in addition to 56 playoff games. You never, not once, missed a single game in your entire career. That's insane. You won two Stanley Cup trophies with the Rangers. After that you went on to have a 27-year career as the coach of Yale University, molding those young students not just to be better hockey players but to be better men."

"Murray, I know after you lost Marie in '74…that it broke you. But I also know you kept going. You just said back in 1927 you encouraged the legendary Lester Patrick to give his son Lynn that jacket. Lynn Patrick went on to have an illustrious hall of fame career as a New York Ranger in his own right. And I know some fifty years later, you and Lynn formed a peewee hockey league together in Connecticut. You and Marie raised a beautiful daughter in Joan. You traveled the world together. Heck, at ninety years of age, you're still doing crossovers."

I put my hand on Mark's knee. "Thank you. Like I said, a life of immense gratitude. But at the same time, except for my daughter, everyone I've ever known and loved, they've all passed."

"Frank's passing was one of the hardest. You know when his playing days with the Rangers were over Lester tapped him to take over as head coach. He loved that job and won the franchise its third Cup. In later years he was also the general manager and that created some tensions between him and both Lester and Bill Cook. But Raffles always did what he thought was best for the Rangers. You know he won the Lady Byng trophy seven times for gentlemanly play. Heck, after he won the award for the seventh time, they just gave it to him to keep and Lady Byng herself donated a new trophy. He was elected to the hall of fame in '58. I was so happy for him. It was a terrible blow to him and Agnes both when they lost everything in a fire in '65. Even his Lady Byng trophy was gone."

"But none of that compared to when he lost Ag. The love of his life. We lost her in '72. Thankfully he had his son Earl and his grandchildren. In retirement he wrote a brilliant book called "When the Rangers were Young." It's an honest account of his long career with the franchise."

"He knew he had cancer by then. We spent a lot of time together after I lost Marie two years later. He was there for me. He understood my pain. We caught a lot of trout together in those last few years. Finally, the cancer spread. He was gone by '77."

"Bill and Bunny lived longer. Did you know that Bill is the only Ranger Captain to lead the team to two Stanley Cup Championships? After his eleven-year career Bill and Bunny both coached several teams. Frank hired Bill to coach the Rangers, but the team performed so poorly under his tenure that as the General Manger, Frankie had to fire his old-line mate and friend. This led to that rift. Eventually, it was forgiven. No one could stay angry at Frank for long. Bill retired to his farm in Lac

Vert, next to his brother Bun's land, of course. He was nearly killed when one of their bulls gored him. Bill was a tough son-of-a-gun. He and Claire had three children. He died of cancer in 1986, at the age of 90. Bunny died two years later at 84. Bill was inducted into the Hall of Fame in 1952. I hear the Veterans Committee is finally getting close to inducting Bunny too."

It was getting late, and several of the young skaters had left with their parents. But there were still a few kids out there who weren't going to stop until the sun went down.

"Murray, I would be remiss if I never ask you about "The Game" in '28. Mark asked with a big grin.

"The Game." I laughed.

"Come on Murray, like you said, you're literally the last person alive who was a firsthand witness. It's arguably the most important game in Ranger history. It was only the second year. Your team fought back after the heartbreaking elimination to the Bruins in '27 and the following year you guys returned to the Playoffs and marched into the Cup Finals. That was fortitude. Tell me, please."

Looking out at the kids, I noticed one young skater with surprisingly good hands. But his skating needed work. His crossovers were weak, and he didn't know how to generate power on his stride.

"I like that word, 'fortitude'. Yes, we rebounded that next year. The team was almost completely intact. Stan Brown and Reg Mackey were no longer on our roster. Stan went back to dentistry. They were replaced by new kids Alex Gray, Laurie Scott and Frank Callighen. As the season ground on, Paul Thompson shifted to center and Alex Gray played with us on the second line."

"We beat Pittsburgh in the first round."

"Our rematch with Boston was satisfying and we sent them home to go fishing." I laughed.

"Now we were in the Stanley Cup Finals verses the Montreal Maroons. It was a best of five series and all the games were played in Montreal." I explained.

"All of them? Was that because the Maroons finished with a better record? All the games in Montreal, with those fans. That's one heck of an advantage."

"No, it was nothing like that" I said laughing. "The circus was in town and the Garden was reserved for the Elephants."

"You've got to be kidding me?" Mark protested with a smile.

"Honest to God!" I assured him.

"We lost the first game 2-0. Lorne was brilliant but their star defenseman Red "Comet" Dutton and goalie Clint Benedict were the difference in that first game."

"But you're asking about the famous Game Two in the series. It was a pivotal game. If we lost, coming back from two down would have been a tough ask. I remember the visitor's locker room had terrible ventilation."

Chapter Fifty-One
April 7, 1928

The room was thick with cigarette smoke.

"It's hotter than Hades in here" Taffy complained.

"You're right about that. I bet it's like this on purpose." Ching added while wiping the many beads of sweat from his forehead.

Thankfully, Harry came into the room and announced it was time for us to line up and head out to the cooler ice.

The 14,000 residents of Montreal were being treated to truly beautiful, fast, and crisp play from both teams. The first game, two night earlier, was largely clean hockey and the same must be said about the first period tonight.

Both teams played at tremendous speeds. Passes were on the tape. Ching and Taffy's skills were equally matched by Dutton and Munro. Benedict and Chabot were moving and flopping around like precise acrobats at both ends of the ice. The crowd was appreciative, loud, and as usual, generally polite.

As the period was winding down, Bunny was moving like his namesake down the boards. He curved towards the net, maneuvered around their defenseman, and sent a backhand shot which Benedict knocked away. It was a beautiful flourish to end the first period.

We went back to our smoke-filled sauna wondering if we wouldn't get more rest if we'd simply stayed on our cool bench.

The second period started like the first. As the first line of Nels Stewart, Hooley Smith and Babe Siebert attacked our zone, Nels sent a bullet on net. The puck was rising, and as it reached Chabot, he spun violently around and backwards.

There was a sickening sound.

The puck went harmlessly into the corner.

Lorne went to his knees, dropped his gloves, and covered his face. His back was to the bench. But immediately, players on both teams were yelling for help. Harry and Lester rushed out.

Harry only needed a glance to immediately order our guys to help Lorne to the locker room. The refs halted the game. The Maroon players dropped to one knee as Lorne was lifted and dragged by Ching and Taffy. The crowd was in stunned silence.

As they approached the bench, I now saw the blood. A lot of blood. A trail was left along the ice from the net, onto the bench. Harry never left Lorne's side and as they passed, he said to us nervously, "It's bad, it's his left eye."

I glanced around the ice and noticed Maroon players were surrounding Nels, who was clearly shaken and upset.

The refs ordered everyone to their respective locker rooms, and they followed us to ascertain what was happening in ours.

A couple doctors from up in the stands rushed into our locker room just as we walked into chaos. The league president Frank Calder burst into the room with both Connie Smyth and Odie Cleghorn in tow, Toronto and Pittsburgh's managers respectively who were in attendance. A few reporters and several people who I didn't know filed into the already hot and uncomfortable space.

The doctors immediately called for the ambulance. A hemorrhage was forming, and the situation was deathly serious. He needed to be transported to the nearby Royal Victoria Hospital straight away.

It's a small, tight room under the best of circumstances. We could all see Lorne, semi-conscious laying on the medical table in the supply room. The area around his left eye was a mess. The doctors worked to control the bleeding while Harry gently removed his pads and skates.

Bill and Ching had both seen worse in the war and gathered us together and settled us down.

The stretcher was wheeled in within a few minutes, but the space was so packed Harry was screaming at everyone to get out of the way. Lorne was loaded and strapped down. We all said words of encouragement and support as he was wheeled away but I don't know if he could hear us.

We were shaken. I was literally shaking.

A few minutes passed and the refs started discussing the dire situation with the Lester and Frank Calder. Smythe and Cleghorn we're advising President Calder on the rules.

"Frank, the Ottawa Senator's goalie Alex Connell is sitting five rows behind our bench. Let us substitute him in." Lester pleaded.

"Not a chance" Smythe protested. "He isn't signed to a Rangers contract, and he is under contract to Ottawa."

I watched as Calder gathered his thoughts.

"Lester, although I cannot order any changes to the rules, I will not object if the Maroons care to consent to the Rangers using a borrowed goaltender."

Lester nodded to the league's President and said, "Thank you."

With that, Lester left in the direction of the Maroons' locker room to discuss this with their coach Eddie Gerard.

I noticed Bill and Raffles drifting into a corner to get away from all the strangers in the room, all offering unwelcome suggestions and opinions.

Bill gave me a quiet nod to join them. They were discussing options and I listened. They were trying to figure out who on our roster should wear the pads in an emergency. Not one of us had ever put on goalie pads. Plus, whoever was chosen would seriously weaken either our offense or defense. We were barely holding our own against the Maroons tonight. We simply had no one to spare and as we went through the list there were no good options. Then Frank suggested the craziest idea.

After several minutes, Lester returned into the chaotic locker room and announced he had spoken with their coach.

"Gerard didn't feel the request was fair but agreed to put it to a vote among their players. They discussed it and they voted no. Their feeling is we chose not to carry an extra goalie and we must live with the consequence. They propose we forfeit. Which I declined."

With this news, Bill Cook motioned for Lester to join our huddle in the corner.

Frank looked nervously at Bill and said, "you tell him."

Bill gave Frank an annoyed look but put both hands on Lester's shoulders and presented the only viable option.

"Lester, Frank here thinks it's a good idea for you to don the pads and get in the net for us."

To his credit, Bill delivered this with a straight face.

Lester's eyes went wide and realized we were serious.

"You've played net during practice. You played a game with us last season on defense. The Maroons can't protest. Plus,"

"Enough". Lester interrupted.

He tried to pace, but the room was too crowded.

"Harry…Harry…Harry! Come here." Lester barked over the crowd.

Harry, visibly shaken and wiping blood off his hands, pushed through the interlopers, and rushed over.

At the sound of Lester's voice everyone in the room went dead silent.

"Harry, grab all of Lorne's gear. I'm going in the net myself." Lester proclaimed.

The noise and chaos erupted anew.

The team immediately started getting everyone out of the room. But who would manage the team with Lester on the ice. Lester looked at his two options, Smythe or Cleghorn and had no trouble choosing.

"Odie, would you kindly take over the bench duties while I stop some pucks?" Lester joked.

"Lester, it would be my pleasure."

Ten minutes later, Lester Patrick led us back onto the ice.

The crowd, first in utter stunned confusion and silence slowly turned to an applauding sustained roar.

"Let them shoot" Lester joked to us.

"For god's sake, don't let them shoot!" Odie Cleghorn, our substitute manager yelled back.

The second period resumed. For several minutes the Maroons were overly confident of their inevitable victory. I couldn't blame them. Our 44-year-old silver haired coach had never played goalie in an actual game before.

But Lester inspired us to our finest hour.

We never played a more perfect or nearly impenetrable defense.

Taffy and Ching played the greatest game of their careers. They stood up every maroon sweater that came into our zone. Our forward lines backchecked and stole pucks before they got into our zone. Frank was poke-checking the moment a Maroon tried skating up ice. The wingers backchecked.

In all fairness, Lester hardly faced any shots that second period. But when a shot did trickle towards the net his smile lit the Forum.

He would drop to his knees and smother it as if putting out a small fire. The Montreal fans behind his net could hear his deep laugher. He was having the time of his life.

The hurricane pace resumed for both teams as the Maroons realized their error in underestimating the old fox.

In the last minute of the second period, Leo broke free and pushed through their defense and put a strong shot on Benedict. Clint barely made the save and the Maroons counterattacked.

At top speed, Red Dutton fed Hooley Smith a sharp pass. Hooley blasted it and Lester never flinched. He caught the puck in midair like he was catching a baseball from his son.

As the period ended, the Montreal fans stood and showed their respect to Lester with a loud ovation.

Both teams were scoreless as we started the third and Bill Cook was determined to change that. Thirty seconds into the period he bullied a path between Dutton and Munro and put a quick wrist shot that got past Benedict.

We now had a 1-0 lead.

Now our mission was not to let them score.

Ching Johnson and Taffy Abel completely took over the game. They sent bone curling shivers through the entire arena with every check. If either needed a breather, Leo Bourgault held the line in relief.

Siebert made the mistake of trying to swing wide around Ching.

Johnson cleanly checked him into the boards and the shaken Maroon left the ice.

With only seven minutes left Nels Stewart was skating thought center ice. Frank had a bead on him, and feeling the pressure, Nels sent the puck towards the net from behind the blue line. It was a weak, harmless shot.

Lester watched it approach and calmly dropped to his knees to smother it. Only it somehow sneaked through his pads, and the score was suddenly tied.

1-1 with seven minutes left in regulation play.

Was there ever a faster or intense contest from this point on? Not one that I

had seen.

Both teams did everything possible to end this before regulation time ran out. But every foray was stifled and snuffed out.

The third period ended tied 1-1.

Referee Marsh announced that we would play until one team scored.

I realized that our team was spent. Every player had given everything on the ice,

and we were gassed and gasping for air.

Lester stood in front of us on the bench, fresh as a breeze in the forest, and asked "Is everyone having fun?"

Taffy, who was perhaps the most exhausted and battered, stood up off the bench and replied, "I have never had more fun in my life boss."

We all smiled at each other. "Let's get this done." Our Captain added as he leaped over the boards.

Both teams played with desperation and high risk. Long passes led to turnovers but also produced some penetrating attacks that led to chances. After three minutes Odie called for a line change on the fly.

When it was safe, Bill, Frank, and Bun each came to the bench as Alex, Paul, and I took their place. As we had done all game, we put our bodies in front of every shot we could. I knew that blocking a shot was never more important and as Munro sent a bullet toward our net I dropped to the ice and blocked it with my leg. I collapsed but had to get back up. Stewart was now going after the puck and I raced him to the boards. We tangled each other up and wrestled for the prize. Odie had sent us out against their first line. If I could outlast their best player in Nels Stewart along the boards, maybe I could tire him just enough to make a difference later. It's the small victories that matter I reminded myself as I dug down and found the raw power to push him back and gain control. I sent the pass back to Taffy and knew it was time for my change.

Taffy skated the puck up through center ice as I safely raced to the bench so that Bunny could get back on. Paul Thompson already used the time I had Nels tied up to wisely make his change with Frankie. Alex was the last to the bench and Bill leaped over the boards and our first line was assembled and rested.

Here came the Maroons. Stewart passed across the ice to Hooley Smith. Hooley slipped a lateral pass to Nels just as Taffy checked Smith. Nels let another shot fly and Lester knocked it down. The puck lay at his feet. He threw himself to the ice and covered it with his glove hand. Smith, having recovered from Taffy's hit crashed the net and stabbed at Lester's glove with his stick.

Lester took no chances and dropped his whole body to cover it now. In that same moment Ching put his shoulder into Hooley Smith and sent him flying backwards.

Lester looked up and saw the ice. No one was near him now, and some of the Maroons were attempting a change. The refs hadn't stopped play.

He yelled "Ching!" and flipped him the puck.

Ching took off up the length of the ice like a runaway freight train. In unison, Frank, Bill, and Bun crossed the blue line with him. From twenty feet away, Ching sent a stinger that Benedict blocked off to the side.

Ching had the momentum and he yelled "I got it" as he chased after the puck along the boards. Bill and Frank crashed the net. Bun stayed high. Munro was all over Bill in front. But Stewart was a step late covering Frank.

The crowd, which never sat down all period watched in awe as the talented Mr. Johnson swooped in, retrieved the puck, and knowing right where everyone was, blindly backhanded the puck to Frank, wide open at the far side of the net.

The red light came on as Frank buried the winning goal.

We had just won our first Stanley Cup game and we raced back to our net so we could celebrate with Lester.

Chapter Fifty-Two
February 1994

I beamed at Mark. "It was our finest game. Our proudest performance."

I continued, "we learned later that night that Lorne would be in the hospital for the remainder for the series. It was a serious injury, and they were doing all they could to save his eye. We visited him the next morning. He was in terrible discomfort but wanted to hear every detail. Despite the pain, he laughed as we shared with him Lester's crazy exploits."

"Fortunately, Lorne recovered from his horrific injury. He only played those two seasons with the Rangers before being traded to Toronto. He won a second cup with the Maple Leafs in 1932 and he won the Vezina Trophy for best goalie in 1935. After his retirement, Lorne was bedridden with arthritis and developed Bright's Disease. He died in Montreal, five days after his 46th birthday."

"That is so young" Mark commented. "Did Lester stay in goal for the rest of the series?" he asked.

"Heck no, did you not hear me say he gave up a slow dribbler from out past the blueline? He was a terrible goalie. But darn if he didn't find a way to get it done that night. He saved our skins." I laughed and continued.

"There was a meeting between Lester, the Maroons' exccutives, and President Chandler on the next move. Tempers were high and Maroons resisted every proposal and solution suggested. Finally, they agreed to let us draft a backup goalie from the Americans named Joe

Miller. The players on his own team nicknamed him Red Light Miller in leu of the fact he was arguably the weakest goalie in the league. But he lived locally, and the old bootlegger and owner of the Amerks, Big Bill Dwyer consented. Never was there a more accommodating gentleman gangster then Big Bill." I chuckled.

"We lost the third game as Clint Benedict shut us out again. 2-0."

"But we didn't quit, we found a way. We won Game Four 1-0. Frank scored the only goal in that one. And then, two nights later we played the deciding Game Five, which we won 2-1. Frank scored both our goals. Joe "Red Light" Miller got the job done."

"We won Lord Stanley Cup's in only our second season. The promise Lester made to us when we first meet him came true. Our names were engraved onto the Cup for all time."

"As our head coach, Lester guided us to our second Stanley Cup Championship in 1933. In 1939 he handed the reins over to Frank Boucher. Lester was the team's general manager when Frank coached the team to their third Stanley Cup in 1940. As you well know, we haven't won the cup since."

"Lester retired as general manager of the Rangers in 1946 but assumed the position of Vice President of Madison Square Garden until 1950. He was inducted in the Hockey Hall of Fame in 1947.

"Lester was not only the father of Lynn Patrick but also the grandfather of Craig Patrick, the Assistant Coach under Herb Brooks during the Gold Medal 1980 Lake Placid 'Miracle on Ice'. As you know Lester's younger son Mazz also played, coached and was the general manager of the Rangers."

"In the late 1950's Lester was diagnosed with lung cancer. He died on June 1st, 1960, in Victoria when he was 76."

"Mark, Lester Patrick's contributions to the sport of hockey cannot be overstated."

Mark took a deep breath. "Murray, this has been the most incredible day. Thank you. Skating with you on a frozen pond, playing with the kids, learning about Taffy's lineage. I feel rejuvenated."

Mark reached down and untied his laces as I watched the action out on the pond.

"Can I get you to a game this season? I'll make all the arrangements and send a car for you?" he asked.

"No Mark, thank you. My last visit to the Garden was when you were named team Captain. This is your team now Mark."

He now had his boots on, and I stood up. He also stood and even with my skates on, Mark towered over my ninety-year-old body.

"Are you taking those off?" He asked, pointing to my old skates.

"Not until I have too." I said, smiling.

We gave each a long, loving, last embrace.

I whispered into his ear "It's time Mark. It's time for the Rangers to have a new finest moment. It's been fifty-four years and the team, and the fans need new memories to last their lifetime and beyond. Bring the Cup home."

I stepped back onto the ice, gloves on and stick in hand.

"Where are you going Murray? The sun is all but set." Mark Messier asked in wonder.

"There's a kid over there with some skills. But someone needs to teach him how to use those edges."

I give Mark a wave goodbye and I push off.

I hear the gift.

Epilogue

Original Rangers Bill Cook, Frank Boucher, Bunny Cook, Ching Johnson, and Lester Patrick were all inducted in the Hockey Hall of Fame. They, and Murray Murdoch, all won two or more Stanley Cups for the Rangers. Taffy Abel was inducted into the United States Hockey Hall of Fame. Today he is recognized as the first Native America to become an NHL regular with the New York Rangers.

Yet none have banners hanging in Madison Square Garden. Nor have they had their numbers retired, as the franchise does for their former greats.

They have largely been forgotten to time, until now.

On June 14, 1994, Murray watched as Mark Messier and the Rangers hoisted Lord Stanley's Cup, the most glorious trophy in professional sports.

It was the team's first championship in 54 years.

John Murray Murdoch passed away on May 17, 2001, in Georgetown, South Carolina. At 96-years old, he was the Last Original Ranger of New York.

Acknowledgements

I would not have accomplished this novel without the unwavering support and love of my beautiful wife, Tia. After reading an early draft, her positivity gave me the motivation and courage to keep going. I asked much of her, and tested her patience often, but I cannot thank her enough. I know how blessed I am.

Without the guidance and experience of M. Rutledge McCall this novel would have been nothing more than unpublished fanfiction. Any aspiring writer would be lucky to have McCall in their corner. I hope I can someday repay him, or at least pay it forward. Please visit MRutledgeMcCall.com

A very heartfelt gratitude goes to Denise Montgomery. Denise tenaciously connected me with Mark Messier's agent, Aldo Esposito. In addition, Aldo serves as the Director of Messier Management and President of the Messier Foundation. Please visit the Markmessierfoundation.org

Our beautiful children, Sydney, Quinn, and Madison. Mom and Robert. My brother Erik, Steffi, Sophia, and Maria. My friends, mentors and counselors who all contributed, Mike Aronstein, Glen Silverstein, Keith Schenenga, Evan and Caroline Brodie, Lou Curcio, Carmin Romanelli, Jaimie Roberts, Wayne Wasserman, Scotty Bakay and Todd Eizikowitz. Mike Scaccalossi, Will Gensburg, Glenn Harris, Paul Graham, Craig Marshall, and all my current and former teammates on the Phantoms, Hornets and Eagles.

No single source was more important than Frank Boucher's "When the Rangers were Young". It is Raffles first-hand account of his years with the team. Unfortunately, only a small portion of the book dealt with the first season. Nevertheless, I leaned very heavily on his memories of his teammate's personalities and exploits. I admittedly took liberties and used a few of his tales from later years because they were too good to pass up.

I started my research in the New York Public Library. I spent weekends going through unopened boxes of microfilm and reading newspaper articles from that first season. The New York Herald Tribune, The New York Times and Daily News had excellent sports coverage thanks to writers Kerr N. Petrie, Will Murphy, Seabury Lawrence, Paul Gallico, W.J. Macbeth, and road games filed by uncredited writers for the Associated Press. Writers for the New York Times Dave Anderson and William Wallace. The New York Times now has the entire archive on-line. Any reader can view the original box scores with a few clicks.

Several other books and websites also provided me with invaluable information. John Halligan's Images of Sports The New York Rangers, Joe Pelletier's Greatest Hockey Legends.com, NHL.com and Dave McCarthy with the NHL, Hockey: A People's History by Michael McKinley, Brian McFarlane's History of Hockey, 100 Ranger Greats by Russ Cohen, John Halligan, and Adam Raider. John Halligan's New York Rangers: Seventy-Five Years. Greatest Jerseys of All-Time by the Hockey News. No One Wins Alone, Mark Messier's memoir.

Special thanks to George Grimm for catching at least some of my errors and his good advice. He wrote “We Did Everything But Win” and “Guardians of the Goal”. Both of which are excellent and I’m excited for his new book “Forgotten Blueshirts: The Frank Boucher Era New York Rangers 1940-1955” for obvious reasons. He is also the host of podcast “Retro Rangers.”

While this book is a work of fiction, I took great pains to get the facts right. If I wrote that Bunny Cook scored a goal off a pass from his brother at 8:13 into the 2nd period, he did. Any errors of fact are unintentional and purely my fault. Much of the action and dialog is my own imagination based on my readings of the game and my own experience playing adult league hockey.

I tried so very hard to get the personalities right. If someone alive remembers meeting Ching, or Taffy, or Murray, please let me know if I captured their spirit. At all times, I wanted to be respectful of their memory.

My passion was ignited when I was at a Ranger game with my son, Quinn. During the pregame festivities, the Garden had a photo montage on the jumbotron to get the crowd excited. They were showing photos of the Rangers through the years. I had been blessed with a long career in sports photography and I instantly recognized all the “modern-day” players, from Harry Howell, Jean Ratelle, Andy Bathgate, Eddie Giacomin, Vic Hadfield, Brad Park to Rod Gilbert. But I was surprised at how few of the faces I could name in the sepia toned images. That bothered me. I’m a life-long Rangers fan. How could I not know who these guys were? I did a little research and quickly learned about Lester, Bunny, Ching, Taffy, Frank, Bill, and Murray. All had incredibly illustrious careers with the Rangers. I was befuddled as to why they weren't recognized by the Rangers with banner's hanging from the rafters with the other Ranger greats. It is my sincere wish this book plays a small role in acknowledging our shared proud history.

As we prepare to commemorate the New York Rangers 100th anniversary in 2026, my hope is that we can honor the men from 1926.

In memory of

Jimmy LoRusso

He shared our passion for the game.

"Shoot them pucks and score them goals."

Made in the USA
Middletown, DE
13 December 2023

45443592R00246